For One Man's Honor

A Broken Lawyer Novel

By

Donald L'Abbate

Also by Donald L'Abbate

"Was it Murder?"

And

The Broken Lawyer Series
"The Broken Lawyer"
"A Murder Under the Bridge"

DEDICATION

Always, for Rose who gives me the courage and strength to do this, and for my children.

Table of Contents

CHAPTER 1

Did you ever get one of those phone calls when, after it begins, you're hoping it's a dream? But it isn't. That's how it was with the call from Laura Simone, my buddy Richie Simone's wife.

Richie Simone was a New York City Detective, working out of the 7th Precinct on Pitt Street in the Two Bridges section of Lower Manhattan. I've known Richie for a long time, all the way back to when I was still a high-flying Assistant

District Attorney, and Richie was a young undercover street cop.

That was in the early 1980s when New York City was a battleground. The murder rate was reaching all-time highs, the subway system was the most dangerous transit system in the world, and crack addiction was epidemic. Fires raged nightly in the ghetto sections of the city as tenement buildings, one after another, were abandoned and left derelict.

New York City was at war, and the City Assistant District Attorneys and street cops were the foot soldiers in that war. Being in the trenches together, Richie Simone and I naturally formed a bond, and we became friends. Good friends.

I almost destroyed that friendship when I started drinking heavily, but to Richie's credit he never lost faith in me. Even during the worst of my drinking days, Richie would keep tabs on me and reach out every now and then to offer help. Of course, I wouldn't admit I had a problem, and I'd get angry at anyone who thought otherwise. But since I got sober nearly seven years ago, Richie and I have gotten close again.

I'd like to say that I was responsible for Richie being promoted to Detective, but that's only partially true. My role did put him over the top, but it wouldn't have happened if Richie hadn't been a good cop.

But back to the phone call. Laura was frantic; Richie had been shot which, given his job, didn't shock me. Knowing how Richie operated, I was surprised it hadn't happened sooner. But what Laura said next did shock me.

Richie was under arrest for murder, and he wanted me to be his lawyer. For the record, it was the part about him being under arrest for murder that I found shocking.

It took a bit of doing to calm Laura down, but once I did, I was able to piece together some of the story. Richie was at New York Downtown Hospital; he'd been shot three times, twice in the back and once in the leg. Fortunately, he'd been wearing his bulletproof vest, and the bullets hadn't pierced the vest. The two shots to the back resulted only in some very nasty bruising.

The shot to the leg had been a through and through, missing the thighbone, and it wasn't likely to leave Richie with any mobility problems.

That much of the story I understood. What I was having a problem understanding was why Richie was under arrest for murder, and Laura wasn't helping me with that. All she kept saying was Richie had shot someone. She didn't know who he had shot, why he shot the person, or even where it happened.

They say it's all in the details, and I was missing the details. Laura was either too upset to think straight, or she just didn't know anything more. I needed to talk with Richie. But even before I did, I was sure of one thing. Richie was no murderer. He was a straight shooter, no pun intended, who took his job seriously and always played by the rules.

I told Laura I'd be at the hospital in twenty minutes and asked for Richie's room number. She hesitated a moment, then she said Richie wanted us to meet in the lobby. I couldn't imagine why, but if that's what Richie wanted that's what we'd do.

Whatever had gone down, I had no doubt Richie was innocent. All I had to do was prove it, a job that turned out to be more difficult than I could have imagined.

CHAPTER 2

New York Downtown Hospital, formerly known as Beekman Downtown Hospital, is at the foot of the Brooklyn Bridge on the Manhattan side. It's not a long walk from my office on Mott Street in Chinatown, but I was across town just leaving Gracie's place when I got Laura's call, so I jumped into a taxicab.

In case you don't remember, I have this thing about riding in taxicabs. I call it a "thing," but some people say it's a phobia. Others, like Gracie, don't call it anything; they just call me nuts. But that morning I was so focused on Richie, nothing else mattered.

Approaching the hospital, I wasn't surprised to see a swarm of police cars and a cluster of media trucks chaotically parked around the building. The shooting of a New York City cop is big news, so when it happens, the local TV and radio stations turn up at the hospital in full force with their reporters and film crews.

With so many vehicles double-parked around the building, the closest the taxicab driver could get was a block from the hospital's entrance. So I paid him and walked the rest of the way.

The lobby was crowded with media people and cops. Most of the cops wore white shirts, which meant they were lieutenants and above. Rank and file street cops wear blue shirts.

White shirts and blue shirts don't play well together, which explained why all the white shirts were on one side of the lobby and all the blue shirts were on the other. The news people were buzzing around both groups like bees around a flower, but apparently not finding any pollen.

I wasn't happy seeing all the white shirts. When a lot of white shirts are gathered together outside of the Ivory Tower, which is how the rank and file refer to NYPD headquarters, it generally means a cop is dead or in trouble. I was hoping Richie wasn't dead, but if he wasn't, he was definitely in trouble.

With the lobby so crowded, it took me a few minutes to locate Laura. I finally spotted her in a corner standing by herself trying her best to look inconspicuous. Obviously, none of the media people had figured out who she was. If they had, she would have been surrounded by a crowd of reporters and a bunch of TV cameras. As for the white shirts, they were too busy jabbering amongst themselves to bother with her.

Laura spotted me approaching and ran to meet me. She gave me a quick hug and pulled me toward the elevators. I started to say something, but Laura shook her head. She didn't want me saying anything, so I kept my mouth shut and tried to look inconspicuous. With all the confusion in the lobby, nobody paid much attention to us as we waited for an elevator to arrive.

In the elevator and heading up to the 10th floor, Laura finally spoke. All she knew, besides what she had told me on the phone, was that Richie had sent her outside the hospital to call me. He told her not to talk with anyone else, especially not any cops, and he didn't want me talking with anyone until I spoke with him. That was why she met me in the lobby, to make sure I didn't talk to anyone. I didn't like what I was hearing. If Richie didn't trust his fellow cops, something was very, very wrong.

CHAPTER 3

Compared to the lobby, the 10th floor hallway was empty. There were a few nurses and orderlies roaming about, but no one who looked like a media type. Apparently, the press wasn't being told Richie's room number, and so far, no one had leaked it. Sooner or later someone would spill the beans, then the 10th floor would be just as congested with cops and reporters as the lobby. But for now, it was quiet and that was good.

The only cop around was a uniformed officer sitting outside of Richie's room. Normally a cop is posted outside the hospital room of an injured cop to keep out unwanted visitors. I suspected in Richie's case, he was there for a different reason. The same reason a cop is posted outside the hospital room of a wounded suspect.

The cop stood as we approached. At first, he tried to turn us both away, saying the prisoner wasn't allowed visitors. I noted his use of the word "prisoner." Then he recognized Laura and said she could go in, but I couldn't. I could tell from his tone of voice that his heart wasn't in it, but he had his orders. I handed him my business card and said I was Richie's lawyer. He looked at the card, shrugged his shoulders and let me pass.

Richie was alone in the room, handcuffed to one of the bed rails. His left leg was bandaged and elevated, but otherwise he didn't look bad. He gave me a little smile and nod of his head. Laura sat on the edge of the bed and held her husband's hand. I sat on a chair at the other side of the bed.

I started to say something, but Richie motioned for me to be quiet and come closer. I moved my chair closer to the bed and leaned toward Richie. In a voice that was little more than a whisper, he told me he was being set up to take the fall for some boss, and he wouldn't be surprised if the hospital room was bugged.

Talk about sounding crazy. Frankly, if I didn't know him better, I might have walked out at that point. But I did know him better, and I wanted to hear the whole story before I reached any conclusions.

There was a sink not far from the bed, so I walked over and turned on the water. The noise of the water hitting the bowl and running down the drain would help to cover our conversation if the room was bugged. It was crazy, but better to be safe than sorry.

So far nothing was making sense. First, there was no PBA lawyer around. In other situations like Richie's, there was always a PBA lawyer present. I asked Richie what had happened to the PBA lawyer, and he said he sent the guy away because he didn't trust anyone associated with the department. Hearing that, I started to wonder if being shot had affected Richie's thinking.

CHAPTER 4

When you encounter a situation that defies reality, it can throw you for a loop, and that's what was happening to me. I couldn't wrap my mind around the fact that Richie Simone was under arrest and charged with murder. To me, it was like watching the sun rising in the west. It went beyond being simply unbelievable; it was unreal.

To appreciate why I found the situation so unbelievable, you have to know Richie. So, before I tell you what Richie said that day, I must tell you a little bit about him.

Richie Simone isn't just a good cop, he's one of the most honorable men I know. Everything I knew about him told me he was incapable of killing someone in cold blood.

Richie loved being a cop and had dedicated twenty-nine years of his life to the job. Next to his family, which always came first, the job was the most important thing in his life. Now the job he loved was betraying him, and everything he believed in was on the line.

Richie grew up in Flushing, a solid middle-class neighborhood in New York City's outer borough of Queens. His father, now deceased, had been a New York City fireman and his mother, who recently moved to Florida, had taught grammar school. They were about as solid a middle-class American family as you could find. Real Norman Rockwell material.

Richie had attended the Catholic grammar school around the corner from his home. It was the school where his mother taught second grade. In the eighth grade, he developed a crush on Laura Walters.

When he graduated from grammar school, his parents expected him to attend the local Catholic high school, but Richie had something else in mind. He didn't want to attend the all-boys Catholic high school. He wanted to go to the coeducational public high school so he could be with Laura Walters.

According to Richie, it was the first time he challenged his parents' authority, and it turned into a major battle. But when Richie made up his mind about something, he usually got his way. In the end, his parents gave in and

Richie went to Bayside High School with Laura Walters, who eventually became his wife.

For as long as he could remember, Richie wanted to be a New York City cop. The week he turned twenty, the minimum age for joining the force, he applied for the job. That was in 1982 when, after years of being understaffed because of the city's financial crisis of the 1970s, the NYPD was finally beefing up its ranks.

The increase in the number of cops came in response to the crisis conditions that existed at the time. By 1981, the number of cops on the force had dropped by nearly 10,000, a third of the force, and the crime rates were spiking to record heights. Finally, the city had no choice but to address the problem. In 1982, for the first time since 1974, the NYPD hired more officers than retired. Richie was one of 2,600 rookies to graduate from the Police Academy that year.

To combat the growing street crime, nearly half of the 1982 class, including Richie, was put on foot patrol the day after their graduation. It was while on foot patrol in Spanish Harlem a month later that Richie broke up an armed robbery, earning his first commendation. Six months later, he was transferred to plainclothes and doing drug buy and busts. That's when we met.

I was a year on the job at the DA's Office handling drug cases, working with the undercover cops, most of whom I didn't like. They thought they were hot shit, and their arrogant attitude made working with them difficult. But Richie wasn't like that. He was easy to work with, and I liked him from the start. He always showed up on time, and he never skipped out on a court appearance, even when it fell on his day off. In fact, he never complained about anything.

A year after being on the job, Richie married Laura. I wasn't invited to the wedding, but I was at the bachelor party. As time passed, Richie and I became closer, and he started inviting me to his house for barbecues. That's how I got to know Laura.

Eventually, Richie and Laure started inviting me to spend holidays with them. When Richie and Laura's daughters, Cathy and Lucy, were born, I was invited to their christenings. I felt like I was a member of the family and not having a family of my own made the relationship that much more important to me.

Then I went into my dark years. I guess I started drinking alcoholically sometime around 1989. It was in 1990 that things started to really come undone That's when the incident occurred that caused Laura to say she didn't want me coming around anymore.

As I recall, I got drunk at one of the barbecues and made a scene. I don't remember exactly what I did, but I believe it had something to do with Laura's attractive cousin, her ample bosom, and her dopey boyfriend. There may have been some diced watermelon and baked beans tossed about, but my memory on that is a bit hazy. Whatever it was, it got me blacklisted. To be honest, it didn't bother me that Laura didn't want me around anymore, because the more I drank, the less I wanted to see anyone anyway.

By the time I got bounced from the DA's Office in 1991, I was only seeing Richie when we had a case together, and it was always a little awkward. As I said, though, Richie never gave up on me. After I got fired and was working out of the backroom of Shoo's Restaurant, Richie would drop by occasionally or give me call. I can't say I was hospitable when he did.

When I got sober seven years ago, I hooked up with Richie, and we renewed the friendship. Laura forgave me for being an asshole, and things went back to where they had once been. After I started going out with Gracie again, I introduced her to Richie and Laura, and now we're all good friends.

So, now that you know about Richie, I can tell you why he was arrested and how the whole siltation came to be.

CHAPTER 5

That morning at the hospital, with the water running in the sink and Laura sitting on the bed holding his hand, Richie told me his story.

It all stemmed from a Joint Task Force involving Richie's 7th Precinct and the 5th Precinct in Chinatown. The Task Force had been formed to investigate and close a high-priced brothel operated by one of Chinatown's infamous Tongs.

The brothel operated in a renovated tenement building on Madison Street in the Two Bridges neighborhood, so technically it was in the 7th Precinct. But the cops in Chinatown's 5th Precinct had more experience dealing with the Tongs and had more Chinese officers able to work undercover, so a Joint Task Force had been formed. Richie headed up the Task Force under the watchful eye of a Deputy Bureau Chief from One Police Plaza.

The operation began with the Task Force surveilling the building and photographing everyone entering and leaving. Things moved along slowly until an undercover cop from Chinatown's 5th Precinct managed to get a job at the brothel as a bartender. Getting an undercover cop on the inside was exactly the break the Task Force needed. With a man inside, the Task Force quickly confirmed the brothel was operated by Sam Yeoung, boss of the Hop Sing Tong. But more importantly, he learned how the brothel operated. It was the information the Task Force needed to conduct a successful raid.

The brothel catered to wealthy well-placed clients who paid, depending on the girl's age, anywhere from $2,500 to $10,000 an hour for servicing. The younger the girl, the more she cost. All the girls were Chinese, and most didn't speak English. But that didn't seem to bother the patrons who obviously weren't there for conversation.

What I had heard so far was interesting, but I wanted to know about the murder. I interrupted Richie and asked him to give me the condensed version of the story, and get to the part where he shot someone. He threw me a nasty look and told me to be patient, but he did get to the interesting parts of his story.

Richie said the operation was peculiar from the start, when Deputy Chief McNulty took a much more active role than was typical. Ordinarily Deputy Bureau Chiefs weren't involved in operational details. They usually only left the Ivory Tower for photo ops after the operation ended well. But this Deputy Bureau Chief insisted on knowing all the details, and he was in the habit of showing up during active operations.

Although the interference bothered Richie, he hadn't given it much thought at the time. But now he saw things differently. He recalled something that happened early in the investigation that might be important.

One day he had been working a robbery related stakeout on Pell Street when he saw McNulty go into the Golden Palace restaurant. He was with a man who looked a lot like Sam Yeoung, the Task Force's biggest target. At the time, Richie wasn't certain it was Yeoung, so he never mentioned it to anyone. But now looking back on things, and putting it all in perspective, it seemed important.

I was anxious to hear about the murder, but Richie insisted I listen to the whole story first. He said if I didn't hear how things went down, I couldn't appreciate what we were up against. What could I do? I sat back and let Richie continue his story.

After two months working as a bartender at the brothel, the undercover cop had learned enough about the physical layout and security operations for Richie to believe the Task Force could pull off a successful raid. The key was for the raiding teams to quickly breach the premises and disperse throughout the building.

The ground floor housed a bar and a lounge, where clients relaxed and met the girls. There was a small kitchen in the basement, where snacks were prepared for the clients, as well as meals for the girls who worked double shifts. The second floor had five bedrooms and an office. The third floor had seven bedrooms, making a dozen bedrooms in all.

Having decided the Task Force had all the intel it needed, Richie began preparing for a raid. But when McNulty heard about it, he nixed the idea, saying they needed more time. In telling me the story, Richie was adamant there was no reason to put the raid off. But the raid was put off, and as it turned out, the delay led to new charges.

The undercover cop bartender had befriended one of the brothel girls, a Li Chin, who told him about a human smuggling operation. The Task Force expanded the scope of its investigation into the human trafficking aspect. With Li Chin's help, it didn't take long to find out how the girls were being smuggled into the country and where they were being held. Still, McNulty insisted that raiding either location was premature.

Finally, with Richie and others pushing for a raid, McNulty had relented and last night they conducted simultaneous raids at the brothel on Madison Street and a warehouse in Brooklyn where the young Chinese girls were held captive.

Richie led the raid at the brothel. McNulty surprised everyone by showing up to be part of the operation, and he went with Richie and his crew. The idea was to hit the brothel hard and fast. Half of the raiding force would break into the front door, while the other half hit the back door at the same time.

The raiding force was divided into teams of two. Each team had a specific area to secure. Richie and his partner, Jimmy O'Brien, were to secure the office on the second floor. Any customers present at the time were to be arrested and charged with patronizing prostitution, a class A misdemeanor. Later I learned no patrons were arrested.

According to Richie, the raid should have taken everyone inside by surprise, but it hadn't. The moment the raid teams breached the place, they were met with gunfire and forced to take cover. Richie, using cover fire from his partner, Jimmy, had managed to reach the staircase, and he raced to the second floor. At the top of the stairs was a hallway, and directly across the hallway was the office.

The door to the office was open. As Richie approached the office, he saw Kim Lee, the brothel's madam, kneeling near a safe behind her desk. It seemed to Richie she was removing something, something small, but he couldn't be sure what it was.

Entering the office, gun in hand, Richie yelled to Kim Lee to raise her hands. The last thing he remembered before being pounded on the back and passing out, was moving toward Kim Lee whose hands were raised.

The next thing he remembered was lying on the office floor and being treated by the paramedics. From his position on the floor, he could see Kim Lee's body lying in a pool of blood next to the open safe. Since there were no paramedics working on her, he figured she was dead. It turned out he was right.

Richie was just starting to get his bearings when McNulty told him he was under arrest for killing Kim Lee and read him his Miranda rights. It took him a minute to catch on to what was happening, but when he did, he wisely decided to keep his mouth shut. He didn't say a word after that until Laura arrived at the hospital, and he told her to call me. I was the first and the only one who had heard his side of the story.

It was a hell of a story, but it didn't explain how Kim Lee wound up dead, or who killed her. It didn't even explain how Richie came to be charged with her murder. Obviously, Richie thought McNulty was behind the whole thing, and he might be right. But being right and proving it are two different things.

If Richie was right and McNulty was behind all of this, we could be up against a major conspiracy with a lot of weight behind it. I'd be swimming upstream all the way on this one. But what the hell, nothing in my life had been easy.

I spent most of my life fighting the odds, like coming out of Hell's Kitchen and becoming a lawyer. Or getting sober after a dozen years of alcoholic drinking. Or putting back together a legal career that had been left for dead among the empty scotch bottles. Not to mention my relationship with Gracie Delaney. But those are all other stories.

Richie wanted me as his lawyer, but he said he wasn't sure he could afford my fee. He and Laura had just finished putting their two daughters through college, and there wasn't much left in their savings account. They owned their home, but he figured he'd have to put it up to make bail.

Richie was my friend, a good friend, and there was no way I was going to turn him down over money. I told him not to worry. I'd work cheap, and he could always work it off by doing favors for me. He laughed, then grimaced, and said it hurt to laugh. I figured with the trouble he was facing, laughing wasn't going be much of a problem.

I patted Richie's shoulder, gave Laura a hug and left. I had a lot of work to do, and the sooner I got to it, the better it would be for Richie. To be honest, I was busy as hell with other cases, but some of those cases were going to the back burner.

That day as I left the hospital, nothing made sense, but I knew I had to make sense of it if I was going to help Richie.

CHAPTER 6

Leaving the hospital, I was approached by Jimmy O'Brien, one of Richie's Detective partners from the 7th Precinct. Jimmy and I didn't know each other well, but he assumed I'd be representing Richie, and there were some things he wanted me to know. He wasn't comfortable talking while at the hospital, especially with all the white shirts around, so we arranged to meet at the Worth Street Coffee Shop at noon.

The Worth Street Coffee Shop is my second office. A convenient place to meet clients before going to the courthouses across the street. In Lower Manhattan, the old

Federal Courthouse, the New York County Supreme Courthouse, and the Criminal Courts Building are all in a line on Centre Street. The Manhattan District Attorney's Office is just around the corner, and my office on Mott Street in Chinatown is a short walk away. It's all very convenient.

But back in the days when I was drinking heavily, I didn't have a real office. I worked out of the backroom of Shoo's Chinese Restaurant on Mott Street, where I rented a desk and shared the space with old man Shoo's grandson. It had one big advantage; it was cheap. Let me correct that. It had two advantages: one, it was cheap; and two, it was a good place for lunch and dinner.

Of course, with a dozen cases of fortune cookies surrounding my desk, and a bunch of chefs constantly screaming at each other in Chinese, it wasn't a particularly professional atmosphere in which to meet with clients. That was why I met all my clients at the Worth Street Coffee Shop. At least the clients who made bail.

Since I got sober in AA several years ago, things have changed. I have a real office on Mott Street, not just a desk in some backroom. I also have a lot of paying clients, as opposed to the 18B Panel assigned clients I used to rely on to survive.

Now I hold meetings at the Worth Street Coffee Shop for convenience, not because it's the only place where I can hold meetings. I still do favors for the coffee shop's owner, and he keeps the back booth open for my use. Everyone working at the coffee shop knows about the arrangement. They even refer to the booth as *Jake's place.*

After my brief chat with Jimmy O'Brien, I decided to walk back to my office. I had to clear my head and start thinking logically. I had a lot of questions that needed answers, starting with how the undercover operation was compromised, as well as McNulty's role in the whole affair. It certainly seemed like a case of police corruption, which begged the question of how deep and how high it went.

Was McNulty at the top of the scheme, or did it go higher? Investigating a Deputy Chief wasn't going to be easy, and based on what had happened to Richie, it might even be downright dangerous. Then again, if this thing went higher than McNulty, it was certainly going to be more dangerous.

One of the many things that puzzled me was why Richie had been arrested at the scene. Normal procedure, when a cop shot someone, is to have the Patrol Borough Shooting Team investigate the incident and determine if it was a good shooting. After that, it's up to the District Attorney to decide whether to bring charges against the cop. So, why wasn't that procedure followed in Richie's case?

Then it hit me. All of that changed if there had been an eyewitness to the shooting. It didn't take a genius to conclude McNulty was not only the arresting officer, but the eyewitness as well. Of course, there was always the possibility he was also the murderer.

I called Tommy Shoo, my private investigator, and asked him to meet me at my office in an hour. I didn't say why because if I had, Tommy would have asked a lot of questions, and I wasn't in the mood to answer questions. I needed time to think, and besides, I didn't have any answers to give him.

Next, I called Gracie, my longtime girlfriend. Gracie heads up the Special Victims Bureau at the Manhattan District Attorney's Office. I was hoping she had heard something about Richie's situation that she could share with me. Nothing confidential, of course, just office talk. The kind of general office talk that goes on after an incident like this one. It was a long shot, but anything she might know would be a hell of a lot more than I knew.

I should mention that Gracie doesn't like me calling her my girlfriend. It's a Gracie thing. I'm not sure why. After all, we've been together for almost twenty years, with a little break in the middle, when I was spending most of my time emptying scotch bottles. Technically we don't live together. We each have our own place, but we spend most nights together. I think we're closer than a lot of married people, but Gracie still doesn't want me to call her my girlfriend. So, forget what I said about her being my girlfriend.

Needless to say, Gracie was shocked when I told her the story. She hadn't heard anything about the arrest, which was strange, because news about a cop being arrested usually spreads quickly through the DA's Office.

For the record, I don't normally ask Gracie for any favors because I don't think it's fair to take advantage of our relationship like that. But this was different. This was Richie Simone, and something about the situation wasn't right.

Before I could ask Gracie for help, she volunteered to check things out and get back to me. That's Gracie, as straight as an arrow, but never one to put up with any bullshit. She knew, as well as I did, there was something wrong here, and she wasn't going to ignore it. I wasn't sure how much help Gracie could be, but I needed all the help I could get.

The best-case scenario would be if McNulty was a corrupt cop, operating on his own. As a Deputy Chief, he ranked only three grades down from Chief, the highest-ranking officer in the NYPD. In New York City, the Police Commissioner and his deputies are not uniformed members of the department, simply civilians appointed by the City Mayor.

McNulty's rank would give him a lot of pull in the department, and maybe some in the DA's Office, but he'd also have his own vulnerabilities to worry about. If McNulty was acting on his own, it would be a one-on-one fight.

On the other hand, if the conspiracy ran deeper and involved more cops, either up the line or down the line, or both, we had big, big trouble. Exposing one corrupt cop was tough enough. However, exposing a whole group of corrupt cops was even tougher, but it could be done.

I was working at the DA's Office in 1986 when the "Buddy Boys" scandal at the 77th Precinct broke. Thirteen cops were indicted and later convicted for running their own crime sprees. They got the name, "Buddy Boys," from the radio signal, "Buddy Bob, meet at 234," which they used to call their crew when hitting a target.

Then in the 1990s, there was the widespread corruption in Harlem's 30th Precinct which was called the "Dirty Thirty." Led by Sergeant Kevin P. Nannery and known as "Nannery's Raiders," this group of corrupt cops conducted their own unauthorized and illegal raids on drug dealers. They stole cash and drugs which they later sold on the street. That crew was so brazen they sold the drugs right out of the precinct house.

But I was getting too far ahead of myself. I needed to stay in the present and not project. Projecting is something I do really well. It's a common habit of alcoholics, a habit that's hard to break even after years of recovery.

Left to my own devices, I could work myself into a completely frenzied state of mind over even the smallest problem. And Richie's problem was far from small.

I probably don't have to tell you that projecting is not a good thing. It's like suddenly finding yourself in outer space and not knowing how you got there, or how you're going to get back to earth. So, to avoid projecting, I go to AA meetings and talk with my sponsor, Doug. That's what I was doing, talking to Doug, when I passed a newsstand and noticed the headline in the *New York Post*: *"CATHOUSE RAIDED IN BIG SHOOTOUT – FOUR DEAD INCLUDING THE MADAM – COP UNDER ARREST FOR MURDER."*

CHAPTER 7

I quickly hung up with Doug and bought a newspaper. It seemed everybody in New York City now knew more about the case than I did. I had some heavy duty catching up to do.

Rather than standing in the middle of the crowded sidewalk trying to read the paper, I popped into a Starbucks and found an empty seat in a far corner. Nobody seemed to notice or care that I hadn't bought a cup of coffee, so I just sat there and read the paper.

It was a long article, with police photographs of the crime scene and quite a few details, most attributed to Deputy Chief William McNulty. There were two or three quotes from Detective Chen of the 5th Precinct, but all the pertinent information had come from McNulty. No surprise there.

According to McNulty's account, the Task Force had been established to close a brothel on Madison Street, operated by the Hip Sing Tong. Unfortunately, the raiding teams had encountered "unexpected resistance" in the form of hostile gunfire. The teams returned fire and in the ensuing battle, three men, presumed to be members of the Tong, were killed as was the brothel's madam, Kim Lee.

Then came the part about Richie. Citing Deputy Chief McNulty as the source, the article stated that Detective Richard Simone had been arrested at the scene for the murder of Kim Lee. As I suspected, McNulty claimed he had witnessed Richie kill an "unarmed and non-threatening" Lee. It was all very convenient, given the fact that Richie was unconscious at the time. It was also a very big problem.

McNulty had done quite a job on Richie, and it didn't end there. The article went on, again citing McNulty as the source. It claimed that no business records or any incriminating evidence was found on the premises, probably because word of the raid had been leaked to the Hip Sing Tong by a member of the Task Force. Apparently, when asked by the reporter about the open safe shown in the police photo, McNulty said it was empty.

The empty safe raised a question in my mind. Was McNulty signaling the brothel's well-to-do and politically powerful patrons that their identities were safe? Or was he warning them somebody would be in touch with them shortly?

The article didn't mention any patrons being arrested, so either they had been warned prior to the raid and left, or some of the cops on the raid were walking around with extra pocket money.

I'm not a cynic; I'm a realist. I don't blame a cop who turns a blind eye and makes a couple of bucks on a prostitution charge that's going to be dropped sooner or later. With rich guys like those patronizing the brothel, it's either pay the cop and walk away now, or pay some high-priced lawyer and walk away later. Maybe walking with a limp if their wives found out about it. The "Johns" weren't really my concern other than it meant having less potential witnesses.

I knew I had to get out in front of this thing fast, so the sooner I had my PI, Tommy Shoo, working on the case, the better. I left the Starbucks with the newspaper tucked under my arm and double timed it to my office.

CHAPTER 8

Before leaving the hospital, I called Connie, my secretary, to let her know I would be late coming in, but I didn't tell her why. Connie has been my secretary for almost seven years, and over that time, she's gotten to know Richie well. She can also be very emotional, so I was sure the news of Richie's arrest would upset her. That was why I had decided to wait and tell her in person.

Now that I was in the office, I explained it all to her. Connie just kept shaking her head and saying, "It can't be. It can't be." I agreed, and now it was our job to prove it.

When Tommy showed up and I told him what was going on, he was equally surprised. Tommy didn't know Richie as well as I did, but he had met him enough times to know he wasn't a murderer. Tommy also knew Richie and I were close, not as close as he and I, but close enough to warrant pulling out all the stops on the investigation.

I met Tommy Shoo almost fifteen years ago, when he and I shared the backroom in his grandfather's restaurant on Mott Street. Back then I was barely surviving on 18B Panel assigned cases, and Tommy was selling knockoff Rolexes. We've both come a long way since then. I'm sober going on seven years and Tommy, who did odd investigative jobs for me back then, became a full-fledged licensed private investigator.

Tommy was raised in Chinatown by his grandfather after his parents were killed in the 9/11 attack. As a result, he is very much a part of the Chinatown world. Chinatown is a closed and very private world, operating by its own rules. If you're not Chinese, that world is closed to you. That's why the 5th Precinct is manned mostly by Chinese cops. It's also why Tommy is such a good investigator when it comes to Chinatown cases.

About two years ago, with his business doing well, Tommy had moved his office from the backroom of his grandfather's restaurant to a building on Elizabeth Street, right down the block from the 5th Precinct. He had also hired Linda Chow, a computer wizard, who could find her way into just about anyone's computer in a matter of minutes. Whether the entry was legal was another matter and a question I usually left unasked.

Tommy and I had just started working when my cell rang. It was Gracie. News of the raid on the brothel and Richie's arrest was circulating through the DA's Office. The word was, McNulty had called from the scene and demanded an ADA from the Special Litigation Bureau be sent to deal with an arrest. When the ADA arrived, McNulty gave a sworn statement, saying he witnessed Detective Simone shoot and kill Kim Lee. He claimed Kim Lee was unarmed and not threatening Richie at the time he shot her. Based on that statement, Richie was arrested and charged with murder.

Gracie said she'd try to get me a copy of McNulty's statement, but it wouldn't be easy. Everybody knew we were a couple, and rumor already had it that I was representing Simone. I wasn't sure how the rumor got started, but I figured someone saw me at the hospital and put two and two together.

I told Tommy I needed a complete investigative work up on Deputy Chief William McNulty. That meant everything he could find on the man and everything Linda could dig up. I wanted to know about his finances, how much money he had, where he kept his money, and where it all came from. If he had any secret bank accounts, I wanted to know about it. It was a tall order, but if McNulty was dirty, the easiest way to prove it was through his finances. Always follow the money.

I also needed to know everything about the brothel's operation. Who was Kim Lee? Where had she come from? Was she part of the Hip Sing Tong, and did she have any connection to McNulty?

This was where Tommy's intimate knowledge of Chinatown paid dividends. He knew a lot about the Hip Sing Tong. For years, the Hip Sing had run all the prostitution rings in Chinatown. They also did a big drug trade, working with the Flying Dragons youth gang.

When I mentioned the Golden Palace restaurant on Pell Street where Richie thought he saw McNulty with Sam Yeoung, Tommy smiled. He said the Golden Palace was a Hip Sing hangout and was owned by Sam Yeoung, the Tong's top boss.

There was a lot of work to do, and Tommy was anxious to get started, so I sent him on his way. He had just left the office when Gracie called again to let me know that Richie's arraignment was scheduled to take place at the hospital at three o'clock that afternoon.

Arraigning a prisoner in a hospital bed is not unusual, but the speed with which it was being done was unusual. Most times it's a logistical problem, getting a judge, a prosecutor, a court reporter, and a defense attorney, all in the hospital room at the same time. The judge is usually the toughest one to get into the room, and most times, it takes days before it happens. But for some reason, Richie's case was being expedited.

I gave Laura a call to let her know about the arraignment. She was still at the hospital with Richie, and we talked briefly about possible bail arrangements. I told her I'd help her find a bail bondsman after the arraignment. I was being optimistic. I really didn't know if the judge would grant bail. In class A felony cases bail isn't always granted; it is up to the judge. I didn't know what the District

Attorney's position on bail would be, but there was no legal reason that bail couldn't be granted. I was just hoping if there was a conspiracy, it didn't reach all the way up and into the District Attorney's Office. I'd just have to wait for the arraignment to find out.

CHAPTER 9

I was about to head to the Worth Street Coffee Shop to meet with Jimmy O'Brien when Connie reminded me of the Delgato sentencing hearing. In all the excitement over Richie's case, I had forgotten about it. Jose Delgato was an 18B Panel client scheduled to be sentenced by Judge Goldstein at three o'clock. It was just a simple appearance, with nothing for me to do except pretend I was listening, look sympathetic, and nod my head occasionally. Still, I was expected to be there.

It was time to call Abe Fishman. Abe has been practicing criminal law in Lower Manhattan for decades and is a legend in the Criminal Court. Years ago, when I was a young ADA, Abe was just hitting his stride and making a real name for himself. Almost everyone in the DA's Office hated going up against him, but not me. I believed the best way to learn was to go up against the best.

The first time we crossed swords, he kicked my butt royally. But I learned more from that trial than I had from any of the past trials I had won. The next time we met, I won. But I have to say, in fairness to Abe, he had a bad case. His client was guilty as sin but refused to plea bargain. Even at that, Abe made it closer than it should have been. The jury was out for three days before returning a guilty verdict.

At the time, I was drinking heavily and had earned a reputation as a "smart-ass." So, when the jury returned with the guilty verdict, I said to Abe, "I guess that makes us even." I remember to this day his reply, "In your dreams, kid. Only in your dreams will you and I ever be even." It wasn't for a number of years that I learned Abe really liked me. He thought I was a bit cocky, but talented, and after I got sober, we became good friends. The fact that getting sober was a humbling experience for me undoubtedly helped our relationship.

A few years ago, Abe retired, and he and his wife moved to Florida. Sadly, after six months of retirement living, his wife died of a heart attack. Abe didn't play golf, didn't play tennis, and hated the beach and hot weather. Other than the early-bird specials, there wasn't anything about Florida Abe liked, so he moved back to Manhattan.

It turned out there wasn't much Abe liked in Manhattan either, other than practicing law. But he didn't want to return to full-time practice, so he began doing per diem work. Per diem, which means, "for the day," is a fancy way of saying he handled appearances for lawyers who, like me, found their calendars overbooked.

I called Abe, and fortunately, he was free that afternoon. He had just finished an arraignment hearing and had nothing on for the rest of the day. I explained my predicament and told him what I needed. It was a simple job. Basically, all Abe had to do was show up and take my place at looking sympathetic while the judge sent Delgato off to prison for fifteen years.

Looking sympathetic at sentencing hearings is something criminal defense lawyers learn to do early in their careers. It doesn't do anything to change the judge's ruling; it just makes the client feel better knowing his lawyer isn't indifferent to his plight. That's particularly important if there is still an outstanding fee due and owing. But looking sympathetic is not so important with 18B Panel clients, so most 18B Panel attorneys do it strictly for the practice.

CHAPTER 10

When I reached the Worth Street Coffee Shop, Jimmy O'Brien was already there, seated in my private booth in the back. We ordered some lunch and got down to business.

Jimmy had worked with Richie on the brothel case from the start and was with him on the night of the raid. Other than Richie, he had the most information to offer about what happened, and I wanted to hear the whole story. I told Jimmy to start at the beginning and not to leave out any details.

As Jimmy recalled, word of the brothel's existence first came from a confidential informant. After the information was confirmed by a second source, the Precinct Detective Squad had been ordered to investigate and close down the operation. But the brothel was in the ever-expanding Chinatown section of the 7th Precinct, and the Caucasian Detectives of the 7th Precinct were having difficulty infiltrating the place.

Frustrated by the lack of progress, the Precinct Captain suggested to the Deputy Chief of Bureau that a Joint Task Force be formed with Chinatown's 5th Precinct. The idea was approved by Deputy Chief McNulty, and the Task Force was created.

Using the Chinese undercover cops from the 5th Precinct, the Task Force got the break it needed when an undercover cop not only managed to get a job in the brothel as a bartender, but cultivated a relationship with Li Chin, one of the brothel's working girls.

At some point, Li Chin told the undercover Detective how the girls were being brought from China and being kept at a warehouse in Brooklyn. That's when the investigation was expanded to include the human smuggling angle.

Jimmy remembered it was after that when McNulty began taking an active role in the Task Force operations. According to Jimmy, McNulty's involvement got unusually heavy-handed, and that pissed off Richie and the other guys who felt McNulty was stepping on their authority.

Things reached a head when Richie and Detective Chen from the 5th Precinct decided it was time to raid the brothel and shut it down, but McNulty nixed the plan. A few weeks later, Richie and Chen brought up another plan to raid the brothel. When it seemed McNulty was going to nix that plan as well, Richie threatened to take the matter "upstairs," and that was when McNulty relented and agreed to the raid. Richie hadn't mentioned that part to me, but other than that, his story and Jimmy's story matched up. At least that far.

On the night of the raid, everybody met at the 5th Precinct. There were three teams—two raided the brothel, and the third raided the warehouse in Brooklyn, where the girls were being held. Richie led one of the teams raiding the brothel. The other team raiding the brothel was led by Chen. Richie's team rushed the brothel's front entrance, while Chen's team hit the back door.

The plan was to hit the brothel from the front and back simultaneously. With the element of surprise working in the raiding teams' favor, they hoped to quickly overpower the little resistance they expected to encounter. Jimmy was the second one to enter the brothel, right behind Richie. Once inside, Richie and Jimmy were supposed to move immediately to the second-floor office and secure the location to prevent anyone from destroying any records.

There had been no reason to suspect that the operation had been blown, so no one was expecting any problems. The only unexpected event before the raid was that McNulty showed up and announced he'd go with Richie's team. Jimmy knew Richie wasn't happy about McNulty being there, but there was nothing he could do about it.

When the teams hit the brothel, things went sideways immediately. The security goons inside apparently had been warned about the raid and were prepared and waiting for them. The moment Richie and Jimmy went through the doors, they were met with gunfire.

Richie had been the first one through the door and hollered for everyone to take cover. Jimmy had come through the door right behind Richie, and McNulty had come in right behind him. The three men dove behind some heavy furniture and took cover.

The rest of the raid team, facing a barrage of bullets, had no choice but to take cover outside the front entrance of the brothel. Richie ordered his team to hold their positions outside the brothel and called dispatch for a SWAT team backup. Then with Jimmy and McNulty providing cover fire, Richie ran to the staircase. From his position, Jimmy saw Richie reach the top of the stairs.

Jimmy knew the office was just across the hall from where Richie was standing, and it seemed to him that Richie had a good view into the office.

Jimmy was about to ask McNulty to lay down some cover fire, so he could break for the stairs when McNulty made his own move toward the staircase. That left Jimmy with no option but to lay down cover fire for McNulty.

Once Jimmy stopped firing his weapon, return fire started, and all he could do was drop back into his covered position and wait for the SWAT team to arrive.

When Jimmy looked over at the staircase, Richie was no longer on the stairs, and McNulty, who had reached the top landing, was apparently moving forward toward the office.

Jimmy held his position until reinforcements arrived. When the SWAT team arrived ten minutes later and laid down heavy rounds of cover fire, Jimmy was finally able to make his way up the stairs.

Once at the top of the stairs, he could see inside the office. Three people were down, and McNulty was kneeling over a woman's body. Entering the office, he saw Richie was on the floor, not moving. Just beyond him was the woman Jimmy presumed was Kim Lee, and behind Richie, near a second doorway, laid a Chinese man. The smell of exploding gunpowder hung heavily in the air.

Jimmy's mention of a second doorway puzzled me, and I had him stop his story for a minute. I knew from the newspaper account that there were some dead Chinese guys, but Richie hadn't mentioned anyone in the room. This was the first I was hearing of it, and it complicated things. I suspected he might have come into the room after Richie was shot. But why hadn't Richie seen the man after he regained consciousness? He saw Kim Lee lying on the floor, so why not the Chinese guy?

And why hadn't he mentioned the second doorway into the office? I had to figure that after entering the office, he had surveyed the area to make sure it was secure. So, either he didn't think it was important to tell me about the doorway, or he hadn't seen it. I made a quick note to ask Richie about that and told Jimmy to continue.

Jimmy ran to Richie, asking McNulty what had happened. McNulty said as he was getting to the office, he saw Richie shoot Lee Kim three times in the chest. Then the Chinese guy came through the side door and fired three shots at Richie who went down. McNulty fired four shots at the Chinese guy and took him down. So, now I had another supposed shooter to deal with. Things were getting much too complicated.

Richie was unconscious, but breathing, and McNulty said he had called for an ambulance, so there nothing more Jimmy could do for him. Looking around the room, Jimmy saw only one gun on the floor. It was a .38 caliber revolver, and it was next to the Chinese guy. He asked McNulty where Richie's gun was, and McNulty said he had it in his waistband, and he pulled back his jacket and showed him. When Jimmy asked him why he had Richie's gun, McNulty said it was because Richie was under arrest for murdering Kim Lee.

I asked Jimmy how many shots he heard fired, hoping that might help me figure out what had happened. But he said the scene had been chaotic, and shots were being fired all over the place. He really couldn't tell where the shots were coming from. In thinking more about it, he said that most of the shots sounded like they came from 9-millimeter pistols, but there were a couple, maybe three or four shots, that sounded more like they came from a small caliber pistol. Maybe the .38 caliber gun that was next to the dead Chinese guy.

I was trying to envision the scene and put together a scenario that didn't include Richie shooting an unarmed woman, but I was having a problem. When the murder took place, there had been three people in the room, in addition to the victim. One was dead, another was Richie, who was unconscious most of the time, and the last was probably a corrupt cop. That meant there was just one eyewitness, and obviously, he wasn't going to do me any good.

Maybe when all the forensic evidence was in, it might tell a different story, but that was a long shot. At the moment, everything in my mind was pointing to McNulty as the shooter, but there was no evidence to prove it. Still, Richie's best defense was nailing McNulty as a crooked cop. I just had to figure out how I was going to do that.

Jimmy, of course, didn't believe Richie had murdered Kim Loo, and he had no doubt McNulty was crooked and behind the frame-up. He didn't have anything to back up his theory, just his instincts after twenty years on the job. Still, hearing him say it made me feel better.

I asked Jimmy if any of the brothel's records had been captured in the raid. I wasn't surprised to hear that none were, or at least none were logged into evidence. If whatever Richie saw Kim Lee removing from the safe hadn't been logged into evidence, who took it and where was it? The answer to those questions would elude me for a long time.

There was something else bothering me about this whole safe issue. If the brothel had been tipped off about the raid, how come the safe hadn't been cleaned out earlier? Jimmy said it bothered him, too, and the only thing he could figure was that the tip-off came only minutes before the raid.

That was more or less confirmed when Jimmy spoke with Chen afterwards. Chen told him that his team had seen several half naked men and women in the alley behind the brothel. Clearly, there hadn't been a lot of time to dress and escape.

I asked Jimmy what happened to the "Johns" in the alley, and he said none were charged because there was no proof they had been inside the brothel. Like there was another reason why half naked Caucasian men would be cavorting with half naked Chinese women in an alley outside of a Chinese brothel while it was being raided by the cops? Just sheer coincidence and colossal bad luck for the guys, I guess.

We were done. Jimmy had told me everything he knew, and I couldn't think of any other questions to ask. It had been a good start, but it was just a start, and l needed a lot more help than that.

Jimmy said he'd stay in touch and do whatever he could to help Richie. I believe he meant it, but we both knew if this conspiracy went higher up the line of command, helping Richie could be a career killer. I couldn't be sure Jimmy would risk his job and his pension to help a friend, and I can't say I'd blame him if he didn't.

I left the Worth Street Coffee Shop with plenty of time to get to the hospital for the arraignment, so I decided to walk there. Along the way, I called Gracie to see if she had any news and to make plans for dinner.

Gracie had seen McNulty's statement and hoped to have a copy for me in a day or two. She said it was a straightforward eyewitness account of the murder, and nothing in it stood out as unusual. That made sense. McNulty knew his statement was going to be questioned by Richie's lawyer, so he'd keep it simple. That was always the best way to go, especially if it was a lie. It's always better to keep as close to the truth as possible and limit the details of the lies. Lies with too many details are hard to keep straight.

Gracie wanted to know if I'd be free in time for dinner. I said I would be, and I suggested we meet for a sushi dinner at the Japanese restaurant she likes. I don't like sushi, but I was feeling horny, so that's why I suggested the Japanese restaurant. You're probably wondering what being horny has to do with a sushi dinner, so let me explain. As I said, I don't like sushi much, but Gracie does, and over the years, we've developed this unspoken rule that after a sushi dinner, we go to her place and have sex.

CHAPTER 11

When I got to Richie's hospital room, the same cop was sitting outside the door. This time he made no effort to stop me from going in; he just nodded his head and smiled.

Laura was sitting and reading a book, and Richie was reading the newspaper. Nothing particularly unusual, but I sensed something was off. It didn't register right away, but then it hit me. Laura was sitting in the chair farthest away from the bed, and Richie had his back to her. It was something that might have gone unnoticed if I didn't know them as well as I did. But seeing them turned away from each other, I knew right away something was going on between them.

Under other circumstances, it would have been none of my business, but with Richie about to be arraigned on murder charges, it was my business. The way I saw it, my job was to get them through this mess, and if that included an attitude adjustment or two, so be it. Besides, they were my friends.

When I asked what was up, neither of them said anything right away. I was about to change the subject when Laura spoke up. She said she had wanted to call Cathy and Lucy to let them know what was happening with their father, but Richie didn't want her to do that. I looked at Richie, and he just grunted, confirming his opposition.

Both girls were married and lived out of state, so it was unlikely they had heard anything about the case, at least not yet. Richie felt it was better if they waited a while before contacting the girls. Laura thought it best to call them right away, and she asked what I thought.

Richie wasn't happy that Laura asked my opinion, and he was throwing daggers my way. But his stare didn't intimidate me, and I happily gave my opinion. Call them now; don't let them hear about this from someone else. Richie didn't argue which meant he knew I was right. He just looked at Laura and agreed as soon as the arraignment was over, they'd call the girls.

Things seemed to be warming up between Richie and Laura, but I thought it best to change the subject, so I asked Richie about the dead Chinese guy and the second doorway into the office. Richie thought about it for a minute, then he said before entering the office, he had surveyed the area and saw no one else inside except for Kim Lee. When he regained consciousness, he was lying on his back, and his field of vision was limited, so he never saw the Chinese guy who was lying on the floor behind him. As for the second doorway, he had seen the door when he entered the office, but it was closed, and he didn't know if it was a second entrance or a closet.

That explained things, but it didn't help the narrative I was starting to create in my head. I was thinking McNulty had shot Richie, then he shot Kim Lee, but now it wasn't that simple. I had to figure out how the dead Chinese guy figured into all of this. Did he come in before McNulty shot Kim Lee or after, and how had McNulty managed to shoot Richie and kill Kim Lee and the Chinese guy before Jimmy arrived? I had a lot of work to do.

Sensing the thaw between Richie and Laura had hit a wall, I decided a story from the old days might loosen things up. Seeing Richie in handcuffs reminded me of an old war story from our early days. Knowing the situation could benefit from a little levity, I said that the last time I saw Richie handcuffed, it was to a hooker. Not something you'd expect me to say in front of a friend's wife, but the story was innocent enough, and Laura had probably heard it anyway.

Richie remembered the incident and started to laugh. Laura either hadn't heard the story before or, more likely, she didn't remember it and wanted to know all about it. Especially the part about the hooker. She had a very serious look on her face, but I could tell she was just playing along, and she wasn't really upset. Not yet anyway.

It was a good story, and we needed something to break the tension, so I told it even though I wasn't sure Richie wanted me to.

It happened years ago, when Richie was a newly minted plainclothes cop, and he was assigned to the vice squad working around Times Square and 42nd Street. In those days, Times Square was known as Slime Square. Gone were the days of Damon Runyon's Guys and Dolls, replaced by nights of Sodom and Gomorrah.

Times Square's transformation from a world-class tourist attraction to a hellhole happened quickly. It began with the movie theaters lining 42nd Street running porno films instead of the usual Hollywood hits. Not surprisingly this attracted hustlers and perverts to the area, and soon tourists were avoiding Times Square and 42nd Street like the plague.

With the tourists gone, the small souvenir shops on the block were forced to close, and they were quickly replaced by peep show joints and sex shops. Prostitutes openly and brazenly paraded the streets, while barkers enticed passersby to enter the slime palaces. The transformation was complete.

The situation worsened as the sex trade spread to neighboring streets. Finally, public outrage reached the point when the mayor was forced to take action and clean up the area. But doing so turned out to be more difficult that he expected. Closing down the porno palaces raised freedom of speech issues, and simply arresting the hookers didn't discourage them for plying their trade.

It seemed most of the hookers knew the vice cops and simply avoided soliciting them. But even when the cops managed to make an arrest, all that happened was the hooker paid a fine and went back to work. As far as the hookers were concerned, being arrested was just an inconvenient cost of doing business. For the cops, cleaning up Times Square was like trying to empty the ocean with a sea shell.

Then a genius in the Office of the Mayor came up with a plan to deal with the hookers. They called it a "crime deterrence program," which was just a fancy name for a plan to harass the hookers. The idea was to arrest them daily until they tired of the process and left the area. The theory being, if the ladies of the night were spending most of their time locked up waiting to pay their fines, the loss of income would encourage them to work elsewhere.

In theory it was a good plan, but there was a problem. The hookers knew the vice squad cops too well and simply avoided them. For the plan to work, they needed new faces that the hookers didn't recognize. So, scores of plainclothes cops, including Richie and his partner, were assigned to run what amounted to buy and bust stings on the Times Square prostitutes.

It was a simple operation, with two cops working as a team. One cop pretended to be the customer, and the other made the arrest as soon as the cash changed hands. It never went any further than the cash changing hands. I mentioned that to put Laura's mind at ease.

To keep the hookers from realizing the cops were pulling a sting operation, and blowing the one cop's cover, both parties were arrested and taken to the station house for processing.

It was working out fine, with Richie and his partner taking turns being the customer. Then one night Richie, playing the role of the customer, approached a woman who said her name was Sugar. Sugar offered her services, money changed hands, and Joe, Richie's partner, arrested both of them. He handcuffed them together and put them in the back seat of the police cruiser.

Everything was fine until Joe inadvertently referred to Richie as his partner, and Sugar figured out she had been duped. She turned on Richie, and with the two of them handcuffed together in the back of the police cruiser, she began to scratch, claw, and bite the crap out of him.

She continued to maul poor Richie until Joe was able to pull the cruiser over to the curb and untangle the pair. Before Sugar was subdued, she had done a pretty good job on poor Richie. When I saw Richie later that night at Sugar's arraignment, he looked like he had gone ten rounds with a big bad alley cat.

Laura remembered the incident and recalled Richie coming home all scratched up. We still had a good laugh over the retelling. Even Richie, who complained that his ribs hurt when he laughed, had a good chuckle over the story.

But it was time to move on. I mentioned that I had met with Jimmy and relayed what Jimmy had told me. While I was recounting my meeting with Jimmy, Laura had gotten up from the chair and was now sitting on the bed, holding Richie's hand.

Laura wanted to know what was going to happen next. Explaining the arraignment process was easy, and Laura didn't have any questions until I got to the part about bail. When I said that hopefully the judge would grant bail, Laura got an anxious look on her face and asked why the judge wouldn't grant bail. I explained it was up to the judge, but I saw no reason why he wouldn't.

Laura still looked worried, and I knew why. Being a cop's wife, she knew what was likely to happen to Richie if he was sent to Rikers Island Jail. Rikers is the infamous New York City jail where defendants awaiting trial are held, and it's where criminals sentenced to less than a year serve their time. It's generally overcrowded and always dangerous, especially for a cop who's sent hundreds of criminals there.

I needed Laura to stay positive, so I lied and told her I was sure the judge would grant bail. I did have a plan in case the judge denied bail, but I didn't mention it. No sense stirring things up if I didn't have to. As for Richie, I was sure he knew if bail was denied, I'd ask that he be held in protective custody, outside of the general population.

Despite my reassurances, Laura didn't look convinced, and frankly, neither was I. So, we sat there waiting and worrying.

CHAPTER 12

When everyone arrived for the arraignment and squeezed their way into the small hospital room, there wasn't enough space left to swing a cat. I know that's an old expression, and for a long time I didn't know what it meant. I kept asking why you would want to swing a cat. Not that I particularly liked cats, but it seemed like an unusually cruel thing to do to poor old Tabby. Then someone explained that it referred to a cat o' nine tails, a multi-tailed whip used as severe physical punishment to discipline sailors on sailing ships. Now it made sense; if there was a crowd, you couldn't swing the whip. It turned out it had nothing to do with old Tabby after all.

Anyway, the room was jammed. The court reporter was seated next to the bed with her stenotype machine squeezed between the chair and the bed. Judge Garcia from the New York City Criminal Court and his law clerk stood shoulder to shoulder at the foot of the bed, using the tray table as a desk. ADA Marty Bowman, stood at the side of the bed between the judge and the court reporter, and I stood on the other side of the bed. Laura positioned herself in the corner between the wall and the nightstand. A court officer stood in the doorway, unable to come any further into the room. That made seven of us, not including Richie, jammed into the small hospital room. I imagined somewhere there was an occupancy warning sign, and as much as I wanted to mention it, I thought it best to keep my mouth shut.

The formalities took less than ten minutes. Marty Bowman read the charge; I waived a reading of the complaint; and the judge asked when the case would be brought before the Grand Jury. In all felony cases, a formal plea isn't entered until after a Grand Jury indictment is issued, so there was no plea entered. If the Grand Jury handed down an indictment, there'd be a second arraignment in Supreme Court at which Richie would enter his formal not guilty plea.

All that was left was the matter of bail. It was up to the judge to decide whether to allow bail, and if so, how much. But before he decided, he'd want to know the District Attorney's position. I hadn't been able to speak with Marty before the arraignment, so I wasn't sure what he had in mind, but I wasn't optimistic. This was a second degree murder case, and the DA normally wants the defendant held in custody pending trial. Technically it's called remand. So, I was surprised when Marty didn't ask for remand, just a high bail.

I didn't know why the District Attorney was being so reasonable, but it suggested he was all-in on the charge. Maybe he was leery because there hadn't been a thorough investigation, and the whole case hinged on McNulty's statement. But it was still a strong case, so maybe it was just the way McNulty had forced the arrest, demanding that a DA take his statement at the scene of the crime. DAs don't like being pushed around, especially by members of the NYPD. And DAs especially hate losing high profile cases like Richie's, and they generally won't bring weak cases or cases with problems. When forced to do so by the NYPD or the mayor, the DA's Office usually sends a message that bringing the case wasn't the DA's idea. That would explain why Bowman hadn't asked for remand. Whatever the reason, it was helping us, and I wasn't going to question it.

When Judge Garcia asked my position on bail, I pointed out that Richie had strong ties to the community, had no past criminal record, was a highly-decorated police officer with a wife and two daughters, and was anxious to appear in court to clear his name. I asked that he be released on his own recognizance, knowing there was no way it would happen. So why ask? You never know what a judge is thinking, and when the DA isn't asking for remand, you take your best shot.

Best shot or not, Judge Garcia wasn't buying it. He set bail at $250,000. It was a bit on the high side, but reasonable given the charge.

With nothing else on the agenda, Judge Garcia adjourned the hearing, and the room quickly emptied.

Things had gone well, but arraignments have a funny effect on people, especially those close to the defendant. Seeing the judge and the court officer turns their nightmare into a reality. Any hope that the nightmare is going away evaporates, replaced by the very real prospect of prison. I don't know why that happens, but I've seen it happen often enough to expect it.

I could tell from the panicked look spreading on Laura's face it was happening to her. Richie was stone-faced, but I knew underneath he was worried. He had reason to be worried. He knew damn well the odds didn't favor him, and if the conspiracy went high enough up the line, his chance of beating the rap was just about non-existent.

The odds may have been against us, but it was important for Richie and Laura to keep a positive attitude. Once a client goes negative, it's tough to bring them back, and that's not good. *Nothing says lovin' like something from the oven*, and nothing says guilty like a dejected defendant.

A dejected defendant gives off a scent of guilt, a scent any ADA can smell, just as an animal can smell fear. If the jurors pick up the scent, it becomes a silent confession of guilt, and the case is pretty much lost.

Explaining this to most of my criminal clients is a waste of time, as most will never face trial, and the concept is probably beyond their ability to comprehend. I say that not cruelly, but from experience. Having once explained it to a client who had opted for a trial, I was amazed when he sat the whole time, staring at the jury with this idiotic grin on his face.

As much as I tried to explain that a big grin didn't seem appropriate for someone facing charges of kidnapping and murder, he just wouldn't listen. I often wonder whether he's still grinning in Attica where he's serving two life sentences.

The only way I know to keep a client's attitude positive is to have him and his family focus on his defense, and that's what I tried doing with Richie and Laura. I wasn't going to give them false hope. I'd simply lay out a defense strategy and a plan of action. No promises, no guarantees, just a strategy, and a plan.

The strategy began with the assumption that McNulty was the only eyewitness. Given the circumstances as I knew them from Richie and Jimmy O'Brien, that was a safe bet. So, our first objective would be to dirty McNulty up as much as we could, and make him out to be an unreliable witness.

It was too early in the case to know what was in the police forensic reports, but we'd have to assume whatever they contained wouldn't be helpful. On the other hand, I couldn't imagine there'd be anything in them that would make matters worse. I know that's not exactly a positive way of putting things, but it was a realistic appraisal, and as I said, I didn't want to give any false hope.

Getting back to McNulty, I said it seemed clear that he was a dirty cop working with Sam Yeoung and the Hip Sing Tong. With that in mind, I had Tommy investigating the Tong and Sam Yeoung, as well as McNulty's finances. Whatever connection there was, Tommy would find it. As for McNulty's finances, I explained how Linda Chow was working on that aspect of the case. I didn't mention exactly what she was doing. It's always best to keep those sorts of details secret.

As I'd hoped, talking about the defense lifted the mood in the room. It was a good time to talk about Richie's bail. I reminded Richie that in a second degree murder case, the DA usually asks for remand, and Bowman hadn't, which I took as a good sign. Richie agreed. Laura wanted to know why it was a good sign, and I explained it to her.

But none of it mattered at that moment. What was important was getting Richie out of custody before he was sent to Rikers Island. I made a call to my buddy, Sal, at A-1 Bail Service and told him I needed to arrange a quick $250,000 bail bond. He laughed. A quick $250,000 bail bond is like a cheap apartment in Manhattan. People often talk about them, but they don't actually exist.

You can get a $5,000 bond, quickly, but a $250,000 bond is going to take time and a bit of doing. Fortunately, Richie was going to be in the hospital for at least another day, so that gave us a little time to work things out.

Sal owed me big-time, but no bail bondsman is going to issue a $250,000 bond without backing. That meant Richie and Laura would have to put up their house as collateral. Luckily, they had recently paid off the mortgage. I told Laura to make a copy of the deed and bring it with her to my office the next morning. I'd help her with the paperwork, and then we'd go together to A-1 Bail Service. Even with full backing, the bond fee would be 10%, so Richie and Laura were already in the hole for $25,000, and the case had just gotten underway.

No one ever said justice was cheap. At least no one who's ever been arrested.

CHAPTER 13

Laura arrived at the office bright and early the next morning, anxious to arrange Richie's bail. She had a copy of the deed to their house and had transferred $25,000 from their savings account into their checking account to cover the fee. Hopefully, once the paperwork was done, we'd be good to go.

It was important that Laura keep a positive attitude. Things were going to get a lot worse before they got better, and if she couldn't keep it together now, she'd never make it through to the end.

I was glad to learn that after I had left the hospital, she and Richie had called their daughters and told them what was going on. Both girls wanted to fly to New York right away, but Richie convinced them there was nothing they could do, and it would be better for everyone if they stayed away for the time being. It was a good call. Having the girls around would peak media interest, and we didn't need that.

I think having to explain the situation to the girls had forced Laura into a more positive attitude, at least temporarily. But I was worried because she didn't have that look of strength and confidence I was accustomed to seeing.

The first time I met Laura, I could tell right off she was a strong person. Now, after living with Richie, a street hardened cop, for more than twenty-five years, she was even stronger. That was why, as we sat drinking coffee waiting for Connie to make copies of the papers, I was surprised and a little worried that Laura looked so fragile. Or maybe the look was one of fear. Either way, it was trouble, and we needed to talk about it.

At first, Laura didn't want to talk about it, but I pressed her. Not hard, just gently like an old friend. Finally, she relented. After she told me her story, I knew why this strong, confident woman was suddenly so frightened.

Shortly after she and Richie were married, she started having panic attacks every time Richie left for work. At first, they thought it was normal; after all, he had a dangerous job. Richie tried to reassure her, but the attacks got worse, not better, and soon they began to completely overwhelm her. That's when she sought professional help.

With the help of a therapist, she learned to cope with the dangers of Richie's job, and her panic attacks eventually went away.

But this situation was different for her. While she could live with the possibility of Richie being killed on the job, she couldn't face the possibility of him going to prison for the rest of his life. She said it probably didn't make sense, but that was how she felt. I said it made sense to me, and it did. It also explained why this woman, who was usually strong, looked so fragile.

I hoped that by knowing what was bothering her, I could help her face this new set of fears. I started by explaining that with a little luck, Richie would be free on bail by late afternoon. This seemed to make her feel better, but she questioned what would happen if we didn't get Richie out that day. I told her not to worry because even if it took until tomorrow, Richie would still be in the hospital and not facing a stay at Rikers Island.

Laura nodded, but I could tell by the look on her face she was still anxious. I wasn't surprised. This was one of her big fears about Richie going to jail. She knew, as well as anyone, if Richie wound up in Rikers, he might be locked up with some of the scumbags he had put there. It was one of those worries she never had to face before.

I wasn't going to lie to her because her fear was rational, and lying wouldn't help. The best I could do was to tell her again that I didn't think Richie was going to Rikers, but even if he did, I'd see that he was kept out of the general population and in protective custody.

To be honest, I was concerned about it myself. Rikers Island was run by the Corrections Department, and while it has no direct link to the NYPD, McNulty could have connections in the department or at the jail. If Richie was placed in the general population and someone recognized him, or someone sent word that he was a cop, he'd get beaten badly and maybe killed. But it wouldn't be a problem as long as I got him out on bail, so I wasn't going to dwell on it. I was going to concentrate on arranging his bail.

CHAPTER 14

Connie had just finished making copies of the papers, and Laura and I were getting ready to leave when Abe Fishman showed up. Abe was handling a plea conference for me that morning. It was another case I had to toss his way to make time for Richie. Not that I was complaining, mind you. I asked Laura to sit in the reception area with Connie while I spoke with Abe.

There wasn't much to talk about. Abe had picked up the file the day before, so he knew all about the case. It was a simple, but serious domestic violence matter, and Abe knew how the bargaining on this one was going to go.

The client, Juan Sanchez, was charged with assault in the first degree, a class B felony, for beating up and stabbing his wife. On that charge, he faced five to twenty-five years in prison. This was not the first time Juan used his wife as a punching bag, and since he had a record for assaults outside the home as well, he was looking at a long stretch. Not that the thought of Juan rotting in jail bothered either Abe or me.

I looked at Abe, then he looked at me and said, "Anything less than twenty-five years is a gift." That said it all. Nothing more needed to be said. Abe would argue for less than the maximum, and he'd do a good job of it. But what was there to say? Abe couldn't argue the facts; they were all but admitted and confirmed by the hospital records. He couldn't argue Juan's past record because it sucked. If he threw Juan on the mercy of the court, he'd be inviting a maximum sentence. Juan had no redeeming social value whatsoever. So if Juan got twenty-five years, Abe wouldn't cry or lose any sleep over it. And why should he?

Abe left for the conference, and Laura and I went to meet with Sal Martinez, my friend, the bail bondsman. Every criminal defense lawyer knows at least one bail bondsman and probably more than one. Bail bondsmen are your friends so long as you send them good clients. Send them a skipper, and you no longer exist.

Many of my clients are 18B Panel referrals, and they can't make bail. If they could, they wouldn't qualify for 18 B Panel representation. My non-18B Panel clients, on the other hand, have money and can afford bail. If they didn't have money, they wouldn't qualify for my representation.

Clients who are good for the legal fees generally aren't skippers, so I send them to Sal. So far, no one I referred to him had skipped, so we were still friends. At least as far as I knew. With Sal you could never tell; he's funny that way.

Sal Martinez has been in the bail bond business, operating out of the same rundown storefront, for as long as I can remember. It's not a big operation, but it's big enough to keep Sal in cigars and those expensive cowboy boots he likes to wear.

The bail bond business and the practice of criminal law have one thing in common. Our clients are all either criminals, or at least accused of being criminals and probably can't be trusted. But that's where the similarity in our businesses ends.

Criminal lawyers realize their clients can't be trusted and demand to be paid in advance. Money up front or no work. That's smart. A bail bondsman, on the other hand, does the opposite. He puts his own money up front, relying on the guy to show up in court. That's not so smart.

Make a couple of mistakes as a bail bondsman, and you can lose a lot of money in a hurry. That's why Sal, like all bail bond agents, does whatever he can to minimize his risk. He chooses his clients carefully, makes most of them put up collateral, and even has some clients sign an agreement to visit his office once a week. And, of course, he only takes referrals from lawyers he trusts. Lawyers like me.

That's all good and well, but the risk is still there.

Sal's biggest deterrent against a client skipping is physical intimidation. Sal is six feet six inches tall and weighs 310 pounds. As a licensed Bail Enforcement Agent, commonly called a "bounty hunter," he is authorized to hunt down and return to custody anyone skipping out on bail.

On the wall behind his desk are a half dozen pictures of him with runaway clients in handcuffs, all looking the worse for wear. Over the pictures is a banner declaring, "A few have tried, but none have ever gotten away!"

I told Sal he should include a health warning on his application forms. Something along the lines of, "Skipping bail is definitely hazardous to your health and can result in loss of limbs, mobility, damage to internal organs, and in some cases, death." He liked the idea, but thought it had more impact if he issued the warning verbally.

I brought Laura here because Sal is fair and smart, plus he owed me a favor. Still, I wasn't expecting him to simply put up the bail money without conditions. The questions were about how many conditions he was going to impose, and how bad those conditions were going to be.

I made my pitch. Richie was a cop, a good man, a husband, a father, and in my humble opinion, innocent. He had no intention of skipping out, and there was no reason to get crazy with the conditions. Plus he owed me a favor. Simple and to the point. As I spoke, Sal sat listening and puffing on his cigar. I considered reminding him that his office was a public space, and smoking was prohibited by law. But I thought Sal might take my comment the wrong way.

When I finished my little speech, Sal wanted to know what Laura had to offer as collateral. I took a chance and asked if collateral was really necessary. Sal just laughed and puffed on his cigar. Okay, that hadn't worked, but the important thing was that I had tried.

I explained that Richie and Laura owned a mortgage-free home on Long Island, valued well in excess of the bail amount. Sal puffed and said as a favor to me that he'd accept the property as collateral without doing a formal record check to find out if it was actually free and clear and how much it was worth. Who said Sal didn't have a big heart?

The only thing left was the matter of the fee and some paperwork. For a $250,000 bond, the fee, set by statute, is slightly less than 10%. Usually Sal requires a bank check or a money order, but as another "favor" to me, he accepted a regular check. In less than an hour, we were done. Bail would be posted by early afternoon, so as soon as Richie was discharged from the hospital, he could go home.

Out on the sidewalk, Laura gave me a big hug, and for the first time in two days, I saw a look of hope in her eyes. My job now was to keep it there.

CHAPTER 15

By late afternoon bail had been posted, and technically Richie was no longer in custody. He was still in the hospital, but he was no longer handcuffed to the bed, and there was no cop sitting outside his door. Other than that, nothing had changed.

When I got to Richie's room, Laura was sitting on the chair next to the bed, and Richie was pacing around the room, or I should say, limping around on his wounded leg. A copy of the *New York Post* was on the bed, so obviously Richie had read the article.

"It's a setup, and I never saw it coming," he said, shaking his head. I knew how he felt, and there wasn't much I could say to make him feel better. All I could do was tell him we'd get to the bottom of it. Not that I necessarily believed we would.

In most criminal cases, the truth doesn't matter. That's because most criminal cases are resolved by plea bargaining, and plea bargaining isn't about the truth. Plea bargaining isn't even about justice. It's about efficiency and who has the stronger hand.

If you had told me when I was in law school that justice was a negotiable commodity, I would have laughed and said you didn't know what you were talking about. But once I was out in the real world, it didn't take long for me to find out how naive I had been. In fact, it happened almost overnight.

When I graduated from law school in 1981, New York City was in the grips of a crack cocaine epidemic. The crime rate was soaring and the NYPD, as I mentioned, was badly understaffed and struggling just to hold the line. The DA's Office was drowning in cases, and the jails were filled beyond capacity.

Justice wasn't an option; it was all about survival. For the cops, it was survival in the streets, and in the DA's Office, it was the survival of a court system so overburdened it was close to collapsing.

You couldn't blame the cops when they occasionally pushed the Constitutional envelope to take a crack dealer off the streets. For us, plea bargains were the norm, and the faster they were worked out the better. You hoped the punishment matched the crime, but if it didn't, no one cared because no one had time to care. I quickly learned it was circumstance, not justice, driving the system, and I wasn't going to change it. More importantly, I realized that I didn't want to change it.

Whatever idealism I had when I started the job was gone, and I began working the system for my own good. Being a hardnosed bastard and taking cases to trial didn't help clear the system, but it got me noticed and it got me promoted.

That's when I learned that everybody lied at trial, and "the truth" was as fictitious as Santa Claus and the Easter Bunny. In the end, the truth was whatever you convinced a jury to believe.

As an ADA, my job was to convince twelve people the defendant was guilty beyond a reasonable doubt. Not an easy task. The defense attorney, on the other hand, only had to convince one juror of reasonable doubt, and the case would end in a mistrial. I thought it was a lot easier being a criminal defense attorney; that was up until I actually became a criminal defense attorney.

There are times you don't appreciate something until it's gone. It wasn't until I handled my first case as a defense attorney that I realized what I had going for me as an ADA. I had the help of 31,000 cops, an army of criminal investigators, crime scene technicians, and the entire Office of Chief Medical Examiner helping me out. As a criminal defense attorney, there was me and that was it. Maybe I only needed to raise reasonable doubt, but I didn't have a lot of help doing so. I still don't. Well, that's not exactly true. I do have Tommy Shoo and Linda Chow, but that's it.

Proving something beyond a reasonable doubt sounds like a tough burden and sometimes it is. But when you have things like DNA evidence, eyewitnesses and even video recordings to help you, it's not really that difficult. In the end, it all depends on the facts, and sometimes the facts are as illusory as "the truth."

In Richie's case, the DA had to prove beyond a reasonable doubt that Richie had killed Kim Lee. I simply had to give the jury a reason to doubt he had. Easily accomplished if I had a solid alibi to offer or testimony from a witness who saw someone else killing her. Unfortunately, I had neither.

I hadn't seen the forensic reports yet, but I knew instinctively that the reports wouldn't be much help. I was sure the ballistic report would show the bullets that killed Kim Lee had come from Richie's gun. The setup had been too good for it to be otherwise.

The best and maybe the only strategy, under the circumstances, was to convince the jury McNulty was lying. Jimmy O'Brien's testimony would help, but it might not be enough to discredit McNulty's story. If there was no other witness to the shooting, relying solely on O'Brien's testimony to discredit McNulty's claim was risky at best, and at worst, unlikely to work at all. If I wanted the jurors to believe McNulty was lying, I needed to give them a reason for him to have done so.

I had a reason, and it was simple. McNulty lied to cover the fact that he himself had killed Kim Lee.

Technically the strategy is termed "offering an alternate theory of the crime." In defense lawyer slang, it's called TODDI, "the other dude did it." It's simply offering evidence that someone other than the defendant had committed the crime.

The defense can't be based simply on speculation or guesswork, There has to be evidence showing a reasonable possibility that the "other dude did it." Evidence showing opportunity and motive are generally enough, but a lot depends on the quality of the individual giving the evidence.

It's a good defense if you don't have an alibi or an eyewitness and an insanity plea is out. But I only had half of the defense, the opportunity part. I still needed a motive and a credible witness. Motive I figured might be tied in some way to the contents of the safe. As for a credible witness, that wasn't going to be as easy.

Sitting there in Richie's hospital room, I was fairly certain that TODDI was still our best defense. Actually, as much as I hated to admit it, the way things stood, it was our only defense.

I was in a tough spot because my options were limited, and that was a big problem. Usually my clients are guilty, and I'm working toward a plea deal. But in Richie's case, I believed he was innocent, and knowing him as I did, I knew there wasn't a plea deal in the world he would find acceptable. That meant we were going to trial no matter what, and that wasn't a good thing.

In a plea deal, there's always a compromise offer, no matter how small your bargaining chip is. The smaller your chip, the less the offer, but it's rarely an all or nothing situation. Both sides walk away feeling they won a little, and they lost a little. But going to trial is an all-or-nothing situation. One side wins and the other side loses.

At that moment, based on what I knew, I estimated Richie's chances of winning at trial were less than 50%. Richie had to know that, too, but neither of us would say it because Laura didn't need to hear it. It was more of a psychological thing because the odds didn't mean anything at that point.

All cases start off with the odds seemingly against the defendant, and it's the job of the defense attorney to turn those odds around. When the facts started coming in, I was confident the odds would change. How much they'd change and the direction they changed, might depend on just how well I did my job.

CHAPTER 16

That night I met Gracie at Pino's, one of our favorite Italian restaurants. Pino's serves a linguini with Calamari Fra Diavolo that's to die for, and believe me, with my heartburn I almost do. But it's so good the heartburn is worth it.

Gracie had brought me a copy of Deputy Chief William McNulty's sworn statement. As anxious as I was to read it, I knew instinctively I couldn't very well sit there and ignore Gracie. Actually, I could do that, but I'd wind up eating alone and not getting laid for a month. So, I put the statement away, made small talk and ate my Calamari Fra Diavolo with half a loaf of crusty Italian bread.

As we were finishing dinner, Gracie suggested we stroll over to Ferrara's Bakery on Grand Street for cappuccino and cannoli. I wanted to go home and read McNulty's statement, but what could I do? Gracie had done me a big favor by getting me a copy of the statement, so how could I say no? But when we hit the street, Gracie started to laugh and said, "Come on, we'll go back to my place. I'll make some coffee, and you can read the damn statement."

You see, that's a big difference between Gracie and me. In court, I have a great poker face, but when I'm with Gracie I wear my emotions on my face, and she can read me like a book.

Gracie, on the other hand, never shows her emotions. She always has the face of a seasoned poker player. I have a better chance of reading ancient hieroglyphics than reading Gracie's moods. I should add that it's not necessary to read Gracie's moods. She makes her feelings known by her actions, and believe me, she doesn't hold back. I have the scars to prove it.

I remember one time we were watching a news show on TV, and the commentator said that most woman hold back about 20% of their feelings, and that's why so many had heart attacks. I just looked at Gracie and said, "Please tell me there's not another 20% you're holding back because if there is, I'm buying a tranquillizer gun." Gracie never answered the question. She just laughed, and I slept with one eye open for the next month.

But I wander. McNulty's statement was important because, as far as I could tell, the DA's entire case hung on his testimony. There was probably forensic evidence proving the bullets that killed Kim Lee came from Richie's gun, but that evidence alone didn't put the gun in Richie's hand. Without proof that Richie pulled the trigger, there was reasonable doubt he was the murderer, and McNulty's testimony was the only evidence that he had pulled the trigger.

That was why every sentence and every word in McNulty's statement was important. If I could find discrepancies, I could use them to discredit McNulty's testimony and create reasonable doubt.

I didn't expect discrediting McNulty to be an easy job. After all, he had risen to the rank of Deputy Chief which meant he wasn't stupid. I wasn't likely to find any outright contradictions in his statement, but that wasn't what I was looking for. I was looking for discrepancies between his story and Jimmy O'Brien's account. Small discrepancies in sworn statements are like cracks in concrete. One or two by themselves are generally harmless and can be ignored, but develop enough of them and they'll bring down an entire building.

I'd start by comparing McNulty's story with what I knew and could prove. One thing I knew for certain, the night of the raid nothing went as planned. Jimmy confirmed Richie's claim that the moment they hit the brothel, everything went sideways. Once the shooting started, whatever plans the Task Force had went out the window, and from that point on, it was basically a free-for-all.

I could safely assume McNulty was operating on the fly like everyone else. So, maybe in the chaos he overlooked some details that might prove important, once all the facts were better known.

Haste is the enemy of accuracy. Given that McNulty hadn't had much time to come up with his story might be helpful. I had to believe somewhere in that statement were inaccurate details, and I was determined to find them.

I started my search by comparing McNulty's statement with what Jimmy O'Brien had told me.

I read McNulty's statement slowly, studying each word. That was something they taught us the first day in law school. If you were a speed reader, don't do it because, under the law, every word is important, and you need to focus on each and every word.

McNulty was good; I had to admit that. His statement was detailed where he had to be detailed, but it was also vague where he could afford to be vague. The less details he gave, the less likely he was to make a mistake. Still, he needed to include enough details to make the charges against Richie stick.

I had taken detailed notes of my conversation with Jimmy, but they were in the office, so I was working strictly from memory. From what I could remember, there was at least one detail that didn't match up. McNulty said in his sworn statement that he saw Richie's gun on the floor next to his hand, and he picked it up and put it in his pocket, fearing if Richie regained consciousness he might try to use it on him. Jimmy had told me when he entered the room, he didn't see Richie's gun, and he asked McNulty where it was. According to Jimmy, McNulty said it was in the waistband of his pants, and he opened his raid jacket to show him.

It wasn't much of a discrepancy, but I thought it might be important. I knew instinctively the ballistics report would show the bullets that killed Kim Lee came from Richie's gun. McNulty would have made sure of that. But if I was right, and McNulty had shot Kim Lee using Richie's gun, his fingerprints would be on the gun, and he'd need to explain how they got there.

The simplest explanation is usually the best, and McNulty claiming he picked up the gun to keep it out of Richie's reach after Richie shot Kim Lee made sense. But what didn't make sense was putting it in the waistband of his pants and not in his pocket.

Unlike what happens in the movies, cops don't put guns in the waistbands of their pants. It's a dangerous and stupid thing to do. So, why would McNulty have done it? I figured McNulty was busy setting the scene and probably wasn't finished when Jimmy arrived. If he hadn't already put Richie's gun in his jacket pocket, he might have had no choice but to jam it into the waistband of his pants. Then afterward, knowing it would look suspicious if he kept it there, he moved it to the pocket of his jacket the first chance he got. He probably didn't expect Jimmy to remember the gun being in his waistband or if Jimmy did remember, he didn't think Jimmy would mention it to anyone.

It was a good theory, but it wouldn't carry the day. The discrepancy might work to shake McNulty up a bit during cross-examination, but it wasn't going to break him, that was for sure. I needed more, and I was hoping I'd find something else in the statement. If it wasn't there, I'd have to look elsewhere, or to be more accurate, Tommy would have to look elsewhere.

At that point, Gracie was giving me one of her "that's enough" looks, so I knew it was time to put away the statement and start paying attention to her. I said, "I think I'll stop working now," and Gracie replied, "Who said you didn't have a brain?" I took it as a compliment. Experience has taught me life is better when I do.

CHAPTER 17

The next morning, I was at my desk reading McNulty's statement for the tenth time when Abe Fishman arrived. He was there to pick up three assignments for that day. It seemed I was turning my entire practice over to Abe to make time for Richie's case.

Hiring Abe to handle a case now and then when I had a conflict was one thing. But turning over nearly all my cases to him could be a problem. The 18B Panel cases were assigned to me, and I was expected to handle them, not hire someone else to do the work. Of course, the 18B Panel clients didn't care who represented them; it was the administrators I was worried about. Not so much Joe Benjamin, the Chief Administrator, but the clerks who handled the paperwork.

I needed to call Joe and let him know what was going on. I've known Joe for a long time. The truth be told, he was the one who forced me into AA, which saved my career and probably my life. Over the years, we've become good friends, and I knew he'd cut me some slack, but I also knew I was pushing the limits.

I was dumping so many cases on Abe that even he thought it was unusual and wanted to know what was going on. I wasn't comfortable telling him the whole story, so I told a little bit, but nothing about my relationship with Richie. Abe is no fool. He knew immediately I was being evasive, and there was more to the story than I was telling him.

"So, what makes Richie Simone so important that you're giving up the rest of your practice and going broke to represent him?" One thing I liked about Abe, he always got right to the point. No beating around the bush.

I had two choices, brush off Abe's question or tell him the whole story. Abe has one of the best legal minds I know, and I was eager to hear his ideas, so I told him the rest of the story. He listened quietly, and when I was done, he shook his head and rolled his eyes. As I said, Abe gets right to the point.

Then he said, "Jake, you've got a problem." Like, I didn't already know that. I had an eyewitness saying my client committed murder, a likely damning forensic report, and no alibi or other viable defense. Of course, I had a problem. Actually, I had a boatload of problems. But as it turned out, none of those problems was the one Abe was referring to.

"You've got something by the tail, and you don't know what it is." He was right. All I had at the moment was McNulty, and I didn't know if he was the whole animal or just the tail. Once I started pulling on the tail, I was likely to find out in a hurry what I had. Whether I'd be able to handle it was the big question.

I had to figure out who and what I was up against and hope that it didn't turn out to be half of the NYPD. If it was, I was doomed. But, whatever and whoever I was up against, I still needed a strategy.

Abe suggested I take a hard look at Sam Yeoung and the Hip Sing Tong. Whether McNulty was acting on his own, or there were other cops on the take with him, the relationship with Yeoung could be exploited to Richie's benefit.

The way Abe saw it, if I put a wedge between Yeoung and McNulty and got them at odds, something good might come out of it. It was the old "split'em' and pit'em" tactic used by the cops and ADAs to get one defendant to roll over on a co-defendant.

It sounded like a good idea. That was until I realized I'd be putting myself in the middle of a war between a Chinese gangster and a high ranking corrupt cop. A corrupt cop who had already murdered two people and might have half of the police force working with him. When I thought about it that way, it had some shortcomings. Like me being killed in the cross fire. But I had nothing else to work with at the time, and I was getting desperate, so I decided to go with it. I even had an idea where to start.

A few years back I had worked a case with Detective Richard Chen of Chinatown's 5th Precinct. It turned out he was the same Detective Chen on the Task Force with Richie. I hadn't seen or spoken to Chen in years, but I remembered him as being a good guy. Hopefully he remembered me the same way.

Knowing Chen led the team raiding the back door of the brothel, I wasn't counting on him seeing what happened on the second floor. But that was okay because that wasn't what I was looking for. What I hoped to get from Chen was information about Sam Yeoung. Chen had worked in the 5th Precinct for years, so I was sure he knew something about Yeoung and his operation. It was just a question of whether he'd talk to me.

When Abe left, I called the 5th Precinct and asked to speak with Detective Chen. He was out on call but expected back shortly. Rather than leave a message, I decided to walk over to the precinct house on Elizabeth Street and wait to see Chen in person.

Tommy's office was down the block from the 5th Precinct, so I stopped there to kill some time. The office isn't large or fancy, but it's quite a step up from the backroom of his grandfather's restaurant that he and I shared back in the day.

Tommy was busy putting together a resume on McNulty. There was a sizable amount of information available, most of it coming from public records. It was good background material, but none of it was incriminating, nor did any of it help prove McNulty was a dirty cop. In other words, it was basically worthless.

The information I needed was more likely to come from Linda, who was at her computer searching the deep web to track down McNulty's financial situation. To be honest, I have no idea what that means. I didn't even know there was a shallow web. I was just repeating what Linda said when Tommy asked her what she was doing.

Whatever it involved, tracking McNulty's finances was the way to go. When a cop is dirty, there's always a financial trail. The problem is finding it, and I was hoping Linda could do that.

I tried reading over Linda's shoulder, but she quickly shooed me away. It was just as well. From what Tommy said about Linda's work, the less I knew, the better off I'd be. Don't get the wrong idea. Tommy never said what she did was illegal. On the other hand, he never said it was legal.

In a way it's like the old argument of "Is the glass half empty or half full?" In the end it didn't matter because I had a Sergeant Shultz defense, "I know nothing!" If you don't know who Sergeant Shultz is, you can Google "Hogan's Heroes."

Anyway, I had other things to do, but before I left to go see Detective Chen, there was one more item I wanted Tommy to check out. Richie had mentioned seeing McNulty going into the Golden Palace restaurant on Pell Street with Sam Yeoung. If he was right, and I was betting he was, we might be able to catch McNulty and Yeoung together. Before you can "split em," you should make sure they're together.

I wanted Tommy to put a tail on McNulty and hopefully get some photographs of him with Yeoung, or at least going in or coming out of the Golden Palace. Tommy had a part-time guy who could do the job, but he reminded me that I was running up expenses at a pretty good clip. It was Tommy's way of asking me if I knew what I was doing.

When I hire Tommy to do investigations, the client pays the bill. So far, I was paying the bill on Richie's case. It was still very early in the case, but I had given Tommy a retainer fee, and he and Linda had already done a lot of work. Tommy is good, but he isn't cheap. He was giving me a discount because it was for Richie, but he couldn't afford to work for free, and frankly, neither could I. If I kept throwing my cases off to Abe Fishman, before long I wasn't going to have a cash flow.

It was a problem of my own making. It wasn't like Richie didn't expect to pay me or didn't want to pay me. No, quite to the contrary. Richie insisted on paying me and offered to pay a large retainer, but I said I'd bill him when the time came. I just wasn't sure when that would be. I figured after having to put up the house to make bail, and with the uncertainty of his future, Richie and Laura didn't need financial pressure on them. I'd wait to bill him.

I told Tommy to put the tail on McNulty, and send me the bill. Then I left and went down the block to the 5th Precinct station house.

I gave the desk sergeant one of my business cards and told him I wanted to see Detective Chen. He didn't ask why; he only asked if I had an appointment. I said no; he shrugged and rang the Detective Squad. I couldn't hear what the desk sergeant said, but the conversation was brief, and when it ended, he told me to take a seat on a nearby bench and wait.

I wasn't waiting long when Detective Chen came down the stairs. The grin on his face suggested he remembered me from our last encounter. In fact, he did remember me, and we spent the first couple of minutes catching up before I got to the point.

I told Chen I was representing Richie Simone, and I was there looking for help with his defense. Chen gave a little nod, but he said nothing. Maybe he was trying to decide if he could, or would, help me. Then he grabbed my arm, pulled me into a nearby interrogation room and closed the door.

CHAPTER 18

When a cop grabs you by the arm and pulls you into a dark room, it's not necessarily a good thing. For a minute I thought I had misjudged Chen, and he might be mixed up with McNulty. But my fears were misplaced. The reason Chen had pushed me into the interrogation room was so we could talk privately, and our conversation wouldn't be overheard.

When we were alone in the room, Chen said he knew damn well Richie wasn't a murderer. He'd like to help

Richie, but he didn't see how he could. The night of the raid, he led the assault on the back of the brothel and never got to the second floor. That I already knew, and I told Chen I wasn't interested in him as an eyewitness, but he might be able to help in other ways.

I could tell Chen was starting to get uncomfortable with the conversation. I figured it had something to do with McNulty, but I wanted Chen to say it out loud, so I leaned on him. I said he owed it to Richie to help him, and if he wasn't going to help, I wanted to know why.

Chen didn't answer; he just turned away and stared at the wall. I said nothing. I just kept looking at him, waiting for an answer. Finally, he turned back, looked me in the eye, and said he wanted to help, but it could cause him a lot of trouble. He was twenty-five years on the job and planned to retire very soon. He knew McNulty was dirty, but he couldn't prove it, and he didn't know if the corruption went further up in the chain of command. If it did, that was a problem because getting sideways with the brass meant they'd screw him out of his pension, and he couldn't chance that happening.

I told him I was sympathetic to his situation, and I assured him if he helped me, I would do everything possible to shield him. I wasn't asking him to be a witness or do anything that would expose his involvement. All I wanted was for him to tell me about the Task Force and to give me information on Sam Yeoung and the Hip Sing Tong. If he did that, I'd do the rest, and he'd never have to say a word publicly. It sounded good, but we both knew what would happen if anything he leaked to me was traced back to him.

Chen was in a tough spot, but to his credit, he did the right thing and agreed to help. Unfortunately, he didn't have much to offer in terms of the Task Force operation. He said that he knew something wasn't right with the operation from the start. McNulty was too involved in the details, and he overrode Richie too often. The night of the raid McNulty had stopped at the 5th Precinct before going to the 7th Precinct to join Richie. Chen remembered McNulty seemed on edge, and he thought McNulty was going to call off the operation. When I asked him what made him think that, he said it was the way McNulty was acting. He was pacing and seemed very agitated. But then he made a phone call on his cell and left for the 7th Precinct. That was the last time Chen saw McNulty that night until after the raid. Other than that, there wasn't much else he could tell me.

It wasn't much, but I hadn't expected it to be. I was more interested in the information Chen could give me on Yeoung and the Hip Sing Tong. He promised to give me everything he had on them, and he warned me to be careful because Yeoung and the Tong were vicious. I appreciated the advice, but I'd been working in Chinatown long enough to know that on my own.

There was one last thing I needed to know. What had happened to Li Chin, the Chinese girl who had alerted the Task Force to the human smuggling operation? Chen believed she had been taken into custody by Immigration and Customs Enforcement. He said that NYPD, knowing there would be undocumented immigrants at the brothel, had notified ICE in advance of the raid. ICE agents didn't take part in the raid, but they were on hand afterward to deal with the undocumented people. Chen had seen two ICE agents talking with Li Chin, and he presumed they had taken her into custody with the others.

I was about to leave when Chen remembered something else. The undercover cop who had befriended Li Chin told him that on the night of the raid, she had been on the second floor. He hadn't said if she saw what went down in the office at the brothel, but Chen said it might be worth looking into. He was right about that; now all I had to do was to find Li Chin.

CHAPTER 19

When I returned to the office, there was a message from
Marty Bowman. Richie's case was scheduled to go to the
Grand Jury on Monday. It was nice of Marty to notify me of
the hearing, but there was nothing I needed to do, or for that
matter, could do. Grand Jury hearings are one-sided
proceedings at which the District Attorney presents the
evidence without anyone there to challenge it. It's not
surprising indictments are returned in 99.9% of the cases,
and Richie's case would be no exception. An indictment

would be returned on Monday, as surely as the sun would rise that morning.

Once the indictment was returned, Richie would be formally arraigned, and I could demand to see the DA's evidence. That would include all the forensic reports and witness statements. Of course, McNulty's statement was the primary, and presumably only, eyewitness statement, and thanks to Gracie, I already had a copy. It would be interesting to see if the DA listed any other eyewitnesses or if McNulty's statement had undergone any revisions. If I was right and McNulty had killed Kim Lee, there wouldn't be any other eyewitnesses on the list. McNulty had made sure of that.

Still, after talking with Detective Chen, I began to wonder if Li Chin had witnessed the killing. If she had, and I could get her to testify, her testimony would be enough to break the case wide open. That was if I could find her and if she wasn't too frightened to talk.

There were a lot of "ifs," and they didn't include what might happen to Li Chin if McNulty knew she was a witness. I figured the odds were good he didn't know because had he seen her at the scene, he would have killed her to keep her quiet. God knows he wasn't shy about killing people.

But what if he found out afterward, or Li Chin had somehow managed to slip away the night of the murder? Then Li Chin's life could be in danger. If McNulty or any of his friends had an in with ICE, Li Chin could end up dead in a hurry. I had to find her, and I had to do it fast.

I called Tommy, but he had no contacts at ICE and no way to find out where Li Chin was being detained. Then I remembered that Abe Fishman used to handle immigration cases, so I rang his cell and left him a message.

Waiting for Abe to call me back, I began thinking that maybe McNulty had committed the perfect crime. Deep down inside, I knew there was no such thing as the perfect crime, that criminals always made some mistake, but if there was such a thing as a perfect crime, this might be it. So far, I had nothing solid to build a defense, and now I was about to start chasing down a lead on nothing more than a hope and a prayer. As much as I didn't want to admit it, I was getting desperate.

But then Abe called with some good news. He checked with a friend at the ICE Detention Center in Lower Manhattan and learned Li Chin had been taken there the night the brothel was raided. The bad news was he didn't know if she was still there.

CHAPTER 20

Abe's friend had been working the intake desk at the Water Street Center the night of the brothel raid, and he had helped process Li Chin and seven other female Chinese nationals. That was how he knew she had been there. Unfortunately, he had no idea what happened to her after she was processed.

Water Street is a first stage processing center, and it only holds detainees until they can be transferred to other facilities. As a general rule, detainees weren't held for more than a couple of days before being transferred. Because it had only been two days since the brothel raid, it was possible Li Chin was still at the center. Abe said I was probably right, and the attorney visiting hours at the center were from 8:00 am to 9:00 pm. That was Abe's way of suggesting I get my ass over there right away, and that was exactly what I intended to do. I wasn't sure what I was going to say when I got there, but I'd figure it out along the way.

I couldn't say I was Li Chin's lawyer because I wasn't, and lying to a Federal Agent can get you thrown in jail. I don't like lying to anyone, especially if it can land me in jail. Gracie says I don't look good in stripes. It has something to do with my build.

When I got to the center, I discovered that ICE didn't actually operate the facility. It was operated by a "rent-a-cop" company under a contract with ICE. That was good news for me because it meant I wouldn't have to lie to a Federal Agent, just a rent-a-cop, and lying to a rent-a-cop won't land you in jail. Lying to a rent-a-cop is like telling your girlfriend how much you love her new hairdo when you wouldn't have even noticed if she hadn't mentioned it. It can be dangerous, but only if you don't do it well.

At the detention center, I gave the guy manning the reception desk my business card and told him I needed to see my client, Li Chin, right away. He gave the card a quick look, handed it back to me and punched some keys on his computer. He stared at the screen with a perplexed look on his face, and then he punched a few more keys. The look on his face didn't change, and he punched some more keys. I was getting the impression things weren't going well.

Finally, he looked up at me and said. "She's not here anymore; she's been transferred." That wasn't good news, but it wasn't necessarily bad news. It confirmed she was alive and hadn't been killed by McNulty or the Tong. At least not yet.

When I asked where she was, which to me seemed like the next logical question, the rent-a-cop looked at me as though the question had taken him by surprise. Then he went back to punching keys on his computer. After punishing the keyboard for a few more minutes, he looked up and said, "I don't know."

I was getting nowhere fast, and I was about to lose my temper when I remembered Doug's advice, "You can't punish a fool for being a fool; it's too late; and you just have to deal with it." So instead of blowing my top at this fool, I asked if there was someone around who could tell me where Li Chin had been sent. He thought about it for a while, then he said that maybe Director Quinn would know, but she wasn't there.

I could have waited until the next day and talked with Director Quinn, but I had to believe she wouldn't be as easily taken in by my claimed representation of Li Chin. If I was going to get any information about Li Chin's whereabouts, it was going to have to come from the rent-a-cop.

One of my talents, which are admittedly few, is the ability to draw people out and get them talking. Some people say it's my Irish gift of gab, but Gracie says I'm just nosy and pushy. Call it what you will, but it is a talent refined during my many hours of socializing in bars.

When attempting to pry information from someone, the first step is finding what interests them. More often than not, it's them, but sometimes it's another topic. You must just keep at it until you find the right topic. Once you do, it's only a matter of time until you build up a good rapport, and then you're in. It's like safecracking; you keep turning the dials until you hear the clicks. Not that I know anything about safecracking, but that's what I've heard.

I noticed the newspaper on the desk was opened to the sports page, and since it was football season, I could safely assume the guy was likely either a Giants or a Jets fan. I took a chance and started talking about the New York Giants. Before long, the rent-a-cop and I were engaged in a deep discussion over the pros and cons of the Giants' defense. Fifteen minutes of sports talk, and we were bosom buddies.

Step two, once rapport has been established, steer the conversation to the topic you want to explore. In this case, it was working at the detention center. Feigning interest in my new friend's job, I asked him all about his work. The trick during this step is not to fall asleep or look bored.

Finally, sensing the time was right, I casually broached the topic of Li Chin's whereabouts. It turned out most of the detainees from the Water Street Detention Center were sent to one of four jails in New York or New Jersey, depending on available space. Most went to the Bergen County Jail in New Jersey, but there was no record of Li Chin having been sent there, or to any of the other three local detention centers.

That news was bad enough. But when I asked where she could have been sent, the news got worse. ICE has 961 detention and processing centers in the United States, and theoretically, Li Chin could have been sent to any one of them.

I suspected McNulty might have had a hand in losing Li Chin in the system, but my new friend informed me it wasn't uncommon for the records to be incomplete. It wasn't necessarily due to sloppiness on the part of the clerks, but it was often simply a matter of bad timing.

The Water Street Detention Center was generally filled to capacity, and it had a list of detainees being held in local county jails waiting for processing. When a detainee at the center was scheduled for transfer, his or her bed was immediately assigned to a new waiting detainee. Sometimes the facility scheduled to receive a detainee from Water Street notified them at the last minute because it was overcrowded and unable to accommodate the detainee. This created a problem because the detainee no longer had a bed at Water Street and had to go somewhere. The staff then scrambled to find a new location, and sometimes when this happened, the paperwork wound up incomplete.

As my new friend explained it, when an agent on duty was advised a planned transfer had to be canceled, the agent would delete the name of the designated detention facility from the record. It was then the job of a different agent to find a new facility for the detainee. Once a new facility was located, someone was supposed to enter the name of that facility into the record, but sometimes that didn't happen. So, in Li Chin's case, the missing transfer information could have happened innocently, or it could have been intentional. Either way, it didn't really matter because I couldn't find her.

Somewhere in the vast government bureaucracy, there had to be a record of Li Chin, and I needed to find it and find her before she was deported to China or killed by McNulty. But it was Friday afternoon, and the bureaucracy was about to close down. My rent-a-cop friend assured me there weren't many detainee transfers happening during weekends. Wherever Li Chin was, she was likely to be there the following week. I resigned myself to the fact there wasn't much I could do until then and left the detention center.

It was getting late, and I wasn't in the mood to go back to the office, so I gave Connie a call to check for messages. Laura had left a message. Richie had been released from the hospital and was back home on Long Island. He wasn't taking any calls, but he would contact me tomorrow. I couldn't blame him for not taking calls. His life had been turned upside down by the very people who should have been on his side. Naturally, he didn't know who to trust, and he was being cautious.

Gracie was attending an office retirement dinner, and I was on my own for dinner and free to choose where to eat. It was time to visit Vincent's Clam Bar on Mott Street and the corner of Hester in Little Italy.

Vincent's has an interesting history dating back to 1901 when Giuseppe and Carmela Siano began selling clams and scungilli from a pushcart. In 1904, they moved the operation indoors to 119 Mott Street, and Carmela started serving her now world-famous Vincent's Sauce, either sweet, mild or hot.

Nothing much has changed in more than a century since Vincent's has been in business. The menu today is expanded, but the sauce is still made from Carmela's original recipe. My favorite meal is the combination plate of calamari and scungilli in the hot sauce.

One more thing about Vincent's Clam Bar. A lot of people confuse it with Umberto's Clam House, originally on the corner of Mulberry Street and Hester, just one block away from Vincent's Clam Bar.

Umberto's became famous two months after it opened in 1972 when gangster, Crazy Joe Gallo, was gunned down inside the restaurant, then staggered outside and died in the street. It was all very dramatic, the stuff legends are made of.

I was fifteen years old at the time, and I remember every detail. How could I not? The press coverage was unrelenting. Pictures of Crazy Joe lying in the street in front of the restaurant with its name prominently displayed were plastered all over the front page of the local newspapers for days.

The publicity made Umberto's Clam House famous overnight. The place did well until the owner was sentenced to six years in prison for skimming over $2 million, not only from Umberto's, but from other businesses he owned, including the famous Peppermint Lounge. Hey, nobody's perfect.

Little Italy holds a lot of memories for me, so eating at Vincent's isn't just dinner. It's a reminder of things past. Some good, some not so good and some downright terrible. But that's what life is, a collection of events that make us who we are.

Speaking of who we are, I realized I hadn't spoken to Doug or attended an AA meeting in a while, both of which I needed to do.

CHAPTER 21

Monday morning Tommy arrived with a handful of papers and a smile on his face. From his smile, I knew he had something good to report, and I was guessing it had to do with the papers in his hand. I was right on both counts. Linda Chow had worked all weekend hacking into McNulty's financial records. Actually, she had hacked into Chase Bank's and Merrill Lynch's records, but that I didn't want to hear. I just wanted to know about McNulty's financial situation, not how Linda got the information.

Ignoring how she did it, I learned that Linda found out McNulty had three checking accounts with JP Morgan

Chase Bank, and one money market account with Merrill Lynch. One Chase checking account was a joint account with his wife, all seemingly on the up-and-up. No unusual or suspicious transactions.

The third checking account was more interesting. It was a business account in the name of Promotion Test Tutor, Inc. Unlike in the other two accounts, this account had numerous transactions exceeding $10,000. That wasn't necessarily unusual or suspicious since it was a business account. But the consistent absence of smaller transactions raised suspicion.

The Merrill Lynch money market account was in McNulty's name alone and had a balance of $210,000. Nothing in that account was necessarily suspicious. It seemed like a dead-end. But Linda never gives up, and after tracing money from the Chase business checking account through a web of sham transactions, she discovered an offshore brokerage account in Grand Cayman with over $2.2 million in assets. That account was suspicious, to say the least.

The account had been opened seven years earlier with an initial deposit of $25,000. Over the ensuing years, the amounts of a number of deposits made into the account matched the amounts of checks drawn on McNulty's business account. The remainder of the deposits made into the account were checks drawn on foreign banks, nearly all of which were Chinese.

Linda was also able to trace the source of those deposits to companies owned or controlled by Sam Yeoung. It was all fitting together nicely. Unfortunately, the information had been illegally collected, and using it in court was going to be a problem.

Linda had more, and it involved McNulty's income tax returns. How Linda had accessed McNulty's tax returns was something else I didn't want to know. But she had, and as I suspected, there was no mention of the Cayman account or the interest paid on the account anywhere in the return. Again, it was good information, but illegally collected.

The way things were going, I was beginning to think that Richie wasn't the only one who might wind up in jail before this case was over. Lying to Federal Agents, hacking into banking computers, and hacking into the IRS could put me away for as long as Richie.

At least the information Linda had about Promotion Test Tutor, Inc., came from public records. Promotion Test Tutor, Inc., had been formed seven years earlier, the same year McNulty opened the offshore stock account. The incorporation papers filed with New York State stated the company was formed to provide tutoring services to NYPD police officers taking promotional examinations. McNulty was the sole shareholder and sole director of the corporation.

The business was legitimate, at least to the extent it did offer tutoring classes, paid its taxes, and maintained its license. But there was nothing to suggest it did anything near the business necessary to produce the $2.2 million nest egg in the offshore account.

McNulty having a side business wasn't unique, nor unusual. Lots of cops did. But all cops, including Deputy Chief Inspectors, working side jobs are required to file annual Off Duty Employment Applications. McNulty, being the good cop he was, filed his applications each year, and not surprisingly, they were approved.

In the last year, $450,000 had been deposited in the offshore account. A good deal of the money had come from the checking account of Promotion Test Tutor. It seemed like an awful lot of money for tutoring a bunch of cops. The rest of the money came from sources Linda had managed to trace to Yeoung. I don't know how she did it, and Tommy assured me I didn't want to know.

Without access to financial books and records of Promotion Test Tutor, I thought it would be impossible to prove the money was merely being laundered through the company and not actually earned for services performed. But I underestimated Linda's talent.

Linda found a site which listed the number of cops taking promotion examinations during the past year. Then using a fee schedule published in one of the business brochures, she calculated the number of applicants it would have taken to earn fees equaling deposits that the company made into the offshore account. The result confirmed what I suspected. For Promotion Test Tutor to have earned the money it deposited into the offshore account, it would have had to tutor all of the cops who took promotion examinations, not once but twice. How likely was that?

To make sense of it all, Linda had collated all the financial transactions on a series of spreadsheets, tracing McNulty's deposits and payments from one account to another. The resulting exhibits laid out a clear pattern of money laundering. If turned over to the Feds, they would be a road map to an income tax evasion conviction at minimum.

Of course, since the information was obtained illegally, getting convictions might prove a bit tricky. But none of that mattered to me. I didn't intend to turn the information over to the Feds, and I wasn't planning to use the information in court. I couldn't because I couldn't explain how I had gotten it, nor could I authenticate it.

That didn't mean I couldn't put it to good use. I wanted to prove McNulty was a dirty cop, and what could be better than to have the NYPD itself label him a corrupt cop? The way to make that happen was to bring all this information to the Internal Affairs Bureau. Internal Affairs investigates corruption within the department, and it would be the place to go, as long as McNulty didn't have a friend there.

The fact the information had been obtained illegally wouldn't matter in a departmental investigation. McNulty would be hard-pressed to deny the money was his, and he'd have a hell of a time explaining where it came from and how it got into his accounts. The information might not support a conviction in court, but it was more than enough to get McNulty thrown off the police force in disgrace.

There were a number of things I could do with the information, but whatever I did, I needed to think it out carefully.

CHAPTER 22

Tommy and I had just finished going over the financial exhibits when Richie showed up unexpectedly. He was walking with a cane and limping slightly, but other than that, he looked to be in good shape. He tossed a plastic bag on my desk and took a seat next to Tommy. The two shook hands and exchanged greetings, then Tommy, suspecting it was time for him to leave, said his goodbyes.

"A gift for me?" I asked, and pointed at the plastic bag sitting in the middle of my desk. Richie turned the bag over and dumped out two burner cell phones. He said we couldn't afford to take chances, so we'd only use burner phones when talking to each other. Personally, I thought the idea was crazy, and it was out of character for Richie. But it wasn't my life on the line, so I kept my opinion to myself.

I had just started telling Richie where we stood on the investigation when Connie buzzed. Marty Bowman was on the line. The Grand Jury had returned a murder indictment, and Richie was scheduled to be arraigned in Supreme Court the following morning. It was no big deal. Arraignments are simply a formality. The only reason to be concerned was if the DA wanted to revoke bail, but Marty assured me that wasn't going to happen.

The indictment didn't come as a surprise to Richie, and he showed no emotion when I told him about it. He was more concerned with my investigation, and he offered to stake out the Golden Palace restaurant. For the moment, I was tempted to let him do it. After all, he had the knowledge and experience to work a stakeout, but then reality kicked in. What if the cops were staking out the place and saw him sitting there? How would we explain that?

No, we'd leave the stakeout to Tommy's guy. Richie needed to lay low, at least until I got a better handle on what we were up against. I told Richie to go home and relax, and I'd let him know everything I was doing as I was doing it. It was a lie, and Richie probably knew it was a lie, but he didn't make an issue of it. Instead, he reminded me to use the burner phone. I promised that I would, and we arranged to meet at the Worth Street Coffee Shop the next morning before the arraignment.

After Richie left, I kept going over in my head the events on the night of the raid. The discrepancy in the stories about the office safe bothered me, and I knew instinctively that it was important. I just hadn't figured out why.

In the *New York Post* article, McNulty was quoted as saying the office safe was empty. Which made sense if the Tong knew about the raid in advance. But Richie saw Kim Lee taking something from the safe. So, what had Kim Lee removed; what happened to it; and why had McNulty claimed nothing was found at the premises?

I had to assume the Tong had been warned about the raid; otherwise the raiding parties wouldn't have been met with a hail of bullets. But the warning must have come just minutes before it happened. Time enough to move armed security personnel into position at the entrances, and chase the customers out the back door into the alley, but not enough time to remove what was in the safe from the premises. McNulty knew about the raid at least a day or two before it took place, so why hadn't he conveyed the warning earlier?

As I sat there thinking about it, I began to suspect the answer to the question might very well be the key to the case. So far, my best guess was McNulty wanted whatever Kim Lee was keeping in the safe. By giving such short notice of the impending raid, he ensured whatever was in the safe would be there, or at least on the premises, during the raid. In the confusion, he hoped to find and pocket whatever was kept in the safe.

At best, it was a risky proposition with lots of ways for it to have gone wrong. So, what was in the safe that made it worthwhile for McNulty to risk shooting Richie and set him up for murder?

From what Richie saw of it before being shot, it wasn't anything big, so it probably wasn't a book or papers. I doubted it was cash because there couldn't be enough money kept on the premises to make the risk worthwhile. Any cash that might have been in the safe would be chump change, compared to what McNulty was pulling down. More likely, it was a computer disk or something of that nature. Assuming that was it, what information was on it?

It could have been bookkeeping records, but they'd be of little use to McNulty and again hardly worth the risk. I thought maybe it was something that incriminated McNulty and tied him to Yeoung. But if that was the case, why not give the warning earlier so it could be removed from the premises before the raid? No, whatever McNulty was after, he wanted it for himself, and he didn't want Yeoung knowing he had it.

Then it hit me. A client list could be worth a fortune. If clients were paying up to $10,000 an hour for services, they weren't average Johns. They were rich men and probably prominent as well. Perfect targets for blackmail. For that reason, it made sense. But the client list alone wouldn't support blackmail; he'd need some evidence putting the Johns there. It was all very puzzling, and so far, I was just spinning my wheels and getting nowhere.

I was still holding out some hope that Li Chin was a witness to the shooting, and I needed to find her quickly before ICE deported her. But there were over 950 detention centers where she might be held, and I had no idea where to start looking.

If I couldn't find Li Chin, or if she hadn't witnessed the murder, my options were narrowed.

CHAPTER 23

Just when I thought my life couldn't possibly get more complicated, it did. It got a lot more complicated.

I had been turning down 18B Panel cases, and it hadn't been a problem. But all that changed when Joe Benjamin called with a case he said I had to handle. As much as I wanted to turn down the assignment, I couldn't. I owed Joe too much.

If Joe was pushing me to take this new assignment, it was important to him, and I couldn't let him down. I'd figure out a way to handle the workload.

The client was Sasha Jones; she was twenty-one

years old; and she was being charged as a major drug trafficker. There are no drug charges more serious than that one which is reserved for the worst of the worst. It made me wonder why Joe was so interested in this case.

Joe Benjamin has been at his job for a long time, and he's damn good at it. Part of what makes him good is his objectivity, so it's rare when he takes a special interest in a case. Especially one involving a charge of major drug dealing. Don't get the wrong idea. I don't mean that Joe is heartless; he's a realist; and he's not easily swayed by sympathy. Trust me, with his job, he can't afford to be sympathetic. He's not one to fall for sob stories, so when a case bothers him, it's usually for a good reason.

When Joe finished giving me the details of Sasha's case, I asked him why the special interest. He said one of his clerks knew Sasha and after hearing her story, he was convinced she was being railroaded. That was strong talk from a man who was usually more measured in his evaluations.

The way Joe heard the story, Sasha grew up in the Harlem projects with her mother and grandmother. At age 16 she got pregnant, dropped out of school, and started living with her boyfriend. Just before her daughter, Kayla, was born, her boyfriend split, and Sasha moved back in with her mother and grandmother.

Her mother was a good woman who worked two jobs to support her family. But shortly after Kayla was born, Sasha's mother was killed, an innocent victim caught in the cross fire of a gang shoot-out. With her mother's death,

Sasha, Kayla, and Sasha's 83-year-old grandmother were left with no means of support other than welfare.

They say a person is best judged by how they respond to a crisis, and to Sasha's credit she responded well. She got a job, worked hard, and supported herself, her baby and her grandmother. When her grandmother died, Sasha found day care for Kayla and continued to work, supporting herself and Kayla. For the last three years, Sasha had worked as a clerk in the Associated Supermarket on 155th Street. She had even managed to get her GED diploma.

I could see why Joe had taken an interest in her case. Sasha didn't seem to fit the profile of a major drug dealer. But so far, everything was based on Joe's impression. I trusted Joe's instincts, but I'd make up my own mind when I got to meet Sasha.

Joe faxed a copy of the arrest report which added to my suspicion that something wasn't right with Sasha's case. According to the arrest report, plainclothes officers from Harlem's 28th Precinct had been conducting an undercover operation aimed at closing down a drug ring operating out of the 155th Street housing project.

In the course of the investigation, they received an anonymous tip that a large stash of cocaine was hidden in Sasha's apartment. Operating on this information, the cops secured a search warrant and raided her place. On the kitchen counter, they found hundreds of bags of cocaine, with an estimated street value of between $80,000 and $95,000. Three individuals, believed to have been guarding the drugs, escaped when they apparently received early warning of the raid from one of the many lookouts situated throughout the project.

It wasn't surprising that there were no on scene arrests. The smart drug dealers conducted their operations deep inside the project where they were well protected. They posted lookouts on the roofs and at the entrances to the project, making it nearly impossible for the cops to conduct surprise raids. In this case, they must have come close because the gangbangers guarding the stash had run, leaving the drugs behind. They'd only leave the drugs behind if they feared being caught and didn't want to be grabbed while carrying a heavy weight of drugs.

Even if I didn't know Sasha's story, I'd still have problems believing how the case went down. I knew the drug investigation inside the Harlem housing project had been underway for at least a year, and probably longer. The cops had been getting nowhere when, all of a sudden, this cocaine turns up just laying around on a kitchen counter in the apartment of a single mom with no known drug connections. It didn't make sense.

But the real problem with the case was the charge. Because the value of the cocaine exceeded $75,000, it meant Sasha was being charged under New York Penal Code § 220.77 for operating as a major trafficker. The charge is a class A-1 felony, and it carries a prison term of no less than fifteen to forty years, and up to a life sentence.

The charge was a big stretch. Normally a major drug trafficking charge is reserved for the known big-time dealers. The really bad dudes, who are making a lot of money pushing drugs. But with the mayor on one of his "I'm tough on crime" kicks, everyone arrested was being charged with the highest degree of the crime possible. It didn't matter that the facts didn't fit the charge. In the end, the case would plead out at a downgraded charge, but it would take time to get there.

In Sasha's case, it wasn't that simple. Due to the amount of drugs involved, even reducing the charge from major trafficking, still makes it a major felony. Not quite as bad as being a major drug trafficker, but almost as bad.

Sasha had been arrested two days earlier, and she was being held for arraignment until the authorities decided if she was going to be represented by Legal Aid or by an 18B lawyer. At the moment, she was at the Rose M. Singer Center for women on Rikers Island. I needed to see Sasha as soon as I could. I had Richie's arraignment the next morning, and the earliest I could see her was the next afternoon.

I don't mean to sound callous, but she wasn't going anywhere. With a 220.77 charge, Sasha's bail, if the judge even agreed to bail, would be astronomical. So, whether I saw her that day or the next afternoon, it wasn't going to mean a lot. Like I said, I wasn't being callous, just a realist.

CHAPTER 24

Richie's arraignment went off without a hitch. He pleaded not guilty; the judge continued his bail; I served my demands for forensic reports and witness statements; and we were done. Afterward, Richie suggested we go to my office to work on his defense. I practiced law long enough to know that "*working on his defense*" meant him telling me what to do, and that was not going to happen. Not even with Richie.

You'd be surprised how many clients think they know better than me when it comes to their defense. I can't tell you how many times I've heard, "Here's what I think," or

"Do you want to know what I think?" I tell them all the same thing, *I'll listen to what you think after you've gone to law school for three years, passed the bar and practiced for twenty-five years. Until then, I really don't care what you think.*

You realize, of course, that most of my clients come to me through the 18B Panel and have no choice but to accept my services. I can afford to talk to them that way. As for my paying clients, I simply tell them, *You're paying me to think for you. You can tell me what you think, but I'm still going to charge you for my thinking. And if I must listen to what you think I'm going to charge you for, that too.*

There is one universal truth about all paying clients; they don't like to pay. Let's face it, nobody likes to pay for a lawyer and everybody has a reason they shouldn't have to pay. Most clients claim they're innocent, and so, if you work out a plea deal, they think you sold them out. Of course, if you happen to get them acquitted, they don't want to pay because they say that they shouldn't have been arrested in the first place. When it comes to getting paid, 99% of the time it's a no-win situation. Client gratitude is like true love; it's rumored to exist, but it's rare when you find it.

I've accepted the fact I'm not going to get rich practicing criminal law. I knew that coming out of law school, when I decided on a career in the DA's Office. But back then, I had the satisfaction of taking bad guys off the street and putting them in prison. Now that I've been on the other side of the fence for the last fifteen years, I don't get that same satisfaction. Well, that's not entirely true. I've had some cases where the client didn't deserve to go to prison, and I felt good when I managed to keep them out.

Also, I'd be lying if I said I didn't get some satisfaction when a repeat violent offender client is sent away for a long, long time. Not that I did anything to make it happen. My satisfaction comes from knowing the criminal justice system is working, and we have one less thug on the streets to worry about.

But I'm ranting a bit, aren't I? Usually when that happens, Gracie tells me to call Doug, or go find an AA meeting.

With Richie's arraignment out of the way, it was time to go visit Sasha and find out how deeply I was going to be sucked into that case.

CHAPTER 25

I prefer using the subway and bus when going to Rikers Island, but I didn't have time to spare, so I had to take a taxi instead.

I know that I keep bringing up this thing I have about taxicabs, and by now you probably think I'm crazy. But try riding in New York City taxicabs, and you'll quickly find out I'm not entirely out of my mind. I read somewhere that more people have been brought to God by New York City taxicab drivers than by Billy Graham. It's true. The two phrases most uttered in New York City taxicabs are, "Oh my God," and "God help me." Third is, "Holy shit," but I'm not sure that phrase qualifies as a true religious incantation; I'll leave that for you to decide.

I won't bore you with the details of my ride. I'll just say, I made it to Rikers Island in one piece, but I took the bus and subway back to Lower Manhattan when I was done.

If first impressions mean anything, the minute I saw Sasha, I knew she wasn't a major drug dealer. A drug dealer, possibly, but there was no way she was a major dealer. There are very few big-time female drug dealers, and all of them are gangbangers. Sasha didn't look like a gangbanger. She had no tattoos, no visible piercings, or any other body mutilation, all of which are part of the mandatory gangbanger dress code.

She wasn't a hardened drug dealer; she was just a scared kid. I've seen my share of big-time drug dealers, and believe me, they're harder than rocks. Nothing shakes them. I watched one client smile as he was given two life sentences. That's hard. Of course, maybe he was smiling because he didn't get the maximum, four life sentences. I said they were hard. I didn't say they were smart.

Sasha was anxious, but not like someone coming off drugs. I'd been around druggies enough to know when someone was suffering withdrawal symptoms. Sasha wasn't. She was just scared; I mean really scared.

Speaking to her confirmed my impressions. Her voice was shaky, but the first thing she wanted to know was what was happening with Kayla, her daughter. Concern for others is not a trait you'll find in big-time drug dealers.

I was glad I could give her good news about Kayla. Joe Benjamin had done some checking, and he discovered Sasha had an aunt in the Bronx. He had contacted the aunt and arranged with Children's Services for Kayla to be placed with her. When Sasha heard that, she settled down a bit, and I was able to get her story.

It was a simple story. The drugs weren't hers. Unfortunately, that's what everyone caught with drugs claims, and the cops don't buy it. Most times, neither do I. But there was more to Sasha's story than simply "They're not mine."

Sasha wasn't certain how the drugs wound up in her apartment, but she had good reason to believe they belonged to Jerome White, her ex-boyfriend's brother. Jerome was the big-time drug dealer in the projects, and he transacted business in the courtyard just outside of Sasha's building. She suspected Jerome was using her apartment as a stash house, but swore she knew nothing about it.

Stash houses are common in the drug business. Smart drug dealers, like Jerome, don't keep a large stock of drugs on their person, or close to where they're selling, for fear of being ripped off, or caught in a buy and bust sting. Instead, they keep the drugs in stash houses, close enough to the point of sale to be convenient, but far enough away to be safely out of reach. The stash houses are always well guarded, and they are usually where the boss of the operation hangs out, protecting his stock of drugs and the incoming cash.

It's only the small-time dealers, selling to support their habit, that carry the drugs on their person, and get personally involved in the street side of the transaction. The major league dealers insulate themselves from the transaction by using runners. It's a simple and effective scheme. The runner conducts the street side of the transaction, taking the buyer's order and money, and then bringing it to the dealer who's waiting in the stash house. The dealer gives the runner the drugs, and the runner brings them to the customer. The buyer never sees the dealer.

The dealers use underage kids as runners. That way if they're caught, they're treated as minors, and they're sent to Family Court, where most times they face nothing more than a slap on the wrist. Without the threat of jail time for these kids, the cops have no leverage to get the runners to turn on the dealers.

The reason Sasha suspected Jerome was using her apartment as a stash house was because he had done so in the past. Not recently, but back when she and her ex-boyfriend, Jamil, were living together, before Kayla was born. At the time, they lived in a ground floor apartment just off the courtyard, making it an ideal location for a stash house.

Sasha and Kayla now lived in a different apartment, but its location was similar. It was a ground floor unit, just a little further off the courtyard than the old apartment. With Sasha often working ten-hour shifts at the Associated Food Market, including overtime night shifts on the weekends, and Kayla at a day care center in the project, or with a baby sitter, the apartment was empty as much as it was occupied.

DONALD L'ABBATE

To that extent, Sasha's story made sense. But there was something about the story that bothered me.

I was having trouble believing Jerome could have been using the apartment as a stash house without Sasha noticing something suspicious. Stash houses are well-guarded, meaning there would be at least two or three well-armed gang members sitting watch with Jerome. It was highly unlikely that a bunch of gangbangers sat in an apartment for seven or eight hours without leaving some signs of having been there.

Sasha wasn't a major drug dealer, or for that matter, a drug dealer at all, but I wasn't sure she was an innocent bystander in all of this. The questions were, how deeply involved in this mess was she, and when was I going to find out the truth?

I had done my best to convince Sasha she needed to level with me, but she stuck to her story. Working with what she gave me, I was confident I could get the major drug trafficking charge reduced. But if we hoped to do better than that, I needed to know the truth.

When I got back to the office, I called Joe Benjamin and told him about my visit with Sasha. Joe was disappointed to hear the news and wanted to know if I thought Sasha was using again. It was a logical question. If she was using, it would explain how and why she got mixed up in selling drugs. But she wasn't exhibiting any withdrawal symptoms, so I didn't think she had been on drugs. Something was going on that Sasha wasn't telling me about, but I was pretty sure it had nothing to do with her using drugs.

Joe said whatever was happening, we needed to get to the bottom of it, and he told me to have Tommy investigate Jerome and his drug operation. I wanted to keep Tommy working exclusively on Richie's case, but I couldn't afford to do that. I was going broke as it was. Besides, Tommy was on the 18B Panel list of approved investigators, so Joe had every right to demand I hire him, and there was nothing I could do to stop him. Tommy was going to work on Sasha's case, and that was all there was to it.

CHAPTER 26

I needed to focus on Richie's case, and I started by studying the locations of the detention centers where ICE might be keeping Li Chin. Assuming they intended to send her back to China, it made sense to hold her in a city with an international airport that serviced China. Of course, this was the federal government, so I couldn't count on anything making sense.

The rent-a-cop at the Water Street Detention Center had said most of the detainees were sent to one of four local jails. The day after visiting the detention center, I had Connie check those jails, using an online prisoner search engine. She ran the searches, but Li Chin's name didn't turn up. I figured Li Chin had been shipped elsewhere; now I was looking for a needle in a haystack.

But as I sat at my desk, it dawned on me that the ICE detainees weren't criminal prisoners, and they might not turn up in a computerized prisoner search. A phone call to the first facility confirmed my suspicion. I needed to call each jail and ask about ICE detainees, not prisoners.

When I made the calls, I didn't actually lie about who I was and why I was calling, but I was deceptive. I simply gave them my name, said I was a lawyer, and I was trying to locate Li Chin. It was all true, except for the implication that she was my client. I spoke basically to clerks, none of whom questioned my story.

After striking out on the first three calls, my luck changed on the fourth call. Li Chin was being held at the Orange County Jail in Goshen, New York, under an ICE detainment. The woman I spoke with was friendly and very helpful. She told me that attorney visiting hours were from 8 am to 7 pm daily, and as long as I had a valid New York State Attorney Identification Card, I could get into the facility. She never said I had to have an actual client in detention to get in, but I thought it was probably the case, so I needed to work on that.

I asked Connie to find out where the hell Goshen, New York, was and how I could get there. While she did that, I tried to figure out how I was going to convince the people at the jail I was Li Chin's lawyer. Lying was the obvious option, but probably not the best.

131

It didn't take Connie very long to find out that Goshen was about 65 miles north of Manhattan and most easily reached by car. That was a problem, I don't own a car. I don't drive, and 65 miles in a New York City taxicab wasn't going to happen. As usual, Connie had a solution. Her cousin, Vince, drove a limousine, and she was sure she could convince him to drive me to Goshen at a discounted rate.

I didn't want to go to Goshen, and I certainly didn't want to be in a car with Connie's cousin, Vince, for three hours. Not that I had anything against Vince; I just don't want to be in a confined space with anyone for three hours. Gracie excluded, of course. Well, maybe not, but don't tell Gracie.

In the past, I probably would have just said the hell with it and gotten drunk. But that was no longer an option, so I told Connie to make arrangements for Vince to take me to Goshen in two days.

As much as I hated the idea of going to Goshen, I didn't have much of a choice. If Li Chin had seen what happened in the brothel office the night of the raid, she'd clear Richie of the murder. Even though it was a long shot, I had to find her and talk with her. All I had were long shots, and if one of them didn't come through, Richie was going to prison for a long time.

Then I called Tommy about Sasha's case. I told him what I knew and asked him to investigate this Jerome White character. Tommy said he'd get on it as soon as he could. I reminded him Richie's case was still our priority, and he assured me he understood. I felt badly having to say that, but it was the truth. Sasha's case was just beginning, and Richie's case was closer to trial, so I felt justified in saying it.

I told Tommy to watch out for himself. The housing project gangs are vicious, and I didn't want Tommy getting hurt. Until I knew all of Sasha's story, I didn't want Tommy getting too deeply involved.

That night I was supposed to meet Gracie at Pino's for dinner, but I got wrapped up going over Linda's spreadsheets, and at the last minute, I called and canceled. Usually Gracie understands these things, but that night she got angry and told me not to bother coming to her place. That pissed me off because I thought she was being unfair. I wasn't canceling because I wanted to. I was canceling because I had to.

I explained to Gracie she should focus on the cause, not the effect. I don't know if she did or she didn't, because she hung up on me. It wasn't the result I was hoping for, but it was okay because it justified my anger. At least in my mind it did.

CHAPTER 27

I hadn't called Doug in a while and hadn't been to an AA meeting for even longer. So, it wasn't surprising that, as I sat at my desk the morning after the mini fight with Gracie, I was in a bad mood. Bad moods, like good moods, pass. I know that. The problem is that I still look for instant gratification, so they don't pass fast enough for me.

I was sitting there having a pity party for myself when I should have been on the phone with Doug. When I get into one of those moods, I tend to make bad decisions and that morning was no exception. I decided to call Gracie, not to apologize, but to justify myself. For some unknown reason, alcoholics feel the need to justify themselves about everything, especially when they're wrong. Unfortunately, some recovering alcoholics, such as me, never break the habit.

As you might expect, the call to Gracie didn't go well. To start with, she accused me of being a jerk, which was probably true, but it didn't improve my mood. Then she warned me there'd be no more sex until I went to a meeting and changed my attitude. That pissed me off even more, so I called her a bitch and hung up the phone. I can be very immature for a 54-year-old.

I sat there stewing for a while and muttering to myself, something I do when I'm out of sorts. But when I finally calmed down, I thought about what Gracie had said. Gracie wasn't one to make hollow threats, and she had never used sex as a weapon before, so I had to assume this whole fight wasn't over my blowing off dinner the night before. There was something much more serious going on, and I wasn't seeing it.

I knew I hadn't been myself for the last couple of days, but I blamed that on the pressure I was under from Richie's case. It was true; his case was taking a toll, financially, mentally, and emotionally. But I had faced similar situations in the past and never had this problem. That's when it dawned on me that the problem wasn't the pressure. The problem was how I was responding to that pressure. I was isolating myself. I was building a wall around myself. A wall I wasn't seeing but one that Gracie saw and felt. That explained why she was so angry with me.

Now, at least I knew I was isolating, and it was a problem. What I didn't know was why I was doing it. It was time to call Doug. He wasn't very sympathetic and sounded very much like Gracie. Not the thing about no sex, of course, but he said I needed to get to a meeting, and soon. I wasn't left with much of a choice. I had to go to a meeting.

But first there were a couple of details I needed to clear up with Jimmy O'Brien. I was putting two and two together, but I kept coming up with five, and I thought Jimmy might be able to help straighten me out. I reached him on his cell phone, and he agreed to meet me at the Worth Street Coffee Shop in an hour. In the meantime, I checked the meeting schedule and decided to attend the four o'clock meeting on East Houston Street.

Walking to the coffee shop, I felt better than I had in a couple of days. I still hadn't gotten back to the place in my head where I needed to be, but I was getting closer.

Jimmy O'Brien was already at the coffee shop, seated in my private booth, when I arrived. We ordered coffee, and after we chatted briefly, I got down to business. I wanted to go over some things Jimmy had told me the first day we met.

He had said when he got to the office on the second floor, McNulty was kneeling over Kim Lee's body. I needed to know if he saw what McNulty was doing. Jimmy thought for a minute, then he said that McNulty had his back to him, but he might have been checking to see if she was alive. He couldn't be sure. When I asked if there were any papers or things on the floor, it jogged something in Jimmy's memory, and he said that he saw something in McNulty's hand. It wasn't papers or an envelope; it was something small, but Jimmy didn't know what it was. He only saw it for a second before McNulty moved his hand, so whatever he was holding was out of sight. When he turned and faced Jimmy, the thing was no longer visible.

The pictures in the *New York Post,* taken the night of the raid, showed McNulty wearing a standard issue NYPD raid jacket. It was the same raid jacket worn by Jimmy and the other cops working the case that night. When Jimmy confirmed the raid jackets had inside breast pockets, we both had a pretty good idea of where the thing had gone.

Jimmy agreed that McNulty claiming nothing of value was found at the scene, was odd, especially given the open safe. You use a safe to store money or other valuable items, and you open a safe to take them out or put them in. It was obvious that Kim Lee had opened the safe when the raid started. The only reason she would have done that was to take something out of the safe or put something into the safe. But according to McNulty, there were no items recovered at the scene. So, what happened to whatever it was that Kim Lee was taking out of the safe, or putting into the safe?

My gut and common sense said Kim Lee was trying to retrieve something from the safe before the cops got to it. Unfortunately Jimmy had no idea what that something was, and neither did I.

We both agreed that whatever it was, it had to be valuable. Valuable enough for McNulty to kill two people and shoot Richie. If it was that valuable to McNulty, it had to be that valuable to Yeoung as well. So how did McNulty explain its disappearance to Yeoung, and why wasn't he having his fingernails pulled out in some Chinatown basement?

The only way McNulty would not be on the hot seat with Yeoung was if he had claimed someone beat him to the safe. But who could he blame? If Richie had taken it, it would have been in his possession when he was arrested, and listed on the inventory sheet. The same was true for the dead Chinese guy and Kim Lee. Since the item didn't appear on any crime scene inventory, did that mean somebody else was there, somebody like maybe Li Chin? Maybe, but I'd still bet my life the thing had gone into McNulty's jacket pocket.

There was something else that didn't make sense to me. Jimmy had said when he entered the office, he saw a .38 caliber pistol lying next to the dead Chinese guy. McNulty claimed he had witnessed the Chinese guy shoot Richie, and then he, McNulty, shot and killed the Chinese guy. So why hadn't he followed standard practice and moved the gun away from the gunman? Even if he thought the Chinese guy was dead, it was still standard practice to move it away from the shooter. He had taken Richie's weapon, so why not the .38 caliber?

Jimmy agreed none of it made sense, but he had no idea why McNulty had done it. There were just too many things about this case that didn't make sense.

CHAPTER 28

I was sitting with Jimmy when I felt this strange vibration against my leg. It startled me, and I was about to throw Jimmy a look when I realized it was Richie's damn burner phone in my pants pocket vibrating. Earlier, I had left Richie a message, asking him what he knew about Li Chin, and apparently, he was reporting back to me. I excused myself from the table and answered the call.

Unfortunately, Richie knew very little about Li Chin, other than she had given the Task Force information on the human smuggling operation. Richie had never met her because she had worked only with the one Detective from the 5th Precinct and no one else. He knew what she looked like because he had seen her in some surveillance photos. That was it. I was getting nowhere fast.

I told Richie I'd get back to him soon and ended the call. When I got back to the table, I asked Jimmy what he knew about Li Chin, hoping against hope he knew more about her than Richie knew. But he didn't. The only way I was going to find out anything more about Li Chin was to track her down in the ICE system.

Jimmy was getting anxious to leave, which was okay, because I was almost out of questions. There was one topic left, a touchy topic I had purposely left until the end. The Internal Affairs Bureau, and the name of someone in the Bureau who could be trusted.

The Internal Affairs Bureau are the cops who investigate cops, so naturally they're hated by everyone. That's why I had left the topic until the end of our discussion and why I wasn't surprised when Jimmy said no one in IAB could be trusted. He, like the rest of the rank and file referred to IAB as the Rat Squad. But Jimmy understood if I was going after McNulty I might eventually need IAB's help so he agreed to check around. That was all I could ask for and all I wanted.

We were done, Jimmy promised to keep his eyes and ears open and to let me know if he learned of any more details. I thanked him for his help knowing he could be putting himself on the line trying to help Richie.

I ordered another cup of coffee and tried to make sense of the whole Li Chin situation. My gut was telling me that chasing Li Chin was leading to another dead-end, but I was desperate. The only way I could prove McNulty, and not Richie, had killed Kim Lee was to produce an eyewitness to the murder, and so far, Li Chin was the only candidate who might fit the bill. But I didn't know if she witnessed the murder or even where the hell she was. There was just too much I didn't know and too many scenarios I didn't like.

With my meeting with Jimmy over, I had nothing on my schedule until the AA meeting at four o'clock. It wasn't quite noon, so I intended to go to the office and work. But when I left the coffee shop, the warm sunshine hit my face, and suddenly an urge overtook me to play hooky. I don't why. Possibly the beautiful weather reminded me of the times my buddies and I ditched school on the first nice day of spring and hung out down by the docks. It was a springtime ritual. Something to look forward to, like opening day for the Yankees, or the last day of school.

I don't have a lot of good memories growing up in Hell's Kitchen. But lying on those old docks, looking out across the Hudson River while the sun warmed my face, and I talked bullshit with my buddies, was one good memory. Leaving the coffee shop that day, I wanted that feeling, that connection again. Actually, when I think about it, it wasn't so much that I wanted that feeling. It was more that I needed that feeling.

It was strange, because most of my adult life I tried to erase my childhood memories. Memories like, my father abandoning my mother and me, and my poor mother working herself half to death trying to support us. Or the memory of people looking down on us because my old man wasn't around. There were good times, I'm sure; I just can't recall many of them. So, when a good memory does pop up now and then, I try to make the most of it.

I called Connie, told her I was going off the grid for a while, and not to call me unless it was a real emergency. For the first time in nearly half a century, I was about to play hooky.

CHAPTER 29

For a couple of hours, I was free, and I intended to make the most of it. As I walked to the East Side by way of Water Street and South Street, I let all the problems that had been weighing me down slip from my mind. I did so, knowing they weren't gone for good, simply out of the way for the moment.

It wasn't noon when I came across a Sabrett hot dog cart open for business. You know, I can't resist Sabrett hot dogs. So, I ordered two hot dogs with sauerkraut and mustard, a Dr. Brown's cream soda, and I sat by the edge of the East River and ate my lunch. As I sat there gazing out over the river, I decided if I was going to act like a kid and play hooky, I needed to have a real adventure.

Growing up, one of my favorite books was *The Adventures of Huckleberry Finn*, so it wasn't surprising that the thought of an adventure recalled Huck Finn and his raft. What better adventure could there be than riding on Huck Finn's raft?

Of course, there were some problems with the idea. I didn't have a raft, and even if I did, there was no way I was going on a raft in the East River. I was nostalgic, not crazy. But that didn't mean I couldn't have a river adventure.

The Staten Island Ferry has been crossing the New York Harbor from Lower Manhattan to Staten Island since 1905. During the week, five ferry boats made 109 trips between the Whitehall Ferry Terminal in Lower Manhattan and the St. George Ferry Terminal on Staten Island.

In the past, you were able to take your car onto the ferry, but not anymore. Now it's just passengers. The five-mile trip takes about twenty-five minutes, and unbelievably, it's free. Yes, free, no charge, nada, nothing. Just get on board and ride.

It costs you nothing to take a one-hour round trip across New York Harbor, and enjoy the most incredible views of the Statue of Liberty, Ellis Island, and of course, the New York City skyline than you've ever seen. That day, I made two round trips on the ferry, looking out at the New York Harbor, while the sun warmed my face. For two hours, I felt like a kid again, playing hooky, and laying on the docks, looking out over the water.

But then my little interlude was over. It was time to grow up once again and deal with my problems. It was okay, though. The problems were still there, but they didn't seem as insoluble as they had before. As I headed to my four o'clock meeting, it was with a new attitude. I still needed to find out why I was isolating myself. If I didn't deal with the problem, I knew the bad attitude would return.

Alcoholics are complicated people, and when we skid sideways, it can take a lot to get us straightened out. But, sometimes we get lucky, and it can happen at one meeting. That afternoon, I got lucky again. As I started to share, it hit me like a ton of bricks. I was isolating because I was afraid of losing Richie's case, not because the case was a loser, but because I was a loser.

It was the same old insecurity that haunted me when I drank. The fear that whatever success I had resulted from luck, not skill, and everything would come tumbling down around me at some point.

Back then, I drank to drown those feelings, but this time around I was trying to drown them in work. If that didn't do the trick, and I wasn't careful, I could go back to drowning them in scotch. That thought scared the shit out of me.

When I left the meeting, I called Doug and asked if he could meet me for dinner. Gracie was probably still mad at me, so I wasn't planning to see her. Not that I didn't want to see her, it was just that I wasn't sure what to say. I figured I needed to sit down with Doug and work out a few things before I faced Gracie.

Luckily, Doug was free that evening, so we met at the Bowery Meat Company, a nice steak house on First Street just a block from East Houston Street. When we started talking, I got the impression Doug knew all along what my problem had been. I say that because when I told him what happened at the meeting, he gave me one of his smiles. One of his, *"So you finally figured it out,"* smiles.

I had seen enough of those smiles to know what they meant. They weren't conceited or malicious smiles; they were more like the smile a teacher gives to a student when the student finally understands what the teacher has been saying. It was a smile that makes you feel good.

Doug doesn't practice criminal law, so he's never been able to give me any practical advice about my cases. But, I didn't need that kind of advice. I needed the advice only another alcoholic could give me. An alcoholic who had been through the same levels of hell that I had been through. That was the advice I needed that night, and that was the advice Doug gave me.

Doug understood what I was feeling, and he knew why. He said I had to trust in myself. I wasn't lucky; I was good at what I did; and my fears were irrational. But if I didn't deal with them, they could cause me to drink, especially if I isolated myself and didn't go to meetings or call my sponsor. It wasn't much advice, and it doesn't sound very insightful, but it was my trust in the messenger, and not the message, that made it work.

In AA, we have an acronym, KISS. It means, keep it simple stupid. Alcoholics can complicate the simplest things to the point that the smallest problem can become seemingly insoluble. Then we drink. It works out well for active alcoholics, but not so much for those of us in recovery. That's why we need to keep it simple. It sounds easy enough to do, but trust me, it isn't. I needed Doug to get me back on track that night, and he did just that.

When we left the restaurant, I felt good, and I knew that feeling would last. I promised Doug I'd call him every day no matter what, and I'd attend meetings. After that, I just wandered around feeling good, because I knew I'd be okay, and I knew I was doing everything I could for Richie. All that remained was to convince Gracie I was okay.

I owed Gracie an apology, which I was pretty sure she'd accept, but it was going to involve my eating a lot of sushi. A small price to pay for domestic peace. So that night I called her, and we spent over an hour on the phone talking about us. Actually, it was a lot of me talking about me and apologizing. Gracie, of course, forgave me, and if it hadn't been so late, I'd have gone over to her place for the night. But it was late, and the next day I was going to Goshen, so we agreed to get together the following night.

My serenity was back, and that night I slept better than I had since Laura called about Richie.

CHAPTER 30

The next morning, I waited anxiously in front of my apartment building for Vince, Connie's cousin, to arrive in his limo. I was anxious for many reasons, and in case you're wondering, they were all justified. First, I was worried because I wasn't certain I'd be able to con my way into seeing Li Chin. Then there was my natural fear of riding in motor vehicles, particularly taxicabs. You may think that fear is irrational. God knows many do, but irrational or not, to me it's very real. Finally, believe it or not, at fifty-four years old, I've had only ridden in a limo once. That was when my mother died, and I rode in a limo to the cemetery in Flushing. Obviously, I don't associate riding in limos with anything pleasant.

So, let's just say I was ambivalent when a stretch Cadillac pulled up in front of my apartment building, and a smiling Vince jumped out to greet me. Despite my less than accommodating attitude, Vince was friendly, and it turned out he had the same sharp sense of humor as his cousin, Connie.

It didn't take long for me to realize a limousine is nothing more than a fancy oversized taxicab. Yes, it did have a bar and a TV, which you don't find in taxicabs, but other than the amenities and its size, it was nothing more than a taxicab.

You know how I feel about taxicabs and that I compiled a list of taxicabs I have vowed on my dearly departed mother's soul, never to ride in again. Before we were even halfway up the West Side Highway, Vince's limo made the list. With an asterisk and underlined, I might add.

Apparently, the distance between the back seat and the driver's seat was such that Vince was unable to hear me say there was no need to rush. I tried speaking louder, but at that point a window between us went up, and I don't think Vince could hear me yelling at him.

The next day, when I told Connie her cousin's limo was on my list, and I wouldn't be riding in it again, she said that wasn't going to be a problem. It seems that Vince had his own list, and I was on it. I guess that made us even.

Anyway, somehow, I made it to Goshen in one piece. I still hadn't decided what I was going to say when I got to the jail. I knew if I said I wanted to talk to Li Chin as a possible witness in a case pending in Manhattan, my chances of seeing her were slim to non-existent. On the other hand, if I said I represented her, and she said I wasn't her lawyer, not only wouldn't I not get to see her, I might end up in the cell next to her. I decided to try the old half-truth, half- bluff routine.

At the jail's registration desk, I put down my New York State Attorney Identification Card and said, "I'm here to see Li Chin who's being held on an ICE detainer." The officer behind the desk took my ID, looked at the picture, looked at me, and handed the card back. He gave me a friendly smile and said, "Good morning, counselor." At that point, I was feeling confident. But then things took a bad turn. After checking his computer, the officer said Li Chin had been released to ICE the day before.

I started to ask him if he knew where ICE had taken her, but he interrupted me, asking why I didn't know she had been transferred. It was a good question. He was justifiably suspicious, and he wasn't about to give me any information. The best thing I could do at that point was get my ass out of there as quickly as possible, so I blamed the whole thing on an administrative screwup and walked out.

On the way back to Manhattan, I kept thinking how things might have turned out differently if the day before I had gone to Goshen instead of taking my mental health day. But I hadn't, and there was no sense dwelling on what might have been. The only good it did was to keep my mind off Vince's driving.

CHAPTER 31

I was sitting in my office trying to recover from the return trip from Goshen when Abe called. In his own inimitable way, Abe had parlayed his relationship with one clerk at the ICE Detention Center into a whole network of clerks, and he had new information about Li Chin. She was in the Northeast Ohio Correctional Center, but would be leaving there shortly for the Fremont County Jail in Canon City, Colorado.

What the hell was going on? Li Chin had been moved from New York City to Goshen, New York, then to Northeast Ohio, and she was about to be moved to Colorado. It sounded to me like someone was trying to lose her in the system, and if that was true, it was good news. It meant someone didn't want her found, and I was betting that someone was McNulty. If McNulty didn't want her found, it was because she knew something.

I was just starting to get excited when Abe burst my bubble. According to Abe's source, she was being moved in stages to the West Coast for deportation to China. Asked why she wasn't simply deported from New York, the source explained she had been smuggled into the country through California, and ICE agents there wanted to interview her before she was sent back to China. As for the route, it was dictated by the availability of transportation. When you thought about it, not in a logical way, but in the context of how the federal government operates, it made sense.

Abe had more news. His contact confirmed neither NYPD, nor any other government agency, had inquired about Li Chin. That meant McNulty wasn't interested in Li Chin's whereabouts. Either she wasn't a threat to him, or he didn't know she was a threat. That left me nowhere.

The only reason McNulty would consider Li Chin a threat was because she had seen something the night of the raid. Either she witnessed the shootings, or she saw McNulty take whatever it was that had been in the safe. Either way would make her a threat to McNulty and give him a reason to find her. It didn't necessarily mean he'd have to kill her; having her deported to China was probably enough to neutralize her. But at a minimum, he was likely to keep tabs on her location and status.

But McNulty wasn't tracking Li Chin's whereabouts or status, which meant he wasn't worried about her. It was possible she had seen something, and McNulty didn't know she had. But without something positive to go on, there was no way I was going to fly to Colorado or anywhere else on the chance I could catch up with Li Chin, and if I did, that I'd be able to see her. I had already wasted too much time chasing ghosts. I had to accept the fact that Li Chin was turning out to be a dead-end.

Accepting that a promising lead isn't promising, after all, is never easy. You get your hopes all up, and then suddenly they're dashed, leaving you nowhere. In Richie's case, accepting that Li Chin wasn't going to be the savior I had hoped was an exceptionally bitter pill to swallow, because it left me with nothing to be hopeful about.

I'm no fool. I knew all along that I was clutching at straws, but that was okay because it gave me hope. I figured at some point something would break our way, and I'd have the proof that I so desperately needed. Maybe the forensic evidence would contain a surprise, or maybe some new witness would turn up. But none of that happened, and Li Chin became our Hail Mary pass, our last-ditch chance for a miracle ending. Now that was gone.

McNulty was still a corrupt cop, and I could prove it, but that alone might not be enough for an acquittal. It would be a good bargaining chip in a plea deal negotiation, but Richie refused to consider a plea deal. I think, at that point, if I hadn't gotten my head straightened out a couple of days earlier, I might have just had a drink. But instead of thinking that way, I called Doug.

CHAPTER 32

That night Gracie and I had dinner at yet another new sushi restaurant. It seemed sushi restaurants were popping up all over the city. I was surprised there were any fish left in Manhattan. But I had been a jerk, and now I had to pay the price. Gracie had, of course, accepted my apology, but as always, my absolution required a penance. So, there we sat with a platter of raw fish between us.

I still don't understand this fascination with raw fish. It's not particularly tasty, and wrapping it in seaweed doesn't make it any more attractive to me. I figured the first one to try sushi was either starving to death, or had lost a bet. How it caught on after that beats me. But mine wasn't to reason why; it was simply to eat sushi or not get laid. It wasn't a question of whether I'd eat sushi, that was a given under the circumstances. It was only a question of how long I'd have to eat it.

Given the seriousness of my sin, I imagined I'd grow fins and gills before I saw a pizza again. But Gracie was happy, and when Gracie is happy, I might not be happy, but at least I'm safe from physical injury. Besides, we were inside what I call a safe zone. Of all the food Gracie has thrown at me over the years, she's never thrown raw fish, so I feel safe in a sushi restaurant.

Hoping to keep the topic of conversation away from my recent ill-advised behavior and maybe create a little sympathy for myself, I mentioned my frightful limo ride. It didn't surprise me that Gracie wasn't very sympathetic. I just wasn't sure if her callousness resulted from residual anger, or simply from having ridden with me in numerous taxicabs. She rolled her eyes and said, "I guess we're lucky to have you here tonight."

Figuring I was still on thin ice, I didn't come back with one of my snappy repartees, like "Oh yeah." Besides, Gracie was more interested in what happened when I got to Goshen than she was in the limo ride there.

I have to admit after I told Gracie the story, she was much more sympathetic. I won't bore you with the details of what happened after dinner. Let's just say that we followed our usual post-sushi tradition, and I was a happy man.

One thing I have to say about Gracie, she doesn't hold grudges. She gets angry, blows her top, throws food, then most times it's over. If she's really angry, there might be a couple of days of not talking to me, but that's generally it. Of course, I've never done anything that warranted her getting mad at me. If you tell her I said that, I'll never speak to you again.

I love Gracie because she puts up with me, and I'm the first to admit that I'm a handful. I don't mean to be. It's just something that comes naturally. Other than my mother, Gracie and Doug, I can't think of anyone else who puts up with my craziness. Maybe Connie, but I pay her salary, so she might not count.

My dear mother had little choice but to love her only child. It's a biological imperative. As for Doug, he doesn't have to live with me, so that sort of leaves Gracie in a unique category.

For the seventh year in a row, the award for putting up with Jake Carney goes to Gracie Delaney.

CHAPTER 33

It had been a week and a half since Laura called about Richie, but it seemed like yesterday to me. Maybe that was because, other than visiting Sasha at Rikers Island, I hadn't worked on anything but Richie's case since the phone call. In the process, I was making Abe's year a financial success, and draining my own cash account at a record speed. It wasn't what you'd call a great business model.

The point was dramatically driven home when earlier that day, I had to transfer money from my personal savings account into my business operating account. If I hadn't, Connie's last paycheck would have bounced like a rubber ball. If you think Gracie gives me a hard time, you have no idea what Connie can be like when she's upset.

Connie does our bookkeeping, and she is well aware of our financial state of affairs. So when I handed her the deposit slip, she gave me a curious look. A large deposit from something other than a fee payment was curious, to say the least. Connie is no fool; she knew right away where the money came from, but she was smart enough to know not to make an issue of it. She just gave me one of her looks.

Connie has worked for me since I opened the office on Mott Street. She's rather like a feral cat, which may seem like a rude thing to say about her, but it's not meant to be rude. She has an edge about her, much like her boss, which is probably why she's survived at the job all these years. Like a feral cat, she fiercely protects her territory, which luckily includes me.

To be completely honest, Connie's secretarial skills are just adequate, which she will readily admit. But she's as honest as the day is long and a hard and dedicated worker. You can't ask for better than that, and I don't. Besides, Gracie likes her.

My problem that morning wasn't with Connie; it was with money, or rather the lack of cash flow. I had the money to cover everything for a while, and if I had to, I could invade the retirement account I opened a couple of years back. I didn't have a great deal of money in it and going to it would be a last resort. It was just good to know it was there, and I'd use it if I had to.

It wasn't as though I needed to cover everything for Richie up front. Laura kept pestering me to send her a bill, but I kept putting it off. I knew after paying for the bail bond, money was tight for them.

If a lawyer in a similar situation asked my advice, I'd tell him he was crazy if he advanced that much money on behalf of any client, including his own mother. Okay, maybe not in his mother's case. At least not if she was innocent. If she was guilty, he'd have to consider how she'd be able pay the fee if she was sent to jail.

It sounds cruel and crude, but when you work alone, that's how you have to think. You can't work for free forever. If you try, you'll end up bankrupt, and then you're not going to be any good to anybody.

I knew all of that, and I knew I was ignoring my own best advice, but it was Richie Simone, and I'm a fool, so I refused to take a retainer. Case closed.

I was still standing by Connie's desk in a stare down over the deposit when Tommy showed up. He had an armload of papers and a smile on his face that told me he had good news. I gave Connie a shake of my head, letting her know our little stare down was over, and then I escorted Tommy into my office. I was anxious to hear what he had to say, but I was also happy that the stare down with Connie was over.

CHAPTER 34

Linda Chow had been working overtime, tracking McNulty's finances, when she stumbled on an interesting, but curious item about his son, George. It was a *Wall Street Journal* article about real estate management companies. It named George McNulty as the president and sole shareholder of GM Properties, a real estate holding company with properties in Manhattan, East Hampton, South Beach, Hong Kong, and the Bahamas.

Curious as to how George McNulty came to own and manage these properties and suspecting there might be a tie between George McNulty's ownership of GM Properties and his father, Linda did some further digging. Not surprisingly, she found nothing in George's background suggesting even remotely that he had the education, experience, or financial ability to have created a multi-million-dollar real estate empire. Based on his education, job history and background, he wasn't qualified to run a candy store, no less a real estate empire.

Convinced there was a connection between GM Properties and the senior McNulty, Linda dug deeper. On the surface, the GM Properties operation appeared legitimate. It listed twelve properties on its books, valued at a total of $81.8 million. You wouldn't think there was anything suspicious in that, but that's because you don't know Linda.

Linda knew we were looking for a connection between William McNulty and Sam Yeoung. So, when she saw that one of the properties owned and managed by GM was located in Hong Kong, it raised a red flag. It was while investigating the Hong Kong property that Linda discovered something much more important about another one of GM's Properties.

The building owned and managed by GM Properties in Manhattan was on Madison Street. Recalling that the brothel operated in a building on Madison Street, Linda cross-checked the addresses. Bingo! It turned out Sam Yeoung was operating his brothel in a building owned and managed by McNulty's son and GM Properties. A coincidence? She didn't think so.

As Tommy explained all of this, and I followed along with the paper trail, the adrenalin started to flow, and my heart began beating faster. This could be the smoking gun I was looking for. But I didn't want to get my hopes up too high, at least not until I heard the whole story.

Knowing she was on to something with GM Properties, Linda dug deeper into the company and its operation. According to public records, GM Properties had been incorporated in New York seven years earlier, coincidentally the same year William McNulty opened his Merrill Lynch and his offshore accounts.

I'm no expert on corporate law, but it didn't take an expert to recognize that GM Properties had been set up with minimal assets and no properties. It wasn't until a week later that GM purchased all twelve of the properties it now held and managed.

What had been merely curious was suddenly becoming extremely interesting. All twelve properties were purchased on the same day from different companies. But when Linda checked out the twelve companies, they all traced back to Sam Yeoung. The connections were buried in a mountain of financial transactions, but as Tommy will tell you, when Linda gets onto something, she's like a dog with a bone. She just won't let it go. It took her a while, but eventually she sorted through it all and found that Yeoung had been the actual owner of the properties.

Why Yeoung sold the twelve properties to McNulty's son was an interesting question. But the big question was where McNulty's son got $82 million to buy them. It turned out the answer to that question was a matter of public record. GM Properties borrowed the money from Silver Star Assets to buy the properties.

Silver Star was a Hong Kong corporation, licensed to do business in the United States. It, in turn, was a wholly owned subsidiary of South Sea Enterprises, owned and operated by Jimmy Yeoung, Sam Yeoung's brother. Simply put, Jimmy Yeoung loaned George McNulty the money to buy the properties owned by his brother, Sam Yeoung.

It's amazing how much information is on the Internet and available if you know where to look. It also helps if you're a world-class hacker like Linda Chow. Somewhere between the public domain and privately held information, Linda found all twelve mortgages and all the paperwork associated with them.

The mortgages secured loans totaling $81.8 million, the total amount paid for all the properties, leaving GM Properties with a net equity of zero dollars. That was a bit odd, but not necessarily evidence of wrongdoing. However, there were a couple of things in the mortgages that suggested something wasn't on the up-and-up. One, the interest rates were exceptionally high for the then current market, and two, there was a streamlined default clause that allowed the mortgage company to foreclose title in the event of a default, without having to go through formal legal proceedings.

Without seeing the bookkeeping records of GM Properties, it was impossible to tell what was actually going on, so I figured at that point we were done. But Tommy had that smile on his face again, so I knew there was more.

Tommy always claimed that Linda could access anything on a computer if it was online, but until that day I didn't believe him. Now I do. I don't know how Linda got hold of the financial statements of GM, and I never want to know, but I was glad she had. The statements gave us a clear picture of what GM Properties was up to.

All twelve properties owned and managed by GM were rented or leased to client companies, producing a total annual income of $9.8 million. But the unusually high interest payments on the mortgages and other expenses, including George McNulty's annual salary of $2.75 million, reduced the company's annual profits to a mere $50,000. With no equity in the properties and no significant profits, GM Properties was nothing more than a shell corporation.

The companies leasing the properties were identified in the financial statements, but they proved to be sham corporations. When Linda dug deeper, she found all twelve were directly or indirectly linked to the Yeoung brothers.

All the money flowing through GM Properties was Yeoung's money. It was nothing more than an intricate money laundering scheme. GM Properties existed to create a circular flow of money that laundered cash from Yeoung's illegal businesses. It was also how Yeoung paid William McNulty for protection.

Money laundering happens in three phases. In the first phase, called the placement phase, cash generated from illegal activities is put into the financial system. Yeoung did this by taking the cash from his illegal Tong ventures and paying it to GM as rent. GM deposited the money into its own account, recording the transaction as rental income on its books. With the money now legitimately in the financial system, it was on to phase two called layering, or camouflaging the money's origin.

GM Properties passed the money on to Silver Star, labeling the transaction as mortgage payments. Silver Star passed the money on to South Sea Enterprises, its parent company. That way the money passed through three layers of legitimate sources before it was ready for the final phase, integration. That's the phase where Yeoung takes back his cash, now legitimate and no longer traceable to his illegal activities. At least not easily traced to his illegal activities.

The salary paid to George McNulty was the payoff to the senior McNulty for the police protection he provided for Yeoung's New York operation. By paying McNulty off through his son, Yeoung added a layer of insulation for both men. George McNulty collected the money as legitimate salary, then he presumably passed it on to his old man, after probably keeping a share for himself. William McNulty then did his own laundering by passing the money through his Promotion Test Tutor company.

The way money was getting laundered all over the place, you'd think we were in a laundromat. It was all very neat and all very illegal. But it might not be as helpful to Richie's case as it seemed.

Nothing we had found tied William McNulty directly to the scheme. Yes, it made sense that the money was going to him for protection, but if I couldn't put the money into McNulty's pocket, it was just argument. If we couldn't find solid evidence that the money was going to McNulty, we at least needed evidence tying William McNulty to Sam Yeoung. Something as simple as a photograph of the two men together would at least keep McNulty from denying he knew Yeoung.

A photograph might not seem like much, but as the old saying goes, *a photograph is worth a thousand words.* If, at Richie's trial, McNulty denied knowing or socializing with Yeoung, which he was likely to do, a photograph of the two men talking together would seriously damage McNulty's credibility. It also bolstered our claim that the money young McNulty was collecting was going to his father in exchange for senior McNulty doing Yeoung favors. It wouldn't be a smoking gun, but it was something.

The problem was how to get a photograph of McNulty and Yeoung together. I couldn't afford to have McNulty under twenty-four-hour surveillance, and simply hoping we'd catch them together sometime wasn't going to work. Tommy was sure that any meeting between the two would take place at Yeoung's headquarters, the Golden Palace restaurant. That was standard operating procedure for the Hip Sing Tong. But, just knowing where a meeting would take place wasn't enough. There had to be a reason for McNulty and Yeoung to meet, and we needed to know when they planned on meeting.

That's when Tommy came up with an idea. Rather than trying to guess when the two men would meet, why not force them to meet? GM Properties was the cornerstone of the McNulty-Yeoung operation, and they couldn't afford to have it exposed. Just the hint that it might be exposed would have to be taken seriously. So, if McNulty knew we were investigating GM Properties, he'd have to alert Yeoung, and Yeoung would demand a meeting.

It sounded good, but I wanted to know how Tommy could be so sure there'd be a meeting. He explained. Some years ago, Yeoung had been charged in a drug case based on a wiretapped conversation, and since then he's had a strict rule to never transact business over the phone. Anything other than the most innocent sounding conversations were held face-to-face at the Golden Palace restaurant.

I agreed it made sense, and then it was just a question of how we put the plan into action. Once again it was Tommy who came up with the idea.

GM Properties had an office in Midtown Manhattan. Tommy would go there, claiming to be an investigator working on a murder case and ask questions about the building on Madison Street. No doubt young McNulty would put two and two together and figure out it had something to do with Richie's case. He'd call his old man, and his old man would call Yeoung.

Okay, I agreed that would probably work, but it still didn't tell us if there'd be a meeting or when it would be. Tommy grinned, and I got the feeling he was about to tell me something I didn't want to hear, and I was right. Linda had put a wiretap on William McNulty's cell phone.

The tap was on a burner phone. Apparently, McNulty didn't use it often, but when he did, it was to speak with either his son or Yeoung. He used a burner phone, so there wouldn't be any records connecting him to Yeoung. McNulty, like Yeoung, didn't talk business over the phone, but used it to set up meetings.

I didn't want to know how Tommy knew about the burner phone in the first place, or how Linda managed to tap it. If I didn't know, I couldn't be a witness against him or Linda if the thing blew up in our faces. Otherwise, it didn't

167

matter if I knew or not, because we wouldn't use any intercepted conversations at trial.

Tommy would go to GM Properties' office later that morning, and Linda would monitor McNulty's cell phone. Hopefully by the end of the day, we'd be making plans to photograph McNulty and Yeoung together.

CHAPTER 35

When Tommy left, Connie said we needed to go over some bookkeeping matters. I hate bookkeeping matters. Maybe it's because I'm not very good at that stuff. I always had trouble balancing my checking account, and as long as I came within a couple of bucks either way I was happy. As a lawyer, I'm required to keep a separate account, called a trust account, for clients' money, and I must maintain very accurate records of that account. Coming close doesn't cut it.

When I worked in the DA's Office, I didn't need to keep a trust account. All I had was my personal checking account. It never balanced, but nobody cared. When I opened my own office, the desk in the backroom at Shoo's Restaurant, I had to maintain a trust account. All of my clients at the time were from the18B Panel, and none of them had enough money to hire a lawyer. If they did, they wouldn't have qualified for 18B representation. So, luckily for me, I never had any client money to put into the trust account. I dread to think what might have happened if I had to handle client money back then. I can tell you this, when you're drinking alcohol in excess as I was, keeping track of the time is a challenge. Forget about keeping very accurate bookkeeping records. I was just damn lucky I wasn't disbarred.

But once I got sober, things changed. I didn't become any better at bookkeeping, but at least I started taking it seriously. I still have trouble balancing my checking account, but when it comes to my trust account it balances to the penny. That, thanks in no small part to Connie and Michael Yee, my accountant.

Anyway, Connie had the business checkbook and a bunch of checks she had just written to pay some of our monthly bills. Before I signed the checks, she wanted me to know that even with the money I had just deposited into the account, the balance, after paying the bills, was going to be lower than usual. It was Connie's not so subtle way of pointing out, once more, that my handling of Richie's case was putting us in the poorhouse.

Eventually I'd have to face facts and either bill Richie or stop spending all my time on his case. If I didn't do one or the other, I'd wind up going broke, and it wouldn't be because I didn't have enough cases to work on. There was plenty of work to do; I just kept farming it out to Abe to make time to work on Richie's case.

It was definitely a problem, and I could tell from the look on Connie's face she wanted to talk about it. But I wasn't ready to deal with it, so we were about to have one of our "discussions." However, before either of us could say anything, Abe arrived to pick up a file. He was scheduled to handle a plea bargain conference for me later that afternoon.

That gave me the perfect opportunity to kill two birds with one stone. I'd handle the damn conference myself and earn a little money, while at the same time putting off the "discussion" with Connie.

I hated cutting Abe out of the job, but it turned out he was happy to be off the case. He couldn't stand the client who he called a "miserable gonif." Gonif is the Yiddish word for a swindler or a crook. To be honest, I couldn't stand the miserable bastard either. Calling Julio Castro a gonif gave gonifs a bad name.

Julio Castro was a con artist, who ran cons on elderly poor people in Harlem. He peddled "get rich" investment schemes and counterfeit lottery tickets, and he sold fake gold coins.

Then he came up with his ultimate scam. First, he printed bogus gift certificates with $250 values. Then he went door-to-door, claiming he worked for the Visa credit card company and offered elderly couples a gift certificate as a reward for applying for a credit card. He claimed the certificate could be used against their first credit card bill. In other words, it was like a free $250 gift certificate.

Castro helped his victims complete their applications, making sure the applications would pass muster with the company. He even supplied the stamps and offered to mail the applications himself. He was quite the little helper.

Once the applications were mailed, Castro waited for the credit cards to arrive. When he saw the postman put the Visa card in the victim's mailbox, he'd simply wait for the postman to leave, then jimmy open the mailbox door and steal the card.

Most of the cards had $500 limits, but some had limits as high as $2,500. Castro took cash advances, bought easy to sell electronics and even took special orders for clothes and furniture from friends and family.

Castro ran the scam successfully for nearly a year until fate intervened, and he scammed Roberto Guzman's grandmother. Guzman was a particularly vicious drug dealer who, upon learning that Castro had preyed on his grandmother, vowed to make him pay dearly for his crime. There was talk of Guzman cutting off Castro's manhood, cutting off all his fingers, or both. Guzman offered $50,000 to anyone who brought him Julio alive and $25,000 if they brought him dead.

Petrified of being grabbed up on the street and having no way to escape from Guzman's revenge, Castro turned himself in to the police and confessed to several crimes. In exchange for his confessions, Castro was guaranteed a prison stay, safe from Guzman and his buddies.

If Castro thought his luck was bad to that point, it was nothing compared to what happened next. Shortly after he had signed all the confessions, Guzman and his top

FOR ONE MAN'S HONOR

lieutenants were killed by a rival drug gang. Gone was Guzman and gone with him was the threat and the contract on Castro's life.

Castro decided to withdraw his confessions and plead not guilty. That's when I was assigned as his lawyer. Castro claimed the confessions were coerced after he had been beaten into submission by the cops. It sounded good, but only if you ignored the facts. The problem was there were ten confessions, all signed, all given on different days, all taken by the same ADA, but with different police officers present. If that wasn't enough, each session had been videotaped.

Castro had the right to change his plea to not guilty, but if I couldn't get the confessions suppressed, the DA could use them against Castro at his trials. Castro was smart enough to know the videotaped confessions would seal the deal and guarantee a conviction. The only way out was to challenge the validity of the confessions.

I advised Castro that challenging the confessions by claiming they were coerced wasn't going to work, but he insisted we try. We went through ten Huntley hearings trying to suppress the ten confessions and lost every one of them. We didn't have a chance in hell of winning any one of those hearings, but we tried.

Seven of the ten hearings were held before Judge Wallace, who by the third hearing, had no patience for either Castro or for me. Finally, after we lost the tenth hearing and Judge Wallace ripped Castro a new one for wasting the court's time, Castro got the message, and we negotiated a plea deal. The DA agreed to drop three of the lesser charges, and to reduce three of the more serious charges to a lower degree. That still left Castro facing seven charges, three of which carried seven- to fifteen-year prison sentences.

Castro's luck didn't improve after we cut the plea deals. When we showed up in court to enter his seven guilty pleas, the judge was none other than Judge Wallace. It wasn't a good day, not for Castro. Now we were going to court, and Judge Wallace was going to sentence Castro. I could hardly wait.

When it was time for sentencing, Castro was naturally nervous, especially after noticing how Judge Wallace was glaring at him. I can't say that I wouldn't have been nervous if I was in Castro's shoes. The Probation Department Report wasn't good at all, and I was hard pressed to find anything to say on Castro's behalf. I did my best, relying on the old "he's repentant and given the opportunity, he will become a better person." That's when Judge Wallace started glaring at me.

When a sentencing judge glares at a defendant and says nothing, then smiles before he begins speaking, you just know it's going to be bad. Judge Wallace began by naming all of Castro's victims. Senior citizens who could little afford to have their credit ratings thrashed. People who were supposed to be enjoying their golden years, but who, thanks to Julio, were reduced to fighting for financial survival. By that point, everybody in the courtroom, including me, were glaring at Castro.

Then came the sentence, maximum terms on each of the seven charges. But Judge Wallace wasn't finished punishing Castro. The sentences were to be served consecutively, meaning one after another, so Castro wouldn't be eligible for parole for twenty-five years. I don't think he fully appreciated the meaning of consecutively because he didn't react to it. But everybody else in the courtroom did, and I thought for a moment there might be a round of applause for Judge Wallace as Castro was dragged off by the court officers.

You might not agree that Castro deserves to spend twenty-five years in prison for a non-violent crime. But ask yourself whether you'd feel that way if he had stolen your life savings and ruined your credit rating. Every now and then it doesn't hurt to look at things from the victim's prospective.

The way I see it, the pain and misery Castro inflicted on his victims wasn't much different from the pain and misery inflicted by violent felons. Castro wasn't stupid; he was smart. If he was smart enough to figure out how to swindle people out of their money, he was smart enough to know how devastating the result would be. He had the brains to earn an honest living, but instead he chose to steal. That made him a lazy bastard with no shame. Just because he didn't use force didn't make him any better than the thugs who mug people in the street.

Sometimes I wonder why I stay in this business.

CHAPTER 36

I was on my way back to the office after Castro's sentencing when Tommy called my cell. He'd gone to GM Enterprises' office, introduced himself as a private investigator, and asked to speak to George McNulty about the murders at the company's Madison Street building.

Standing next to the receptionist's desk, he overheard her pass on his request to Mr. McNulty personally. Fifteen minutes later, a woman claiming to be Mr. McNulty's secretary, informed Tommy that Mr. McNulty was out of the office and not expected to return anytime soon.

While Tommy was at George McNulty's office, Linda Chow was monitoring the elder McNulty's cell phone. Shortly after Tommy asked to speak with George, George called his father and asked him what he should do. William McNulty told his son not to talk to Tommy and suggested George have his secretary brush Tommy off, claiming he was out of the office.

After hanging up with his son, William McNulty called Yeoung. The conversation was cryptic as expected, but it clearly concerned Tommy's visit to George's office. It ended with McNulty and Yeoung agreeing to meet at the Golden Palace that night.

Tommy's plan had worked. We had forced the meeting, and now it was just a question of having people in position to photograph the two men together. Tommy wanted to lead the stakeout team, but I vetoed the idea. I thought it was too risky because McNulty or Yeoung might have seen Tommy with me at some point, and that could tip our hand. It wasn't likely, but why take the chance? We had nothing to gain by sending Tommy, but everything to lose if we spooked them. Tommy reluctantly conceded I was right and agreed to send his team alone. We'd both sit this one out.

As much as I would have liked to be there when McNulty and Yeoung met, I knew I couldn't be. Besides, of all the practical reasons for not being there, that night was movie night, and I couldn't miss movie night. Not without a lot of unpleasant consequences.

One night a month Gracie and I eat in and watch old movies. One of the things we do on movie night is turn off our cell phones. It's not something either of us likes doing, but we do it anyway. Why? Because it gives us a couple of uninterrupted hours together and affirms the importance of our relationship. At least that's what Gracie said when she told me to turn off my cell phone.

So that evening when Tommy called, he was going to get my voice mail, and I wouldn't know what happened at the Golden Palace restaurant until the movie was over. To make matters worse, it was Gracie's turn to pick the movie, and she'd probably choose some Hallmark movie. Not only would I be miserable wondering what was happening with McNulty, I'd have to sit through a chick flick. The only way things could be any worse would be if Gracie ordered sushi for our dinner.

I spent the rest of the day trying to figure a way out of movie night, but I couldn't come up with anything I thought Gracie would believe. In a moment of sheer desperation, I thought of telling her that old man Shoo was getting married, and Tommy was throwing a surprise bachelor party for him. You can see all the holes in that story, right? To start with, the man's in his mid-eighties and hates parties, not to mention I'd then have to explain why we weren't invited to the wedding. I mentioned it only to give you an idea of how desperate I was.

That evening I did get one break. Gracie ordered Chinese food for dinner. Thank God, it wasn't sushi. Had it been sushi I might have considered killing myself.

The Chinese food for dinner was the only break I got. The movie was a Hallmark classic. I don't remember the name, but the plot was the same as in all the other

Hallmark movies Gracie has made me watch. It's the standard formula for all chick flicks, and it comes in four parts.

Part one, boy meets girl; boy and girl fall in love. How, when and where it all happens doesn't matter. It could be a blind date in Manhattan, a car crash in Paris, a crowded supermarket in Los Angles.

Part two, something happens that causes boy and girl to break up. The breakup could be caused by a lie, another lover, or an unfortunate misunderstanding. It doesn't matter so long as it's the boy's fault.

Then we come to part three; boy and girl are miserable apart. Here the director can be creative in portraying the poor girl's misery and the boy's self-loathing over his own stupidity.

After twenty minutes of misery, finally, and at long last, comes part four, the reconciliation and happy ending. By this point, I have lost all interest, and I'm trying to recall the names of the state capitals, just so I don't fall asleep and start snoring. Gracie says snoring sends a bad message.

But getting back to that particular night. The movie seemed unusually long, and I was dying. I considered putting my phone on vibrate instead of turning it off and going to the john if I got a call. But Gracie was wise to my tricks, and I didn't want to risk pissing her off. I had enough problems, and I didn't need a pissed off Gracie on top of everything else.

When the movie finally ended, I was fumbling furiously, trying to get my cell phone out of my pants pocket, when Gracie said she was going to bed and asked if I was coming. It was clearly an invitation, and for a moment, I was filled with uncertainty. Lust is a powerful emotion, but curiosity at times is stronger. Trying to be as casual as I could be, I told her I'd join her shortly, but first I needed to check my cell phone and possibly make a call or two.

Happily, I had only one voice mail, and it was from Tommy. It was short and sweet. He had news and wanted me to call him as soon as I could. I called his cell immediately.

The news was good. Tommy had three operatives staking out the Golden Palace restaurant. One stayed outside keeping watch, while the other two, a man and a young woman, went inside posing as customers. Concealed in the woman's purse was a video camera. The couple selected a table with a view of the entrance, as well as a clear view of a door marked "OFFICE."

The stakeout had been operational for an hour when McNulty showed up at the Golden Palace. Tommy's outside man took a series of pictures of McNulty approaching and entering the restaurant. His face was clearly visible in all of the pictures. Inside the restaurant, Yeoung greeted McNulty and led him back to the office. All of it was captured on video with both men's faces clearly visible. The two men hadn't hugged, but I hadn't expected them to. They didn't look like huggers to me.

It had been a good day and for the first time, I was feeling a bit more optimistic about Richie's chances. Now if I was lucky, Gracie was waiting for me in the bedroom. As I approached the bedroom door, I heard noises. It turned out Gracie was right; snoring did send a bad message.

CHAPTER 37

As if Richie's case wasn't enough to keep me busy, I now had to deal with Sasha's case as well. Handling multiple cases isn't really a problem. Most of the time I have a dozen or more active cases. But these two cases were far from the typical cases I usually handle.

Most of the cases I handle follow a simple pattern moving from start to finish in a straight line. The case starts with the client telling me his story, then it moves on to arraignment, followed by some plea bargaining and ends with the client going to jail. That may sound cynical, but that's just the way it is. It isn't my doing; it's simply how the system works. Why? Because 99% of my clients are clearly guilty, and guilty people go to jail. With them the question isn't "if," the question is for how long.

But things are different if your client is in that magic 1% of innocent clients. Then the case doesn't move in a straight line. It zigzags, and you have to stay on top of it and not let it get away from you. It always involves a lot more work than when you represent a guilty client, and it's a lot more stressful. One innocent client is a handful; two at the same time is a definite overload. Knowing Richie was innocent and now believing Sasha was also innocent had me mentally and emotionally taxed to the max.

Maybe that was why I was having trouble sleeping. Whatever was disturbing my sleep pattern, I was up early and had gotten to the courthouse for Sasha's arraignment much earlier than usual.

As I sat waiting, the ADA assigned to handle arraignments that day arrived. She was young and looked nervous. I suspected this was her first time in a courtroom. She had that look, the look everyone has the first time they're in a courtroom by themselves. It's the "What the hell am I doing here?" look. I can't tell you how many times I'd seen that look on the faces of young ADAs. I hate to admit it, but it was probably the look on my face the first time I was sent into Arraignment Part alone.

On the calendar she was listed simply as M. Martinez. I hadn't recognized the name, but that wasn't surprising. Arraignment Part is where the DA sends the newest ADAs, the ones fresh out of law school. That's where the newbies get courtroom experience. Arraignments are simple, probably the simplest part of the whole criminal justice process, and there isn't much that can go wrong. So, young lawyers can get used to being in a courtroom without doing any damage.

As M. Martinez approached the prosecutor's table, I walked over to introduce myself. It's a simple courtesy, nothing more than that, but to me it's important. When you're a prosecutor or a criminal defense lawyer, you deal daily with the worst of the worst, and if you're not careful you'll get sucked into their world. A world without civility, a world of indifference, and a world of constant hostility. To avoid being sucked into that world, lawyers need to be courteous, which I am most of the time. Of course, if the ADA is an asshole, then all bets are off, and the ADA gets what he or she deserves. But M. Martinez didn't seem to be an asshole, just a scared new lawyer.

As I approached M. Martinez, I stuck out my hand and introduced myself. She flashed a warm smile and said her name was Maria Martinez. Then as she shifted the pile of files she was holding in her arms to free her hand to shake mine, the files began to slip. A look of panic spread across her face. I reached out and steadied her files. Then leaning in toward her, I said, "Relax Maria, you're going to do fine." She smiled and seemed to steady a bit.

I walked back to my seat and waited for the calendar to be called. The arraignment calendar can run upward of forty cases and take the better part of the morning to call. That Sasha's case was second on the list that morning wasn't by luck. The calendar clerks assign the first five or so slots to those defense attorneys smart enough to treat them respectfully and occasionally indulge their appetites. Coffee and donuts every now and then, and bottles of wine at Christmas ensure you don't spend most of your day in Arraignment Part.

Just before Sasha's case was called, the court officers brought Sasha up from the holding cells and into the courtroom. She seemed calm and composed, which was good. It meant she was adapting well in jail. I spoke with her and explained what was about to happen. I explained the proceeding wouldn't take more than ten minutes, and once it was over, she'd be taken back to Rikers Island. Sasha nodded. She understood from our last conversation that she would be in jail for a while. All I wanted her to do was remain calm, keep her mouth shut and look innocent.

The arraignment went off without a hitch. Once Martinez got going, she gained confidence and from then on, she was fine. Courtroom work is no different than anything else in life. The first time you try it, it's scary, but if you're prepared, it gets easier. Martinez was obviously prepared, and by the time she finished the first case on the calendar and got to Sasha's case, you wouldn't know it was her first day in court.

As we were finishing up, I asked Martinez who in her office I should talk to about Sasha's case. It's the polite way of asking who's really handling the case. I was happy to learn it was Sarah Washington. I had worked with her on other cases, and we got along well. She was tough, but fair. She knew the law, but she was street smart enough to be practical.

In the few minutes I had before the court officers took Sasha away, I explained to her what was going to happen next and promised I'd be out to see her in a day or two.

Sasha understood why she had to stay in jail, and that didn't bother her. The only thing that bothered her was not being able to talk with her aunt and with Kayla. Sasha tried setting up a prisoner phone account, but without money in her prison account, she couldn't do it.

The only other way to set up the account was to have someone on the outside do it with a credit card. Her aunt had agreed to do it, but the old lady kept screwing it up. Either she'd hang up in the middle of the process, or she'd say "no" when she should have said "yes."

I felt badly for Sasha, so I told her the 18B Panel would set up and fund the phone account. It wasn't true, but I had something in mind.

When the court officers had taken Sasha away, I left and headed over to see ADA Sarah Washington.

I wanted to see Washington before she had time to study the case. If I got to her before she read the file in depth, I could put a good spin on it. She'd know I was spinning, but she'd also know I was giving her my baseline. In other words, I was letting her know where I stood on the case.

The first step in positioning a case for a plea deal is setting expectations. I was about to let Washington know the kind of deal I was open to. I've found it's always best to know if you're on the same page, or at least in the same book, before you start serious negotiations.

The District Attorney's Office is just around the corner from the courthouse, and on my way, I called Connie and told her to set up a prisoner telephone account for Sasha. I didn't tell Sasha I'd be the one funding the account because it set a bad precedent, and it could hurt my reputation.

I found Sarah Washington at her desk buried in files. We exchanged pleasantries and caught up a bit. Then I brought up the reason for my visit. Sarah was handling two dozen cases, and Sasha's was naturally at the bottom of the pile. That was good. I was there before Sarah had studied the file and formed an opinion. It was spin time.

Sarah gave the file a quick once-over, and after I made my pitch, she agreed that charging Sasha as a major drug trafficker was a long reach. But she pointed out that even if the charge was dropped down to simple possession, the weight involved made it a first degree charge, which was also a class A-1 felony. She was right; simply reducing the charge to a lower felony wasn't going to do the trick. That's why I needed more than just dropping the major trafficking charge.

I suggested if the charge was dropped down to possession in the 7th degree, it would be a class A misdemeanor, and we could live with that. Sarah laughed and said I was dreaming. But her laugh wasn't one of those "over my dead body" laughs. I've gotten those laughs on more than one occasion, so I know them well. No, Sarah's laugh was more of an "I don't think so" laugh which meant I at least had a chance.

I wasn't going to push the issue until I knew for sure how Sasha was involved. So far, the only evidence the DA had was the drugs found in her apartment. It was circumstantial evidence, but not proof that the drugs were hers, and that she was selling them. If that was the extent of the case, then I might be able to work out an acceptable plea deal. But if there was evidence tying her to Jerome and the drugs, then Sasha was likely going to prison for at least five to seven years.

We were about done when Sarah, who had been continuing to look through her file, asked if there was any chance Sasha could roll on Jerome White. It was an odd question because there was no reason why White's name would be in the file. The only connection was the Harlem housing project. The drugs were seized in the Harlem housing project, and White was the big dealer in the Harlem housing project.

Having worked in the DA's Office, I knew right away what was going on. I used to call it the Moby Dick syndrome. It happens when the DA, acting like Captain Ahab, becomes fixated on some elusive bad guy and focuses everything on his capture and conviction. Jerome White was apparently the new Moby Dick. Why not? The cops spent two years trying to nail his ass and had gotten nowhere.

It would take more than the cops to bring White down. They needed an informer, a top-level informer at that. The slug able to bring him down would earn a big bargaining chip. The ADA who arranged it would do pretty good for his or herself as well, and I wasn't surprised that Sarah was looking to score that prize.

I said there was a chance my client could help, but I needed to talk with her first. I wasn't exactly being honest, but then again neither was Washington. We weren't telling each other outright lies, we were just fishing. That's how the game is played.

When you're dealing with drug cases, you can't rely on anything anyone involved says. Everybody lies. Some tell big lies; some tell little lies; but everyone lies. Why? Because the addicts start it. They lie; that's what addicts do. They use, and they lie. When I was drinking, I lied. I lied even when I didn't have to lie.

In most drug cases, even the cops and the lawyers lie. But I figure you can't blame them for lying. After all, everyone else is lying, so why not them? When the cops do it, I call it counter-lying. Lies told to offset other lies. It's a balancing of the books. When the lawyers lie, it's called lawyering, unless you do it under oath. Then it's called perjury, and you go to jail.

I should be able to cut Sasha a good deal, but if I wanted to get her off entirely, she'd have to give the DA Jerome White. If the cops couldn't nail his ass after two years of trying, it wasn't likely Sasha could bring him down. But it was a possibility, and Tommy Shoo and I had pulled off a couple of miracles together.

Before anything else happened, I needed to talk with Sasha and get her to level with me.

CHAPTER 38

When I got back to the office I was surprised to find the preliminary forensic reports on the brothel shootings on my desk. Under an archaic New York law, the District Attorney isn't required to inform a defendant of the evidence against him or her until the eve of trial. It supposedly protects witnesses from potential intimidation and harm, but that's bullshit. It just makes the defense attorney's job more difficult.

Delivering the forensic reports early was another indication the DA's Office wasn't happy prosecuting the case against Richie. The case had trouble written on it from the start. It began when McNulty demanded an ADA come to the scene to take his statement. Then McNulty ignored the standard protocols in a cop shooting incident, and without consulting anyone from the DA's Office, he arrested Richie. He had totally circumvented the District Attorney and taken the case out of the DA's control. Now the District Attorney was striking back. It was all petty, but it had a purpose. It sent a message to the NYPD and McNulty that the District Attorney was back in charge.

Whatever the reason, I was happy to have the reports and anything else the DA was willing to give us. But in the end, none of it mattered. The case was going forward and handing us a small favor here or there to piss off the NYPD wasn't going to change the outcome.

I quickly scanned the reports looking for highlights and maybe a surprise here or there. But I didn't see anything I didn't already know or hadn't expected. Of course, I still had to read the reports carefully, but I wasn't expecting anything to change.

I started with the ballistics report. The two slugs recovered from the body of the still unidentified Chinese man had been fired from McNulty's Glock 19-millimeter pistol. The two slugs embedded in Richie's bulletproof vest were too mangled to be identified, but each weighed in as a .38 caliber slug. A third .38 caliber slug was removed from the wall and was believed to be the slug that passed through Richie's leg. That slug had definitely been fired from the S&W revolver found next to the body of dead Chinese man. Finally, the three slugs removed from Kim Lee's body had been fired from Richie's Glock 19 pistol.

The fact the bullets that killed Kim Lee came from Richie's gun didn't prove Richie was the one who shot her. Of course, that argument wouldn't fly if the jury believed McNulty's eyewitness testimony. That was why I needed another eyewitness, or I had to discredit McNulty. Now with Li Chin having become a dead-end, I was left with discrediting McNulty.

The next forensic report I read was the fingerprint report. I didn't expect the report to contain any good news, but I was hoping there was something in it I could at least work with. There wasn't much.

The report was fairly cut and dry. Fingerprints lifted from Richie's Glock 19 were Richie's and McNulty's. No surprise there, right? But it wasn't all bad news. There were no identifiable prints on the trigger, just on the butt of the gun. There was nothing in the report which conclusively proved Richie had fired the weapon, but on the other hand, there was nothing to suggest anyone else had. Again, it all came down to McNulty's testimony.

The fingerprints lifted from the .38 S&W matched those of the deceased Chinese man. But as with the Glock there were no identifiable prints on the trigger, and there was some smearing of the palm prints on the butt.

The report didn't offer any explanation for why the palm prints were smeared or why there were no identifiable prints on the triggers of either weapon. It could be important, although I suspected if I tried raising the point, the DA would claim the smearing was the result of careless handling of the gun by the forensic team while collecting the evidence at the scene.

Marty Bowman had wisely included dozens of crime scene photographs, knowing if he didn't provide enough photographs of the scene I was likely to ask the court for permission to visit the premises with my own investigator.

DAs hate when a defense attorney and his investigator go snooping around a crime scene. They worry the attorney will find something the forensic team missed and the whole case will blow up. In my experience that only happens in movies and television shows. Still, it was obvious Marty Bowman had done his best to keep me from seeking a crime scene visit, and he had done a good job. With all the photographs he provided I'd be hard pressed to show the special circumstances needed to justify a visit to the brothel.

I really would have liked to have gone to the place, if for no other reason than to be able to say I had been in a brothel. Ever since I heard The Animals' hit song, *House of the Rising Sun,* I've been curious about brothels. I was only a kid when the song came out, but even as a kid I knew what it was about. My buddies and I actually vowed that someday we'd go to a cathouse. I never made it to one, and Gracie would definitely kill me if I went to one now, so I guess I'll just have to scratch it off my bucket list.

I was reviewing the forensic team's photographs when Tommy arrived and tossed the photographs of Friday night's meeting between McNulty and Yeoung on my desk.

His people had done a great job. Both men were clearly pictured. I was enjoying the pictures when Tommy pulled a disk from his pocket and said if I liked the photos I'd love the video.

He was right. As good as the photographs were, the video was better. It started with McNulty entering the restaurant, and Yeoung greeting him and shaking his hand. Then the camera followed the two men walking across the dining room and entering the restaurant's office. As they walked, they had their heads close together conversing. Clearly, they weren't strangers.

When McNulty testified at Richie's trial, you could bet he'd never admit knowing Sam Yeoung. And since he wouldn't know the photographs and video existed, he'd have no reason not to lie. Not that you'd expect someone like McNulty to tell the truth. I mean, he was a corrupt cop, a murderer, and a thief, so what are the odds he's going care about committing perjury?

Once he denied knowing Yeoung, I'd press him on the point, and I'd keep pressing him until he lost his cool or the judge stopped me. Then I'd pull out the photographs and after that, the video. It would be a critical point in the trial. If I was going to convince the jury that McNulty was lying about what happened the night of the raid, and that he was the murderer, that's where it was going to start.

But simply showing McNulty to be a liar wouldn't prove he was a murderer or, for that matter, even a corrupt cop. There are a lot of explanations why an NYPD Deputy Chief Inspector was meeting privately with a notorious Tong member. I was offering the jury a reason, but until I could prove that reason it was just speculation.

Richie's trial was starting in less than three weeks, and all I had for a defense were bits and pieces and not much tying them together. To put it together, I needed to answer two questions: what was in the safe, and why hadn't McNulty given Yeoung more advanced notice of the raid?

No matter how many times I asked myself those questions, I came up with the same answers. I couldn't be sure what had been in the safe, but I knew it had to be valuable. Why hadn't McNulty warned Yeoung of the raid earlier? McNulty wanted whatever was in the safe for himself, and that was the only way he could steal it. That much made sense. It was when I got to the next step that I had a problem.

By all accounts, on the night of the raid, McNulty was in the best position to steal whatever was in the safe. In fact, he was probably the only one in that position and Yeoung had to know that. Yeoung was no fool, so he had to suspect McNulty stole whatever it was that had been in the safe. But, looking at the video taken at the Golden Palace during the Friday night meeting, there didn't appear to be any tension between the two men. Why?

I had to believe McNulty laid the blame on someone else, and Yeoung bought his story. But who did McNulty blame? It would have to be someone who knew what was in the safe, and that would mean it was someone on the inside. But it would also have to be someone now beyond Yeoung's control. Someone like Li Chin, or one of the other girls rounded up by ICE and now being deported.

It was like being on a merry go round. I was covering a lot of distance, but I kept coming back to the same place over and over.

CHAPTER 39

You build a defense in a criminal case by linking together a bunch of facts. The tighter you can link them together the better the defense. In Richie's case I had a bunch of facts; that wasn't the problem. The problem was I didn't have the evidence to link them together. I had a theory, but that and an unshakeable belief that Richie hadn't killed Kim Lee, was all I had.

The theory was simple. The way I figured it, McNulty brought the .38 caliber gun with him the night of the raid. He intended to be the first one to reach the second-floor office. Once there, he'd force Kim Lee to open the safe. If she hadn't already done so, then he'd kill her using his Glock. He'd drop the .38 caliber next to her body to justify his killing her. But things didn't go as planned when Richie made it upstairs to the second floor before he did.

Richie had gotten to the stairs under the cover fire provided by O'Brien. Then McNulty followed while O'Brien continued to provide cover fire. With both Richie and McNulty gone, there was no one left to provide cover fire for O'Brien to reach the staircase until reinforcements arrived. McNulty knew he'd be alone in the office with Richie and Kim Lee for at least five to ten minutes.

When McNulty reached the office, he saw the open safe and realized he couldn't kill Kim Lee with Richie there. So, he did the only thing he could do. He shot Richie with the .38, and he took Richie's Glock and killed Kim Lee. He probably intended to claim Kim Lee had shot Richie, and Richie had returned fire killing her.

But then McNulty had a couple of problems. Richie was wearing his vest so he wasn't dead, and the facts didn't match up. If Kim Lee shot Richie with the .38, how was it that he was shot in the back? Had he entered the office backward, or had he turned his back to her once he was in the room?

That's when McNulty got a big break. The Chinese guy arrived unexpectedly before McNulty had a chance to retrieve whatever had been in the safe. McNulty shot him, then he probably put the .38 in the Chinese guy's hand to get his fingerprints on the weapon before he left it next to the body.

For McNulty, having a dead suspect to blame for Richie's shooting was unexpected good luck. But setting up the suspect delayed McNulty getting to Kim Lee. That explained why he was still kneeling over Kim Lee's body when Jimmy arrived on the scene and why he didn't have a chance to put Richie's gun in his pocket.

It was speculation on my part and without an eyewitness, I wouldn't be able to prove much of it. Li Chin had been my only hope, and once she turned out to be a dead-end, my options narrowed considerably. You might say they were narrowed to one option, "the other dude did it" defense. All I had to do was prove McNulty was a corrupt cop, and he had shot Kim Lee in order to steal the item from the safe.

Proving McNulty was a corrupt cop wasn't a problem. I had the evidence to do that. Proving the rest of the story would be a problem, but fortunately I didn't have to prove it. I just needed to convince the jury it was a reasonable possibility. Doing that would be a lot simpler if McNulty wasn't the only eyewitness.

The truth be told, I would have loved having an eyewitness of my own, but I didn't. The next best thing would be no eyewitnesses at all. Since McNulty was the only eyewitness, if the jury didn't believe his testimony and disregarded it, there would be no credible eyewitness testimony in the record, and we'd all be in the same boat.

I haven't forgotten about the forensic evidence, but as I said before, it only proves the bullets that killed Kim Lee came from Richie's gun. It doesn't prove he pulled the trigger. It was only McNulty's testimony that put the gun in

Richie's hand. With no eyewitnesses, a jury normally believes the story that makes the most sense to them. In such a situation, the burden of proof works entirely in our favor

Marty Bowman had to convince all twelve jurors that Richie had killed Kim Lee, and he had to convince them beyond a reasonable doubt. I didn't have to convince anyone of anything beyond a reasonable doubt. I simply had to convince the jury there was a reasonable possibility that McNulty had killed Kim Lee. I'd need evidence to support the claim, but if I could convince the jury, it would create sufficient doubt in the jurors' minds to result in an acquittal.

The first step was to make sure the jury wouldn't believe McNulty's testimony. That meant I had to dirty him up and do it so well that even his mother wouldn't believe anything he said. The material Tommy and Linda had come up with so far was great, but I wanted more. I wanted enough evidence to put McNulty behind bars.

Convincing the jury that McNulty was a dirty cop would be easier than getting them to believe he was a murderer. For that I had to show he had opportunity, and more importantly, a motive. It was the motive part that was giving me trouble. I had a motive in mind, McNulty wanted whatever was in the safe. The problem was I didn't know what McNulty had stolen.

The crime scene photographs established that the safe was open at the time of the murder. I was counting on Jimmy O'Brien's testimony to bolster the photographs and verify that McNulty had taken something from the safe. It was a bit of a stretch from what Jimmy had told me, but it made sense, and I figured I could sell it. It wouldn't hurt that by the time Jimmy testified, I should have blown McNulty's credibility out of the water.

I had to convince the jury McNulty double-crossed Yeoung and killed two people in the process to steal something, but I didn't know what it was he stole. Again, I was back to the same question, what was in the safe?

Back in my dark days, when things got to this point I'd get drunk. Now I don't drink so there's nothing left for me to do but bang my head against the wall. Either way I'm going to end up with a headache, but now I don't have to wonder if I had done something that might get me arrested, disbarred, or banned from another bar.

CHAPTER 40

The next morning, I had a call from Detective Chen. A few days earlier he had dropped off a file on Sam Yeoung and the Hip Sing Tong. He said at the time it was all he had. Frankly, it wasn't much, so I assumed Chen had decided not to get too involved. I couldn't blame him for that. That's why I was surprised when he said he had some new information I might find interesting.

Chen and his squad had arrested a Hip Sing Tong member named Joey Peng on a murder charge. It was an open-and-shut case, so Peng was looking at spending the rest of his life in prison. During the initial interrogation,

Peng claimed he was on the outs with Sam Yeoung and asked about cutting a deal. He had information about Yeoung and the Tong he was willing to trade for a shorter sentence and witness protection. A deal was struck, and during the debriefing Peng had revealed some information about the brothel operation.

I was getting excited, but then Chen explained it had nothing to with the raid. But it did involve police protection and visits to the brothel by high placed politicians. There was more, but Chen didn't want to talk over the phone, and knowing I had a connection with old man Shoo, he suggested we meet at Shoo's Restaurant. It was close to lunchtime, and I figured that played into Chen's thinking. I said I'd make the arrangements, and we'd have lunch there in half an hour.

After calling the restaurant, I called Tommy and Abe. I explained what was happening and asked them to meet me at the office in two hours. If I picked up any useful information at the meeting with Chen, I wanted to get on it right away.

When I got to the restaurant, old man Shoo came out of the kitchen to greet me. He was always happy to see me, and the feeling was mutual. He didn't speak much English, and I spoke no Chinese, but somehow we always managed to communicate. He had a knack for communicating using the least possible number of words. What little English he knew didn't include adjectives, adverbs or articles, making his sentences much more economical.

"Hello, come," he said, smiling and pulling me by the arm into the private room he had set up for my meeting with

Chen. He pulled me to a table set for two and said, "Sit." Then he smiled and said, "Friend come, I bring. Okay? Bring food, you eat, good. Okay?" I smiled, nodded and said "Okay." Shoo just smiled, bowed his head, and left.

If I'm not mistaken, that made a total of twelve words exchanged, only one from me, yet there was a lot of information passed on. And a lot of warmth.

The waiter had just poured a cup of tea when Detective Chen arrived. We exchanged pleasantries, then got down to business. Until recently, Joey Peng had been the number four guy in Sam Yeoung's crew. That was until he knocked up Yeoung's daughter.

The daughter was twenty-four years old, so it wasn't as bad as it sounded, but for Yeoung it was still a matter of honor. Yeoung wasn't about to kill Peng over the incident, but the indiscretion had cost Peng his status in the crew. Between being reduced to a nobody in the crew and facing a long prison sentence, there was nothing left for Peng on the streets of Chinatown. He wanted out, and that was why he had cut a deal.

Peng had overseen security at the brothel but wasn't on duty the night of the raid, so he didn't know what happened that night. Shortly after the night of the raid is when Yeoung found out Peng had impregnated his daughter and banished Peng to the streets.

I was beginning to wonder why Chen was telling me all of this since nothing he had told me up to that point helped Richie's case. Chen must have realized I was losing patience because he said Peng did say some things I would find interesting.

Chen had shown Peng pictures of McNulty and asked him if he had ever seen McNulty at the brothel. Peng said he had seen him there on only a couple of occasions, but he had seen him with Yeoung at the Golden Palace many times. According to Peng, Yeoung and McNulty were close, and he knew they did a lot of business together. When McNulty wasn't around, Yeoung would brag how he owned the cop. He said he paid the guy a lot of money, but he got good protection.

I asked if Peng said anything about the office safe. He had but it didn't help. According to Peng, the safe in the office belonged to Kim Lee, and he had no idea what she kept in it. He did know it wasn't the brothel's books and records because they were kept in the safe at the Golden Palace restaurant. At the end of each night's business, Peng took the receipts and the records, and delivered them to the Golden Palace.

What Peng had said about Yeoung and McNulty being friends and doing business might be helpful. I could call Peng as a witness and have him tell his story to the jury. That would go a long way toward establishing McNulty as a dirty cop. But relying on someone like Peng to testify honestly is always risky, and juries tend to discount their testimony. Still, it was a potential area to explore.

Of course, there was also the risk that Peng wouldn't be alive and available to testify. Much of that depended on how soon Yeoung found out Peng had rolled on him and how quickly Peng was put in witness protection.

I asked Chen if McNulty knew Peng had been turned. If McNulty knew about Peng's deal, I was sure Yeoung knew. Chen smiled and said not yet. He knew McNulty was dirty and after the disastrous raid on the brothel, he figured McNulty would do anything to protect himself and Yeoung. He didn't want McNulty to know about the Peng situation, but at the same time he was in no position to take on McNulty head-to-head.

Not sure what to do, Chen had initially kept everything in house at the 5th Precinct while he sorted things out. Then when Peng started talking about Yeoung's drug smuggling operation, another of Yeoung's numerous illegal activities, Chen came up with a brilliant idea. Instead of charging Peng with the murder and having the DA's Office write up the case, Chen called a friend at the FBI and offered him Peng. The FBI jumped at the opportunity to close down the drug smuggling ring it been investigating for years, but hadn't been able to take down. Peng was no longer in NYPD custody; he was in Federal custody being charged with conspiracy to engage in drug smuggling.

Chen and his buddy at the FBI wrote up their reports so it looked like Peng's arrest had been a joint operation to explain why the Feds had Peng. The deal with the Feds had just taken place that morning, and Chen wasn't sure when McNulty would find out about it, but he assumed it would be soon. When he did there'd be blowback, but unless McNulty had pull all the way up the chain of command, there wasn't anything he could about it. There wasn't much he could do to Chen. I was glad to hear that. I liked Chen; he was a good a cop, and he was doing the right thing.

I appreciated Chen sharing the information with me even if I couldn't use it. It was just good to know there were honest cops who were willing to stick their necks out for a fellow cop. I was sure Richie would be happy to hear he had Chen's support.

CHAPTER 41

Tommy and Abe were waiting for me when I returned from my meeting with Chen. I told them about Peng and his connection to Yeoung, and we discussed how we might use the information.

Abe agreed that calling Peng as a witness was risky. If he testified honestly, his testimony would definitely hurt McNulty and the DA's case. But it was doubtful he'd agree to testify since there was nothing in it for him. I could subpoena him and force him to testify, but I'd have no way to keep him honest.

When he testified for the Feds, he had to tell the truth, or he'd lose his deal. But that condition only applied in cases where the Feds called him as a witness. It wouldn't apply if I called him as a witness in Richie's case. Once I put him on the witness stand, I had no way to keep him honest. He could lie his head off, and there would be nothing I could do about it. And worse, if he lied, he could sink our case.

Abe and I argued the point back and forth for about an hour, each of us taking turns as the devil's advocate. But we kept coming to the same conclusion. Putting Peng on the witness stand was just too risky.

I was frustrated. It seemed every lead we found that could tie McNulty to Yeoung turned into a dead-end. First Li Chin, now Joey Peng. I was about to end our little meeting when Abe came up with an idea.

Even if we couldn't use Peng as a witness, we might be able to use the threat of his testifying to our advantage. If McNulty learned Peng was going to testify for the defense, he'd have to be worried. Peng claimed he never worked directly with McNulty, but McNulty had to know who Peng was and where he ranked in the Tong. That alone should set off alarm bells in McNulty's head when he heard Peng was going to be a witness for the defense. One thing McNulty would certainly want to know was how much Peng knew about him and the operation. Where would McNulty go to find that out? To the only source possible, Yeoung.

That could mean another meeting between the two men and another opportunity to photograph and videotape them together. McNulty might be able to explain away one meeting with Yeoung, but he'd have a lot more difficulty explaining away two meetings.

You've got to love the way Abe thinks. The plan wasn't much, but we didn't have a lot going for us, so every little bit helped. I was excited about the plan until it dawned on me I might be breaking my word to Detective Chen. Chen had gone to a lot of trouble to keep Peng's arrest under wraps, and he had done me a favor telling me about it. Now here I was about to let the cat out of the bag.

When I mentioned my concern, Abe laughed. He said I was overthinking the situation. In the first place we weren't saying Peng was under arrest, or that he had turned on Yeoung. I said that may have been true, but the implication was there. It was a tip-off to Yeoung that Peng was up to no good. Abe laughed again and said I was naive to think Yeoung didn't know by now that Peng was up to something.

Tong members don't just disappear the way Peng had. They don't take long unannounced vacations. If a high-ranking member of a Tong goes missing, he's either dead or up to something that could make him dead. Tommy nodded in agreement. Yeoung might not know exactly what Peng was up to, but he had to know it wasn't good.

Put that way, I had to agree. Besides, Chen wanted to keep everything quiet because he was concerned about Peng's safety, but Peng was now well protected in federal custody. At least as well protected as you can be when the Tong is out to get you.

Having been convinced that I wouldn't be double-crossing Detective Chen, I agreed to the plan. But I wasn't sure how we'd get word to McNulty that we'd be calling Peng as a witness. The smart play with a witness like Peng is to keep his identity under wraps until the last possible minute and then take the DA by surprise. Putting his name on the list early would be suspicious and might signal a ploy of some kind.

Abe assured me it wouldn't be a problem; he had a plan. Abe suspected someone in the District Attorney's Office has been tipping off McNulty as to what we were doing. I had to agree. Abe planned on using the leak to send McNulty word that Peng was going to testify at Richie's trial. Once the information was out, we'd just sit and wait. Abe wouldn't say how he was going to put the information out there; he simply smiled and said to leave it to him.

Tommy was still monitoring McNulty's cell phone, so he would know if and when McNulty talked with Yeoung. The surveillance on McNulty was part-time, but once Abe dropped the information about Peng, we'd up it to 24/7. We couldn't take a chance on missing a meeting between him and Yeoung.

In the meantime, I asked Tommy to check with his sources to find out if Yeoung had put out a contract on Peng's life. If he had, it would confirm he knew Peng was working against him.

With a plan now in place, we were done with Peng, and Abe left to go do his thing. I needed to talk with Tommy about Sasha's case so he stayed on.

Tommy was splitting his time between Richie's case and Sasha's case, but so far he had nothing new to report about Jerome White. He was working a street contact in

Harlem, and he was sure he'd have something to report in a couple of days.

CHAPTER 42

Later that day as I thought more about the Peng situation, I realized it could be helpful in more ways than one. If Abe's plan worked, we would get additional photographs of McNulty and Yeoung meeting together. That was good. But beyond that, there was a chance we could learn if McNulty was working alone, or if there was a conspiracy in the NYPD that went up the chain of command. I admit, it was a small chance, and maybe my reasoning was more wishful thinking than it was logic, but it was a chance.

Detective Chen had been careful to keep the Peng information within his own chain of command and out of

McNulty's reach, so there was no legitimate way McNulty could know Peng had been arrested or what he had said during his interrogation. The only way he could know any of that was if there was a widespread conspiracy within the department.

If McNulty called Yeoung when he heard Peng was going to testify, he was probably in the dark about Peng's arrest. But if he didn't call Yeoung, it meant he already knew about Peng's arrest, and if he knew that much, it was safe to assume he also knew what Peng had to say.

As I said, this wasn't a foolproof test, and maybe it was just wishful thinking on my part. But knowing if there was a conspiracy, and if so, how deep it ran was important. Eventually I had to decide whether to contact the Internal Affairs Bureau and knowing if anyone in IAB might be working with McNulty would affect that decision.

I had enough evidence to paint McNulty as a corrupt cop without help from IAB. My only concern was the jury questioning how McNulty was getting away with all this. It was a fair question and one I couldn't really answer. On the other hand, if IAB got involved and at least had an investigation into McNulty's conduct underway, the question would never come up.

I had to decide soon whether to approach IAB or not. Figuring the Peng situation would play out quickly, it was time to act. I had already reached out to Jimmy O'Brien, now I called Richie and asked him for the name of someone in IAB he trusted. It wasn't any easy conversation, and I hadn't expected it to be. No rank and file cop likes or trusts IAB which they call the rat squad. It's a universal thing, so I wasn't surprised when Richie said, "nobody on the rat squad can be trusted." But I was surprised when he said under no circumstances did he want me talking to IAB.

Richie was making my job a lot harder than it had to be, and it was hard enough to begin with. He knew damn well we were behind the eight ball, but he didn't seem to care. I didn't know if he had just given up, or he was readying himself for the worst. It didn't matter; I had run out of patience.

Richie was acting like an asshole and making it impossible for me do my job. Knowing him as well as I did, I had no trouble telling him off, and I knew exactly where to start. I said he might not care what happened to him, but he had damn well better care what happened to Laura and his daughters. He was being an asshole and a jerk and needed to get his act together before he destroyed his family.

I finished saying my piece and was prepared for Richie to curse me out or hang up on me, but he did neither. He said nothing for a long while, and then he asked what I needed him to do.

I explained, once we claimed McNulty was on the take, IAB would have to get involved because it was department policy. But it was better for us if they got involved now and that was why I wanted the name of someone he trusted. That's when he gave me the name of Joe Hadden.

Hadden was a sergeant in the IAB Command Center on Hudson Street. Richie and Hadden had been cadets together at the Police Academy, and for a short time, served together as patrolmen. They weren't as close as they used to be, but they still kept in touch. Richie hadn't seen or spoken to Hadden in a while, but he believed Hadden could be trusted.

That was all I needed, but I wanted to keep Richie talking because I was starting to worry about his state of mind. He was his usual pain in the ass self, but I was beginning to sense something dark was slipping into his thinking. It wasn't anything in particular I could put my finger on, but it was something subtle I might not have noticed if I hadn't known the man for all those years. Maybe having gone through very dark modes myself when I drank alcoholically made me more sensitive to the situation, but whatever it was, I was worried. I hoped to give Richie a little therapy, but he wanted no part of it and ended the conversation.

After our conversation ended, I started to wonder if my own experiences were causing me to overanalyze Richie's state of mind. But my concerns would soon be justified.

CHAPTER 43

It wasn't more than an hour after I spoke with Richie when Laura called. She claimed to have a question about the bail bond, but I knew right away she had something else on her mind.

After I answered her question about the bond, Laura broke down and said she was worried about Richie. He wasn't handling things well.

Richie had been suspended from the job which was standard operating procedure in these situations. It really didn't mean anything, but knowing Richie as I do, I was sure he hadn't taken it well. I expected him to have been upset by the suspension, but things were worse than I imagined. A lot worse.

Frankly, what Laura told me had me worried. Richie was sitting around the house all day obsessing over his case. That may have been understandable, but his behavior wasn't. He was short-tempered and argumentative, and Laura was frightened because he had never behaved that way.

In all the years I had known Richie, I never once heard him raise his voice to Laura or his daughters. On the job he was as tough as they come, but at home he was a pussycat.

Laura said things had gotten so bad she had been afraid to call me from home and was making the call from a friend's house. She was frightened and didn't know what to do. That made two of us.

I wanted desperately to help Laura, but there wasn't much I could say. I knew what Richie was going through, and I knew he was thinking that he was going to jail. The way things looked he was right about that. But I couldn't tell that to Laura. It was bad enough having his spirits in the tank; I didn't need hers down there with his.

I needed to say something, so I said it was common for defendants to get anxious, and for that anxiety to manifest itself at times in hostile ways. I had read that somewhere, and I thought it sounded good in the situation. I left out the part about Richie's anxiety probably being due to him knowing he was going to prison.

That seemed to make Laura feel a little better. I knew from AA that when someone's going through a crisis, they feel a little better knowing their situation isn't unique. If I could convince Laura that Richie's behavior wasn't uncommon in these circumstances, it would give her hope.

We chatted until I felt Laura was feeling better and had things under control. Then I offered to talk to Richie about his behavior, but she said it was probably better if I didn't, at least not yet. Having just spoken to him, I agreed. But I let Laura know if things didn't improve soon, I'd have no choice but to talk to him.

I didn't think Richie would ever do anything to hurt Laura, but I've know people to snap under less pressure. I was concerned, but not worried enough to make an issue of it. I'd simply keep on top of it, and if I thought it necessary, I'd step in and talk to Richie.

That night during dinner at Pino's, I told Gracie about my conversation with Richie and Laura and my concerns about their mental states. Gracie thought I might be too emotionally invested in the case and putting too much pressure on myself. She said I needed to step back a bit before I lost my objectivity.

I suspect there's a fine line between being totally committed to a client's case and being so emotionally invested in the case that you lose your objectivity. But as I explained to Gracie, I hadn't lost my objectivity. I knew exactly the odds we were facing. It was Richie who wasn't being objective when he refused to consider a plea deal. By doing that, he put me in the position where I had no option but to try the case, no matter what. It was Richie's loss of objectivity, not mine, that brought us to that point.

Gracie admitted that was true, but said it didn't matter how we got to where we were. No matter whose fault it was, or how it happened, I was getting too emotionally involved for my own good. Gracie was worried if I lost the case, I'd question my decisions and blame myself.

She might have been right. The thing with representing someone you know is innocent is you feel you must win. Sometimes that makes you think of a plea deal as a loss. But in circumstances like those in Richie's case, a plea deal is the best way to go.

When I have serious doubts about winning a case, I advise a client to take a plea deal, so the client does less time in prison than if convicted. I consider that a win. What I consider a loss is going to trial and having the client convicted and sentenced to the maximum. If that happened to Richie, I could blame it on his refusal to consider a plea deal, but I knew I wouldn't. Gracie was right; I'd blame myself.

Representing guilty people is so much easier. When you represent someone who's guilty, a plea deal is the only rational option. If a guilty client is dumb enough to refuse a plea deal, that's his problem, not mine. My job is making sure the client gets the best deal possible. It's not a difficult job, and it doesn't require much soul searching.

In my career as a criminal defense lawyer, I've only had four truly innocent clients, and that includes Richie. So far things turned out okay for all of them. One was convicted, but the conviction was overturned on appeal.

That's how I know what it feels like to lose. Even after the conviction was vacated, I still wondered what I could have done differently at trial.

The more I thought about what Gracie said, the more I knew she was right. If Richie was convicted, I'd have a hard time getting over the loss. It wouldn't matter that I had done everything humanly possible to win. Nothing would cushion the blow of losing Richie's case.

CHAPTER 44

Richie's case was now in pretty much of a holding pattern. Until McNulty contacted Yeoung or until I contacted IAB, there wasn't much else for me to do. That was good because I needed the time to concentrate on Sasha's case. It had been a couple of days since her arraignment, and Tommy had called to bring me up to date on the results of his investigation.

He had been working almost full-time on Sasha's case the last couple of days and had developed a pretty good dossier on Jerome White and his drug operation. He also developed a working plan to take him down, and he wanted to meet so we could talk about it.

Without even knowing the details of the plan, I knew it wasn't going to be easy, and it was definitely going to be dangerous. Of course, Tommy would never let on how dangerous any operation would be; that was just the way he was. But I didn't need him or anyone else to tell me that skulking around a bunch of drug dealing gangbangers was dangerous. Deadly dangerous.

I still wasn't sure how Sasha fit into all of this and until I did, I didn't want Tommy getting too deeply involved. Unlikely as it seemed, it was still possible that Sasha was working with White and if she was, there was no way I'd approve of Tommy going into the projects to take him down. So I told Tommy to put everything on hold until I got back to him.

Tommy doesn't always listen when I tell him to put on the brakes. Most times he doesn't stop; he just slows down, so I wasn't surprised when he started arguing with me. The only way I was able to get him to agree not to do anything was by promising I'd see Sasha that morning and meet with him that afternoon. With that, Tommy reluctantly agreed and promised not to do anything more until we met.

Being pressed for time, I had no choice but to take a taxicab to Rikers Island. God, I hate taxicabs.

You would not believe what that ride to Rikers Island was like that day. I'll spare you the details and simply say I tried to jump out of the taxicab when Abdul was forced to slow down in order to avoid ramming into the rear of a city bus. Had Abdul not swerved violently to the left, throwing me back into the center of the taxicab, I swear, I would have leapt out into moving traffic.

Abdul Singh and his taxicab now hold top position on my list of banned taxicabs and drivers. Not only does Abdul top the list, his name is underlined three times and has four asterisks next to it.

I now have this reoccurring nightmare in which Abdul is driving me through the gates of hell, which happen to be closed and strangely resemble the back of a city bus.

But I'm rambling again. The point is that I made it to Rikers Island to see Sasha. It was Sasha's first time in jail, and I was worried she might not be handling it well. I've found people react differently to being jailed. Some simply withdraw into themselves, while others lash out in an attempt to assert control. In my experience the ones that withdraw usually do better, and I hoped Sasha was one of them.

When they brought Sasha into the conference room, she looked okay. She didn't have that wild-eyed look I'd seen so often on clients jailed for the first time. I was glad she was calm and apparently rational because we were about to have a very frank discussion, and I needed her focused.

I told Sasha about my meeting with Sarah Washington and how I was working on a deal to have her released without a jail sentence. That brought a smile to her face. But the smile disappeared when I told her the deal wasn't going happen if she wasn't honest with me and so far, I didn't think she was telling me the truth. I didn't say anything more; I just waited for Sasha's reaction. After a few seconds, she dropped her head and said simply, "Okay, I'll tell you the truth."

Jerome was Jamil's brother, and he had used their apartment as a stash house back when she was living with Jamil, just as she had told me. What she hadn't told me the first time around was when she moved into her current apartment with Kayla, Jerome had approached her about using the apartment as a stash house. She had refused.

A few weeks after that conversation, Sasha began suspecting someone was using her apartment when she was at work and Kayla was in day care. Things were out of place; there was the smell of tobacco; and the toilet seat was left up. The last thing being a sure sign someone had been there.

It didn't take Sasha long to figure out it was Jerome and his gangbangers using the apartment as a stash house. She confronted Jerome and threatened to go to the police, and that's when he threatened to kill her and Kayla if she did. She knew he meant it, so she didn't go to the police. That was it. But I knew it wasn't.

As I said before, I don't trust anything anyone in a drug case says. I could tell from Sasha's body language that she hadn't told me everything. She wasn't looking me in the eye, and she was fidgeting with a tissue in her hand.

I said nothing. I just sat looking at her. Occasionally she'd look up at me, but she wouldn't say anything. I suspected she wanted to tell me the rest, but she was embarrassed. I just waited.

Early in my career in the DA's Office, I learned a few things about interrogating witnesses. When you face a reluctant witness who is obviously nervous, as was Sasha, you don't press for answers. You just sit patiently and say nothing. The silence makes most people uncomfortable, and they'll start to talk just to fill the void.

Eventually Sasha started talking, and she told me the rest of the story. Realizing that Jerome was going to use the apartment anyway, she worked a deal with Jerome to get paid. For the last six months, Jerome had been paying her $500 a week to use the apartment. Now that was it, the whole story. Maybe, maybe not, but it was enough, at least for now.

The situation wasn't great, but neither was it fatal. Accepting the payments tied Sasha to the drug deals, but it was small-time compared to Jerome's part. The payments had been in cash which normally would have been a good thing for us since there would be no proof of payment. But Sasha had put most of the money in a bank account, so there was a financial trail. That didn't necessarily mean the DA would find it, and we were under no obligation to point it out.

The situation wasn't as bad as I thought it might have been, and it wouldn't matter if the DA found out about the "rent." I was confident if I could hand over Jerome to the DA, the DA would overlook the "rent" payments and give Sasha a deal with no prison time. After all, Captain Ahab would have his Moby Dick.

CHAPTER 45

When I got back to the office, by bus and subway I should mention, Connie announced Tommy was waiting for me. Actually, he was sitting at my desk drinking coffee and reading my newspaper. I asked him what he was doing, and he said he was there to report on Jerome White. That was good and well, but what the hell was he doing behind my desk, drinking my coffee and reading my newspaper? Tommy just shrugged off the question and asked if I wanted my chair. I did.

Once we were properly repositioned, with me behind my desk and Tommy on the other side, he began his report.

Jerome White's street name was Stinger; he was twenty-seven years old; and he ran the cocaine business in the project. He had a long juvenile record, but only one arrest as an adult and no convictions. The arrest had been for assault with a deadly weapon and attempted murder, but the case was dismissed when the complaining witness disappeared. Unfortunately, witnesses disappearing or refusing to testify is a common occurrence when gangbangers are involved, and all too often, gangbangers rule the New York City housing projects.

According to Tommy's source, everyone in the Harlem housing project knew Stinger had a short fuse and a vicious temper. He was extremely violent and controlled his crew through fear and intimidation. No one dared cross Stinger. He operated primarily in the housing project, but his drug clientele came from all over the city.

The cops had been trying for two years to take down White's drug operation, but so far, they hadn't made a dent in it. The operation was set up for maximum protection and almost impossible to raid undetected. The drugs were sold in the courtyard of the southeast building, easily accessible from both 155th Street and the Avenue. But White had lookouts posted on the roofs and at the entrances into the project, so there was no way to enter the courtyard without being seen. Even when the cops got in quickly and knew the location of the stash house, as they had during the recent raid, they weren't likely to catch anyone and certainly not Jerome White.

The cops were able to find and raid the stash house this last time only because somebody had tipped them off.

That didn't happen often because snitches didn't have long lives in the projects. They used to say, "Snitches get stitches," but now they just disappear.

Word was, the recent raid had been set up by a local street dealer who went by the name, Snorty. Snorty gave the cops the location of Jerome's stash house in exchange for a pass on a buy and bust arrest for selling marijuana. What seemed like a good deal at the time turned out to be not so good a deal in the end. Jerome quickly and easily found out who had ratted out his stash house and put out a contract on Snorty. No one had seen Snorty in a couple of days, and Jerome was smiling. End of story, or I should say, end of Snorty.

When Tommy was done, I told him what I had learned from Sasha, and the only way I could work out a generous plea deal was to bring down White. Sasha didn't have enough information to bring him down, and I didn't see any other way of doing it. Tommy said that Sasha might not have enough to offer, but he had his own plan.

Since the raid on Sasha's apartment, Stinger had opened a new stash house in the same section of the housing project, and it was business as usual. But Stinger was still upset. He was out nearly $100,000, and Tommy figured he was looking to make it up. Tommy's plan was to offer him the opportunity to make some quick big money as a wholesaler and that way set him up for a big bust.

I had to admit it would do the trick, but I didn't like the idea because I thought it was too dangerous for Tommy. Tommy laughed at my concern and said I was being ridiculous. That's what I usually hear from Gracie when she doesn't like one of my ideas.

Tommy argued it was the only way to keep Sasha from going to prison. I had to agree, but I was still worried, and I wasn't being ridiculous. The plan involved Tommy getting deeply involved with gangbanging drug dealers. Not to mention the fact that he didn't exactly fit in with the crowd and could hardly expect to mingle without being noticed. Tommy said it was better that way. His plan was to act as a Chinatown drug dealer looking for a new supplier. He didn't want to come off as a threat to Jerome, but as a business opportunity. It was a good plan.

However, before Tommy did anything, I wanted to check with Sarah Washington just to make sure we could work out a deal. There was no sense putting Tommy at risk if I couldn't come to terms on a plea deal. That being said, I called Sarah and gave her a rough account of the plan.

Sarah Washington liked the idea of taking down Jerome White and his drug operation, but she wasn't crazy about letting Sasha completely off the hook. Even with the Moby Dick syndrome in play, a complete pass on a drug rap with that much crack cocaine involved was a lot to ask. I think Sarah would have gone along with the deal if I pressed her, but I knew she'd need her boss' approval. Rather than get her boss involved right away I thought it best to wait until we had something more concrete to offer. If you're offering a bird in the hand, you should at least be holding a few feathers.

I wasn't expecting to cut the deal right then. I just wanted some assurance Sarah would take the deal to her boss if Tommy was able to set it up. I would have been happy with that assurance alone, but I saw an opportunity to hedge my bet and took it.

You never want to be in an "all or nothing" position when you negotiate, especially if you're in a weak position like I was. You need a fallback position. In your fallback position, you give a little to make you look reasonable, and you prompt the other side to give a little as well. But you don't necessarily have to give away the prize. The key is keeping what's important in play, and in this case, what was important was keeping Sasha out of prison. With that in mind, I suggested to Sarah that if we delivered Jerome on a major drug trafficking charge, the DA would reduce the charge against Sasha to possession in the seventh degree, a misdemeanor, and no prison time.

Sarah thought reducing the charges was possible, but she didn't think her boss would agree to no prison time. After some skillful negotiating on my part, I got Sarah to agree that a one-year sentence was in order. Then I pushed the envelope and suggested suspending the sentence would be justified. With a suspended sentence, Sasha would be on probation for three years, but she wouldn't go to prison if she stayed out of trouble. Sarah rolled her eyes at my suggestion, but she didn't reject it. As long as the door to a suspended sentence was open, I was happy with a one-year sentence.

Worst case scenario, if the one-year sentence wasn't suspended, Sasha would do her time at Rikers Island and be eligible for parole in nine months. That sentence beat the hell out of twenty-five years in the penitentiary that she was now facing.

I felt confident that I had covered all the bases, and Sasha probably wouldn't go to jail if we nailed Jerome White. Sarah agreed it would be best to have all our ducks in a row before we went to her boss for approval. That didn't worry me because I knew Sarah's boss was likely to follow her recommendations. Now all that remained was for Tommy to go to work, and it wasn't going to be easy work. I still didn't like the idea, but it was the only chance we had of keeping Sasha out of prison.

As soon as I was off the phone with Sarah Washington, Tommy began to explain his plan for taking down Jerome White. The plan involved two stages. In the first stage, Tommy would reach out to Jerome through his street contact. He'd pose as a dealer looking for a new supplier and offer to buy a kilo of cocaine. At a kilo, the buy would be well above normal street volume and should be enough to get Jerome's attention.

When he made the buy, Tommy would suggest a possible buy farther down the road but a much bigger buy. At the second buy, Tommy would be wired, and once the sale was made, the NYPD would make the bust.

It was a plan, and it was simple. But I didn't like it because it was dangerous. Still, I had to admit it was likely to work. Tommy said he'd start putting things together, and he'd get back to me as soon as he could.

That's when Abe arrived with some news.

CHAPTER 46

Abe's friend at ICE had called. Li Chin had been deported, and as we spoke, she was on an Air China flight to Beijing. Our one possible eyewitness was now ten thousand miles away somewhere in the land of a billion people. I knew that was going to happen, and I had already written Li Chin off as a possible witness. But the news still stung a little bit. I guess I had been holding onto some irrational hope that Li Chin would be that mythical surprise witness all trial attorneys dream about. The witness who suddenly shows up in the middle of a trial and turns a losing case into an instant winner. We've all seen it in the movies and on television shows, but trust me, that's the only place it happens.

At least Li Chin was finally history, and I didn't have to agonize over her any longer. I couldn't afford to send Tommy to China, and even if I could, we had no idea where to look for her. Trying to locate someone named Chin in China was like trying to locate someone named Smith in America. It could be done, but it might take years, or even decades. Li Chin was gone, and that was that.

Then as I sat there with Abe, it hit me. Maybe Li Chin could still help us. I had an idea how we could use Li Chin in absentia.

Although I was now convinced Li Chin hadn't witnessed the murder, there was no way for me to be certain. If I couldn't be certain, then neither could McNulty or Yeoung. True, McNulty was in the room, but that didn't mean Li Chin couldn't have witnessed everything without McNulty having seen her. There was the room next to the office where the Chinese security guard had been before bursting onto the scene. Based on Jimmy O'Brien's account of events that night, McNulty wouldn't have had time to search that room, so he couldn't be certain Li Chin hadn't been in there with the security guard.

My plan was to make it appear she had witnessed the murder by floating her name as an eyewitness. We could pass that on the same way we passed on the Joey Peng information. You might be asking yourself how pretending I had an eyewitness who I didn't really have, and who, if I did have, probably wasn't an eye-witness, was going to help

Richie's case. That's a good question, and it deserves a good answer. But I don't have one.

I was doing some more of what I like to call pot stirring but on a higher level.

I figured that suggesting Li Chin was an eyewitness for the defense was big news and would definitely get Marty Bowman's attention. It was important to my plan that I had Bowman's attention and not just McNulty's.

If I were in Bowman's shoes, the first thing I'd do when I heard about a new eyewitness would be to check with McNulty to find out who this Li Chin was, and why she wasn't mentioned in McNulty's statement. That would be fairly standard operating procedure, so I was counting on Bowman doing it.

As long as Bowman asked McNulty about Li Chin being a witness, it didn't matter if she had actually witnessed the murder, or what McNulty knew about it. Either way he'd have to be worried. Worried because he knew she had, or worried because he thought she might have. That would give him at least three things to be worried about, Li Chin, Joey Peng, and us knowing about GM Properties.

Worried people make mistakes, and I intended to keep McNulty plenty worried. If I could get him to make enough mistakes, maybe it would break the case. All right, that wasn't likely to happen, but two things could happen.

One, it was another potential wedge between McNulty and Yeoung. More questions might add urgency for the two to meet. We were still waiting on the Peng thing; maybe throwing Li Chin into the mix would speed things up.

But what I was really hoping was to put the idea in Marty Bowman's mind that McNulty was hiding something. I had the impression Marty didn't like the way McNulty had manipulated the case from the start and that matters had gone downhill from there. McNulty's press interviews had definitely irked Marty who made no effort to hide the fact.

Discontent between the prosecutor and his star witness is not going to produce a smoking gun moment. But it can lead to mistakes that create an opening for the defense. That was basically the best I could hope for. Let's be honest, this idea was simply a scheme you come up with when you've run out of ideas, and you're getting desperate.

Abe said he liked the idea although he may have just been humoring me, but he pointed out it was still too early in the case to file a formal witness list. As for Peng, filing now was likely to arouse suspicion, and that we definitely didn't want to do. But Abe would handle the situation the same way he was handling the Peng matter.

My curiosity got the best of me, and I demanded Abe tell me how he could be sure the information got to the right people. He smiled and said simply, "Tea and a muffin with Mrs. Goldberg."

I should have known better than to question Abe's ideas, but I was hopelessly baffled. I had to ask, what the hell he was talking about? Who is Mrs. Goldberg? He chuckled and said Mrs. Goldberg, who he'd known for years, was his connection to the grapevine at the DA's Office. She worked for a Senior ADA and was a very useful source of information, as well as a conduit for delivering unofficial messages.

That was enough of an explanation for me, but Abe went on and confided that since the passing of his wife, Mrs. Goldberg had become even more helpful. I was getting disturbing pictures in my mind and really wanted to change the subject.

Still, you just have to love Abe. I don't know anyone else who gets away with more stuff than Abe. Legend has it that anytime there was an elderly Jewish widow on a jury, Abe won the case. I don't know if that's true or not, but I tend to believe it is.

Abe reminds me of Max Bialystock, in *The Producers*. I'm talking about the original film released in 1967 with Zero Mostel playing Max and not the musical version released in 2005 with Nathan Lane in the role. Both movies are great, but the original is my favorite. I pick it for movie night at least twice a year.

CHAPTER 47

The next day I decided to walk from Gracie's apartment to my office. It takes about twenty-five minutes, and on a nice day maybe a little longer. I like to walk because it gives me time to think. That morning I was thinking what Gracie had said at Pino's a couple of nights earlier about my being too emotionally involved in Richie's case. At first, I thought she was wrong, but the more I thought about it, the more I began to think she could be right. Maybe my emotions were blinding my own objectivity.

I had to ask myself a simple question. If the client wasn't Richie Simone, would I be doing things differently?

Instead of looking for a possibly non-existent "bulletproof defense," would I be convincing the client to cut a plea deal? One thing was for sure, I wouldn't be putting myself in a hole financing the case. Maybe I wasn't being objective, but that didn't necessarily mean I couldn't be objective.

A good lawyer is able to argue either side of a case. That's a good quality when it comes to representing a client, but not such a good quality when it comes to judging yourself. For years I had been able to convince myself I wasn't a drunk. I'm over that, but I'm still able to convince myself I'm right whenever I argue with Gracie. Since Gracie's also a lawyer, we generally finish with a standoff, or most times, with a plea bargain on my part.

But Gracie was dead right about one thing. If Richie was convicted, I'd blame myself. I'd question everything I had done and everything I didn't do. I'm not sure I could withstand the guilt if that happened, and my fear was that I might just try and drown it.

It may sound funny, but the idea of me getting drunk is a sobering thought. It's the nightmare that occurs occasionally for no apparent reason other than to perhaps remind me of the horrors of being a drunk.

They say that awareness of the problem is half the solution, and I was good with that. I'd just call Doug later and find out what the other half was. With that, I dropped the thought from my head and just enjoyed the walk.

CHAPTER 48

Abe had done his thing with Mrs. Goldberg, and a few days had passed without anything happening. I was beginning to think it had been a waste of time, but then Tommy called and said McNulty had contacted Yeoung, and a meeting was set for that night at the Golden Palace. Tommy had already arranged for his people to be in position to photograph and video the two men, just as they had done the last time the two had met at the Golden Palace.

I figured the meeting was prompted by us floating the idea that Peng and Li Chin were testifying as defense witnesses, and Tommy confirmed my suspicion. He said

McNulty told Yeoung they needed to talk about two individuals, and while he didn't mention their names, we both knew he was referring to Peng and Li Chin. From the way McNulty worded things, Tommy said it was clear McNulty didn't know who they were and was looking to Yeoung for information.

That was good news on two fronts. First, it would get us more pictures of McNulty and Yeoung together. Second, it appeared McNulty hadn't known anything about Peng before we floated his name. If McNulty hadn't learned of Peng's arrest through department channels, it probably meant we weren't facing a widespread departmental conspiracy. The odds were McNulty was acting alone, and that was really good news.

Our plan was working well. The additional photographs and videotape of the two men together would go a long way toward convincing a jury that McNulty was a dirty cop. But showing McNulty to be dirty was the easy part. I still had to convince the jury that there was a reasonable possibility he was the one who killed Kim Lee. I also had to explain how the bullets that killed Kim Lee came from Richie's gun if McNulty was the one who killed her.

Ultimately, it would all come down to credibility and motive. If the jury believed McNulty, Richie was done. But if they didn't believe McNulty, we had a chance. It would come down to convincing the jury McNulty had a good reason to kill Kim Lee. No matter how I twisted it or turned it, it came back to motive and the damn safe. What was in the safe?

I wasn't having any luck finding out what was in the safe, and I didn't have time to spend worrying about it. Not at that moment, anyway. It was first things first, and with the expectation of more photographs of McNulty and Yeoung together, it was time to consider how I would approach IAB.

I had the name Joe Hadden from Richie, but earlier I had asked Jimmy O'Brien for a name and I had yet to hear back so I decided to give him a call. When I had asked Jimmy if he knew somebody at IAB he trusted he first gave me the standard line, *nobody in IAB can be trusted, they're all rats.* But once I explained why I needed a name he had agreed to do some checking.

When I finally got hold of Jimmy, he said the only person he'd consider trusting was Joe Hadden. It wasn't a coincidence that Jimmy mentioned Hadden. Jimmy knew Hadden through Richie. They had met a couple of times after work at a cop bar in SOHO. Jimmy never worked with Hadden, but based on what Richie told him, and from what he could tell by talking with the guy, he thought Hadden was a good cop. That was all I needed, so I thanked Jimmy and asked him to stay in touch.

Now I had a name of someone at IAB I could talk to, and soon I'd have a second set of photographs of McNulty and Yeoung. Add those to the financial spreadsheets laying out McNulty's finances and the GM Properties information, and I had plenty of incriminating information to take to IAB. So, what was I waiting for?

It was simple. I was worried what would happen when I told Richie of my plan. I knew he didn't want me talking to IAB, and I was afraid he'd forbid me from doing so. It could be argued it was his decision to make, but technically it was a strategic issue. While I usually consulted with clients on strategic matters, I was the one who made the final decision.

Involving the IAB wasn't just a strategic move; it was a critical element in the defense. One thing I was sure of, the dirtier I made McNulty, the easier it would be to convince the jury he could have murdered Kim Lee. In other words, if I was light on motive, I had better be heavy on the dirt, and that's where IAB came in. I could make McNulty look really bad, but IAB could blow him right out of the water.

If IAB investigated McNulty, it would absolutely help our claim that McNulty was a dirty cop. If they arrested McNulty, which was a long shot, but a possibility, I thought it could make our case.

Richie's objection to involving IAB was strictly emotional and irrational. With everything we had at stake, I couldn't allow emotion to decide the issue. Still, I hated to go against Richie's wishes.

CHAPTER 49

I was still struggling with the IAB issue when Tommy arrived with the photographs from the McNulty/Yeoung meeting the night before. The pictures were excellent. Both McNulty and Yeoung were clearly visible in all of them, including the one showing them entering the restaurant's office. We now had indisputable evidence of a high-ranking New York City Police Officer meeting on two separate occasions with a Chinese gangster. What it proved was another question.

McNulty would have to come up with a reason why he was meeting with Yeoung, and saying he liked the egg rolls at the Golden Palace wasn't going to cut it. But McNulty was no fool, so I couldn't be overconfident.

Tommy said the meeting lasted for nearly two hours. One thing was certain; neither man looked happy leaving the office. After the meeting, McNulty called his son and said he didn't like Yeoung's answers. The message was cryptic, and to be honest, we couldn't make a lot out of it. Still, it seemed we might have succeeded at putting Yeoung and McNulty at odds. If we had, something good might come of it.

I now believed McNulty hadn't seen Li Chin the night of the raid. Had he seen her and not been able to kill her that night, he would have been after her all along. But there was no evidence that he had searched for her, and he seemed surprised to learn she was on our witness list. As for Yeoung, Li Chin didn't represent a threat to him, but McNulty could have made her the prime suspect in the theft of whatever was in the safe. Now I suspected that both men wanted Li Chin, but one wanted her dead, and the other wanted her alive.

Fortunately for Li Chin, she had already been deported and was safely out of McNulty's reach somewhere in China. Yeoung might be able to find her in China, but he wasn't likely to have her killed. Tortured maybe, but killed, unlikely. There was no reason to kill her so long as she was in China and unavailable to testify. Besides, what did Yeoung care if she sent McNulty to jail? At that point, McNulty was probably becoming more of a liability than an asset to Yeoung. I had to believe Li Chin would be okay even if Yeoung found her.

Tommy had also managed to dig up some interesting information on Yeoung or more precisely, Yeoung's history with the Hip Sing Tong. It was the type of information that could have only come from someone inside the Tong, so I was curious as to how he got it.

I can't say I was surprised when he said it came through his grandfather, old man Shoo. But I was wrong when I suspected the old man had been a member of the Tong. According to Tommy, the old man had never been a member of the Tong, but as a restaurant owner he knew a lot of guys who were.

A couple of the old retired Tong guys still hung out at the restaurant and with his grandfather's help, Tommy had been able to coax them into telling him some stories about the good old days. Nothing about present goings on, but some good background material, particularly about Sam Yeoung and his rise in the Hip Sing Tong.

Putting together the information Tommy learned about Yeoung with information Linda dug out of McNulty's NYPD personnel records, painted an interesting picture.

Sam Yeoung had grown up in Hong Kong where he and his brother became members of a major Triad, a criminal organization with worldwide reach. When the United States Congress passed the Immigration and Naturalization Act in 1965, abolishing the restriction on Chinese immigration, Sam moved to Chinatown in New York. There he joined the Hip Sing Tong, a longtime crime syndicate similar to the Mafia in its operation and organization.

Sam quickly became an up-and-coming member of the Tong. He was ruthless and vicious, two qualities highly admired by Tong leaders. Taking on the Mafia in Little Italy, Yeoung expanded the Hip Sing Tong's drug trade well beyond the boundaries of Chinatown at the time.

Yeoung's exploits were legendary. The story is often told how Yeoung killed three top Mafia hit men sent to assassinate him at the Golden Palace restaurant singlehanded. According to the legend, the Mafia Don had invited Yeoung to a sit-down to discuss his expansion of the Chinatown drug trade north into Little Italy. Needless to say, the Don wasn't happy, but in the interest of keeping the peace, he was willing to grant Yeoung a small territory outside of Chinatown on the Lower West Side. Yeoung, who had been frisked for weapons before being seated, listened politely to the proposition. When the Don was done talking, Yeoung grabbed a steak knife from the table, slashed the throats of the Don's two bodyguards, and fled the restaurant before they could pull their weapons.

Naturally angered by Yeoung's audacity, the shaken Don immediately dispatched his three best hit men to the Golden Palace restaurant to kill Yeoung. While the three men sat outside the restaurant waiting for Yeoung to come out, Yeoung left by way of the alleyway and came up behind them. He slashed the throats of two of the men. The third he sent back to the Don with his tongue cut out and a message pinned to his shirt, "I'll take what I want. I won't take it all unless you try to stop me." Supposedly that was the end of the war.

That was the start and by the mid-1970s, Yeoung's exploits had earned him a high-ranking position in the Tong.

During the 1970s and 1980s, the Tong ruled Chinatown and had the New York City Police Department in its pocket. Most cops working the beat in Chinatown in those days were on the Hip Sing Tong's payroll, and those who refused to play ball were given such a hard time that they eventually transferred out of the 5th Precinct.

McNulty started his police career in the 5th Precinct, walking the beat on Pell Street, home of the Golden Palace restaurant and Hip Sing headquarters. Eventually McNulty became Captain of the 5th Precinct and remained at the precinct until promoted to Deputy Chief in 2006.

In 2004, Sam Yeoung became head of the Hip Sing Tong in a bloody coup that lasted a month. During that month, there were a dozen murders on Pell Street alone. All the murders were investigated by Detectives from the 5th Precinct, but no arrests were ever made.

In the meantime, Sam Yeoung's brother, who remained in Hong Kong, had risen to head the Triad. The two brothers then joined forces with the Chinatown Tong, acting as an agent for the Hong Kong Triad.

That same year, 2004, McNulty started his tutoring business and opened his Merrill Lynch account. It was all tying together, and there was more.

Following up on my suggestion that she check into McNulty's spending habits, Linda had hacked into his credit card accounts. Apparently, McNulty was a cautious man, so there wasn't anything overtly suspicious. But Linda, being

Linda, kept looking until she found an interesting connection between McNulty and Yeoung.

McNulty's credit card charges showed that he and his wife had vacationed on Anguilla, a small exclusive Caribbean island, for two weeks each of the last five years. On the face of it, there was nothing suspicious or out of the ordinary about the trips. But Linda noticed that while there were restaurant charges and transportation charges on the credit cards, there were no hotel charges. She wondered why and started checking.

That's when she discovered Sam Yeoung owned a condominium on the island. Linda hadn't been able to find any direct proof that McNulty stayed in Yeoung's condominium, but he had to stay somewhere and apparently it wasn't in a hotel. Tommy offered to go to Anguilla to investigate, but I told him it wasn't in the budget.

Tommy had one other thing to report, and it wasn't good news. Yeoung had put out a $500,000 contract on Joey Peng. Apparently no one yet knew Joey was in federal custody, but Yeoung suspected Peng was up to no good and wanted him dead.

I had no intention of calling Peng as a witness, but so long as he posed a threat to McNulty, I preferred that he kept breathing. I had to assume, if Tommy knew about the contract, so did the Feds. That was comforting, but we both knew there was no guarantee Peng wouldn't turn up dead. People in federal custody had been murdered in the past.

When Tommy left, I called Richie on the burner phone. I was now convinced that there wasn't a department-wide conspiracy and using the damn burner phones was just plain stupid. Of course, I wouldn't say that to Richie who was in no mood to hear it. After letting him know what was happening, I mentioned that I was considering calling Hadden at IAB. Richie insisted it wasn't a good idea. He still believed this whole thing went well beyond McNulty, and IAB might be in on it as well. As hard as I tried, I couldn't convince him otherwise, so I just dropped it

.

CHAPTER 50

I spent a restless weekend deciding what to do about IAB. Should I go, or shouldn't I go? If I went, should I give them everything I had or hold back some of it? And if I went, when would I go, and what would I say?

Gracie was very good about letting me stew and didn't complain about my moody behavior. Well, at least she didn't complain much. She did demand that I go to an AA meeting on Saturday and suggested I go to one on Sunday, sure signs she wasn't thrilled with my attitude.

I spoke to Doug twice, but he wasn't much help. He just kept telling me to do what I knew was right. Why did he always assume I knew what was right? Had he forgotten I used to be a drunk? But I wasn't being fair. I wanted Doug to make my decision for me, and I knew he wasn't going to do that.

Saturday morning, Gracie decided I needed to take my mind off my problems, and since the weather was so nice, we should take a walk to Battery Park.

It was a beautiful day, and the walk did me good. By the time we reached Battery Park, I had nearly forgotten about Richie's case and was starting to enjoy myself. Battery Park is at the tip of Manhattan Island, where the Hudson River meets the East River. It overlooks the Upper New York Bay with the Statue of Liberty rising majestically on Liberty Island, formerly known as Bedloe's Island.

I have to tell you, changing names of things for no good reason bothers me, and sadly it's been done a lot in New York City. I grew up not far from 6th Avenue. It was called 6th Avenue because it came between 5th Avenue and 7th Avenue. It made perfect sense and insured that when somebody said 6th Avenue, you knew right away where it was. But then for no good reason they changed the name to Avenue of the Americas.

The same thing happened with 7th Avenue which they decided to re-name Fashion Avenue. Why, I don't know. Actually, I do know why; I just don't care; and I think it's stupid.

I'm not alone in protesting this practice of indiscriminate re-naming of things. Most Manhattanites over the age of forty continue to refer to the two avenues by their numeric designations. Someone even wrote a song when Constantinople was re-named Istanbul. Too bad nobody bothered to write a song when they re-named Ceylon, Sri Lanka. Did you know that the New York Jets were originally named the New York Titans?

I could go on, but now I'm just ranting, so let me get back to my day with Gracie in Battery Park. We spent an hour or so just sitting on a bench, looking out over the water and enjoying the view. Then Gracie suggested we grab a nice lunch. I agreed, eying a nearby Sabrett hot dog cart. But Gracie had something else in mind. She wanted to walk up to Battery Park City, just north of Battery Park, to some fancy Sushi restaurant.

Pointing out that we had eaten sushi twice that week already, I suggested we flip a coin, and the winner would choose where we eat. It was a risk, but a mutual and reasonable one to which Gracie readily agreed. I don't usually do well in games of chance, but that day Lady Luck shined her light on me, and I won.

I think Gracie assumed we'd be having Sabrett hot dogs, but I had grander plans. My choice for lunch was Mighty Quinn's Barbeque, home of the Brontosaurus Rib and other fine delicacies. I had never eaten there, but as Gracie would always say, I had heard good things about it, and I was excited to try it.

Gracie didn't share my enthusiasm for Mighty Quinn's, and after she looked over the menu, whatever enthusiasm she may have had vanished. When Gracie couldn't find much on the menu that appealed to her, I was going to suggest she could order the Brontosaurus Rib served raw. You know, playing on the sushi and all, but I thought better of it. Having won the coin toss and gotten my way, there was no reason to gloat. Besides, I was wearing a new shirt and didn't want to leave the restaurant covered in lunch.

But Gracie is a good sport, and she eventually ordered the brisket, with pickled cucumbers and sweet potato casserole. I'm sure you know what I ordered. The Brontosaurus Rib, fries smothered with Burnt Ends, chili-lime sauce, red onions, and spicy scallions. Gracie frowned at my choice, but kindly said nothing. Of course, she would smile later when my heartburn kicked in, but it was worth it. I learned to live with heartburn a long time ago. It's a small price to pay for an unhealthy lifestyle.

Our little adventure did take my mind off Richie's case, at least temporarily. But by Saturday night, I was obsessing again, and that's when Gracie sent me off to an AA meeting. As usual, going to a meeting put me in a better mood, even though it didn't help me decide what to do about the IAB.

It wasn't until Sunday night that I finally reached a decision. I'd call Joe Hadden at IAB and ask him to meet with me as soon as possible. For what it's worth, I'd make it an unofficial visit.

I knew in my heart and my head that calling IAB was the right thing to do. Even so, I wasn't in the mood for any arguments from Richie, so I had no intention of telling him about the meeting in advance. If it cost me his friendship, so be it. It was better than not contacting IAB, losing the case, and second-guessing myself for the rest of my life.

Once I made my decision, I slept like a rock. It was the first good night's sleep I had in two weeks. For the record, the half dozen Tums I consumed probably helped as well.

CHAPTER 51

The next morning, I was in the office early. Deciding to make the call to IAB was one thing; figuring out what to say when I made the call was something else entirely. Obviously, to have credibility I had to identify myself and disclose that I represented Richie. That was a given. But should I give Hadden everything I had on McNulty right away, or should I hold back details until I was sure IAB was all in?

I decided to do what I always do and that was to play it by ear, trusting my gut and going with it. I called IAB and asked to speak with Sergeant Hadden. Concerned that calls to IAB might be recorded and not wanting any details on the record, I intended to be as vague as possible. I'd keep it that way until I knew where all of this was going.

When Hadden picked up, I identified myself and told him I was representing Richie Simone. I said I had some information that might be of interest to IAB and asked if he would meet me at the Worth Street Coffee Shop. He said a meeting was possible, but he'd like to know what I had in mind. He was fishing for information, but I got the impression he knew what I had in mind.

Not sure I could trust him, I wasn't about to give any details, especially over the phone. I said simply, a meeting would be in both our interests. That was enough. Hadden agreed to meet me at the coffee shop in two hours.

The die was about to be cast; all that remained was to clean up some loose ends, the first of which was to call Detective Chen. When Chen and I had last met, we knew that sooner or later one of us was going to IAB. The only question was which one of us was going. No one on the job likes to be known as an IAB informer, so I'm sure Chen was hopeful it would be me.

I had promised Chen I'd let him know if it was me, and I called him to make good on my promise. When I told him the news, Chen was relieved to be off the hook and even more relieved when I promised to do my best to keep his name out of it.

With the call to Chen out of the way, I had to decide how I was going to handle my meeting with Hadden. Not knowing if McNulty had a hook in IAB was a real problem.

The odds were good he didn't, but it was still a gamble and that complicated matters.

If I gave Hadden everything we had on McNulty and McNulty found out, he might be able to clean some of it up or worse, bury it. On the other hand, if I didn't give Hadden enough information, I might not get him on board.

It was going to require some finesse. I had to give Hadden enough to keep him interested, while keeping enough in reserve to get what I needed.

I made copies of everything we had, and I separated the copies into folders by category. When I was done, I put the folders into my trial bag. That way I'd have it all on hand and ready to use. If things went well, I'd keep pulling files from the trial bag. But if I suspected Hadden wasn't on the up-and-up I'd stop, and he'd never know exactly how much dirt I had on McNulty.

As I walked to the coffee shop to meet Hadden, I couldn't help feeling guilty over not having told Richie about the meeting. As much as I could rationalize the decision I couldn't shake the feeling, but it was done, and I had work to do.

CHAPTER 52

I arrived at the coffee shop early and waited for Hadden in my usual booth. The booth was far enough away from other tables to be private, but still publicly visible. I prefer public places when meeting with someone I know will be carrying a gun. Not that I was worried Hadden was going to kill me. If McNulty or Yeoung wanted me dead, I'd be dead already. Unless they simply hadn't gotten around to it yet.

Hadden showed up right on time and after checking with the hostess, he was directed to my booth. Joe Hadden looked like a Hollywood version of a New York City Detective. I'd say he was in his late forties, maybe five feet nine inches tall, 170 pounds. He had a tough looking face, with a nose that had obviously been broken more than once. He wore a fedora and a wrinkled suit. I wanted to call him Columbo, but I didn't think that would get us off to a good start.

We ordered coffee, then I told Hadden both Richie and Jimmy O'Brien vouched for him being a good guy. Hadden just nodded a couple of times. He said he knew about Richie's situation, but so did everybody else in New York City who could read.

I put my first card on the table. I said we believed McNulty was a dirty cop and working with Sam Yeoung. Hadden said nothing; he just me gave me a nod; it seemed he was a nodder. I went on. I said that McNulty killed Kim Lee and had framed Richie for the murder. This time I didn't get a nod; I got a shrug. A shrug is okay, but it's not as good as a nod. It was time to put another card on the table.

I pulled the first folder from my trial bag. It was the series of photos of McNulty and Yeoung at the two meetings. I gave Hadden the background on the meetings. Hadden nodded. He was good at nodding. As long as he kept nodding, I'd keep putting cards on the table.

I pulled the second folder out of my bag. It contained the materials on McNulty's vacation on Anguilla and Yeoung's condo. Hadden read over everything in the folder. He looked at me and nodded. A look with a nod was good, but enough with the nodding, it was time for Hadden to put something on the table.

I waited and said nothing. Finally, Hadden said IAB had McNulty on its radar for some time. The official investigation was limited to his tutoring business, but Hadden thought there was more to it than that. What I had just shown him confirmed that belief and if I was willing to give him whatever else I had, he was confident he could help me out.

It was back to me. I said that I had plenty more, but my goal was to prove McNulty had murdered Kim Lee and framed Richie for the crime. Hadden nodded and added that he figured that was where I was going.

Hadden didn't believe for a minute Richie had murdered anyone, but IAB's investigation was limited to the corruption issues. Besides, as far as the NYPD was concerned, Kim Lee's murder was a closed case. The only way Hadden said he could help Richie was to take down McNulty before Richie's case went to trial. But to do that he needed more evidence, and it had to come from me.

What Hadden said made sense, and I guess I knew all along that IAB wasn't going to investigate Kim Lee's murder. But if IAB charged McNulty with corruption before Richie's trial started, that would help the defense enormously. I told Hadden I had plenty more on McNulty, but before I turned it over, I wanted some assurances that McNulty would be charged right away.

Hadden tilted his head from side to side. This guy was the master of head moves, but I had no idea what the tilting meant. Then he said he wanted to help Richie, but he couldn't give me any assurances before he saw what other evidence I had.

I couldn't argue with that. How could he give me assurances IAB would move on McNulty right away, if the only information I had was the same information IAB had already? It was time to go all-in. Or almost all-in. I showed him half of McNulty's personal financial records and the GM Properties documents. Hadden looked them over.

The financial records he had probably seen before because he just glanced at them. But when he got to the GM Properties documents, I could tell from his reaction he hadn't seen them before. He didn't just glance over them as he had the financial documents, instead he read them slowly and as he did, he nodded and smiled. I was hoping the smile was a good sign.

When he was done reading, Hadden looked at me, smiled, and nodded. It turned out the smiling was a good thing. The GM Properties documents were the link IAB needed to connect McNulty with Yeoung and the brothel. It wasn't quite a smoking gun because McNulty's son was a buffer, but it was close enough.

Between what IAB already had on McNulty and the GM Properties documents, there was enough evidence to charge McNulty. As soon as IAB confirmed the authenticity of the GM Property documents, IAB would arrest him. When I pressed Hadden on a timetable, he guessed it would be within a week.

That was what I wanted to hear. I gave Hadden the rest of the folders. It was almost everything we had on McNulty. The only information I didn't give him was the information from Detective Chen about Joey Peng. I kept that in reserve in case any further negotiations were needed. Besides, I wasn't going to drag Chen into the IAB investigation unless I absolutely had to.

Hadden and I both left the Worth Street Coffee Shop with something to feel happy about. Hadden promised to stay in touch, and I promised to pass on any more information we developed about McNulty. I hoped Hadden was better at keeping his promise than I was at keeping mine.

It was now simply a matter of waiting for IAB to arrest McNulty. Whether that happened or not, I still had to prepare for trial.

CHAPTER 53

I was feeling mildly optimistic after meeting with Hadden when Tommy showed up with some bad news that killed my optimism. First, Joey Peng was dead. He had been shanked in the shower at the Federal Detention Center. It meant I lost one of my possible leads, but it had never been a strong one. Bad news, but far from devastating except, of course, for Joey Peng.

The next news was potentially worse. When Linda Chow recently tried checking McNulty's Merrill Lynch accounts for new activity, she was blocked. Linda was unable to tell if the block resulted from a routine security update, or if Merrill Lynch had discovered the hack and blocked it. If Merrill Lynch had discovered the hack, it would have been obligated to notify McNulty. That wouldn't necessarily be a bad thing. Anything that kept McNulty worried was good. But if it tipped McNulty off that his accounts were under surveillance, he might try to clean up his financial tracks, and that wasn't good.

So far, nothing turned up on the wiretap about the hacked accounts. Either McNulty didn't know about the hacking, or he didn't intend to share the news with Yeoung or anyone else he called on the burner cell.

Linda Chow was looking for another way into Merrill Lynch's system, but for now we had no access.

It turned out to be one of those days when things just kept getting worse. After Tommy left, Joe Benjamin called. He said we needed to talk about a case I had handled some twelve years ago. It seemed the client was claiming I screwed up his case, and as a result he was serving a longer sentence than he should have.

What he was claiming is technically called inadequate representation, and generally those types of appeal go nowhere. But my former client, Andrew Barrows, had managed to hire a well-known civil rights lawyer, and there was a hearing scheduled. Not what I wanted to hear.

Twelve years ago when I handled the case, I was drinking heavily and Joe, knowing that, was understandably concerned with the allegation. But I remembered the case very well, and I assured him I had done a good job. It had been an open-and-shut case, and there hadn't been any real defenses to the charges.

Barrows was a crack addict living on the streets. To keep himself in drug money, he rolled drunks in the wee small hours of the morning. One night he spotted a man coming out of a bar at closing, and assuming he was drunk, he tried to roll him. The guy wasn't that drunk and started to fight back. As the two wrestled, Barrows grabbed a beer bottle out of a trash can and hit the guy with it. The bottle broke, and then Barrow stabbed the guy in the throat. The jagged edge of the bottle cut through the man's carotid artery and he bled out.

Barrows was arrested a few hours later in an alleyway, two blocks from the murder scene. He was spaced out on crack and covered in the victim's blood. When the arresting officers searched Barrows, they found the victim's wallet in his pocket. If that wasn't enough, Barrows' fingerprints were on the broken half of the beer bottle covered with the victim's blood. The only way it could have been any worse for Barrows was if the cops had a video of the crime.

Barrows claimed someone else had killed the victim, and he had come onto the scene just as the killer fled. Being a good citizen, he tried to help the victim, and that was how he got the victim's blood all over him. But two independent forensic experts concluded the blood splatter pattern on Barrows could only have resulted from being sprayed during the assault and not from casual contact afterward.

Barrows' explanations for how his fingerprints came to be on the beer bottle and how the victim's wallet wound up in his pocket were even less believable than was his blood explanation. He claimed when he went to help the victim, the beer bottle was laying on the victim's chest, and he moved it. That was why his fingerprints were on the beer bottle.

The top whopper, however, was how he explained having the victim's wallet in his pocket. He said the victim was so thankful for his help that he insisted he take his wallet. I gave him credit for being able to say that with a straight face.

I don't know if Barrows was suffering from some form of drug induced break with reality, but he refused to plea bargain, even when I told him his chance of prevailing at trial was less than zero. No matter what I said, he insisted we go to trial.

I, of course, didn't believe a word Barrows said, but I couldn't be certain it was a lie. I can't and won't allow a client to lie under oath. It's called suborning perjury, and not only is it a crime, it could get me disbarred. But if I don't know the client's story is a lie, I must allow him to tell it, even if I doubt it's true.

So we went to trial. Other than Barrows' testimony, we had nothing to offer in support of his claim of innocence. It was pathetic. As Barrows told his ridiculous story, the jurors were shaking their heads in disbelief. One juror actually laughed out loud when Barrows claimed the victim had given him his wallet as a reward. Others just snickered. By the time the ADA finished cross-examining Barrows, there wasn't a single juror who wasn't glaring at him and shaking their head.

The jury deliberation was the shortest I've ever known. I think they may have decided the case in the hallway on their way to the jury room. They were out no more than ten minutes, and they returned a unanimous verdict of guilty.

The sentencing hearing went no better than the trial. The Probation Department Report on Barrows contained nothing to mitigate his punishment and with Barrows still unrepentant, the judge sentenced him to the maximum term of twenty-five years to life. Case closed.

Now, some hot shot civil rights lawyer was trying to have Barrows freed, claiming I provided inadequate counsel. According to Joe, he wasn't claiming Barrows was innocent; he was claiming I was drunk most of the time and never informed Barrows of a plea deal. A plea deal that would have resulted in him serving less time than he was now serving. It was definitely a reach, but a judge had granted a hearing, so I had to take it seriously.

The drunk part may have been true. I can't totally deny it isn't. The failure to tell him about the plea deal was a total lie. But if I couldn't prove it was lie, it would be one of those "he said, I said" situations, and you can never predict how those situations will turn out.

When a client refuses to follow my advice, I know enough to cover my ass. I write a memo laying out the case, the plea deal, and the client's refusal to accept it. Then I have the client sign it. Even when I was drinking heavily, I followed that practice. At least I think I did. Or I hoped I did.

If I'd written a memo in Barrows' case, it would be in the file, but that was a problem. During my drinking days, my filing and organizational skills were a bit lacking. Not to mention the challenge of remembering where I might have put things. When you're drinking heavily, organization and neatness are not top priorities. In fact, they don't rank in the top ten. Drinking takes up the top eight spots on the priority list, and buying booze rounds out the top ten.

When I handled the Barrows case, I was working out of the backroom at Shoo's Restaurant where I had a filing cabinet and some file boxes. The filing cabinet I had taken with me when I moved to the office on Mott Street, but I didn't remember taking the file boxes.

Hopefully the file boxes were still in Shoo's backroom, and one of them contained the Barrows' file and the memo. If I couldn't produce the memo, I didn't like my odds. I was sure Barrows' lawyer could produce any number of witnesses who would testify I was drunk most of the time back then. Hell, half the lawyers and half the judges in New York could tell you that.

Joe suggested I speak to the ADA handling the case. Her name was Jessica McKenna, and she had all the details.

I had worked with Jessie, as she liked to be called, on a couple of cases, and we had gotten along well. She was damn good, and I felt a little better knowing she was the one holding my career in her hands. Still, there was going to be a hearing, so I needed to be prepared.

CHAPTER 54

I'd like to say that I handled the Barrows situation in a calm, cool and intelligent way, but I didn't. The minute I hung up with Joe, I called ADA McKenna.

I admit I was a little upset at the prospect of airing my drunken history in open court. But it was more than that. I've never denied what I did when I was drunk, and I've tried to make amends for the harm I caused. I don't mind being called a drunk, that's what I had been. What bothered me most was the prospect of being labeled a professional incompetent. That I wasn't.

I also knew if we lost, the bastard would sue me for damages. I had malpractice insurance, but the publicity would probably ruin my practice. I just knew nothing good was going to come from all of this.

That was my state of mind when I called Jessie, so you can imagine what I must have sounded like. To Jessie's credit she responded calmly to my rapid-fire questions. *No, this wasn't a joke. Yes, she had read the file. Yes, the claim was ridiculous. Yes, Barrows was as guilty as sin. No, I wasn't crazy.*

When I finally stopped to take a breath, Jessie jumped in and brought the conversation back to earth. Ronald Stein, the notorious civil rights lawyer, wasn't claiming Barrows was innocent, only that he was serving a longer sentence than he should be.

Jessie believed Stein had taken on Barrows' case simply for its publicity value. It had been over two years since Stein's last big civil rights case, and his name hadn't appeared in the newspapers since then. He was probably using the Barrows case to stoke up publicity and get his name in the papers again.

But simply bringing the claim wasn't newsworthy; he'd have to win at the hearing to make it news. That was good for me. If we won the hearing and the judge refused to re-open Barrows' case, the whole incident would recede quickly and quietly into obscurity with no harm done.

Jessie had retrieved the Barrows file from the DA's archives. During her review of the file, she came across a memo outlining a plea deal that Barrows had been offered. The deal involved Barrows pleading guilty to a lower degree of homicide and doing fifteen years to life. If Barrows had taken the deal, he would have been eligible for parole after twelve years. I didn't recall the precise details, but that sounded about right to me.

Jessie had also spoken to the ADA who handled the Barrows case. He confirmed we had discussed a plea deal and as he recalled, it was Barrows who rejected it. The problem was the ADA hadn't heard Barrows reject the deal; he had only heard it from me; and what I told him was hearsay.

It was coming down to my word against Barrows'. Jessie claimed she wasn't worried about that, but I was. I wouldn't be at all shocked if a very liberal minded judge took the word of an admitted felon over the word of an admitted drunk. After all, the poor felon had society to blame for his misconduct; all I had to blame was myself.

Talking with Jesse, I was convinced I had prepared a memo confirming that I had told Barrows to take a plea deal, and he rejected it. If I could find it, the case would be over before it even started. But if I couldn't find it, I wasn't optimistic about the outcome. I promised Jessie I'd look for the memo and get back to her.

Realizing I was on the verge of losing my perspective, I wisely called Doug, and he talked me off the ledge. Worst case scenario Barrows is entitled to nothing more than a re-sentencing, if that much. But even if he were granted a re-sentencing, it wouldn't necessarily mean he'd end up serving less time in prison. The only sentence Barrows would be entitled to was fifteen years to life, which was the sentence offered in the plea deal. That might make him eligible for parole, but it doesn't guarantee he'd get it.

Doug was right, but I still faced the prospect of being humiliated in court, and for that I had nobody to blame but myself.

I'd go to Shoo's and look for the file boxes, and I'd definitely go to my AA meeting that night. It was my regular home group meeting on East Houston Street.

CHAPTER 55

I was still stewing over the Barrows situation when Tommy called. The last two days he had spent working to set up a deal with Jerome White, and it was about to pay off. He wouldn't tell me the details, but said if everything worked out, he'd be in the office the next day with good news.

I hadn't exactly forgotten about Sasha's case, but it hadn't been in the front of my mind. Not that it had to be. There wasn't anything I could do for her until Tommy figured out if we could take down Jerome White. If we could, then Sasha's future looked bright. But if we couldn't take down White, Sasha was probably going to do some hard time. It was sad, but those were the facts. As much as I wished there was something more I could do to help her out, there wasn't.

Drug cases are always the worst. Everyone in law enforcement remembered the crack epidemic, and they weren't going to let it happen again. Sentences were tougher and longer, and there weren't many sympathetic ADAs willing to cut a defendant a little slack. Don't get me wrong, there were some good deals offered to first-time offenders, but they were rare. If it hadn't been for the amount of drugs involved, Sasha might have been a candidate for one of those deals.

Sarah Washington is one of those ADAs who will show a little kindness to a young mother who's gotten herself hooked on cocaine. Had Sasha been caught with a small amount of cocaine and admitted she was an addict, maybe I could have gotten her into a rehab program. But Sasha had nearly $100,000 worth of cocaine in her apartment, and she wasn't even an addict, so naturally everyone concluded she was a dealer.

I hoped like hell Tommy would be able to bring down Jerome White because that was the only way Sasha had a chance of staying out of prison. Unfortunately, all I could do at that point was hope.

Still obsessing over the Barrows matter, I walked down the street to Shoo's Restaurant and went to the backroom to search for my old file boxes.

Nothing much had changed in the backroom. Of course, Tommy's knockoff watches were no longer there hidden under a tarp, but my old desk and his were still there. So were the cases of Chinese fortune cookies from Wonton Foods in Brooklyn, the largest manufacturer of fortune cookies in the world.

The last place I recalled seeing my file boxes was against the back wall. There were stacks of boxes there, but none of them were mine. I checked each one just to be sure. Most were fortune cookie cartons filed with old restaurant order pads, old menus, and some waiters' jackets. Others had the restaurant's business records, and some were cases of soy sauce, but none contained my old files.

I went back into the restaurant looking for old man Shoo, but he was at his weekly Mahjong game. I tried calling Tommy, but the call went to his voice mail. I decided to give the backroom one more look.

Being in the backroom brought back some old memories, not all of them good. Just for the hell of it I took a seat at my old desk. I reached down and opened the desk drawer where I used to keep my ever-present bottle of scotch. Of course, it was empty, the drawer that is, and had been even before I left Shoo's.

Sometimes I forget those days. But I know if I forget them altogether, I might end up reliving them. That's why I go to meetings, and that's why I tell my story.

But I didn't have time for nostalgia. I had to find those file boxes. I took another tour around the backroom, but the boxes were gone.

CHAPTER 56

That night at dinner with Gracie I told her about the Barrows situation and my search for the missing file boxes. Gracie was confident things would turn out okay even if I didn't find the memo. Her reasoning was the same as Doug's, and it made sense. But I was still nervous, and it was showing. So when I told Gracie I was going to my AA meeting, she said it was a good idea. Figuring I needed more cheering up, she said she'd pick up some gelato on her way home, and we could have a little party after the meeting. I didn't know exactly what she had in mind, but I love gelato.

The meeting was exactly what I needed. When I left I was feeling pretty good. But that didn't last for very long. I had walked about a block when someone grabbed me from behind and pushed me into an alleyway.

Whoever it was, he was strong, and he had my right arm twisted behind my back. I don't work out, and at my age I'm not a fighter. I knew struggling would only get me a dislocated shoulder, so I didn't resist. I didn't have much cash on me, and what cash I did have he could have.

When this clown had pushed me halfway down the alley, he shoved me face-first against the wall. He kept my right arm twisted halfway up my back and pressed his other arm into my neck forcing my face against the wall. Then leaning toward my ear, he said, "Keep your nose out of other people's business, or you and your girlfriend are going to get hurt."

I wanted to tell him that Gracie didn't like being called my girlfriend, but I didn't think he'd care. Besides, before I could say anything, he threw me into a pile of trash bags and jogged out of the alley.

I never saw his face, only his back as he left the alley. He was wearing a dark sweatshirt with a hood and a pair of jeans. From where I lay on the ground, he looked to be maybe a little over six feet tall and well built. I figured that only described about five million people in New York City.

I didn't detect any accent, but that didn't rule out the possibility that my assailant was Chinese and sent by the Hip Sing Tong. I knew one thing; it wasn't McNulty. McNulty was shorter than I am and had a gut. Of course, McNulty could have sent the guy to deliver the message.

The garbage bags had cushioned my sudden and rapid descent to the pavement, so I was unhurt. Except for my pride, which I admit was wounded in the encounter. I decided there was no sense reporting the incident to the police because I couldn't give them any details about the assailant, so I dusted myself off and went to Gracie's.

I wasn't going to tell Gracie what had happened because I didn't want her to worry. But then I remembered the scumbag had threatened her as well, and she had a right to know. So when I got to her place, I told her the whole story. I did leave out the part about him calling her my girlfriend.

The first thing she wanted to know was if I was okay. After that, her only comment was, "Screw 'em. You do what you have to do for Richie." Gracie is one hell of a tough woman, so I knew better than to ask if she was sure about that.

My shoulder hurt a little bit, but the gelato eased the pain and by the time we got to "partying," I was feeling fine.

CHAPTER 57

The next morning when Tommy showed up at my office, I told him what had happened. Not that I expected he could do anything about it, I just wanted it on record somewhere. That way if I turned up dead, it'd be harder for the cops to call it a random act of violence.

Tommy offered to get me a gun. High quality and untraceable. But I said no because I have this thing about guns. I like guns in the hands of people who know how to use them, and I'm admittedly not one of those people. I was offered gun training when I was with the DA's Office, but at the time I was drinking heavily and wisely turned the offer down. Who says a drunk can't make a good decision? I'm sure you can come up with your own reasons why it's not a good idea to give a gun to an active alcoholic.

I'm not drinking now, but I still don't want a gun because I'm not sure I could shoot someone. Oh, I'm a tough guy alright, and I'd like to think that in my prime I could handle myself in a physical confrontation, but shooting someone, that's different.

I know one thing; if you pull a gun, you better be prepared to use it. If you're not prepared to use it, bad things can and will happen. I learned that from the cops. When I was an ADA, all the cops told me the same thing; they didn't pull their guns unless they intended to use them, and when they used them, they fired until the target went down. That's what they were trained to do.

The idea that someone can shoot a gun or a knife out of someone else's hand or even intentionally shoot them in the arm or the leg is pure bullshit. In a series of controlled tests, experienced shooters, firing pistols at human sized targets fifteen feet away, missed the targets entirely when their aim was off by as little as a quarter of an inch. And that was under ideal conditions with a stationary target and non-stressed shooters. Remember that the next time you're tempted to think cops should shoot to wound and not to kill.

Anyway, I turned down Tommy's offer of a gun. I'd just have to be more careful and avoid dark alleys.

The incident did tell me one thing. I was on the right track and maybe getting too close for someone's comfort. If I was way out in left field, no one would care what I was doing, and they wouldn't be threatening me. The problem was I didn't know who was worried or what I was doing that was making them worried.

My first thought was McNulty discovered that Linda had been snooping around in his Merrill Lynch accounts. But Tommy said he didn't think that was the case. He assured me Linda was a world-class hacker and had never come close to being caught. That may have been true, but Tommy had to admit even the best hackers leave some evidence that they'd been there. It isn't always easy to find, and it doesn't necessarily reveal the hacker's identity.

But Tommy wasn't there to talk about Richie's case. He had news on Sasha's case. He explained that getting close enough to Jerome White to set him up hadn't been easy. White was smart, shrewd, and careful. He worked behind layers of protection which was why the NYPD was having a tough time arresting him.

Tommy had managed to work his way through those layers and was scheduled to meet directly with White. It started with Tommy and a couple of his friends going into the Harlem housing project to buy cocaine. His friends were there for both safety and appearance. The idea was to look like a drug syndicate and not a bunch of users.

When one of White's runners approached the group, Tommy said his group was looking to score a kilo of cocaine and if the quality was right, they'd pay as much as $30,000. The runner passed on the message to Jerome who sent one of his lieutenants, a gangbanger named Donte, to talk with Tommy.

Tommy told Donte he and his friends were setting up a sales network in the Financial District and needed a supplier, but he wouldn't say anything more until he met with the boss man.

Donte moved away from the group and made a call. Tommy figured he was calling Jerome and passing on the information. When Donte rejoined the group, he told Tommy to meet him at the same place in three days, and they'd talk. Then Donte gave Tommy a dime bag of cocaine so he could judge the quality.

The three-day delay gave Jerome time to check Tommy and make sure he wasn't a cop or a Fed. It also gave us time to secure approval from the DA and the NYPD to set up the operation.

Tommy had set up the plan in phases because Jerome was cautious, and offering to buy too large an amount of cocaine right off the bat might make him suspicious. So, the original buy of one kilo of cocaine was simply to establish Tommy's bona fides as a dealer. If Tommy could do that, he'd arrange for the big sale needed to put Jerome away for life.

My job now was to convince Sarah Washington's boss to cut the deal Sarah and I had worked out earlier. It also involved convincing NYPD that it was worth spending $30,000 to set up Jerome White for a takedown. There was no guarantee the $30,000 would be recovered during the later arrest, or for that matter, that a later arrest would happen, so it wasn't going to be an easy sell.

CHAPTER 58

After Tommy left, I called Sarah Washington and set up a meeting for later that morning. With the Moby Dick syndrome in play, convincing Sarah's boss to approve the deal could be easier than getting the NYPD to go along with the plan.

Jerome White wasn't exactly what you would call a drug kingpin. On the DEA's list of the most wanted, Jerome probably wasn't in the top 100. But he was a major thorn in the side of the NYPD and the Manhattan District Attorney, and thus became a Moby Dick.

If Sarah and her boss agreed to the deal, it would be up to them and the District Attorney to get the NYPD to go along with the plan. I'd supply the details and lend support, but it would come down to a decision by NYPD brass.

When I arrived at Sarah's office for our meeting, she took me to a conference room where Milt Sorenson was waiting. I knew all along the deal I was proposing required approval from someone above Sarah's level, so I wasn't surprised to see Milt.

Milt Sorenson had started at the DA's Office a year or two after I had. I hadn't known him very well back then, which was a good thing, because when I went off the deep end, I burned a lot of bridges with people I was close to. Fortunately, Milt wasn't one of those people. At least I didn't remember him as being one of them, but I could never be sure about anything that happened once I started drinking alcoholically. I lost a decade or so of memory, much of which I'm happy to forget.

Over the years, Milt had risen in the ranks and was now a member of the Executive Staff, which meant he had authority to cut deals. Whether he had the authority to cut the deal I was looking for, remained to be seen. After making the usual small talk, I laid out Tommy's plan. Milt asked a few questions and then excused himself. It seemed my proposal may have exceeded his authority level. Since it required NYPD participation and $30,000 in cash, I wasn't surprised.

When he returned less than five minutes later, which was unusually quick, we had a deal, provided the NYPD was on board with the plan. That was fair since we needed the

NYPD to provide the equipment and manpower to make the plan work. Not to mention the cash to make the buys. Milt didn't think getting NYPD to approve the plan would be a problem, but he wanted me with him when he made the pitch. I agreed, and Milt went straight to the phone to set up a meeting at One Police Plaza.

I wasn't surprised the plan was accepted, but I was surprised how quickly it was accepted and how fast Milt was moving on it. Apparently, my Moby Dick theory was in play but just to confirm it, I asked Sarah how the deal got approved so quickly. She explained the Mayor was pressuring the NYPD and the District Attorney to get the city's drug problems under control. The cops were out making more arrests and the District Attorney's Office was pushing for longer sentences, all of which accounted for the recent rash of higher than usual charging practices.

NYPD and the DA had put together their own top ten most wanted list and Jerome White was at the top of the list. He was the DA's Moby Dick.

All of that was good news for Sasha, and my proposal couldn't have come at a better time. All that remained was to convince the brass at NYPD that the plan would work.

Milt hung up the phone and said we had a meeting at One PP in half an hour, so we needed to discuss our strategy. He suggested that since it was my plan I lay out the details, and he and Sarah would chime in with support where appropriate.

I got the impression we were about to do a dog and pony show that wasn't going to mean anything. When I pressed Milt, he admitted the District Attorney was already on the phone with the Mayor and the Police Commissioner making the deal happen. We were meeting with the brass only for show. No one wanted it to look like the DA had gone over their heads.

I hate politics and I hate politicians and if I hadn't before I would then. We were wasting time and taxpayer money on a charade so that a bunch of high ranking cops could think they were making a decision that had already been made by the politicians. If Sasha's future wasn't at stake I think I would have blown the lid off the charade, but her future was at stake, so I just went along and played my part.

As we walked the couple of blocks from the DA's Office to One Police Plaza, I decided to use the situation to my advantage. The basic deal was already cut and knowing how much the DA wanted it, Milt was in no position to squelch it. I could make a demand or two of my own, and if they weren't outrageous Milt would have to go along.

We met in a conference room on the fourteenth floor, not far from the Commissioner's office. I had been in One Police Plaza, or the Ivory Tower as the rank and file called it, a number of times but this was my first trip to the fourteenth floor. I imagined it was like being down the hall from the Oval Office in the White House.

Sitting around the conference table when we arrived where six individuals, ranging in rank from Deputy Chiefs to Deputy Commissioners. They represented six different Bureaus or departments of the NYPD that would be involved in executing the plan.

The Crime Control Strategies Bureau was there to presumably assess the proposed plan. The Detective Bureau and the Intelligence Bureau would run the operation, while the Information Technology Bureau would provide the surveillance equipment and support. The Legal Matters Department was there to insure the plan was legally sound. Finally, the Community Affairs Bureau was there for some reason no one could seem to articulate.

As I laid out the details of the plan, there was a lot of "umphing" and "humphing," but happily no comments or questions. I wondered if they all knew the meeting was a charade and if they even cared. At the end, I added my demand to be present in the Mobile Command Center when the deals went down, with full access to all audio and video feeds.

Sarah looked a little chagrined by my new demand, but Milt just smiled and nodded. He was no fool, and he knew I wasn't one either. I had the upper hand, and I was playing it to my advantage. It's not often I get the upper hand in these situations, so he couldn't blame me for taking advantage of it.

When I finished, Sarah, Milt and I were asked to leave the room and wait in a smaller conference room down the hall. We had barely settled in when we were called back into the larger conference room. We had a deal. Tommy and I would coordinate with Detective William Evans who would lead the operation. He would arrange for all the personnel and equipment needed to carry out the mission. Lastly, I would be given full access to the Mobile Command Center during all aspects of the operation.

Why did I want to be part of the operation? Because I learned a long time ago that operations like this one can go sideways very quickly, and with Tommy's life possibly at stake, I wanted to be able to pull the plug. I knew from experience that when the cops used civilians in an undercover operation they always gave them a "safe word." A word that would end the operation and send in the cavalry. I wanted to be in a position to use that word if I thought Tommy was in danger.

With the deal cut, Milt, Sarah and I went back to Milt's office to put the agreement in writing. After that, I called Tommy and gave him the go-ahead to deal with Jerome. All that was left was to let Sasha know if things went as I expected, she'd be free in a week or so.

CHAPTER 59

When I got back to the office, it was time to call Richie and tell him about my meeting with Hadden of IAB. I knew he wasn't going to be happy about it, but I couldn't keep it from him any longer.

As I expected, he blew up when I told him what I had done. The good news was that he didn't hang up; he just kept yelling. It took a while, but I was finally able to calm him down enough to let me explain my thinking.

Richie was worried the corruption went beyond McNulty, and if it did, IAB could either be in on it or powerless to stop it. When I explained McNulty was already on IAB's radar, Richie felt better, but he was still upset.

I told him about Joey Peng and how he was shanked, presumably by one of Sam Yeoung's guys to keep him quiet. Then I cautiously mentioned that I had been roughed up. As I expected, Richie went ballistic.

He offered to come live with me and when I turned down that idea, he offered to get me a gun. A nice clean gun, as he put it. I had already turned down a similar offer from Tommy, and there was no way I was accepting Richie's offer.

I told Richie the gun wasn't necessary, and besides, if I got caught with an illegal handgun, I could lose my law license.

I promised to keep Richie in the loop and let him know when I heard from Hadden. It was one of those promises I intended to keep when I made it, but which might prove impossible to keep.

Later that morning, I finally caught up with old man Shoo at the restaurant and asked him about the file boxes I was looking for. As I asked the question, the old man kept nodding his head which was a sign he understood what I was asking. When I finished, he smiled widely and in his own inimitable way said, "Tommy take."

I don't why I hadn't thought to ask Tommy about the file boxes earlier, but I called him right away. Much to my relief, he confirmed that when he moved his business out of the restaurant's backroom, he took all his and my boxes with him. When he hired Linda Chow and needed space for her in the office, he moved the boxes to the Nolita Self Storage facility on Mott Street. He had a list of the stored boxes, and four of them were mine. I prayed to God the Barrows file was in one of them, and it contained the memo about the plea deal.

Tommy was at the Harlem housing project working on Sasha's case, but he could meet me at the storage facility at two o'clock. I was feeling better having at least found the file boxes. Now it was just a matter of time until I found out if my ass was saved.

I had time to kill before I met Tommy and since it was nearly noon, I decided to have lunch at the Golden Palace restaurant. I can't tell you exactly why I decided to have lunch at the Golden Palace, and you probably think going into the lion's den was a crazy thing to do. But I was still angry over being roughed up, and sometimes my anger clouds my judgment. I never said I was smart all the time, just a smart-ass.

All the way to the Golden Palace I tried to figure out what I would do if things didn't go well, but I couldn't come up with a decent plan. I even ran a scenario in my head in which I had a gun, but even that one didn't work out well. In the end I decided to play it by ear which was really just a cop-out.

The Golden Palace is small by Chinatown restaurant standards, so when the hostess seated me at a banquet along the wall, I had a view of the entire place. It was still early, so the place was relatively empty, maybe a half dozen other customers besides me.

I had just ordered the hot and sour soup and Lo mein when Sam Yeoung came out of the office. My heart beat a little faster. Had he come out because I was there?

Yeoung looked around the room, passing right over me and stopped his gaze on two men seated a couple of tables away. Smiling, he walked over to the two and greeted them by name.

After a brief conversation, Yeoung walked back toward the office. Along the way he smiled and nodded at patrons, including me. There was nothing in his manner that suggested he knew who I was.

The Chinese can be very subtle when sending a message. But if that was a message, it was way beyond subtle. Maybe if he had glared or even stared when he looked my way, I could say he sent a message. But he didn't. He just smiled and nodded at me the same way he had with the other patrons. My heartbeat returned to normal.

Maybe Yeoung was smart enough not to tip his hand, or maybe he didn't know who I was, and he had nothing to do with my mugging. By the time I finished my Lo mein, I was convinced he had no idea who I was, and McNulty was the one behind my mugging.

I'm not a great believer in fortune cookies, particularly those made in Brooklyn. But I must admit I have found some to be insightful. For instance, years ago in my drinking days, I had a fortune cookie message, "You will die alone and poorly dressed." Honestly, that's what it said. Either the guy who wrote it knew me, or he was having a really bad day. At the time, the part about dying alone didn't bother me, but the poorly dressed part did.

That day in the Golden Palace, my fortune cookie read simply, "The answer you seek is in another cookie." I thought about asking for another cookie, but then I considered there might be a subtler meaning to the message. Perhaps it meant I was in the wrong place.

Finally, as I finished the last of my tea, I came to my senses. What the hell was I thinking? I was looking to a cookie for an answer. How crazy was that? I paid the bill in cash, no sense using a credit card and leaving my name.

I had just enough time to walk to the Nolita Self Storage facility and meet Tommy.

CHAPTER 60

When I left the Golden Palace restaurant, I thought I had plenty of time to get to the storage facility. After all, it was on Mott Street, so how far could it be? I had ignored the fact that Mott Street runs all the way from Worth Street north to Bleecker Street in the East Village. The storage facility was further north on Mott Street than I realized, so I was a little late in getting there. Besides, as much as I hate to admit it, I was stopping every block, looking in shop windows to see if I was being followed.

I said I didn't think Yeoung knew who I was, but there have been times when I've been wrong. Not many, but a couple. Besides, it doesn't hurt to be a little paranoid. As I see it, there's a very fine line between being paranoid and being cautious. And it might be the same fine line between being dead and being alive.

After getting mugged, I knew I had enemies; the only question was who they were. Since no one seemed to be following me from the Golden Palace, I hoped that meant Yeoung didn't know who I was, or had no interest in me, or both. I'd be happy with any one or any combination of those possibilities. But if that was the case, it left McNulty as the likely culprit, although I have to admit there are probably quite a few people from my past life who'd like to dance on my grave.

Tommy had gotten to the facility early and already sorted through the boxes by the time I arrived. He had located my four file boxes and put them aside. The room was small and cramped, but I decided to go through the boxes right there instead of trying to lug them back to my office. I didn't need them any time soon; I just needed know where they were.

Tommy said that normally he would be glad to help, but he had a meeting back at the housing project and left. I promised to lock up when I was done.

I had been going through the boxes for about twenty minutes when I found the Barrows file. I flipped through it quickly, looking for the memo, and thankfully I found it. It was handwritten and laid out the terms of the proposed plea deal, along with my recommendation that Barrows accept it. I didn't remember writing it, but that didn't matter, Barrows had signed it, acknowledging he refused the deal.

Barrows' signature was on several documents in the file, and I took those as well. That would make it harder for Barrows to claim the one on the memo was a forgery. It looked like my ass was saved.

I'd like to think, I was as good an attorney drunk as I am sober, but that's not true. I was just lucky that day to have done the smart thing. God knows how many times I did the wrong thing. Getting sober doesn't wipe out your past or forgive you of your sins. Sometimes the things you did in the past when you drank come back and bang you over the head. In AA we call them time bombs. This time I was lucky the Barrows time bomb turned out to be a dud. I might not be so lucky next time.

I put the Barrows file aside and stacked the boxes back in place. After locking up the room, I walked down Mott Street to my office. This time I didn't bother stopping to check for tails.

ADA McKenna was delighted to hear about the memo and asked me to send her a copy as quickly as possible. She was going to ask Barrows' lawyer to voluntarily drop the case. I said if he refused, tell him I intended to file a grievance against him with the State Bar Association.

Technically the grievance would be nothing more than a nuisance to Ronald Stein. But under the circumstances, it was a nuisance he'd probably like to avoid. He knew his client was a guilty scumbag who was proving to be a liar as well. So why go through with a case he was sure to lose and then face a grievance charge on top of that?

But the real problem for Stein would be the publicity the grievance was likely to generate. Grievances are published in the legal journals and sometimes the mainstream media picks up the story. Given Ronald Stein's notoriety, any grievance against him was likely to be reported, at least by the local papers. The publicity wouldn't be good, and Stein lived for good publicity.

Contrary to popular belief, not all publicity is good, and some publicity is particularly bad for lawyers. While the general public may soon forget bad publicity about a lawyer, judges don't forget as easily. Believe me, I learned that lesson firsthand. It took a while after I quit drinking for judges to accept the fact that I wasn't drunk when I appeared in their courtrooms.

Stein knew what kind of reputation he could get for pressing a bad case, so he wasn't likely to take the risk. Barrows just wasn't worth it. For the first time since I heard about Barrows' claim, I felt confident the case would be dismissed.

After Connie sent a copy of the memo to Jessie McKenna, I called Gracie and shared the good news with her. She tried to give me one of her "I told you so" speeches, but I could tell she was as relieved by the news as I was.

Then I called Doug and we went through the same routine I had just been through with Gracie. I love both, and both gave me great support, but they knew I faced a big problem. They wouldn't say it, and they both had a rationalization that made sense, but deep down they were as worried as I had been.

It's a natural instinct when someone's in trouble to try and put them at ease. What's the first thing we usually say when something bad happens? "Don't worry, it'll be okay."

Most times when we say it, we have no way of knowing if it's true or not. But we say it to make the other person feel better and because we don't know what else to say.

When you're on the receiving end of the message, it does make you feel better. You want to believe it's true, and you're grateful that someone is there for you. I was happy to have Gracie and Doug there for me.

Just like bad news, good news sometimes comes in bunches too. I had just finished talking with Doug when Joe Hadden called. He wanted to meet as soon as possible. He wouldn't say over the phone why he wanted to meet, but I got the impression it was good news.

Joe didn't want to meet in his office or mine, so I offered to buy him coffee at the Worth Street Coffee Shop. He accepted my offer, and we arranged to meet there in an hour.

Abe Fishman had come to drop off a file, and when he stuck his head in the door to say hello, he asked how things were going. I invited him in and told him what had happened the last couple of days. He was upset when he heard I had been mugged, but he said it was a good sign. We were getting to McNulty and Yeoung, and one of them was losing his cool. I wasn't as quick to call my mugging a good sign, but I wasn't going to argue the point with Abe.

I decided it was time to let Abe know I had gone to IAB.

CHAPTER 61

After letting Abe know what I was doing with IAB, I went to the Worth Street Coffee Shop and met with Joe Hadden. Not knowing why he wanted to meet concerned me, but my concern proved to be unfounded. The news was good. No, it was great! IAB had confirmed the information I had given him on GM Properties. It was the connection to Sam Yeoung they had been looking for, and they were ready to move on McNulty.

There was one small problem. The connection wasn't actually a direct link; it went through McNulty's son, George. But Hadden and his bosses at IAB believed McNulty would confess to spare his son. The plan was to offer McNulty a walk for his son if he pleaded guilty and cooperated against Sam Yeoung., Initially the DA had been reluctant to agree to such a deal, but Hadden's boss had finally convinced him it was the only way to get McNulty and in the end, Sam Yeoung.

I had one question. How much pressure would IAB put on McNulty to admit he killed Kim Lee and framed Richie for her murder? When Hadden looked away, I knew the answer to my question, and I didn't like it. IAB's only interest was taking down McNulty and with the evidence connecting him to Yeoung and the brothel, it was an easy deal. Getting McNulty to admit to murder wasn't likely to happen and making it a condition would jeopardize the deal. The best I was going to get was having McNulty indicted on charges of corruption and dereliction of duty. What I did with that was up to me.

Hadden had another piece of information he thought might interest me. Recent phone taps had recorded Yeoung complaining to his lieutenants about McNulty and looking for someone named Li Chin. It seemed he was very anxious to find Li Chin and was offering a very generous reward to any of his people who found her.

Hadden was right; the information was interesting because it told me two things. First, Yeoung didn't know that Li Chin had been deported. If he knew, he would be looking for her in China and not in Chinatown. Second, Yeoung's interest in Li Chin wasn't as a witness to Kim Lee's murder.

The way things stood between McNulty and Yeoung, it wasn't likely Yeoung was looking to protect McNulty's ass. The only reason Yeoung would be interested in finding Li Chin was if he believed she had stolen whatever had been in the brothel safe the night of the raid. It also confirmed that Yeoung wanted whatever had been in the safe. I still had no idea what it was, but it had to be worth a lot.

Hadden wouldn't say exactly when IAB intended to arrest McNulty, only that plans were in the works, and it would happen "soon." The only issue was whether McNulty would get the full "perp walk" treatment. With the full perp walk, there'd be lots of media coverage and lots of pictures of McNulty in handcuffs being paraded into Central Booking. That would be great.

Unfortunately, the Commissioner's Office wasn't on board with the plan and was leaning toward keeping the arrest quiet. No final decision had been made, but as it stood a perp walk was a long shot.

While I really relished the thought of McNulty being paraded in handcuffs into Central Booking with the media all around, I'd be happy just to have him arrested.

Hadden promised to keep me informed and to let me know when McNulty was going to be arrested. That was about all I needed at that point. I could call off any additional investigation of McNulty and at least stop the meter on that work. I still didn't have any direct evidence implicating McNulty in Kim Lee's murder, but the circumstantial evidence I had would get a big boost with McNulty's arrest. That was about all I could hope for at the moment.

Later that night Gracie and I were celebrating my having found the Barrows memo. During dinner she asked me about Richie's case, and I filled her in on what was happening. She agreed I was in a tight spot, but reminded me Marty Bowman wasn't exactly going to be on easy street after McNulty's arrest. He'd go from having a case that was open-and-shut to a case with a big problem. Instead of his key witness being a high ranking decorated cop, his key witness would be a disgraced piece of crap who was headed to jail. Gracie at times has a great way with words.

In case you hadn't realized it, Gracie likes to tell it like it is. Don't get me wrong. Gracie doesn't often use vulgarity, so when she does it makes an impression. I appreciated her passion and support, but I think her closeness to the situation may have been blinding her to the reality of it all. I asked her if she was a juror on the case, wouldn't she want to know why McNulty had gone to all that trouble to kill Kim Lee? Gracie thought about it for a second or two, and then she said, "You better find out what was in that safe."

Gracie was right about that and about Marty Bowman being in a tight spot as well. I needed to leverage that situation.

CHAPTER 62

The next couple of days went by quickly. I heard from Tommy that he had struck a deal with Jerome to purchase the one kilo of cocaine for $32,000. It was $2,000 more than planned, but it was still within the NYPD's budget. Tommy and Detective Evans had worked out the details, and at Tommy's request, Evans agreed to monitor the buy "loosely" so as not to arouse Jerome's suspicion. I wasn't sure what "*loosely*" meant, but I intended to be in the Mobile Command Unit when the sale happened. As far as I was concerned, it was Evans' job to keep Tommy safe, and I'd be there to make sure Evans did just that.

Tommy was meeting Jerome that Friday night at 11 o'clock inside the housing project grounds. No doubt Jerome would have lookouts posted on the roofs and around the perimeter of the project. Detective Evans planned on setting up the Mobile Command Unit five blocks away, but he would have undercover Detectives on alert just outside the project.

Everyone working the detail was scheduled to meet in the One Police Plaza parking garage at nine o'clock. I told Tommy I'd see him there. Then I called Evans and confirmed that I would be present during the operation. Evans didn't seem particularly pleased, but he understood it was part of the deal, and there wasn't anything he could do about it.

I kept hoping to hear from Hadden that McNulty's arrest was in the works, but so far it hadn't happened. I was never big on patience and while I have gotten better, I still look for immediate gratification.

I was thinking about Hadden and whether I should give him a call when Connie reminded me I had a meeting with Jessie McKenna on the Barrows situation in half an hour. With everything that had been happening, I had nearly forgotten about Barrows. After I sent Jessie a copy of the memo signed by Barrows acknowledging he rejected the plea offer, I had figured the case was over.

Now it turned out the judge wanted a conference on the matter, and he wanted me there. Barrows couldn't claim I hadn't told him about the plea deal or that I told him not to take it, so what was left? Jessie assured me the conference was just a formality, but I wasn't so sure about that.

CHAPTER 63

When I met Jessie at her office, Murray Klein, the ADA who had handled the Barrows case originally, was already there. Murray had left the DA's Office a couple of years earlier and was now a partner in a small midtown law firm. Why the judge wanted Murray at the conference puzzled all of us, but he wanted him there, so Murray showed up.

The three of us walked across Worth Street to the courthouse, and on the way to Judge Marshall's courtroom, we ran into Ronald Stein, Barrows' lawyer. Jessie greeted him and introduced Murray and me. This may surprise you, but I acted very rudely. I refused to shake his hand, turned my back on him, and walked away. I figured I was about to be needlessly humiliated, and it was his fault. In truth it was my own fault, but it was still unfair.

Stein didn't make an issue of it and said nothing to me after that. When we were alone, Jessie said she understood how I felt, but she asked that I try to be civil to Stein during the conference. I understood why she asked and said I would be, and I was.

Judge Marshall greeted us in his courtroom, then he invited us into chambers. He explained the conference was informal and not on the record. That made me feel a little better, and my hostility index dropped 50 points. I felt even better when the judge took out a copy of my memo and asked Stein if he or his client contested its authenticity. The way the judge asked the question suggested he expected the answer to be "no." Stein thought about it for a moment but then said "no."

The judge smiled, then looking directly at me, he said that he understood I had a bit of a history, but as things stood, he saw no reason to go into it. Then he looked at Stein and asked if Mr. Barrows was prepared to dismiss his claim. Stein knew the case was over, and he wasn't about to put his ass on the line for Barrows, so he simply nodded his head. Judge Marshall nodded his approval and said he'd issue the order of dismissal that afternoon.

That was our cue that the conference was over, and we all stood. Stein said goodbye and left immediately. Jessie thanked the judge, shaking his hand. Murray followed suit, and then it was my turn. As I shook the judge's hand, he asked, "Still a friend of Bill W's?" If you don't know, Bill W is

Bill Wilson, the founder of AA, and the question is code for "I'm in AA; are you?" I smiled and said, "A card-carrying lifer." The judge just smiled.

Outside of the courtroom, Jessie asked what my little conversation with the judge was all about. I told her it was just small talk. She left it at that, and we all said goodbye. Little did I know what awaited me as I walked back to my office.

CHAPTER 64

I've lived in New York City my entire life and never been mugged until the incident two weeks earlier. I wasn't even mugged back in the 1980s when street crimes were at an all-time high, and I was living in a high crime area.

So you can imagine my surprise when as I was walking down Mott Street, someone grabbed me and shoved me into the hallway of one of the old pre-war buildings. He wasn't a big man, but he was strong. He twisted my right arm behind my back and pushed me down the hallway and against the wall under the staircase. Then he pressed his free arm against my neck, forcing my face into the wall. It was déjà vu. Only this time it was definitely a Chinese accented voice asking where Li Chin was.

When I didn't answer right away, my attacker pressed his forearm more forcefully against my neck, pushing my face harder against the wall. He asked again where Li Chin was. This time I decided I had better say something because if he pressed any harder on my neck, something was going to break, and it wasn't going to be his arm.

I said I didn't know where Li Chin was. It apparently was not the right answer. I knew that because when I said it, my left arm was pushed further upward toward my collar. None of this was doing my shoulder any good, and I let out a yelp of pain.

My attacker asked again where Li Chin was. I had a feeling he wasn't going to give up, and I wanted to keep my arm attached to my shoulder, so I said she was in China. It was the truth, but I wasn't sure he was going to believe me. I grimaced and waited for the next level of pain, but it never came. Instead, I was pushed to the ground and left there.

I make light of the incident now, but it shook me up when it happened. I sat on the floor in that hallway for a good five minutes collecting myself and waiting for the pain in my shoulder to subside. But it didn't go away, so eventually I got up and walked to my office.

My suit was a bit dirty from sitting on the hallway floor, and my face must have shown I was in pain because Connie kept asking me what was wrong. I didn't tell her what happened; instead, I told her I slipped on the courthouse steps.

Later that night when I told the story to Gracie, she said it probably meant I was making Yeoung nervous which was a good thing. Not necessarily for my health, but for Richie's case. I had to agree and would have offered Gracie a congratulatory toast with my water glass, but I was having problems moving my left arm.

I'm no wimp, and I have a pretty high tolerance for pain. But sometimes I could use a little sympathy. That was one of the times. Unfortunately, I wasn't going to get any sympathy from Gracie. Gracie is very solicitous, but she's not very sympathetic. She'll ask me if I'm okay, which is her way of showing concern. But if I say "no" or hesitate, she'll just ask if I want an Aleve. Then if I say "yes," she'll tell me they're in the medicine cabinet. Gracie is a lot of things, but a Clara Barton isn't one them.

There was a lesson to be learned from all of this. I just wasn't sure what that lesson was. Even if Gracie was right and Yeoung was nervous, I wasn't sure how that was going to help me.

If Yeoung was looking for Li Chin, he probably believed she had robbed the safe, and he wanted to recover whatever had been taken. The only logical reason for him to suspect Li Chin had robbed the safe was if McNulty had told him she had done it. Even if Yeoung didn't believe McNulty, he was leaving no stone unturned.

It seemed clear that the relationship between McNulty and Yeoung had soured. Whether it had deteriorated to the point of open hostility remained to be seen. But it was becoming more obvious that the two men were now on divergent paths, and the contents of the safe were at the center of their falling-out.

I needed to find out what had been in the safe. I doubted Yeoung would tell me, and McNulty sure as hell wasn't going to tell me. My only hope was Joe Hadden, and IAB would recover whatever it was when they arrested McNulty.

CHAPTER 65

At nine o'clock Friday night, I was standing in the police headquarters garage, along with Tommy, Detective Evans and a dozen or so cops. Six were in uniform; they were the tech guys who would operate the equipment in the Mobile Command Unit. The rest were in street clothes. They were the backup unit that would hang out around the edges of the project, ready to move in if things started going badly.

I re-introduced myself to Detective Evans, who at least pretended he was happy to see me. He welcomed me to ride along in the Mobile Command Unit as an observer. His choice of words and his tone of voice made it clear that I was not to say or do anything during the operation. I played along, not wanting to jeopardize my ride.

Earlier in the week, Tommy had met with Evans and was measured for a sport coat. It seemed odd to him at the time, but now it made sense. The sport coat had buttons that concealed a small, but powerful microphone and video transmitter. The transmission range was short, but relay boxes were positioned throughout the project to insure the signals reached the Mobile Command Unit.

Evans didn't think Jerome was sophisticated enough to check Tommy for transmitters, but he wasn't taking any chances. The transmitter couldn't be detected while it was inactive, and it would remain inactive until Tommy thought it was safe to turn it on. Then he would activate the transmitter by buttoning, then unbuttoning, one of the buttons on the jacket. Once the transmitter was activated, we'd have eyes and ears in the Mobile Command Unit.

Evans went through the operational plan with Tommy and the crew one last time to ensure everyone knew what they had to do. The last order of business was the safe word. That night it was "hold on." I was tempted to point out it was two words, but I figured this was one of the times when Evans expected me to be quiet.

If Tommy said, "hold on," the operation was over, and the undercover cops in the area would rush to his aid. Evans also had the option of pulling the plug by using the command "code red," along with the words, "go, go." Those were the words I wanted to know.

With everyone briefed, it was time to saddle up and move out, as they used to say in the old cowboy movies.

Evans gave Tommy an attaché case containing the $32,000 in unmarked bills. Jerome had insisted on old cash, and he was sure to check the serial numbers on the bills for consecutive numbering. Evans wasn't taking any chances, so the money was clean.

The undercover teams left first, traveling in old vehicles not likely to arouse suspicion. Then Evans, the tech guys, and I climbed into the Mobile Command Unit. Tommy would leave later in a BMW, on loan from the NYPD collection of impounded vehicles.

The Mobile Command Unit that night was in a medium-sized U-Haul box truck. On the outside it looked like a typical U-Haul truck, a bit battered and dirty. On the inside it looked like the control room of a spaceship. The walls were lined with sophisticated communications equipment and video monitors. There were six work stations, three on each side of the truck, with chairs bolted to the floor in front of each work station. Behind the chairs, there two long benches where observers could sit and watch the video screens. Hanging from the roof of the truck over the benches was a series of headphones.

Evans directed me to one of the benches. He sat next to me, and reaching up, he handed me a set of headphones. He said, once we were in position and Tommy's microphone and camera went online, I could listen in on the headphones, and watch the action on the video monitor in front of me. Now it was blank.

In those types of situations, I usually have a couple of smart-ass comments to make, but that night I wasn't feeling the need to heckle. I always knew Tommy's work was dangerous, but this was the first time I was literally coming face-to-face with that danger. I was nervous, and I was worried.

We were in position, parked on 155th Street, well before 11 o'clock. Evans used his walkie-talkie radio to check in with the undercover teams, all of whom had worked their way into positions around the project. Two members of the team, posing as drunks, had dropped the relay transmitters into wastebaskets at the predetermined locations, then they moved on. After the buy, they'd go back and retrieve the relay transmitters, but for now, they moved far enough away not to arouse suspicion.

All that remained was for Tommy to arrive.

As 11o'clock approached, the undercover teams began reporting people on the roofs of the buildings. They were the lookouts. Except for the two undercover cops, posing as drunks, none of the teams had gone near the location where Tommy and Jerome were scheduled to meet, for fear of being made and killing the deal.

Just before 11 o'clock, the BMW arrived, and Tommy made his way into the project, passing two of the undercover teams on their way in.

We sat waiting inside the Mobile Command Unit. There was a digital clock on the panel in front of me, and I kept looking at it as I waited anxiously for the video screen to come alive. 11:05, nothing. 11:10, still nothing.

Evans could tell I was nervous and said it was early; he didn't expect any action for a while. 11:15, still no video. I was hoping Evans knew what he was talking about. 11:20, nothing. At 11:27, I was about to shout, *code red., go, go*, when the video screens came alive.

I pulled the headphones on and heard Tommy's voice. There was a good deal of static, making it difficult to understand what everyone was saying. The video was pretty decent, and I could see someone I presumed was Jerome. He was surrounded by six or seven guys, all gangbanger types. Two of them held pistols in their hands, which didn't make me feel any better about the situation.

I listened and watched as Tommy opened the attaché case and showed Jerome the cash. Then he closed the case and demanded to see the kilo of cocaine. Jerome reached back, and one of his goons handed him a bundle. Tommy said he wanted to test the cocaine for quality, and Jerome handed him the brick. Tommy cut a small slit in the package, removed some of the powder, and put it in a test tube filled with liquid. The sample must have passed muster because Tommy handed the attaché case to Jerome.

Then Tommy said he'd be back for more. Jerome wanted to know how much more and when he'd want it. Tommy said soon. As for how much more, he asked Jerome how much he could handle. Jerome laughed and said as much as Tommy could afford. Tommy didn't answer right away. It was like he was sizing up Jerome, then he said next time he'd want ten keys, meaning ten kilos.

Jerome frowned. He looked Tommy up and down, and said he'd need a couple of days' notice, but it was doable. Price was $300,000. Tommy laughed. Evans tensed, and I got nervous. What was Tommy doing? He should have just agreed; there wasn't going to be an actual buy next time, just an arrest.

Tommy said if they were going to continue doing business, he wanted a bulk discount. It was Jerome's turn to laugh. He said he couldn't be blamed for trying, but if it was ten keys, the price was $250,000. The two shook hands, and everyone in the Mobile Command Unit relaxed.

Fifteen minutes later everyone was on their way back to One Police Plaza. It had been a good night's work. Next time it would hopefully end with arrests and Jerome being put out of the drug business.

CHAPTER 66

The next day was Saturday, and I don't usually work on weekends. Since Gracie and I have been together, we've made it a rule to reserve that time for ourselves. There are exceptions to the rule, and Richie's case going to trial in a couple of weeks was one of them.

I wasn't feeling my usual confidence, and that was a bad sign. It meant that, as much as I hated to admit it, I wasn't sure I could win Richie's case. Don't get me wrong. I don't normally think I can win every case, but I usually have options. Options like plea deals. But with Richie refusing to even consider a plea deal, it was an all-or-nothing situation.

Trust me, that's never a good thing, especially when the gamble involves twenty-five years to life in prison.

If it was anybody other than Richie, I wouldn't have been so conflicted. I've been in situations where the client refuses to cop a plea and winds up going away for a long time. Those cases never bothered me because the clients were jerks and besides, I knew they were all guilty anyway. But in Richie's case, I knew he was innocent, and he wasn't a jerk, just pigheaded. Okay, maybe he was being a little bit of a jerk.

So that was my mood on that Saturday morning. It was definitely a mood that makes for a bad day. The kind of mood that always leads to an argument with Gracie. So, rather than hang around and start a fight, I decided I'd go to the office for a couple of hours.

I called Tommy and Abe and asked them if they could meet me there. If I was going to have a crappy weekend, at least I'd have some company. Tommy had gone out clubbing after the drug buy the night before, but he was up when I called and said he could be at the office in an hour. As for Abe, he said he didn't have anything better to do, so he'd be there as well.

The three of us hadn't gotten together in a while, and I thought it would be good if we did. I wanted to let Tommy and Abe know what was happening, and I wanted some fresh eyes looking at the situation. I wasn't sure what good it would do, but everybody knows three heads are better than one. That is so long as the three heads aren't on the same body. When they are, it gets messy.

I had just turned on the Keurig coffee machine when Abe and Tommy arrived. I congratulated Tommy on his performance as a drug dealer the night before. Then I warned him, if next time he took a chance like questioning the price, I'd pull the plug on the operation myself. He said he did it to keep it real. Bargaining the price was something a drug dealer would do. I had to admit that made sense.

Once we had our coffee poured, I told Abe and Tommy about my meeting with Hadden and my second mugging. Abe wanted to know if I had reported the incident to the police. When I said I hadn't, he just shrugged his shoulders. He knew as well as I did that reporting the incident wouldn't have done any good.

Tommy, on the other hand, was furious and demanded I accept his offer of a "clean gun." I assured him there was no way in hell I was going to carry a gun. If I was attacked again, and my next assailant was like the first two, he wouldn't be armed, and I didn't intend to bring a gun to the party. I had to be realistic. I'm no fighter and certainly not a gun guy. So the odds were good that an assailant taking me by surprise would wind up with the damn gun in his hands. Being shot would be bad enough, but being shot by my own gun would be humiliating. Under the circumstances, I think I'd prefer death to humiliation. Well, maybe not, but I was being dramatic for Tommy's sake.

Tommy didn't agree with my logic, and he certainly wasn't impressed with my dramatic take on death. But he was smart enough to know my mind was made up and he dropped the subject.

Having put to rest the subject of my mugging, I explained what I had learned from Hadden. Tommy said the information Hadden had given me confirmed what he was hearing from his contacts. Word on the street was that Sam Yeoung wanted Li Chin, and he was offering big money to anyone who found her.

Abe added that one of his contacts in the DA's Office had called, asking if it was true that Li Chin was going to testify at Simone's trial. Obviously, listing Li Chin as a witness had aroused curiosity.

Tommy also confirmed there been a falling-out between McNulty and Yeoung. McNulty hadn't called Yeoung in a while and hadn't been seen at the Golden Palace. One of Tommy's contacts, a cook at the Golden Palace, told Tommy he'd overhead Yeoung screaming at McNulty.

We couldn't be sure what had caused the animosity between McNulty and Yeoung, but Abe's "pit 'em and split 'em" plan had certainly helped. I had little doubt that the contents of the safe was at the center of the dispute.

Abe suggested that with the trial beginning soon, it was a good time to review where we were, what we had, and where we were going. Abe's a planner; me, I'm more spontaneous, but Abe did have point. We had been moving in a number of directions, and it was time to pick a course and stick to it.

We agreed McNulty was the central figure in the case. As the sole eyewitness to the murder, he was the biggest obstacle we had to overcome. So far, we had done a good job gathering evidence to discredit him and his testimony. If his arrest on corruption charges didn't put it over the top, nothing would.

Once we were successful in discrediting McNulty's testimony, we were relying entirely on circumstantial evidence to prove McNulty had opportunity, means and motive to murder Kim Lee.

Proving opportunity was simple; he admitted he was there. Proving means was likewise simple; he had a gun of his own, and he could have taken Richie's gun.

Up to that point, Abe and I agreed. It was the next step, proving motive, where we disagreed. Not knowing what had been taken from the safe, I felt that we'd just be speculating if we made that the motive, and jurors don't like speculation.

Unable to come up with any other motive, I was thinking maybe I didn't need to prove motive. The District Attorney didn't have a motive for Richie killing Kim Lee, so why did I need one for McNulty killing her? I made my pitch and looked to Abe for his reaction.

Abe rolled his eyes and shook his head. He obviously didn't agree with me on motive. He said I needed to look at the case from a distance because I was missing the whole point.

The case turned on the jury deciding who killed Kim Lee. Was it Richie as McNulty claimed, or was it McNulty as I would claim? One question with two possible answers. So, who wins?

Abe believed the District Attorney had the advantage because of the forensic evidence. While that evidence wasn't fatal to our defense, it definitely gave the District Attorney an advantage. If I was going to overcome that advantage, I had to show McNulty had a motive for killing Kim Lee. And it had better be a good one. One the jury could believe.

When I thought about it, I knew Abe was right. McNulty was an eyewitness, so his testimony would normally carry a lot of weight with the jury. True, we would be able to discredit him and show he was a liar. Convincing the jury McNulty was a liar was one thing, convincing them he was a murderer was something else entirely. I had to give them a good reason. If I couldn't do that, then we'd lose the case. It was that simple.

A jury looks for simple explanations because simple explanations made the most sense. The jury would expect me to explain why McNulty planned this elaborate scheme, brought multiple guns to the raid, and framed Richie. If I didn't give them a reason, they weren't likely to believe my theory, especially if McNulty wasn't charged with Kim Lee's murder.

The reason McNulty killed Kim Lee was to steal whatever was in the safe. But if I wanted the jury to believe that, I had to tell them what was in the safe. Either I would know what it was, or I'd have to speculate, and I liked our chances a lot better if I knew what it was.

Tommy said he'd hit the streets and see what he could learn, but he wasn't confident. The Hip Sing Tong was a tight organization, and it wasn't going to be easy getting information.

There wasn't much I could think of doing other than to pester Hadden to look at McNulty for Kim Lee's murder.

Once McNulty was arrested, IAB would search his home and maybe that would turn up something I could use. Maybe even whatever McNulty had taken from the safe.

Of course, IAB would have no way of knowing if something had come from the safe at the brothel, but it didn't matter. If it looked like something that could have come from the brothel and it had any value, either for blackmailing Yeoung or any of the brothel's patrons, I could use it as motive. I've built defenses on shakier grounds than that.

We tossed the problems around for another hour and having accomplished nothing, we adjourned to Shoo's for lunch.

CHAPTER 67

It had been a hell of a weekend, starting with the ride Friday night in the cop-mobile for the drug buy and the unproductive meeting of the brain trust on Saturday. At least Sunday was uneventful and peaceful. Well, almost peaceful.

It started like any other Sunday morning, with coffee bagels and the *New York Times*. I was still fretting over Richie's case which is a bad habit I've yet to break. Fretting, that is. Some people call it obsessing, and when I say some people, I mean psychiatrists. I prefer my mother's term, fretting. Fretting not only sounds less threatening; it doesn't cost $300 an hour to cure.

As much as I sing the praises of the Serenity Prayer, the truth is there are times when it doesn't work for me. Trust me, the fault lies in me, not in the prayer. So, on that particular Sunday morning, as we sat drinking our coffee and munching on our bagels, I sat staring at the sports section of the *New York Times* and fretting.

I don't believe I behave any differently when I'm fretting than I do when I'm not fretting. But somehow Gracie always knows when I'm fretting. It must be one of those woman's intuition things.

My fretting has turned into something of a weekend game. As we sit having our coffee, Gracie reads my mood. She then confronts me, claiming to know what I'm feeling. I naturally deny I'm feeling anything, and then we duel.

Gracie wins if she gets me to concede my feelings, and she gets to pick our activity for the day. If I'm able to fend off Gracie's assault on my denial, I win, and I get to choose what we do the rest of the day. I'm looking forward to winning someday.

Anyway, Gracie asked me if I was still fretting over Richie's case. I denied thinking about Richie's case, and the game was on. Gracie, master of the sneak attack, surprised me with a direct assault. She asked what I was thinking about.

Caught by surprise, I knew I needed to answer quickly if I expected Gracie to believe me. Desperate, I looked to the sports page at which I had been staring blankly. The first thing that caught my eye was European volleyball scores, and I said that I was fretting over the Kazakhstan volleyball team having lost to Latvia. Gracie laughed and said she hadn't realized I was such a big Kazakhstan fan.

At that point, an intelligent man would have just let it go and accepted defeat. But I'm not an intelligent man, so I added that I'd been a big fan of the Kazakhstan volleyball team since I was a kid. I said I even had all the bubble gum cards for the team from 1967 to 1970. They'd be worth a fortune today, but unfortunately my mother had thrown them away.

As an aside, you're usually safe with the story about your mother throwing away your bubble gum card collection. It seems there's something in the universal mother's manual that requires a good mother to throw away your bubble gum card collection the first time you leave the house for more than two months.

I was in deep, well over my head, and Gracie damn well knew it. She wanted to know the name of the Kazakhstan's star player. Given a minute or two, I might have been able to come up with a good bluff. But she had caught me by surprise, and I blurted out the first name that came to mind, Tigeras Woodistan. Gracie roared, and the game was over. All that remained was deciding the price I had to pay.

Gracie picked up the weekend section of the newspaper she had been reading and announced we'd be visiting MoMa. In case you're not a New Yorker, MoMa is the Museum of Modern Art. It's located on 53rd Street between Fifth and Sixth Avenues, which puts it somewhat in the middle of Manhattan. Despite its convenient location, I prided myself on never having set foot inside its doors during the first forty some odd years of my life. As you may have guessed, I'm not an art connoisseur, and museums aren't my thing. But I lost the game, and I had to pay the price.

Sunday afternoon was spent walking the galleries of MoMa, listening to Gracie utter "ahs" and "ohs," while I just grunted. But Gracie is a good sport, so at the end of our march through the halls of modern art, she announced I could pick the restaurant for dinner.

We were on West 53rd Street, so the choice was obvious, Patsy's, an Italian restaurant on West 56th Street. It's another one of my favorite landmark restaurants. The place opened in 1944 and is still owned and operated by the Scognamillo family. Amazingly, it has had only three chefs in all that time, starting with Patsy, then his son, Joe, and then his grandson, Sal. It was one of Frank Sinatra's favorite restaurants. Need I say more?

As usual, we had a great meal. Afterward, we took the subway back downtown and walked around the East Village for a time. It turned out to be a great day, by the end of which I was no longer fretting over Richie's case, or the Kazakhstan volleyball team's loss.

CHAPTER 68

It had been over a week since the drug buy, and I was scheduled to meet with Tommy and Evans to discuss our next move. But before that, I had an appointment to see Sasha, so I wasn't going to have a lot of time to spend on Richie's case. Not that there was anything to do except fret. And I was doing a lot of fretting.

On my way to Rikers Island to meet with Sasha, I tried calling Joe Hadden again and got the same result. He wasn't available at the moment, but I could leave a message. I left my tenth message. I knew that I was being a pain in the ass, and Hadden was right in not taking my calls, but it still bothered me.

The last time I had spoken with Hadden, he assured me IAB was close to arresting McNulty, but so far nothing, and Hadden wasn't taking my calls. That's why I was worried. When I thought about it rationally, I knew that I was being a little crazy. It was the damn fretting thing. Time to call Doug.

When I called Doug, he could tell I was stressed, and the first thing he asked was when I had last been to a meeting. With all that had been going on, I hadn't been to one in a while, and I guess I needed one. So, right after I left Sasha at Rikers Island, I found a midday meeting and went.

I mention this for a reason. As an alcoholic, I don't always react rationally. Not that I don't want to, it's just part of being an alcoholic. My anxiety over Richie's case is probably normal, but like everything else, I can take it to an extreme. That's what I did when I drank. I didn't drink a little; I drank to an extreme. I didn't lie a little; I lied to an extreme. I did everything to extreme.

Left to my own devices, my alcoholic thinking will push me to those extremes. Maybe I won't drink, but I will fall into my old way of thinking if I'm not careful. I go to meetings because they help me to put things into perspective. Sometimes it works, sometimes it doesn't.

I can't say for sure if it worked that day or not. I did get my mind off Richie's case, but that may have been the result of my meeting with Evans and Tommy. After that meeting, I had something else to fret about.

We met at police headquarters, so all the brass could attend, but apparently none of them were interested, so it was just Tommy, Evans, three of his guys, and me. It was better that way; all the white shirts did was to ask a lot of ridiculous questions and turn a half hour meeting into a two-hour meeting.

Tommy had contacted Jerome White and said he was ready to cut a deal for 10 kilos of cocaine. Jerome wanted to meet in advance to discuss the terms of the buy. Tommy agreed but wanted the meeting to take place on neutral ground. In the end, they agreed to meet in Bryant Park, behind the New York City Library, at noon. The park would be busy, and therefore, an unlikely place for an ambush.

Evans wanted to stake out the location, but Tommy objected, fearing White would sense a setup and pull out of the deal. I preferred having the cops staking out the meeting, but I had to agree with Tommy that the risk was too high. The meeting was going to happen in a public place, so the risk was a lot lower than if they met in the projects. Besides, White had no reason to suspect Tommy was anything but a legitimate dealer.

In the end, Evans agreed not to cover the meeting. Tommy would be on his own. I didn't like it that way, but Tommy could take care of himself.

Tommy would try to set up a deal for the coming weekend. Preferably Saturday night, which would give Evans and his people more time to set things up. This time around, the undercover guys had to be in closer proximity to the buy to make the arrest as soon as the deal went down.

Then we hit a snag. Evans didn't want to put $250,000 in the attaché case. He said they'd put real bills on top of the stacks, but the rest would be fake money. Tommy said that wouldn't work. White was sure to want to examine the money before he turned over the drugs, just as Tommy would want to examine the drugs to make sure he wasn't being scammed before he released the money. After all, it wasn't unheard of for an unscrupulous drug dealer like White to substitute baby powder or baking soda for cocaine. With $250,000 in play, the possibility of a scam couldn't be ignored. The big problem was, if it turned out to be a scam, there'd be no drug crime.

Evans made a couple of phone calls, and in the end, the NYPD agreed to put up the whole $250,000 in used bills. However, a GPS bug would be hidden in the lining of the attaché case containing the cash. Even with that, Evans wasn't a happy camper. His ass was on the line, and if something went wrong and the $250,000 was lost, he'd probably end up walking a beat in Brooklyn.

I was very uncomfortable with the idea of Tommy carrying a quarter of a million dollars and meeting alone in the projects with White, so I threw a monkey wrench into the plan. I said the meeting wasn't going to happen unless Tommy had some of Evans' people with him when he met White.

Tommy was the first to object, but I reminded him he was working for me, and I could pull the plug on the operation anytime I wanted. That shut him up. Evans was ambivalent, and when he realized I was serious, he agreed to send two of his men to the buy with Tommy. Tommy did a little more grumbling, but he knew it was a done deal, and we moved on.

Tommy and I had just left the Ivory Tower when my cell rang. It was Hadden. IAB was getting ready to arrest McNulty. It wouldn't be that week, but probably sometime the next week. He reminded me he was going out on the limb by telling me, and I needed to keep it to myself. I swore I would.

The timing on the news was good because the next call was from Connie, letting me know Richie's case was scheduled for jury selection two weeks from Wednesday. Everything was popping at once, and I must admit I was nervous as hell.

With jury selection scheduled, the trial was right around the corner, and I wasn't ready to go to trial. I had no solid defense that I was comfortable with. It was a form of my worst nightmare, the one where I stand up in court and suddenly realize I'm naked. You'd think I would have noticed it before I got to court, or at least before I stood up, but then it wouldn't be as much of a nightmare, would it?

I was staring reality in the face, and I wasn't happy with what I was seeing. Most of the tactics I had tried failed to produce any solid evidence. Adding Li Chin's name to the witness list hadn't done much other than getting me mugged. Dropping Joey Peng's name into the mix hadn't done much either. If it had put a wedge between McNulty and Yeoung, as we had hoped, it wasn't helping. Of course, it might have gotten Peng killed, which I'm sure he didn't appreciate.

Getting IAB involved had been our best tactic, and the one I was now relying on for a defense. Whether simply discrediting McNulty's testimony would be enough to raise reasonable doubt about Richie's guilt, was questionable. The "other guy did it" defense wasn't a lock, not without a solid motive. Overall, I rated our chances as good, but with so much on the line, good wasn't good enough. I wanted excellent, but would have settled for very good.

That was why I wasn't ready to go to trial. When you're not confident in your case, you want to put off the trial for as long as possible, hoping that something goes your way at some point. That was my state of mind when I got the jury selection notice.

CHAPTER 69

Abe and I were working on a jury selection strategy when Tommy arrived to give us his surveillance report. He had been keeping tabs on Yeoung and any ongoing connection with McNulty, but nothing had turned up. Yeoung had been seen around Chinatown and at the Golden Palace, but there had been no sign of McNulty and no phone calls between the two.

McNulty must have ditched the burner phone he used to call Yeoung, because he sure as hell wasn't making any calls to Yeoung, or for that matter, to anyone else. Whatever was happening, McNulty and Yeoung weren't talking, at least not to each other.

It was rumored in the street that Yeoung and McNulty had a major falling-out. Supposedly, after the raid on the brothel, Yeoung was furious with McNulty. No one was sure why, but some suspected it was because McNulty hadn't given Yeoung enough advance notice of the raid. That made sense, but I was betting Yeoung was upset because he believed McNulty had stolen something from the safe.

Whatever caused the rift, one thing was certain, Yeoung was cutting his ties with McNulty. Linda Chow had been keeping tabs on GM Properties, Yeoung's money laundering realty company, operated by McNulty's son, George. Within two days of Tommy's visit to the company, it had gone dark. Its website was taken down, its phones weren't answered, and its online footprint disappeared.

Digging deeper, Linda discovered that within days of GM Properties closing down, Silver Star Assets, which held mortgages on all the GM properties, had taken ownership under an obscure clause in the loan agreement. The clause giving Silver Star the power to reclaim the properties at any time, without having to resort to legal proceedings. Since Silver Star was a wholly owned subsidiary of Yeoung's South Sea Enterprises, the clause gave Yeoung a simple and fast way to reclaim his properties and cut his ties with McNulty.

Obviously, the relationship between Yeoung and McNulty was over, and it hadn't ended on a good note. At least not for McNulty and his son, who was now out his million-dollar salary.

It was all very interesting, but it wasn't necessarily helpful. I needed to know more. Like, what McNulty stole from the safe and what made it so valuable.

We were tossing around some ideas when Tommy said he had to run. He was meeting with Jerome White in Bryant Park the next day, and he had some logistics to deal with. I asked Tommy what logistics were involved, but he brushed off the question, saying it was just standard stuff.

I wasn't sure what Tommy had in mind, but I felt better knowing he was preparing for the meeting and not going in cold. I worry about Tommy because, at times, he's been reckless, even by my standards. I know he has a gun, and he's an expert in martial arts, which is good. But gangbangers like Jerome White are vicious, callous punks who tend to be unpredictable and that makes them extremely dangerous. In a gunfight, the first one to pull the trigger usually wins, and Tommy's not the type to fire first.

It turned out I had nothing to worry about. The next evening Tommy called and said he had met with White, and everything had gone off without a hitch. The drug sale had been set up for Saturday night. He was meeting with Detective Evans and his crew the next day to work out the final plans. I wasn't needed at the meeting, but I was invited to sit in on the big event.

CHAPTER 70

It was four o'clock in the morning, and I was sound asleep when my cell phone rang. A telephone ringing in the middle of the night scares the crap out of you. You just know it can't be good news, so my heart was pounding as I fumbled to answer the phone.

I was wrong; it was good news. It was Joe Hadden letting me know an IAB arrest team was on its way to arrest McNulty.

Executing arrest warrants is a dicey operation because the arrest team is never certain what they'll encounter. That's why, given the option, they prefer conducting arrest raids during the early morning hours. It adds an element of surprise, which always works in their favor. Plus, someone coming out of a deep sleep is likely be disorientated, making them less of a physical threat.

Hadden said the arrest team wasn't expecting McNulty to put up a fight, but they weren't taking any chances. Knowing McNulty had at least one weapon in his home, the team had secured a "no knock" warrant, allowing them to enter the premises without notice or warning. If things went as planned, it would be a quick and easy takedown.

Hadden estimated the arrest would happen in about twenty minutes and promised to call me as soon as McNulty was in custody. That was the good news. The bad news was, there would be no perp walk. The brass wanted the arrest to be kept as quiet as possible. McNulty would be taken to One Police Plaza, processed there, and then sent quietly to Central Booking. The Commissioner's Office would issue a press release once McNulty was in custody.

The ringing phone had awakened Gracie, and after I explained what was happening, she offered to make coffee while I got dressed. I brought my cell phone along into the bathroom and kept it nearby as I showered and shaved. It wasn't going to take me much time to shower and shave, but I didn't want to miss Hadden's call if things happened faster than expected.

I had finished showering and shaving and was nearly dressed when the phone rang. Everything had gone smoothly, and McNulty was in custody and on his way to One Police Plaza.

I thanked Hadden for the heads-up, finished dressing, and went to have coffee with Gracie. While we were having coffee, I called Richie. I knew it was early, and he was probably asleep, but I figured he'd want to hear the news.

He answered with the groggy voice of someone awakened from a deep sleep, but like most of us, he denied he was asleep at the time. Before I could tell him the news, he started yelling at me for not using the burner phone. But once I got him to shut up and told him the news, he mellowed considerably.

I heard Laura yelling happily in the background when Richie told her the news of McNulty's arrest. I said I'd call him later from the office to discuss our next move.

Gracie poured me a cup of coffee, and I turned on the television, hoping to find some news of the arrest. All of the TV stations were in overnight mode, but I knew they all had news crews on standby. I had hoped someone would have picked up news of the arrest, but apparently no one had.

It didn't matter, because all the news outlets monitored the booking log at Central Booking, and they would pick up the arrest once McNulty was processed. If they didn't, the press release from the Commissioner's Office would certainly get their attention, or so I thought.

CHAPTER 71

When I got to the office and started checking the news sites, the story of McNulty's arrest was nowhere to be found. By noon, the story should have made the news, but it hadn't, and I started to worry. I didn't know what was going on, but whatever it was, it couldn't be good.

I called Hadden, but got no answer on his cell. When I called the IAB office, I was told Hadden was unavailable. I was trying to figure out what to do next when Connie announced Richie was on the line.

Richie was elated over the recent turn of events, but wanted to know why there was nothing on the news about McNulty. I told him the truth. I didn't know why, but I was going to find out. Naturally, Richie wasn't happy with my answer, but he didn't make an issue of it. He just asked me to keep him posted, and then he hung up.

By now, Abe had shown up, and I was filling him in on what had happened when Hadden finally returned my call. Hadden said the arrest had gone smoothly, and everything had gone according to plan, at least until they got McNulty to police headquarters. At that point, McNulty asked to make a phone call, which everyone presumed was to his lawyer. But twenty minutes later, before the booking process started, the FBI and a United States Attorney showed up and stopped everything.

Within half an hour, the Manhattan District Attorney arrived, and there was a closed-door meeting between the FBI guys, the US Attorney, the District Attorney, and Hadden's boss. When the meeting ended, the FBI left, taking McNulty with them.

Hadden had no idea what happened in the meeting, and when he asked his boss, his boss said it was way above his pay grade. Whatever had happened, McNulty was no longer in NYPD custody. That was all Hadden knew. He promised to let me know if he learned anything else.

I relayed the story to Abe, who was just as shocked as I was over the turn of events. We agreed the only way the FBI and the US Attorney would be involved was if McNulty had committed some federal crime, or if he was turning on Yeoung on some federal charge. But even then, the DA still had jurisdiction over McNulty, and there was no reason to turn McNulty over to the Feds.

It was all very puzzling, and none of it made any sense. Abe and I tossed around ideas, and eventually Abe suggested McNulty might have worked out an immunity deal on the corruption charges by giving the Feds information on Yeoung's human smuggling and drug operations. The DA might have agreed to the deal because he needed McNulty's testimony in Richie's case, and McNulty would be a more credible witness if he wasn't charged with corruption.

It made sense, but I wasn't buying it. We were talking about Chinatown and the Tongs. In Chinatown, secrets are more plentiful than grains of rice. Secrets that would never be shared with an outsider like McNulty. Not to mention the Tong's code of silence.

There was just no way McNulty could have gotten enough information about Yeoung to bring him down. Certainly not from Yeoung and not from anyone else in the Tong.

But whatever it was that McNulty had, it was likely a game changer. I knew Richie would be waiting anxiously to hear from me, and it wasn't fair to keep him in the dark. I called him on my office phone. He answered on the first ring, which meant he was sitting by the phone waiting for my call. I told him everything I knew, which wasn't much, and he wasn't happy. He asked what it meant for his case.

He had the call on speaker, and Laura was listening. Regrettably, there wasn't much to say. The DA's case against Richie relied heavily on McNulty's testimony, and we had been counting on McNulty's arrest to discredit his testimony. But, if McNulty wasn't formally charged with corruption, we might lose that opportunity, and that would be bad.

Laura interrupted and asked if the case against Richie would be over if McNulty was charged with corruption. I could tell from the way she asked the question, she was hoping for a positive answer. Unfortunately, I had to disappoint her.

I explained, as gently as I could, that even if McNulty was charged with corruption, the case against Richie wouldn't be over. The DA had forensic evidence proving the bullets that killed Kim Lee came from Richie's gun. But, the forensic evidence alone might not be enough to support a conviction. The evidence that Richie was the one who pulled the trigger was circumstantial, and the odds of the jury believing it was fifty-fifty at best.

All that changed, however, with McNulty's testimony. He put the gun in Richie's hand, and if the jury believed him, a conviction was almost guaranteed. We needed to discredit McNulty's testimony, and our best shot at doing so was to prove he was a corrupt and disgraced cop. But now I wasn't sure what was happening with McNulty.

Naturally, Laura wasn't happy with my analysis. She thought nobody would believe McNulty and wanted to know why I didn't simply ask the DA to dismiss the case.

Hoping not to sound totally negative, I said the DA might be willing to offer a plea deal. Before I could finish the thought, Richie interrupted, and said he would not plead to anything that required him going to prison and hung up the phone.

Abe had overheard most of the conversation, and I asked him for his thoughts. Not surprisingly, he had reached the same conclusion that I had. Until we knew what was going on with McNulty and the Feds, we couldn't be sure how it affected Richie's case. The best we could do was put out feelers and hope we'd learn something before Richie's trial started.

My job had been clear from the start, and nothing had really changed. Since Richie was adamant he wouldn't agree to any plea deal involving jail time, I had to either convince Marty Bowman to drop the case, or I had to prepare for trial, and hope like hell I could, in some way, create reasonable doubt in the jurors' minds.

I hadn't had much to work with from the, beginning, and now the little I did have was fast falling apart. When I said our best chance at an acquittal was still offering the alternate theory of the crime in which McNulty was the murderer, Abe shook his head and said, "It's not your best chance; it's your only chance for an acquittal."

I wanted to call Marty Bowman and arrange a meeting to discuss Richie's case, hoping to learn what was happening. But I didn't want to seem too anxious. As much as I was concerned about the case, Marty had to be concerned as well.

Looking at things from his perspective, his open-and-shut case just took a hit, maybe not as big a hit as I had hoped for, but a hit nonetheless. His one and only eyewitness, the likely key to his case, turned out to be a despicable felon. Or maybe not, depending on what the Feds were doing. That was the big unknown.

I'd just had to wait and hope the Feds brought charges against McNulty, and they did it soon. In the meantime, I'd wait for Hadden to let me know how NYPD was handling McNulty. Until all of that played out, I wouldn't know for sure how badly our defense had been damaged.

Abe agreed I should wait at least a day before calling Marty. We'd wait to see if he called first. If he did, it could be a sign he was more worried about things than we were. Whenever you're in a situation like this one, it's like a chess game, and both sides try to read the tea leaves. I know I just mixed two metaphors, but I've never been very good at metaphors. I must have skipped class the day they were covered.

CHAPTER 72

In the next couple of days following McNulty's arrest, things went from strange to downright weird.

There was no further news about McNulty or his arrest. Neither the NYPD, nor the DA's Office, had anything to say about it. As for the Feds, they hadn't brought any charges or even acknowledged McNulty was in custody. It was as though the arrest had never happened, and I couldn't figure out why that was.

When I called Marty Bowman and asked what was going on with McNulty, Bowman acted as though nothing had happened. He said he was preparing for trial, and as far as he knew, McNulty would be his main witness. If Bowman wasn't blowing smoke, I had a big problem on my hands.

Then things got worse, if you can believe that. I checked the court records and discovered McNulty's case had been dismissed. No indictment had ever been issued, and his arrest record was sealed.

As if that wasn't enough, I learned McNulty had retired. He hadn't been drummed off the force in disgrace, but quietly retired, his rank and pension intact.

My defense was circling the drain and about to disappear entirely. I could still use McNulty's arrest against him when he testified, but now its impact had been seriously marginalized. In a matter of two days, McNulty had been mysteriously transformed from a corrupt cop on the take, and possibly a murderer, to a retired veteran police officer with an unblemished record. Talk about transformations.

If I at least knew why the case against McNulty had been dropped, I might be able to make more of it. I was calling Hadden three times a day, trying to get answers to my questions, but he wasn't taking my calls.

I still couldn't fathom how McNulty wiggled out of the corruption charge. Yeoung was a big fish, but he wasn't big enough to warrant letting McNulty off the hook on the corruption charges and then, on top of it, allowing him to retire on the city's dime. And why turn him over to the Feds?

If I was wrong, and McNulty did have information on Yeoung's human smuggling operation, how come no charges had been brought against Yeoung? And why was McNulty allowed to retire? The DA didn't have the authority to make that part of the deal. That had to have come from the NYPD. So, what was in it for NYPD?

The best defense was still the one where I convince the jury that McNulty killed Kim Lee. The one that was on life support at the moment. That one. It was the best defense, and as Abe had predicted, probably the only defense we had.

All I had to do was convince the jury that McNulty wasn't just a liar, but a murderer. The same McNulty who now wasn't even under a cloud of suspicion. Not only was it a heavy lift, I had to do it with no evidence and no provable motive. Had I still been drinking, you know where I'd be and what I'd be doing. Could you blame me?

But I was sober, and drinking wasn't an option. I'd do what I could, with what I had, and hope for the best.

I would confront McNulty with his arrest when I cross-examined him, even though the case was dismissed. The judge was likely to give me some latitude in my cross-examination, and I had to take full advantage of that latitude. I planned on asking as many questions as I could about the charges before the judge cut me off. It was the only way I could let the jury know what McNulty was actually like, or at least what the DA had originally thought he was like.

After that, I'd be able to ask him about the plea deal that resulted in the dismissal of the charges. He couldn't outright lie about the plea deal because that would open him up to perjury charges, but I was sure he'd fudge it as much as he could. Still, the fact that he took a plea deal would tell the jury he wasn't completely innocent. They would have to decide for themselves just how guilty he was. Of course, it would have worked out a lot better if the charges hadn't been dropped.

With Abe sitting in, I called Richie and explained to him and Laura what was happening. They understood things weren't going well, at least not as well as we had hoped, but when I suggested a plea deal, Richie went crazy again.

I figured Richie would react that way, but I said it, hoping Laura would get the message and might be able to persuade him to change his mind. It seemed to be working because Laura started asking what a plea deal would involve. But before I could answer, Richie hung up the phone.

I sat at my desk in despair. All I had were lots of questions and no answers. I was frustrated, so I did what I usually do when I get frustrated. I called Doug and then went to a meeting. Doug didn't have any answers, and I didn't find any at the meeting either.

CHAPTER 73

I had done everything I could think of to do preparing for Richie's trial, so unless something changed, there was nothing more I could do, except fret. Fret and hope something broke soon. Of course, the only thing left that could break was news from Hadden, and I wasn't counting on that happening any time soon. Whatever the deal had been with McNulty, no one was saying anything about it. Not the DA, not the Feds, and certainly not Hadden.

When Laura called, I can't say I was surprised. I was hoping our last conversation had gotten the point across that Richie was in trouble and needed to consider a plea deal. As soon as Laura said she was at her girlfriend's house and not at home, I knew she had gotten the message.

Laura wasted no time getting to heart of the matter. She asked if I thought Richie was going to prison. It was one of those questions, where the answer is obvious, but you don't want to say it. I tried to soften the blow, but when I began dancing around the point, Laura shut me down. She wouldn't be put off. She demanded I tell her the truth and not sugarcoat it. So, I told her the truth, Richie was probably going to do serious prison time.

Laura took the news better than I expected. She didn't argue the point or question my judgment, she simply gave a little sigh and then asked what a plea deal would involve. I tried to explain that as things stood, I couldn't negotiate a deal because I didn't have Richie's permission to do so. Laura said I shouldn't worry about that because, when the time came, she'd convince him to take a deal. Knowing Richie as I did, I doubted it, but I was hoping she was right.

As for a plea deal, I figured the best we could hope for was a reduction in the charge from murder to manslaughter. That would reduce the crime from a class A felony to a B or C felony, depending on how generous I could convince Marty Bowman to be.

With a conviction on a class A felony, Richie was looking at twenty years to life, but with a class B felony, it was five to twenty-five years, and with a class C felony, it dropped all the way down to three to fifteen years. Worst case, Richie would do twenty years in prison. Best case, he'd do two years.

If things had gone better with McNulty, I might have even been able to negotiate a plea all the way down to criminally negligent homicide, a class E felony with no jail time, or one and one half to four years, at most. But that wasn't likely, given what had happened with McNulty.

Laura listened intently while I explained all of the possibilities. Then she told me to negotiate a deal. I told her I wasn't comfortable doing it behind Richie's back, but I would at least contact Marty Bowman and see which way the wind was blowing. If I thought we had a chance at a good deal, I'd sit down with her and Richie, and we'd try to work it out. That satisfied Laura.

I had just gotten off the phone with Laura when Tommy arrived. His meeting with Detective Evans had gone well, and everything was set for Saturday night. I wanted to know all the details, but Tommy said I didn't need to know them. All I needed to do was show up at the police headquarters parking garage on Saturday night at eight-thirty.

I didn't like being shut out on the details. That was mostly due to my need to be in charge. As you can imagine, with Gracie around, it's difficult for me to be in charge. But we've worked out a reasonable compromise. Gracie is in charge of all the little things, while I'm in charge of the really important things. Things like, going to war and raising the interest rate. I'm sure there are other things; it's just none have come up yet.

Oh, I nearly forgot, picking the movie for movie night every other month. That's a shared power, but when it's my turn to pick the movie, I get this tremendous feeling of being in charge. I used to wander about in the video store on Mott Street for an hour, reveling in my power, as I pondered the titles. But now we stream the movies, so I can't wander about lauding over my minions. Gracie offered to get me a crown to wear while I picked the movie, but I don't think she was serious. I would have liked a crown. Nothing fancy, just a simple crown.

I mentioned movie night because that night was movie night, and it was Gracie's turn to pick the movie.

CHAPTER 74

It had been a rough day, and I and was feeling out of sorts. Between what was happening with McNulty, and worrying about what might happen to Tommy, I wasn't in a very good mood. We were supposed to go to one of Gracie's sushi joints for a quick raw fish dinner before watching the movie. I wasn't looking forward to it, but it was on the schedule for a week, so I couldn't very well complain about it.

I called Gracie to finalize our plans, and I must have sounded pathetic because Gracie suggested, instead of going out for sushi, we bring in a pizza. She even said I could pick the movie. That perked me up, and I volunteered to pick up a large pie with pepperoni and meet her at her place.

If you're down in Greenwich Village, and you want a great thin crust pizza, go to John's of Bleecker Street. John Sasso began making pizzas in his coal fired brick oven on Sullivan Street in Greenwich in 1929. Since then the business moved to Bleecker Street and Sasso sold it, but it's still family owned and operated, and they still make the pizzas in the same coal fired brick ovens. You just can't beat a pizza cooked in a brick oven.

A large eight-slice pie will set you back $20 and $4 more if you add pepperoni, but trust me, it's worth it. Here's another suggestion. If it's date night, don't get the anchovies or the extra garlic.

Anyway, I picked up the pizza, and we ate it on the roof of Gracie's building. We keep a couple of lawn chairs up there, and on nice nights, we watch the sunset and the city light up. Some nights we bring dinner or snacks, other times just a cup of coffee or a cold drink. It doesn't matter. I always find it very calming and reassuring, watching the sunset and seeing the city start to twinkle. I guess it reminds me I survived another day.

After our roof top dinner, we retired to Gracie's apartment and watched "The In-Laws." Not the remake, but the original, with Alan Arkin and Peter Falk. I think it's one of the funniest movies ever made, and it's certainly one of my favorites. That's why I make Gracie watch it at least two times a year. In case you haven't noticed, I have this thing when it comes to movies. I like to watch some of them over and over and over. As I had to remind Gracie on occasion, that doesn't make me a bad person. A pain in the ass maybe, but a bad person, no.

Gracie didn't complain about seeing the movie for the umpteenth time. I know she was sick and tired of seeing the movie and listening to me recite the dialog, along with the actors, but she watched, quietly nestled in my arms. She did it to make me feel better. Which was the same reason she canceled our sushi dinner and suggested pizza. You've got to love a woman like that, and I do.

You might be wondering why we haven't gotten married. It's simple; neither of us wants to screw up a good thing. We're both very independent people and not necessarily in a good way. I think we're both afraid to give up our independence, but don't really know why. Maybe we're both insecure. God knows I am. I put on a good show, but when times get tough, like they were with Richie's case, I can be as insecure as Woody Allen. Well, maybe not that insecure, but close.

Nothing happened that night to change Richie's case, but I felt better, a lot better. Gracie had made me feel better, not because of the pizza and the movie, but because I knew Gracie was looking out for me.

Before I met Doug and got into AA, I felt no one except my mother had ever looked out for me. In AA, I came to realize that part of the problem was I hadn't looked out for anyone besides myself, so I could hardly blame anyone else for not looking out for me. I started to change, and that was when my relationship with Gracie grew.

Right now, our relationship works well for the both of us. Maybe over time, things will change. Who knows? I've learned to live my life one day at time, and I intend to keep doing that.

CHAPTER 75

The day after talking with Laura, I decided to approach Marty Bowman to see if he was interested in working out a plea deal. I knew the District Attorney was being pressured by the mayor to get some headline-grabbing convictions, and Richie's case offered that potential. But the DA hadn't seemed very interested in pursuing the case to begin with, and now with a potential scandal on his hands, everyone might be anxious to put the case to bed.

The media had lost interest in the case, and without all the sensational headlines, public interest faded fast. But the situation was likely to change once jury selection began.

Now was the best time to try to work out a plea deal. Of course, I was doing all of this against Richie's wishes. I was counting on Laura to deliver and convince Richie to take a deal, if I could work out a good one.

Marty Bowman agreed to meet me for lunch at the Worth Street Coffee Shop. He had to know why I wanted to meet. Talking plea deals is part of the process; it's expected. You buy the ADA lunch, or a drink and dinner, when you have the short end of the stick. So, by offering to buy Marty lunch, I was signaling I knew where I stood. I made it the Worth Street Coffee Shop and not a fancy restaurant, so he'd know I wasn't about to throw in the towel. When I have the upper hand, I usually suggest we meet for a hot dog, then if I don't get the deal I want, I stick the ADA with the tab. Not this time.

Since the corruption charges against McNulty had been dropped, my bargaining position had been substantially weakened. I still could raise the specter of corruption and question McNulty on the deal that resulted in the charges being dismissed. It wasn't as effective as if he had been arraigned on the charges, but basically it was the best I had.

Lunch with Marty proved interesting. Marty admitted that, after talking with several ADAs who had worked with Richie, he wasn't convinced Richie had killed Kim Lee. Marty was open to a reasonable plea deal, but his boss wasn't. His boss, a Chief Assistant District Attorney, was under pressure from the District Attorney, and he wasn't going to approve any plea deal that didn't include Richie doing some hard time.

The best deal Marty thought he could push would involve a fifteen-year sentence, which would mean Richie had to serve at least seven and a half years. There was no way Richie would agree to that, and I wouldn't recommend he accept it anyway.

Since Marty seemed to be in a talkative mood, I asked him how McNulty was able to swing his plea deal and have the corruption charges completely dropped. I didn't believe it had been done just to keep him clean for Richie's case, and Marty confirmed I was right about that. But Marty didn't know any of the details. He said whatever went down, it was way above his pay grade and even above his boss' pay grade. All either of them knew was that McNulty had something the Feds wanted badly enough to give him what the guys in the DA's Office were calling the "deal of the century."

Lunch with Marty had been interesting, but not particularly helpful. The only thing I learned was that we weren't going to get a plea deal unless I came up with a hell of a lot better cards. It also left me asking how a crooked cop got the deal of the century.

CHAPTER 76

When I arrived Saturday night at One Police Plaza for the big drug bust, I was surprised at the number of people waiting to be briefed. I knew it was a big operation, but I hadn't expected to see two dozen or more people involved.

When I mentioned my surprise to Detective Evans, he explained that working in the projects presented a unique set of problems, logistics being the major one. Since his people couldn't get close to where the buy would take place, he wanted to be sure he had enough personnel on hand to flood the area when the deal went down, so no one could escape. That was why he had a dozen plainclothes cops, and

Detectives who would be positioned in and around the project, and another dozen or so SWAT team members in two trucks located strategically near the project.

As soon as the transaction was completed, all units would move in and start making arrests.

I wondered how much of Evans' concern was prompted by the $250,000 of the city's money that Tommy would be carrying. Not that it mattered. What mattered to me was Tommy's protection, and even with the load of cops on hand, I was still worried. Yeah, I felt a little better knowing there would be a lot of cops, with a lot of fire power on hand, but Tommy was still going to be alone with Jerome and his gangbangers, and that worried me.

Yes, there would be a large force of cops nearby if things went sideways, and that sounded comforting, but it wasn't. If something went wrong, Tommy and Evans' two guys would be in the middle of it, right at ground zero. This big force would be nearby, but they'd have a lot of ground to cover before they got to Tommy. Evans assured me his people could get to the location of the buy in less than a minute. But a lot can happen in sixty seconds, especially if bullets start flying.

When I said I was still concerned for Tommy and his guys, Evans gave me a strange look. Then he said his guys weren't going in with Tommy; Tommy was going in alone. That had been one of Jerome's conditions.

Now I knew why Tommy didn't want me at the meeting with Evans when the logistics of the operation were being worked out. I told Evans I didn't like the plan and wanted it called off. Evans said it was too late, and it was no longer my decision to make. If Tommy wanted to call it off, that was fine, but he wasn't going to abort the operation on my say-so.

Tommy spotted me and came over to chat. He appeared relaxed, but I knew his nervous smile when I saw it. That's when I laced into him for lying to me. He said he hadn't lied; he just "lawyered" me. That's an expression I hate. Maybe because Gracie accuses me of "lawyering" her whenever we argue.

I wasn't in the mood to play games. I told Tommy I wanted him to call off the operation. He said there was no way he was going to do that, and he walked off. I chased after him. I tried to explain why I thought going in alone was a bad idea, but Tommy wouldn't listen. Finally, knowing I'd never change his mind, I gave up. I didn't want him going into this thing upset, just nervous.

I knew Tommy would be nervous. It was good to be nervous. Let me tell you why I know. When you're a drunk one of the many phases you go through is thinking you're bulletproof. Nothing can harm you, and you have the courage of a lion. But courage has nothing to do with it. It's stupidity that makes you ignore risk. I was glad Tommy was nervous, because it meant he wasn't being stupid.

Evans called for everyone's attention, and after giving general instructions, he divided people up into groups for the final briefings. I stood next to Tommy in a group with Evans and a half dozen undercover cops.

Evans had two attaché cases that Tommy would carry to the meeting. Tommy would show the money, just as he had the last time, and he would demand to see the drugs before turning over the cash. If possible, Tommy wouldn't let Jerome take control of the attaché cases. That confirmed what I had been thinking. Evans was worried as much about the damn $250,000 as he was about Tommy's safety.

Once Jerome produced the drugs, and Tommy confirmed it was cocaine, he would give the signal, and the raid would happen. At that point, Tommy would duck for cover. That was the part that concerned me. The time between the signal and the cops getting to Jerome and his thugs. Once Jerome realized there was a raid, there was nothing to stop him from killing Tommy and making off with the drugs and the money.

When I raised my concern, Evans assured me nothing would go wrong. It wasn't that I didn't believe Evans, but I reminded him, Jerome would be armed while Tommy wouldn't be. To my way of thinking, that made a big difference, but Evans didn't see it that way and assured me his guys would protect Tommy.

I pulled Tommy aside and told him again he didn't have to go through with this. But he insisted he was okay with the plan and saw no reason to cancel the buy. I still didn't like it, but if Tommy was okay with it, I wasn't going to make waves.

After watching the tactical guys gear up in heavy body amor, I suggested to Evans that Tommy be given a bulletproof vest. Tommy rolled his eyes, and Evans replied, "Why not just put him in a NYPD uniform?" When I thought about it, I knew Evans was right, but I was nervous, and when I'm nervous not everything I say makes sense.

With everyone briefed and geared up, Evans called the group together for some last minute details and a final word. It was time to set the "safe word." The word Tommy would say if things went bad and they wanted to abort the operation. Evans suggested they use "brother," and Tommy agreed, brother it would be.

Parked nearby were the U-Haul Truck, housing the Mobile Command Unit and the fancy BMW Tommy had been driving since the first buy. Initially, Tommy was told to leave the BMW in the NYPD garage after the buy. But then Evans, suspecting Jerome might put a tail on Tommy, changed his mind. He said it might look suspicious if Tommy didn't have the BMW.

Tommy liked the arrangement and had grown quite attached to the expensive car. Me, I couldn't see the attraction, but then again, I have no use for cars. To me, cars are nothing more than a nuisance, especially when I'm trying to cross a street.

At eight-thirty, everyone was briefed and geared up, and it was time to get going. Evans, the command team, and I would leave first in the U-Haul. Then the undercover cops would leave in some old sedans, followed by the tactical units in their fancy vans. All teams were to be in place by nine-thirty.

If everything was going as planned, Tommy would be given the word to leave the garage in the BMW an hour later. His expected time of arrival at the Harlem projects was eleven o'clock, right on time for the buy. If everything went as planned, the whole operation would be over by eleven-thirty.

I gave Tommy a hug and wished him luck, then I climbed into the box truck and took a seat on one of the benches. Five minutes later, we were on our way to Harlem.

CHAPTER 77

The box truck or, I should say, the Mobile Command Unit, arrived on schedule and parked on 155th Street. I was sitting on the bench next to Evans, who was busy talking on his radio to the undercover units as they arrived on the scene.

The first order of business was putting the video and audio relays in place between the buy location and the Mobile Command Unit. The relays were needed to pass the signals from the video and audio devices in Tommy's jacket buttons to the Mobile Command Unit. Only one relay was needed, but to be on the safe side, Evans wanted three relays in place.

The same deployment method used for the first buy was used again. The relays were hidden in empty pint-sized liquor bottles. An undercover cop, posing as a drunk, wandered through the project, dropping a bottle in a trash barrel at the three predetermined locations.

To make sure the relays were working, the undercover cop wore the same type of video and audio transmitter as Tommy would wear. As he activated each relay and dropped it in place, we watched and listened in the Mobile Command Unit. Wearing the headphones that hung from the ceiling of the truck, I could hear the cop singing as he headed out of the project. The video equipment seemed to be working fine, except the picture was a bit wobbly. I was about to say something to Evans when I realized it was simply the cop doing his staggering drunk imitation.

Within half an hour, all units were in place, and it was just a matter of waiting for Tommy to arrive. Evans, who had been moving about giving commands and checking the status of his teams, took a seat next to me. He reminded me for the tenth time I was there as an observer and I needed to keep my mouth shut and stay out of his way. I wanted to say something rude, but I didn't want to get kicked out of the truck, so for once, I kept my big mouth shut.

Sitting next to Evans, I sensed that I wasn't the only one who was nervous. I don't know if it was nervousness, or more of an adrenalin fueled sense of anticipation. Whatever it was, it seemed like everyone in the truck was feeling it, and I had to assume everyone outside the truck was also feeling it.

At eleven o'clock on the button, the radio crackled, and an undercover cop reported Tommy's BMW had arrived at the project. The tension level in the Mobile Command Unit went at least up three points. The radio crackled again; Tommy had entered the project. Now it was just a matter of waiting for his video and audio transmitter to go active. That wouldn't happen until Tommy was sure Jerome wasn't using any signal monitoring devices. Until then, the video monitors in the truck would remain black, and the only sounds coming through my headphones were the transmissions between Evans and his teams.

That was usually the point I get bored and start making smart-ass comments, but I was too nervous to do anything except sit and fret. Not that it was doing any good.

After twenty minutes without a transmission, I started getting really nervous and suggested Evans send one of his undercover guys to check things out. Evans pretended he hadn't heard me, and I was about to poke him when the video screens came alive, and I could hear voices through my headphones.

I could see Jerome and four of his gangbanger thugs clearly. Two of them had big guns in their hands. Tommy moved slightly to his left, and I could see three more gangbangers, all holding pistols. I didn't like what I saw.

Tommy and Jerome were talking. Jerome wanted to see the money. Tommy opened the first attaché case, then the other, closing each after Jerome had a chance to see the money. He was asking to see the drugs but, as expected,

Jerome wanted to examine the money first. Tommy handed the attaché cases to one of Jerome's gangbangers.

I watched the video monitor in horror as Jerome pulled out a gun and then the screen went white, blinded by the muzzle flash of the gun's firing. The image normalized just as the ground seemed to jump up to meet the camera lens. Tommy was down. Over the headphones, I heard him moaning.

Evans was yelling into his radio, "Code red, code red! Go, go, everyone go!"

CHAPTER 78

I threw off the headphones and jumped up. I moved toward the door, but Evans grabbed me and told me to take a seat. He said he had enough to worry about without me being in the middle of a shootout. I knew there wasn't anything I could do out there, and I'd be better off in the truck where at least I could follow what was happening. I put the earphones back on, but only over one ear. That way, I could listen to Evans talking on his radio, while still monitoring whatever might come from Tommy's transmitter.

I could hear gunfire coming over the headphones and through the truck's walls. Some of it seemed far off, and some seemed nearby.

Suddenly, the video monitors flickered, and I saw images, then sky. Evidently, someone had turned Tommy over onto his back. The audio was muffled, as though the microphone was blocked. I couldn't make out what was being said. Then Evans' radio crackled, "Need buses, now! Two officers and a civilian down, along with six bad guys!" A bus is police slang for an ambulance. I knew the civilian down was Tommy.

Evans used another radio to call dispatch, and he put a rush on the ambulances. Then he asked his team leaders to report. One by one they checked in. By that point, the gunfire had ended, at least as far as I could hear.

The area had been secured, and the two officers shot had superficial wounds, but Tommy's wound was bad. He had been hit in the upper right side of his chest. The officers on scene had applied pressure bandages, and Tommy was conscious and able to talk. As I listened to the report, I could hear the sirens of the approaching ambulances.

Evans picked up his radio, and he told the dispatcher to order the first ambulance to point one, which was where Tommy was located.

Of the six gangbangers down, three, including Jerome, were dead. The other three suffered injuries of varying severity. At that moment, twenty-two people were in custody, and the sweep was still underway. I told Evans I wanted to go and be with Tommy. Evans nodded and called into his radio for the officer nearest the Mobile Command

Unit to report to the unit immediately. The officer took me to Tommy.

When I got to Tommy, he was still on the ground, and the medical techs were working on him. When he saw me, he smiled and nodded his head, as if to say he was okay. I knelt beside him and took his hand. I had tears in my eyes. I loved that kid, and it broke my heart to see him lying there like that.

Once the techs had stabilized Tommy, they moved him to the ambulance. I moved with them and started to climb into the back of the ambulance, at which point one of the techs stopped me. I was about to argue with the guy, when someone behind me said, "It's okay, let him go with you." It was Evans. I turned and said thanks, he nodded, and said, "Good luck."

CHAPTER 79

Luckily, Harlem Hospital Center, a Level 1 Trauma Center, was only twenty blocks away, on 135th Street and Lenox Avenue. I don't know how long it took to get there, but it seemed like forever. Tommy had started moaning; the EMT was working on him; and I was sitting there going crazy. When we arrived at the emergency room entrance, a team of medics in blue scrubs was waiting. The moment the ambulance stopped, the back doors were yanked open, and the team of medics went to work.

I followed Tommy's gurney into the emergency room, trying to keep pace, but not get in the way. Tommy was wheeled through a door marked "Trauma 1," and when I tried to follow, a nurse blocked my path and said I couldn't come in. I argued with her to no avail, and finally, when she promised the doctor would keep me posted on Tommy's condition, I went and sat in the waiting room.

When I finally collected myself, I called Joey Shoo, Tommy's younger brother and told him what had happened. Then I spotted the doctor who had examined Tommy when we first arrived in the emergency room, but he wouldn't talk to me about Tommy's condition. Something to do with his privacy. I was going to claim I was his father, actually his stepfather, for obvious reasons, but that proved unnecessary.

As I stood there trying to decide what to do, Tommy was wheeled out of the trauma room, and a different doctor came to talk to me. He was the chief surgical resident, and he explained Tommy was being taken to an operating room, where he was going to perform an operation to remove the bullet and repair the damage it had done. He said, Tommy's condition was critical, but he expected the surgery to go well. He anticipated the surgery to last four or five hours, and as soon as it was finished, he'd report back to me. In the meantime, I could wait in the surgical waiting room.

Knowing Joey Shoo and his grandfather were on their way to the hospital, I waited for them in the emergency room. Within half an hour they both arrived. The old man looked me in the eye, but said nothing. He didn't have to, his eyes said it all. I updated Joey on Tommy's condition, and as we made our way to the surgical waiting room, I told him everything that had happened that night. Joey passed on the word to the old man. Then we all sat quietly and waited.

I prayed. And not just the serenity prayer, no, I asked God to make Tommy well. I made it clear I wasn't taking no for an answer.

I had called Gracie and told her what had happened, and of course, she came to the hospital and sat vigil with the rest of us. I think she could tell what I was thinking because she kept reminding me that it wasn't my fault. I was having trouble accepting that, and at some point, Gracie ordered me to call Doug. I spoke to Doug for about ten minutes, and he suddenly begged off the call. Fifteen minutes later he showed up at the hospital.

The operation took nearly five hours, and when it was over, the chief surgeon said it was successful. Tommy was still in critical condition and not out of the woods yet, but he was confident Tommy would recover. He suggested we all go home and get some rest, while Tommy was in the recovery unit. We were all exhausted, so I did argue when Gracie dragged us outside and hailed a couple of taxicabs to take us all downtown.

CHAPTER 80

As you might imagine, I didn't get much sleep that night, or I should say, what was left of the night. By seven o'clock, I was up, and by eight-thirty, I was back at Harlem Hospital. I wasn't surprised to see old man Shoo there, along with Linda Chow. Tommy was still in recovery, but conscious, and he was allowed limited visitors. Old man Shoo made sure I was one of the visitors on the list.

Tommy was groggy, probably from the painkillers, but he managed a smile. I stood next to the bed and took his hand, the one without the IV needles stuck in it.

I tried to say something, but I kept getting choked up. Tommy smiled again and said it was okay. I finally managed to get my emotions under control, and I told Tommy how sorry I was and that nothing like this would ever happen again. He nodded, and I could see tears in his eyes.

Joey had arrived, so it was time for me to leave to make room for him. I said goodbye and promised to come back soon. Tommy smiled and nodded. He was one tough kid, and I loved him.

Joey said that once Tommy had been moved to a room, he'd let me know. In the meantime, he and his grandfather would take turns visiting Tommy. Linda Chow had already been in to see him, so she and I shared a taxicab downtown.

Back in the office, Connie had a million questions about the raid and about Tommy's condition. Connie doesn't usually show her emotions, but all of this had hit her pretty hard, and she started to cry.

I suddenly realized how much Tommy meant to all of us, not just to me. I still felt Tommy being shot was at least partially my fault, and the conversation with Connie wasn't doing anything to change my mind.

Connie and I were sitting and talking about Tommy when Sarah Washington called. The first thing she wanted to know was how Tommy was doing. Then she asked when I wanted to talk about Sasha's case. It sounds crude to be talking business so soon after Tommy was shot, but that's life. Tommy was going to be okay, but Sasha's future was still uncertain, and I had a job to do.

I was still too upset to think straight, and I didn't want to talk about the case over the phone. I suggested we meet at Sarah's office that afternoon and talk then. Sarah checked her schedule, and she said two o'clock was good for her, if it was good for me. It was, so we had a date.

That morning, the phone never stopped ringing. Everyone called to find out about Tommy and how he was doing. It got so crazy I finally told Connie I wasn't taking any more calls. But when she announced that Detective Evans was on the line, I changed my mind. I hadn't spoken to Evans since the night before, and I had some questions to ask him. Connie put through the call, but before I could say anything, Evans asked how Tommy was doing.

I didn't know Evans well, but the way he asked the question convinced me he was genuinely concerned about Tommy. The hard edge was gone from his voice, and he no longer sounded like the tough street cop from the night before. We talked a little bit about Tommy, then Evans asked how I was doing, and whatever hostility I had been feeling toward him, began to fade. I realized my anger at Evans was misplaced. He wasn't any more responsible for Tommy being shot than I was. Yes, we could both blame ourselves or each other, for that matter, but the truth was, it wasn't either of our faults.

Despite the best of plans, things can go wrong. And things had gone wrong. Terribly wrong. That happens sometimes, and it doesn't always mean somebody screwed up. Tommy was alive, and I thanked God for that. Maybe what happened to him wasn't my fault, or Evans' fault. But I still wanted to know what went wrong.

Evans knew where I was coming from, and to his credit, he gave me an honest assessment. He said in retrospect it was clear, Jerome never intended to sell the drugs to Tommy. It was going to be a robbery all along, and Evans and his people weren't prepared for that scenario. No one expected Jerome to shoot Tommy, so when he did, Evans and his teams were left flat-footed. All they could do was to move in as quickly as possible for a mop-up operation. The teams were on the scene in seconds and found themselves engaged in a gun battles with Jerome and his crew. Those who weren't injured or killed were arrested, but no drugs were found. That was why Evans concluded Jerome planned all along to kill Tommy and take the money.

It was obvious that Evans felt badly about the raid, and I wasn't about to make it worse by asking senseless questions. Like, why didn't you see this coming? Shit happened, and it was time to move on. Maybe I just wanted to forgive Evans, so I could forgive myself, or maybe neither of us deserved to be blamed. Eventually I'd work it out, but at that moment, I was beat and had to prepare for the meeting with Sarah Washington.

CHAPTER 81

Sarah Washington was sitting at her desk waiting for me when I arrived. After she asked about Tommy and we chatted about how brave he was, we got down to business.

I figured with Jerome and two of his crew dead and most of the other gangbangers arrested, things turned out better than we had hoped for. We didn't have to worry about Jerome skating on the charges, and there was no doubt his drug selling days were over for good, not just twenty to twenty-five years. If it sounded callous, it was. Jerome White had shot Tommy, and the bastard deserved to die for that. I had no sorrow for White, and neither should anyone else. He deserved the death penalty, if not for shooting Tommy, then for all the misery he caused selling drugs. If thinking that way makes me a bad person, well, then I'm a bad person. I can live with that.

The way I saw it, we had cleared the Harlem projects of scum and vermin. The projects were free of a major drug dealer, the gangbanger population had been dramatically reduced, and the DA had his Moby Dick. Except for Tommy being shot, it was a win all around. Now it was time to set Sasha free.

Sarah is a much kinder individual than I am, and I'm not sure she shared my sentiments that Jerome White deserved to die, but that didn't matter. What mattered was the deal we had. We had fulfilled our part, and now it was Sarah's turn to fulfill her part and arrange for the charge against Sasha to be reduced to a misdemeanor.

For a moment, I thought there was a problem because Sarah was sitting there looking like she was about to deliver bad news. But then she burst out laughing and waved some papers in the air. It was the plea agreement signed by her boss.

Sarah handed me a copy of the agreement, and I started reading the terms. As we had agreed, the charges against Sasha were dropped all the way down to possession in the seventh degree, a misdemeanor. That was fine. It was the next part that was surprising. On a plea of guilty, the DA would ask the court to sentence Sasha to time already served and two years' probation. It was a better deal than we had asked for.

At that moment I wanted to kiss Sarah. But I feared if I did, she'd tear up the agreement, so instead of kissing her, I just shook her hand. Then I signed the agreement just to make it legal and binding. I didn't think anything could go wrong at that point, but after the events of the last couple of days, I wasn't taking any chances.

Once the deal was safely sealed, I asked Sarah why the terms suddenly were better than we had discussed. She smiled and admitted taking Jerome White out for good was a part of it. Of course, the DA would never admit to that. But there was another factor as well, and that was the sympathy everyone had for Tommy. Tommy was a hero.

An arraignment hearing would take place the following morning. The charges would be dropped to a misdemeanor, Sasha would plead guilty, and a sentencing hearing would be scheduled for a week later. That meant Sasha would be free in a week and a day.

I had just enough time to get up to Rikers Island and deliver the good news to Sasha. Of course, it meant taking a taxicab, but I was feeling so good it didn't matter. On the way back, I'd stop by the hospital and visit with Tommy.

Before leaving the DA's Office I dropped in on Gracie. When I told her where I was headed, she said she'd meet me at the hospital after work. She wanted to visit Tommy and suggested afterward we stop for a bite to eat.

Life was starting to return to normal. But Richie's case was still weighing heavily on my mind, and nothing would be normal until his case was over.

CHAPTER 82

The next morning, Sasha's hearing went off without a hitch. She looked better than she had in weeks. It seemed news of her imminent release had done wonders for her outlook, and it was certainly reflected in her appearance.

After she pleaded guilty, the judge set sentencing in a week. Then as the court officers were preparing to take her away, Sasha reached out and kissed me on the check. She didn't say anything; she just kissed me and smiled. Then she looked over at Sarah Washington and said, "Thank you." It was very classy.

It's those moments that make it worthwhile. They don't happen often, so when they do, I treasure them. I would have spent more time enjoying the moment, but I was beginning jury selection in Richie's case the next morning, so I had things to do.

First, I had a meeting with Abe to work out his handling of my cases while I was in trial with Richie's case. He'd have to handle Sasha's sentencing, but that wasn't a problem. It was a done deal; all he had to do was show up and smile. Most of the cases were like that.

When you represent guilty clients, there isn't a lot to do. You figure out the best defenses you have, you line up what little evidence you can find to support those defenses, and then you go beg the ADA for the best deal you can get. Sometimes you make a motion to suppress evidence, or a confession. Most times you lose those motions, but you tried.

Then after you work out a deal, you look at the Probation Department Report for a way to mitigate the sentence. Most times you don't have to read the report to know it's bad for your client. You can tell how long the sentence is going to be from how thick the report is. The thicker the report, the longer the sentence. Over the years, I've learned thick Probation Department Reports never contain anything good for the defendant.

The final thing you do as a criminal defense lawyer is attend the sentencing hearing. You look sympathetically at your client, lie to the judge saying your client is repentant and seeks mercy, then look sympathetically at your client as the judge throws the book at him. Oh, one other thing, send a bill to the 18B Panel.

If you don't know by now that I'm completely cynical, you haven't been paying attention. But before you judge me, try going to criminal court and see what's going on there. Take a good look at the defendants and listen to the charges. After that, let me know what you think about my attitude. I believe you'll understand why I treasure moments like the one I had with Sasha.

When I finished with Abe, I called Joey just to check in. Tommy was getting better by the minute. His spirits were up, and he had just eaten some Jell-O, his first solid food, if you can call Jell-O solid food. It was still too early to know when he'd be discharged, but the doctors were very pleased with his progress.

With jury selection starting the next day, I had scheduled a meeting with Richie and Laura. I needed him to be there during the selection process, and I assumed Laura would want to attend. In truth, I assumed there was no way she wouldn't be there, so I needed to prepare them both.

When Richie and Laura showed up forty-five minutes late, I got the impression Richie wasn't enthusiastic about our meeting. I wasn't surprised that the first topic of conversation was Tommy and how he was doing. That was understandable, but after a while it was apparent Richie was prolonging the conversation to avoid talking about his trial. Every time I'd start talking about the trial, he'd ask another question about Tommy. Finally, I'd had enough and said we were going to talk about the trial.

Richie wasn't happy, but he shut up and paid attention. I knew Laura would probably want to be present during jury selection, but I had to ask. When I did, you would have thought I had asked her if she loved her children. I guess that I should have expected her to react that way, but I hadn't, and I was a bit stunned when she did. I glanced at Richie, and he just shook his head and smiled.

After recovering my composure, it was time to lay down the rules. I've given these rules so many times I can recite them in my sleep.

Dress code, conservative. Richie, a dark suit, white shirt, striped tie. Laura, a conservative dress, not too bright, no wild patterns. No spike heels. No fancy jewelry; wedding rings, yes, watches yes, bracelets no, earrings, okay for Laura, no for Richie.

Demeanor in court - always sit erect, no slouching. Slouching said guilty. When you walk together, hold hands and look lovingly at each other. Smiling, okay, laughing not okay. No reactions, facial or otherwise, no matter what is said. Look at the prospective jurors, but don't stare at them. Don't try to influence with your looks; you're just likely to scare them.

As for your suggestions - I'm not really interested in your suggestions. Don't lean over and talk to me during the questioning, I'll be busy listening. If there is something you want to tell me, write it on the legal pad I'll give you, but don't wave the pad in my face. Simply put it on the table in front of me.

Follow the rules, and we'll be fine. Don't follow the rules, and there's going to be trouble.

That was it for the rules; now came the difficult part of our meeting. The part Richie was expecting and wasn't going to like at all. But whether he liked it or not, we were going to have a serious conversation about a plea bargain. At least I was going to start one. How far it would go I couldn't know, but the conversation was going to be had.

As soon as I said it was time to take a hard look at our defense and consider our odds of winning, Richie tensed. He knew what was coming next, and he didn't want to hear it.

I started to explain that our defense had taken a big hit when the charges against McNulty were dropped, but Richie cut me off. He said that he knew perfectly well where he stood, and if I was going to talk about a plea deal, I could forget about it. He would never accept a plea deal. He was going to take his chances with a jury, and that was that. I was about to respond when Laura exploded.

With tears running down her cheeks, she looked Richie straight in the eye and said, "Richie, I love you, but right now you're being the most selfish bastard I have ever seen, and I can't take it anymore." Richie was stunned and so was I. I had seen Laura angry before, but I had never seen her react with such fury.

Richie began to say something, but Laura cut him off. She said if he loved her and his daughters, he'd better consider how all of this affected them and not just himself. They believed in him, they knew he was innocent, and that wouldn't change, no matter what happened. If he was found guilty, they could live with that because they knew in their hearts he wasn't guilty. If he had to go to prison, they could live with that because they had no choice. But if he went to prison for longer than he had to because he refused a plea deal, they couldn't live with that. That was why he had to consider a plea bargain. Then Laura put her face in hands and sobbed.

I keep a box of tissues in my desk, and I pulled it out and passed it to Laura. I didn't say anything because there was nothing more to say; Laura had said it all. She wiped the tears from her face, and we both sat looking at Richie, waiting for him to say something. But he never said a word; he just got up and walked out of the office.

I started to go after him, but Laura grabbed my arm and stopped me. She said he needed time to think, and I should leave him alone. If he wasn't back in thirty minutes, we'd have our answer and she'd leave. I didn't know if that meant she'd just leave the office, or she'd leave Richie. It was one of those awkward moments that I don't handle well. The only the thing I could think to do was offer Laura a cup of coffee, or tea.

Twenty minutes later, Richie was back. He took Laura's hand, gave her a kiss, and asked me what kind of plea bargain we were looking at. Being honest, I said right now we didn't have much leverage, and the best offer we could expect was manslaughter in either the first or second degree. If it was first degree, the sentence could range from five to twenty-five years, but it was negotiable. With second degree, we were looking at three to fifteen years, again negotiable.

Laura wanted to know how soon I could negotiate a deal. I said I didn't think it was a good idea to rush things. We were behind the eight ball right now, but things could get better. In plea bargaining, you want to deal when you're at your strongest point, not your weakest, and at the moment we were probably at our weakest.

I suggested we wait until after jury selection to see how things were shaking out. By then, we might know more about McNulty's situation, and I'd have a better feel for how well our "the other guy did it" defense would work. If things were looking better, we might even start the trial, but that remained to be seen. All I needed right then was authority to talk about a plea deal at some point.

Richie nodded; he said he trusted me like a brother; and I should do whatever I thought was best for him and his family. Laura started to cry again, then she came around my desk and gave me a big hug. Then we all hugged and agreed to meet the next morning at the Worth Street Coffee Shop. Then we hugged again, and Richie and Laura left the office hand-in-hand.

Sitting there after Richie and Laura left, I felt a sudden sense of relief. Knowing there were options lifted an enormous burden off my shoulders. It didn't mean I wasn't going to take the case to trial. I would if I thought we could win at trial. Options were important because they gave us another way to win. You win if your prison sentence is five years instead of twenty-five years.

I didn't have a lot of confidence we could win the case, but I was still hopeful something might break with McNulty. I had been calling Joe Hadden daily, all to no avail. For some reason, he was ducking me. I thought about paying him a visit, but I figured I'd never get past the desk sergeant.

Sooner or later, the news about McNulty had to break. I just hoped it wouldn't be too late when it did.

CHAPTER 83

With jury selection starting the next day, my life was about to get very busy, and it was likely to stay that way for a while. Once trial began, my days and nights would be tied up, so I called Gracie and suggested we have a nice long dinner at Pino's. Gracie agreed and said she'd meet me there at eight o'clock. That gave me plenty of time to visit Tommy.

When I arrived at Tommy's hospital room, Detective Evans was sitting in a chair next to Tommy's bed. I could tell from the way the two were talking that it wasn't an official visit. Evans was there because he was genuinely concerned about Tommy's condition. My instincts about the man were right; he was a good guy.

I had to wonder, though, if he was there out of a sense of guilt over how things had gone down. Perhaps guilt was a part of it, but I had to believe he was honoring Tommy for what he had done. Tommy had put his life on the line for someone he didn't really know, and he had done it simply because it was the right thing to do. That was something Evans understood because good cops like Evans do that every day.

Old man Shoo was sitting, with his eyes closed, in the chair on the other side of the bed. He looked like he was sleeping, but I knew he wasn't. He does this thing, where he closes his eyes and he looks like he's sleeping but he's not. He's fully aware of everything going on around him. I don't know how he does it, but Tommy says it's some sort of Zen thing.

When Tommy saw me, he flashed a big smile in my direction and Evans, seeing me, stood up. Old man Shoo opened one eye, smiled, then closed the eye. He was keeping track of everything that was happening in the room. I'm telling you, the old man was like a Ninja. You couldn't get anything past him, and you never knew what he was thinking.

I smiled at Tommy and shook hands with Evans. For some reason, it was an awkward moment. Maybe it was too many alpha males in the room. Not knowing what else to say, I told Evans it was nice of him to visit Tommy. Apparently, the moment was as awkward for him as it was for me, because he just shrugged and said he was just about to leave. So why didn't I take his seat?

Evans said goodbye to Tommy and promised to visit again. Then he looked over at the old man, shrugged, and said goodbye. The old man opened one eye, nodded, and closed the eye.

Evans had gotten to the doorway when he turned and asked if he could see me in the hallway for a minute.

Out in the hallway, Evans said, "You know it wasn't your fault. It was my fault. I should have done more to protect Tommy." I appreciated him saying that, but there was enough fault to go around; he didn't have to shoulder it all himself. I said we're all to blame, but mostly that scumbag White, who got what he deserved. Evans smiled, shook my hand again, and walked away. I think we both felt a little better after that.

Tommy looked pretty good and sounded good. He did seem a little frail, but I guess that was to be expected after everything he'd been through. The doctors weren't certain when he'd be discharged, but it would be in the next couple of days. After that, he'd recuperate at home. Home being his apartment upstairs from his grandfather's restaurant. In a way, it was funny how our lives still revolved around Shoo's Chinese restaurant.

I wanted Tommy to rest, but he insisted on knowing what happened with Sasha's case, and how things were going with Richie's case. He deserved to know, so I filled him in on both cases. When I told him Sasha would be released soon, and she was coming to thank him, a big smile crossed his face.

I've got to be honest. To this day, I'm not sure it was worth it. And if I had it to do over again, I probably wouldn't let Tommy do the buy. But I know if Tommy had it to do over again, he'd insist on doing it. That's Tommy, and that's one reason why I love him.

I sat and chatted with Tommy for about an hour, then I took the subway back downtown and met Gracie at Pino's. It had been a long, tough day, but a good day. Now that Tommy was on the mend, and after talking with Evans, I was feeling a lot less guilty. Plus, with Richie agreeing to consider a plea deal, my life was suddenly a lot less complicated. It was no less busy, though, since jury selection was starting the next morning, but I was under a lot less pressure.

Gracie and I enjoyed a great dinner that night. You may find this hard to believe, but I don't recall what we ate. It was just one of those nights. One of those great nights that stick in your memory, but you don't necessarily know why. I don't know if you've ever had one of those nights, but if you have, you know what I'm talking about. And if you haven't, I hope you have one someday soon.

By the time we finished our dessert and espresso coffee, we were both in a romantic mood. Unfortunately, even though I was feeling great, I needed to go to a meeting. Why? Because once jury selection started, I'd be hard pressed to find time for meetings, so I had to attend them when I could. That night was likely to be my last free night for a while, and as much as I wanted nothing more than to go with Gracie, I knew I had to attend a meeting.

Gracie knows what it means to be a recovering alcoholic, and she accepts everything that comes with living with a recovering alcoholic. So that night she sent me off to my meeting with a kiss and promise to wait up for me. Actually, she said she'd be waiting for me in her red hooker outfit. That last part is just between us because if Gracie finds out I told you that, she'd probably kill me.

For the record, the red hooker outfit is just a red bra and a slinky pair of red panties. I don't mean to say the outfit isn't sexy. It is, or I should say Gracie is sexy in the outfit. But I sense that I'm just digging myself into a deeper hole, so I'll quit.

CHAPTER 84

The next morning, I was up bright and early. I'm always up early on mornings when I'm about to start a trial. It's the adrenalin.

Selecting a jury may not sound exciting, but there's a lot riding on it, and that makes it important. That day, and maybe over the next couple of days, I'd choose twelve individuals, ordinary people, who would ultimately decide if Richie is going to spend the next twenty-five years in prison. That's why the adrenalin was flowing that morning.

People think lawyers are looking for a fair and impartial jury, but that's not true. Yes, we want a fair jury, but not an impartial jury. Why? Because an impartial juror doesn't exist. We all have our own beliefs and biases, and as much as we'd like to think we can set them aside, we really can't. So, we get a fair jury by balancing out the biases.

I look for jurors who are likely to see things from my point of view and side with me. The ADA does the same, and if we do it right, the selection process should level out the biases. In the end, the jury might not be impartial, but it's balanced.

Picking a jury is part art, part science, but mostly gut reaction. I know there are people who make a living helping attorneys pick juries, but I think they're useless. Of course, I never used any of those so-called jury consultants; I couldn't afford their fees. But even if I could, I wouldn't use them.

Generalities, like young people being good for defendants and old people being good for the prosecution, only get you so far. After that, it's all instinct gained from experience.

Some lawyers think you have to try to get into people's heads. I don't agree. I don't believe anybody can figure out what's going on in somebody else's head. I've been with Gracie for a long time, and I have no idea what the hell's going on in her head. Gracie claims that's because I'm an insensitive jerk. I don't think that's the reason. I may be an insensitive jerk, but figuring out what's going on in a woman's head has puzzled men far smarter than me for ages. Go back to ancient Greek mythology and Medusa, the woman with living snakes in place of hair. Anyone who looked into her eyes and tried to figure out what she was thinking turned to stone. I rest my case.

But I digress. My point is, I don't think it's possible to read people's minds, and I don't think you have to in order to pick a jury.

I have learned a few things about jurors during my years of practice. First, jurors always try to do the right thing. Second, the right thing is usually what makes sense to them. And third, there will always be a leader in the group. Remember those three things, and picking a jury is easy. Well, maybe not easy, which was why I had Abe sitting with me.

The way Richie's case was shaping up, there was an additional dynamic worth mentioning. The jury's decision must be unanimous, so if I was able to convince one or two jurors that Richie was not guilty, we could end up with a hung jury and a mistrial. A mistrial wouldn't be as good as an acquittal, but it would be better than a guilty verdict.

When a case seems headed for a deadlock, the judge will put tremendous pressure on the jurors to reach a verdict, so it takes a strong juror to resist the pressure and hold out. But during a holdout, ADAs become more flexible in plea bargaining.

Abe and I met Richie and Laura at the Worth Street Coffee Shop, and after a couple of cups of coffee, a lot of reassuring, we walked together to the courthouse across the street. Marty Bowman was waiting for us just outside the clerk's office, and after introductions and salutations, he and I went inside to let the clerk know we were ready.

We spent the better part of the next two days picking the jury. In the end, Abe and I were satisfied we had a jury we could live with. We had at least two jurors we believed would side with us and were potential leaders. Neither of them struck us as being particularly strong leaders, but it was all relative. As they say, in the land of the blind, the man with one eye is king. Whether or not they'd be strong enough to win over other jurors, or to hold out for a mistrial, remained to be seen.

When we finished the selection process, the jurors and the alternates were sworn in, given some preliminary instructions by the judge and sent home with instructions to return in two days to begin the trial.

In two days we'd appear in the Trial Assignment Part where the case would be assigned to a trial judge. We had no way of knowing to whom the case would be assigned. as the assignments were random. The next case up for assignment was sent to the next available judge on the list. Most of the judges were okay, but there were two or three who could be trouble for us. I'd just have to wait and pray.

As we were finishing packing up I told Richie and Laura to go back to my office and wait for me there. I wanted to talk with Marty Bowman before he left.

CHAPTER 85

When Abe and I approached Marty, he smiled. He knew exactly why we were coming to talk, and he also knew he had the upper hand. I invited Marty for a cup of coffee, which he declined, saying we should just take a seat outside the courtroom and talk. Obviously, Marty didn't expect our conversation to last very long. Not a good sign.

With Abe standing by, I made my best pitch. I said I knew a lot about McNulty. I probably knew more about him than Marty and his boss knew, and I intended putting it all on the record during cross-examination. If Marty couldn't convince his boss to offer a more reasonable plea deal, a lot of people, including the District Attorney and the City Mayor, were going to be embarrassed.

Marty wasn't buying it. He said his boss was offering a reasonable plea deal, with Richie doing seven years. That was the fifteen-year sentence, with time off for good behavior. It was the same deal Marty had offered when we met at the Worth Street Coffee Shop earlier in the month.

I didn't think it was a good deal, but it was better than twenty-five years or, even worse, life. Still, I felt we could do better, and when I glanced at Abe and he a gave a little shake of his head, it told me he agreed. I laughed, and told Marty he'd have to do a lot better than that. Marty just shrugged his shoulders and said he'd see us in court.

Some of the younger ADAs get nervous around trial time, and the closer the trial date, the easier it is to work out a plea deal. But that wasn't going to happen with Marty Bowman. Marty was an old hand at this, and he certainly wasn't afraid to take Richie's case to trial.

The bit about Marty needing his boss' approval for any plea deal was basically bullshit. Marty was a senior trial attorney, and I knew damn well his boss would accept any plea deal Marty suggested. Marty was just using the boss routine to give himself some negotiating room.

It was Marty I had to convince to get a better deal, and Marty wasn't going to scare easily. The only way I'd get a better deal from Marty was to get a better defense.

Back in the office, I told Richie and Laura what had happened, and although Laura seemed disappointed no deal had been struck, both were relieved that the decision was put off for at least another day or two. It gave them more time for hope.

I didn't plan to see either Richie or Laura until the trial began in two days, so we went over the courtroom rules one more time, then I sent them home. Unless something came up in the next two days, we'd meet at the Worth Street Coffee Shop at nine o'clock and go to court together from there.

Now I needed to call Jimmy O'Brien. Earlier when I met with Jimmy, no one knew if McNulty was in this alone or if the corruption went higher. Naturally, Jimmy was being cautious, so I hadn't pushed things, and I hadn't asked him if he'd testify at trial. But that was then; now I needed him to testify.

I only had two witnesses I could call, Jimmy O'Brien and Richie. If Jimmy's testimony went well, I wouldn't call Richie. There were some benefits to calling Richie as a witness, but it was risky, and I thought the risks outweighed the benefits.

On the plus side, Richie had plenty of experience testifying, so I was sure he'd make a good witness. Besides, the jurors always like to hear from the defendant.

But there were too many negatives to his testifying. First, there wasn't a lot Richie could tell them, other than the basics about the raid and denying he shot Kim Lee. Then he'd be subject to cross-examination by Marty Bowman, who was no slouch when it came to roughing up witnesses.

When you've been on the police force for as long as Richie had been, there's always something in the record that doesn't look good. In Richie's case, it was two excessive use of force claims. Claims by a couple of drug dealing lowlifes, looking to get even with Richie for arresting them. Richie was cleared in both cases, but that wouldn't stop Bowman from banging Richie over the head with them.

Finally, by putting Richie on the stand as a witness, I'd open the door to Marty calling rebuttal witnesses to impeach Richie's character. I wasn't particularly worried it would do much harm, but it would give Marty the last word in the trial, and that I didn't want to happen.

I kicked the question around with Abe, who agreed I should keep Richie off the witness stand. But if O'Brien didn't testify, I'd have no choice but to put Richie on the stand. I called O'Brien and asked him to meet me.

In the past, O'Brien hadn't wanted to come to my office, preferring instead to meet somewhere else. That I understood. He didn't want the brass knowing he was meeting with Richie's lawyer. It made sense. But this time, he said he could be in my office in half an hour.

When Jimmy arrived, I could see he was more relaxed than he had been at our last meeting. Clearly, something had changed, and I asked him directly what it was. He thought that was funny and said the word was out that McNulty had acted alone. With McNulty gone, he didn't have to worry about getting caught up in a jackpot. Jackpot being cop slang for a disciplinary action.

I told Jimmy I needed him to testify at the trial, and tell what he did and saw on the night of the raid. He agreed, and we discussed briefly what he would say. It wasn't detailed, just a general discussion. After Bowman had put in the prosecution's case, I'd meet again with Jimmy, and that's when we'd get into the details of his testimony. In the meantime, there wasn't much else I needed him to do. Of course, if he came up with anything that might help, I wanted to hear from him.

Things were looking a little brighter, and I was starting to feel a little bit optimistic. Little did I know what was coming.

CHAPTER 86

One day away from trial and I still hadn't heard from Joe Hadden. The last time I had spoken with him was the morning of McNulty's arrest, after McNulty had been released from custody.

Hadden had promised to call and let me know what was happening, but I hadn't heard from him. I had tried calling him a number of times, but he wouldn't take my calls. I had lost hope of hearing from him, when unexpectedly he called. He said we needed to talk, but not over the phone. He wanted to meet somewhere private, so I told him to meet me at Shoo's Restaurant.

When someone says they don't want to talk over the phone, and they want to meet somewhere private, it usually means trouble. Trouble for the person doing the talking, or trouble for the person doing the listening. Either way, I wasn't expecting anything good to come from this meeting.

I got to Shoo's a few minutes before Hadden arrived and arranged with old man Shoo to use the backroom for my meeting. I was sitting there, reminiscing about the old times, when old man Shoo opened the door and ushered in Joe Hadden. Joe looked nervous, and I soon found out why.

After McNulty was arrested, he demanded to speak with either a FBI Agent or an United States Attorney. He claimed to have critical national security information which he would share only with the Feds. Hadden's boss passed the word on to the Police Commissioner, who contacted the US Attorney's Office and arranged for someone from that office and a FBI Agent to interview McNulty.

At that point, Hadden was no longer included in the loop and wasn't told what happened at the meeting. All he knew was that after the meeting, McNulty was hauled off by the Feds.

Then he was surprised to learn the corruption charges against McNulty were being dropped, and he was being quietly retired from the NYPD. He didn't know why, but rumor had it that McNulty was able to trade information for his immunity.

It was only the day before that Hadden learned what information McNulty had, and why it was worth giving him immunity. What he learned was highly classified, and he would lose his job if word got out that he had passed it on to anyone. But he didn't like the idea of McNulty getting a pass, and knowing it would hurt Richie's case, he decided to share the information with me.

McNulty had some very interesting photographs and videos on a thumb drive. Hadden didn't have copies of the videos, but he had used his cell phone to sneak a couple of shots of the pictures the FBI had printed from the thumb drive. Hadden's photographs weren't very clear, and I really couldn't see the details, especially on Hadden's small phone. But there was enough detail for me to know they weren't photographs you'd post on your Facebook page. Not unless they did so under the caption, "Perverted things I have done in my life."

Hadden explained what I was looking at. The photographs and videos weren't valuable for what they showed happening, but rather for who was doing it. The first set of photographs was of a Chinese diplomat engaged in some very compromising activities. In truth, what he was doing, and who he was doing it with, was a hell of a lot worse than compromising. And there was more on the thumb drive, lots more.

The next set of photographs was of an Iranian diplomat engaged in similarly unusual sexual activities. If you're very liberal minded, you might be tempted to call them hobbies; otherwise, you'd simply call them perversions. However you categorized them, the mullahs weren't likely to approve of his actions, if they could even figure out what the hell he was doing.

Then there was the clincher, pictures of the mayor's married brother-in-law having sex with two women, one of whom seemed to be very, very young. That was bad enough, but the man was wearing ladies' underwear and makeup. It was all very bizarre. Hardly pictures you'd expect to find in the mayor's family album and certainly not Christmas card material. But, definitely Page Six material.

Hadden reminded me that, in addition to the photographs, McNulty had full-length videos in "living color" and "surround sound." To the CIA, the pictures and the videos of the Chinese and Iranian diplomats were worth their weight in gold. Their blackmail value was incalculable. As for the video of the mayor's brother-in-law, it was at least worth a pass on the corruption charges, just to keep the already shaky administration out of a family sex scandal.

So, now I knew why McNulty was off the hook. And I knew exactly where he got the pictures and the videos, from the safe at the brothel. Somehow, McNulty found out about them and figured they were kept in the safe.

When McNulty could no longer forestall a raid on the brothel, he knew it probably meant an end to his financial arrangement with Yeoung. He evidently decided to offset his losses by stealing the pictures and the thumb drive. That was why he didn't tip off Yeoung about the raid until the last minute. Had he given Yeoung more notice, the safe would have been emptied and the contents moved out of the brothel before the raid.

That was all Hadden could, or would, tell me, but it was enough. He warned me if I mentioned our conversation to anyone, he'd deny it ever happened. I understood where he was coming from and thanked him for his help. He said he did it for Richie, who didn't deserve to get taken down by a bastard like McNulty. I agreed.

CHAPTER 87

If I could prove in court what Hadden had just told me, it would blow the case wide open. But I didn't have the evidence to prove it, and there was no way Hadden or anyone else was going to give it to me. So, how could I tell the jury the story, and how was I going to get them to believe it?

I didn't have a witness to tell the story, so the best I could do was work it in during my cross-examination of McNulty. I could do that to establish McNulty's motive for killing Kim Lee. The question was just how far I could go with it. Marty was sure to object, and in truth, I was on thin ice. But most judges would give me some latitude, and I planned on pushing it to the limit.

If I was going to convince the jury there was a reasonable possibility McNulty killed Kim Lee, I had to offer evidence that McNulty had a motive for doing so. Stealing something from the safe was the only motive I could offer, and having McNulty admit he had done that, would be a big help.

It would be great if I could get McNulty to tell the jury what it was he stole, but that was never going to happen. If he let that cat out of the bag, his immunity agreement would go down the drain. But, not knowing what it was he stole wouldn't matter so much if McNulty admitted he had stolen something.

I knew McNulty would deny he stole anything, believing there'd be no consequences, and he would be right, except for one small exception. If he lied, he'd put the US Attorney in a bind.

The US Attorney knew McNulty had stolen the items from the safe, and that made him a potential witness. If McNulty denied taking items from the brothel's safe, I'd have the right to call the US Attorney as a rebuttal witness to prove McNulty was a liar. Then, while he was under oath, I could ask him what it was that McNulty had stolen. There was no way in hell the US Attorney was going to face that dilemma, and that left only one choice.

If I threatened to call the US Attorney as a witness, the DA would simply throw McNulty under the bus, and stipulate that he had stolen the contents of the safe, without revealing what it was he had stolen. That alone would not only prove McNulty lied under oath, it would give him motive for killing Kim Lee.

But would the plan work, and would it be enough to get Richie off? If the jury believed McNulty could have killed Kim Lee, that might be enough for an acquittal, but simply showing McNulty to be a liar, might not be enough. McNulty's testimony was a big part of the DA's case, maybe the critical part, or maybe not. Without McNulty's testimony, the DA had the forensic report, proving bullets that killed Kim Lee came from Richie's gun. It wasn't conclusive proof, but it was circumstantial evidence.

There was another possibility I had to consider. Hadden's information gave me new bargaining power for a plea deal. The Feds and the DA had to be concerned that during the trial, details of McNulty's plea agreement might get out. The only sure way to keep that from happening was to avoid a trial, and that gave me some leverage to force a favorable deal. But by taking a plea deal before trial, we lost the chance for an acquittal.

When I got back to the office and told Abe what I had just learned, he agreed it put a new light on things. He thought using it when I cross-examined McNulty was the best way to go, but he reminded me that, without the thumb drive or the pictures, we didn't have evidence to prove any of it.

I was in a tough position. Did I try and use the material now to work out a plea deal, or did I wait and use it at trial and hope to win the case? I had to assume Marty Bowman didn't know about the thumb drive, and if he did, he didn't know I knew about it. The element of surprise worked to our advantage if I used the information during trial. But if I tried using it to work out a plea deal, and we couldn't come to terms, I'd lose that advantage. Not only wouldn't Marty be surprised, he was likely to ask the judge to exclude the matter before the trial even began.

Marty would probably lose the motion, and the judge would likely allow me to raise the issue when I cross-examined McNulty. But I'd have to lay out my strategy when I argued the motion, and that would give Marty an advantage.

Abe and I batted around the problem and finally concluded that, like with everything else in this case, there was no easy answer. But we had to decide on some strategy, and we did. Rather than bringing the new information to Bowman's attention now, and risk the DA trying to quash its use, we'd wait for the trial to begin. If just before McNulty testified, things were going badly, we'd drop the bomb on Bowman and try for a plea bargain. But if things were going well enough, we'd consider using the material in open court and try to win the trial.

Once Abe and I settled on the plan, I called Richie and discussed it with him and Laura. After a long discussion, they agreed the plan was the way to go. I think, at that point, we were all feeling a little more optimistic. Sometimes that's good, and sometimes it's bad. It's good if it gives you the confidence to look strong in court. It's bad if it gives you false hope of winning.

CHAPTER 88

As much as I love trial work, I hate the anticipation of waiting for the trial to begin. The problem is, if I don't keep busy, I start to second-guess myself. The day before the start of Richie's trial, I was doing my best to keep busy so I wouldn't go out of my mind.

It didn't matter that I'd done everything I could possibly do to get ready. With all the unsettled issues, I could have easily worked myself into a nervous breakdown before lunch. I needed to keep busy, and that was why I was going over my opening remarks for the umpteenth time.

I don't write out my opening or closing arguments. I just outline the points I want to raise, and maybe jot down a catch phrase I intend to use. But sitting at my desk, I rehearsed my timing and rhythm. An opening argument is a story;, it's the only time I would get to tell it; and I needed to tell it well.

I planned on opening with one of my strongest points, Marty's failure to mention a motive for the murder. How did I know Marty wouldn't mention a motive? Simple. He didn't have one, and he didn't need to prove one. He wouldn't mention motive because he wouldn't want the jurors thinking about motive, especially when he couldn't give them one. Plus, if he mentioned possible motives, he'd be creating issues I could attack to create doubt about his case. Why take that risk when he didn't have to? So, I was sure Marty wouldn't mention motive.

Why would I talk about motive? Because jurors are conditioned to ask why, and I planned on playing to their curiosity and using it to create an alternative theory of the crime. The argument was simple; Marty hadn't mentioned motive because there was no reason for Richie to have killed Kim Lee. However, there was a motive for McNulty to have killed her. What was McNulty's motive? He wanted something in the safe.

Motive was the central point around which I'd build reasonable doubt,, and at the center of my argument was the contents of the safe. Knowing I probably couldn't prove what had been in the safe, the most I could say was that it was valuable. I was counting on the jurors' common sense to tell them that anything kept in a safe was valuable.

In an opening statement, you never want to promise to prove something you might not be able to prove. So, when it came to the theft itself, I'd limit my comments to what I was sure I could prove. The fact that nothing from the safe was recovered by the police, as confirmed by the NYPD inventory reports and crime scene logs. The crime scene reports would also confirm that McNulty was the only one who left the brothel office that night without being searched and without having his property inventoried.

I was counting on the crime scene photos of the open safe next to Kim Lee's body to help make the point that something was missing. Photographs always made a point more powerful than words. In this case, they also left room for the imagination. An open safe, a dead body, and nothing of value inventoried at the scene.

Of course, I'd talk about Richie and his background as a cop, a husband and father. Knowing Marty was probably going to mention the two excessive force charges, I'd wait to see what he said and then address them.

Next, I'd talk about McNulty and do my best to paint him as a corrupt cop. I wasn't sure how far I could go, or what I could say that wouldn't come back to bite me in the ass. I could say he had been arrested, that was a fact and it wouldn't change. The case having been dropped by the DA was a problem, but not a fatal one. Since McNulty had been transferred to federal custody, I had some wiggle room. Not much, but enough so I could at least say charges hadn't been brought "yet."

How long I talked about McNulty depended on the jury's reaction. I can generally tell when I have the jury's attention and when I don't. Sometimes it's obvious, like the time one juror sat flossing her teeth during my closing argument. Other times it's not so obvious, but after years of trying cases, I know when enough is enough.

I had to address the forensic evidence, but I wasn't going to spend a lot of time talking about it because I didn't want the jury thinking I was worried about it. Yes, the forensic evidence proved that the bullets which killed Kim Lee came from Richie's gun. But it didn't prove who fired the gun. The fingerprint evidence proved nothing except that McNulty had held Richie's gun.

I'd finish by telling the jury what they were going to hear from Jimmy O'Brien. As the only eyewitness I planned on calling, he would be the key in establishing what happened on the night of the raid. His testimony was the bones supporting my argument.

My goal was simply to get the jury thinking there could be another version of the case besides Marty's version. I needed to do that before Marty's version took root in their minds. Once that happened, I'd need a weed whacker to get it out.

I knew my opening argument wouldn't convince the jury that Marty's case was bogus; that would be too much to ask for. A little healthy skepticism was all I was aiming for. If I could plant a seed of doubt in the jurors' minds, I could work on making it grow into reasonable doubt and an acquittal, or at least a hung jury. It all came down to how well I could tie all the elements into a persuasive argument. Something that would make sense to the jury and make them question Marty's theory of the case.

By mid-afternoon, I couldn't think of anything more to do. Rather than sit around driving myself nuts, I decided to go to a meeting, and then go to the hospital and visit Tommy. That would keep me busy until dinner with Gracie. If I kept busy, I'd be okay.

CHAPTER 89

I was still hyped when I got to my AA meeting. AA meetings refocus my attention, which is usually a good thing. When I first started going to AA meetings, they refocused my attention from booze to sobriety. Now that I've been sober a while, the meetings refocus my attention from complicated issues I tend to create in my head to the simplicity with which I need to live my life.

In days when I was drinking, my mind was always racing at a thousand miles an hour, but it got me nowhere. Everything wound up being a confused blur. Since getting sober, I've learned that by throttling back to idle, I actually get somewhere. I see things clearly most of the time. But every now and then I need a reminder to slow down, and that's why I go to meetings.

It's never been my intention to bore you with the details of my life, but I do have to tell you some things about me being an alcoholic. Why? Because those things are part of me, and they're what make me tick. So, if you're going to know me, you have to know those things. You have to understand what makes me and all alcoholics different from other people. Why we do the things we do, and what we need to do to live a sober life.

I'm not looking to make you my best friend; I already have one, Gracie. But if we're going to hang out together, you should know these things about me.

Anyway, by the time the meeting ended, I had my head on straight again, and I was anxious to see Tommy. I had started to accept the fact that I wasn't totally responsible for Tommy having been shot. I don't think I'll ever get completely over it, but whatever guilt I have left I can live with.

That afternoon when I got to the hospital, Tommy was in good spirits and doing well. Old man Shoo was in his chair next to Tommy's bed, and he opened one eye and smiled when I came into the room.

The doctors had just finished examining Tommy and said if his progress continued, he would be discharged in two days. I figured, after taking a bullet in the chest, he'd need some convalescing time at home, but Tommy was already talking about going back to work.

I tried to talk him into taking some time off, but he wouldn't hear of it. He said he was feeling fine, and he needed to work. I knew there was no sense arguing with him. Once Tommy made up his mind, that was it.

Hearing Tommy talk convinced me he was going to be okay. I'd been worried because I'd known two cops who'd been shot and never got over it. They got better physically, but mentally they were never the same. They couldn't take the pressure of the job, and eventually they left the NYPD. But Tommy seemed to be okay mentally, and with the doctors saying he'd be fine physically, everything was turning out okay.

I was going to lecture him on being more careful in the future, but I knew it wouldn't do any good. Besides, I was sure old man Shoo had given him an earful. I was just grateful Tommy had survived and was recovering so well.

CHAPTER 90

It was trial day and at eight-thirty I met Laura and Richie at the coffee shop. Naturally, they were both nervous and trying hard not to show it.

Laura was dressed as I had suggested. She wore a dark dress and no jewelry, other than her wedding ring and a wristwatch. I reminded her that she was to sit in the gallery, directly behind Richie. She was to make eye contact with the jurors, but not make any comments or facial expressions, no matter what was said.

Richie was dressed in a dark suit, white shirt, and blue tie. He looked good. He had enough courtroom experience to know he'd be sitting next to me at counsel table. I didn't have to tell him that. But I did tell him the same rules of conduct that applied to Laura applied to him, only more so. The jurors would be focusing on him, and he needed to appear confident, calm, and composed. As difficult as it might be, it was crucial for him to maintain a calm appearance, no matter what came out the mouth of Marty Bowman or any of the witnesses.

I had learned earlier that morning that Richie's case had been assigned to Judge Simon Morganstern, known to the local lawyers as "Simple Simon," and not in an affectionate way. Morganstern earned his nickname because he's very simpleminded and never lets complications, such as the law, cloud his thinking. His favorite line, uttered after most objections, is "Let's keep this simple." No matter how legally complex the issue might be, you could always count on Judge Morganstern to keep it simple.

But the assignment was good news for us. Morganstern was known to favor defendants, and he had the highest acquittal rate in the city. It wasn't that Morganstern was philosophically liberal; he was just simpleminded. Not surprisingly, most of his rulings were legally wrong.

Being victimized by his erroneous rulings was so common, it came to be called, being "simonized." Every now and then, Morganstern made a correct ruling, but that was more the result of random chance than legal acumen. You know, the blind squirrel finding an acorn occasionally.

The way our system works, acquittals can't be appealed because the government only gets one shot at you. There are a few exceptions, like a hung jury, but once a criminal case ends favorably for a defendant, it's done. It's something called double jeopardy. The result is that errors in favor of a criminal defendant can't be appealed, so they remain uncorrected. On the other hand, errors made in favor of the prosecution can and usually are appealed and corrected by the Appellate Courts.

Frankly, I don't like Judge Morganstern because I think he's a bad judge, and bad judges damage the system. I don't like any bad judges, no matter which way they tend to rule. Call me crazy, but I believe a judge should be fair, honest, and above all, know the law. Or at least have a passing acquaintance with it. But I was never one to look a gift horse in the mouth, so I was happy when Morganstern was assigned Richie's case. Poor Marty wasn't happy.

I could tell from the look on Marty's face he wanted to pull his hair out. The only judge in the courthouse worse than Morganstern might have been Richard Lewis, nicknamed "Rip Van Winkle" because he sleeps through most trials. But we didn't have Lewis; we had good old Simple Simon.

I leaned over to Marty and asked if he'd like to rethink the plea deal he was offering. He gave me a dirty look, but then he laughed. He knew as well as I did that the luck of the draw had gone in our favor, and now the scales of justice were tipping to our side. It was a slight tip, but a tip nonetheless.

Abe, who had just arrived, was all smiles. He knew we had gotten a big break.

At nine-thirty on the button, Judge Morganstern took the bench. If nothing else, the man was punctual. He greeted us warmly and said if we were ready, he'd have the jury brought in and we'd begin. As I said, "Defendant is ready, Your Honor," my heart beat a little faster. It always beat a little faster whenever I uttered those words.

It was the moment of truth. The moment I had been waiting for. All the preparation, all the worry, all the questioning, all the indecision was done. Over. "Defendant is ready, Your Honor," was the battle cry.

The jury was brought in and given introductory instructions. Then the judge invited Marty to make his opening statement.

CHAPTER 91

Marty Bowman made a good opening statement. Marty wasn't flamboyant or dramatic; he was a simple straight talker; and a good one. He took the jurors through the crime, step by step, starting with a description of the crime scene. He told them about the forensic evidence, and then capped it with the eyewitness testimony from his star witness, Deputy Chief Inspector, William McNulty.

He spent time talking about Richie, calling him a good cop who went bad. By calling him a good cop, he was blunting my thunder. Then he mentioned the two times Richie had been charged with using excessive force while making an arrest. Marty knew the charges had been dismissed, and for that reason, he didn't spend much time talking about them. He just threw them out there to see if he could put a little stink on Richie.

I thought Marty might bring up the charges, and I had told Richie and Laura to expect it. I glanced at Richie and did a half turn to look at Laura. As I hoped, neither reacted to any of the inflammatory statements. So far, so good.

Marty concluded by asking the jurors to listen carefully to the evidence and then return the only verdict possible, guilty of murder. As I predicted, he never mentioned motive.

It was my turn to talk to the jury, but even as I stood to begin, I still wasn't sure how much I was going to say about McNulty. Marty had to know I'd be bringing up McNulty's recent arrest, but he must have thought it was a small problem at most because he never mentioned it. As far as Marty was concerned, the charges had been dropped, and McNulty had retired honorably from the police force. He obviously didn't know what I knew. The question was, how much would I tell the jury in my opening?

In the end, I didn't tell them much. I stuck with my planned opening and hammered the lack of motive. I did address the excessive forces charges. Personally, I thought doing so was a tactical mistake because it was weak, and it gave me a chance to take a shot at Marty.

I simply explained that both charges had been fully investigated, then dismissed. Then I looked at Marty and chided Marty for having brought them up. Ordinarily Marty would have rightly objected, but we were before Simple Simon, and objecting wasn't likely to do him any good.

As I took my seat at counsel table, Richie smiled and nodded, letting me know he thought I had done a good job.

The opening statements had taken all morning, so once we were done, the judge adjourned the proceedings for lunch. After the jury had been ushered out of the courtroom by the court officer, Laura gave me a big hug and told me what a great job I had done. Richie echoed her opinion. It was all very flattering, but it wasn't their opinion I was interested in.

I wanted to hear Abe's opinion. Abe had over forty years' experience trying cases, and he could read a jury better than anyone I knew. I looked at Abe, and he smiled. He said he thought the jury was open to my argument, or at least they hadn't rejected it. Richie and Laura were elated, but I cautioned them not to get overconfident. As the judge had told the jurors, arguments aren't evidence; I still had to prove the facts. If I couldn't prove the facts, we weren't going to win.

Eating lunch at the Worth Street Coffee Shop, we were all feeling pretty good about the morning' s proceedings. But I knew the mood would change when court resumed, and Marty called his first witness. It was to be expected; after all, the prosecution's witnesses weren't going to say anything good for the defense. I'd do my best on cross-examination to blunt the testimony, but it was going to sound bad. So, with coffee and dessert, I prepared Richie and Laura for what was about to come.

CHAPTER 92

When court resumed, Marty called Detective Moore from the Crime Scene Investigating Team. Detective Moore described the crime scene, explained what the Crime Scene Investigating Team did, and introduced the forensic reports and crime scene photographs. Or at least some of the crime scene photographs.

Marty spent a good deal of time questioning Moore about ballistic testing. He had him explain how it worked and how it was done. Then he had Moore describe, in agonizing detail, how he determined the bullets that killed Kim Lee came from Richie's gun. I was tempted to object when the testimony became repetitive, but it was Judge Simple Simon, so I just kept my mouth shut and waited. Finally, Marty moved on to the fingerprint reports.

As far as I was concerned, the ballistic evidence was the worst evidence we were facing in the case. McNulty's testimony was potentially worse, but it was assailable. The ballistic evidence was unassailable on its conclusion. It was science and you can't argue with science. That was why Marty had spent so much time on the subject. He knew it was his strongest forensic point and the one forensic point I couldn't really attack. The best I could do was claim it didn't prove who fired the gun. Of course, the implication was that Richie had, but an implication isn't scientific proof.

Whatever you want to say about it, I was just glad when Marty moved on to the fingerprint reports. In a well-rehearsed little show, Moore testified that prints lifted from the murder weapon matched Richie's prints. I say well-rehearsed because Moore was very careful not to use the word "fingerprints," and not to mention where the prints were found. The testimony, on its face, sounded damning, but I'd take much, if not all, of the sting out of it on cross-examination.

On balance, I didn't think it had gone badly. Moore was a decent witness, not great or even good, just decent. His voice was monotone, and he mumbled a lot. Other than the testimony about the ballistics, the rest of his testimony was rather dryly delivered. Toward the end, I thought the jurors were losing interest.

After a recess, I cross-examined Moore. Moore had been around long enough to know he was going to get hammered on a couple of points, and I expected him to be prepared. Not that there was much he could do about it, other than not looking surprised and not wetting his pants.

When I have a point to make, I like to get right to it. Beating around the bush can get you in trouble. So, I confronted Moore immediately about there being no usable fingerprints found on the trigger of Richie's gun. Moore was smart enough not to fudge an answer and conceded that was the case. Then holding the gun so the jury could see it, I said to Moore, "None of your forensic testing was able to tell you who fired the bullets from this gun." Of course, Moore had to agree.

After that, I forced Moore to agree that since the gun belonged to Richie, he would expect to find Richie's prints on it, and merely finding his prints on the gun didn't mean he was the one who killed Kim Lee. Since there were no readable fingerprints on the trigger of the gun, Moore reluctantly agreed that the same conclusion applied.

I was just about done questioning Moore about the forensic reports when it hit me. What good was having Simple Simon Morganstern as the judge if I didn't take advantage of the situation?

"Based upon the results of all of your forensic testing, we can conclude anyone in the brothel office that night could have killed Kim Lee, right?" Marty Bowman jumped out of his chair like he'd been shot from a cannon and objected loudly. Moore knowingly kept his mouth shut, and we all looked at the judge. The question was probably objectionable the way it was phrased, but good old Simple Simon kept things simple and let the witness answer. Moore didn't know what to do, so he answered simply, "Yes."

Reveling in my victory, and under the guise of making sure I understood the witness' answer, I repeated the question and his answer. Poor Marty was seething, while Detective Moore waited anxiously to get the hell out of the courtroom.

Glancing at the jury, I knew they had gotten the point, and it was time to leave the subject alone. It never pays to overdo it. When you've made your point, quit and move on.

The last item on my agenda was to have Moore identify additional crime scene photos, particularly the ones showing the open safe. I'd need them later on in the trial, and by entering them into evidence then, I hoped to send Marty a subtle message.

When I was done with my cross-examination, Marty chose not to ask Moore any further questions. Moore couldn't change his answers, and trying to take the sting out would only reinforce the testimony in the jurors' minds. It was better to move on.

There was just enough time left in the day for Marty to call his next witness, the Deputy Coroner, from the Office of Chief Medical Examiner. He testified as to the cause of Kim Lee's death and the recovery of the bullets from her body. It was all very dry, very quick and inconsequential to our defense, so I had no cross-examination. I was also smart enough to know when not to ask questions. No sense having the good doctor repeat all his testimony, if I had no point to make.

That ended the first day of trial. Outside the courthouse, we were all feeling pretty good about the day's events. Once again, I warned Richie and Laura that things would probably get worse. The next day McNulty was due to testify, so they should be prepared. We arranged to meet again at the Worth Street Coffee Shop in the morning, and then everyone headed home.

I was on my way to Gracie's place when my cell phone rang. It was Jimmy O'Brien; he needed to meet with me right away. I suggested my office, but he said no, it had to be someplace private. That didn't sound good.

CHAPTER 93

A half hour later, I met O'Brien in the backroom of Shoo's Restaurant. I was using the place as much as I did when I had my office there.

Jimmy's news was bad, and it hit me like a punch in the gut. He wasn't going to testify on Richie's behalf. It wasn't that he didn't want to; he couldn't. He'd been warned off the case by the Feds. I asked if it was the FBI, and he said he didn't think so. The guys that approached him had only identified themselves as Federal Agents, but they weren't FBI.

I was betting they were CIA agents. I was sure it had to do with the thumb drive, and the CIA was the one federal agency with the most interest in the thumb drive, and the one agency that had the most to lose if its contents were made public.

The material on the thumb drive gave the CIA leverage over two very important diplomats, but only if the information remained secret. If the information went public, it lost all of its blackmail value. The CIA was the one agency that profited from keeping the thumb drive's contents secret, and I suspected they'd go to any length to make sure it stayed secret.

It was all starting to make sense. McNulty had probably stolen the thumb drive, intending to use it to blackmail the ambassadors. But then he was arrested and had to use it to cut a deal for himself and his son. Knowing how valuable the material on the thumb drive would be to an intelligence agency like the CIA, McNulty had demanded to see the Feds right away. Once the CIA learned what McNulty had to offer, McNulty was in the driver's seat, and he apparently leveraged his position to the maximum.

I had little doubt the CIA had the juice to strong-arm the DA into dropping the charges against McNulty and his son, and to strong-arm the NYPD into allowing McNulty to retire. But the DA and the NYPD had to make sure the deal wouldn't come back and bite them in the ass. That meant McNulty couldn't be linked in any way to Sam Yeoung or the brothel incident. If he was, someone was sure to raise the question of why he hadn't been at least investigated at the time. The DA and the NYPD would be hard pressed to answer that question, and the whole affair would begin looking like a great big cover-up.

Were that to happen, a public outcry would certainly follow, leaving the NYPD or the DA no choice but to go after McNulty. That would breach the deal McNulty had with the Feds, leaving him with no immunity. All McNulty could do at that point was to take his revenge by releasing the information on the thumb drive.

The NYPD had tried to make sure that didn't happen when it quashed the IAB investigation and allowed McNulty to retire. The DA's Office had done its part by never bringing formal charges against McNulty, and then expunging his arrest record. The only remaining threat to the McNulty deal was Richie's trial. If I successfully linked McNulty to Yeoung with credible evidence, it could jeopardize the whole plan. The DA needed to convict Richie quickly and quietly, without any critical mention of McNulty. That was why Jimmy O'Brien was threatened into not testifying.

Even though I hadn't listed Detective Chen and Joe Hadden as witnesses, it wouldn't have surprised me if they had also been threatened. It seemed all bases were being covered. All my possible witnesses were being eliminated, leaving me with only Richie.

Richie's testimony about McNulty wasn't seen as a problem. It was, after all, the word of the accused, looking to place the blame on someone else, and without corroborating evidence, it carried little weight. The photographs of McNulty and Yeoung together were evidence, but McNulty could probably explain them away, and at the end of the day they wouldn't be enough.

I had to believe that neither the DA, the NYPD, nor the CIA knew that I knew what was on the thumb drive. If they did, they'd know they had another big problem on their hands. By pinning me in a corner and leaving me with no options, I was likely to expose the contents of the thumb drive during the trial.

If they even suspected that could happen, things could get a lot worse, and my next mugging might end with me dying. Okay, maybe that's a little over the top, but it was the CIA ,and the CIA has been known to do such things.

I tried to no avail to change Jimmy's mind. I couldn't blame him for refusing to testify; he was too close to retirement to risk it.

One day into the trial, my strategy was taking a big hit. My one independent witness was gone, and gone with him was key testimony. Testimony that Richie's gun was in McNulty's waistband, and testimony that McNulty had something in his hand. On top of that, I now had no choice but to call Richie as a witness.

After Jimmy left, I called Abe and asked him to meet me for dinner at Shoo's. Maybe it was time to drop the thumb drive bomb on Marty to try and cut a deal. Hopefully, once the CIA knew we knew about the thumb drive and what was on it, they'd pressure the DA into cutting a deal with Richie, so the whole thing could be put to bed.

Why just a deal and not a dismissal of the case? I had a good bargaining chip, but it wasn't a "get out of jail free" card. The problem was, I didn't have a copy of the material on the thumb drive, so I couldn't prove the material actually existed. No doubt the accusation would make a big splash, but the DA, the NYPD, and the CIA were all likely to deny it was true. If I couldn't produce evidence to support the claim, the story would die off quickly, leaving the blackmail value of the material intact.

I knew Richie and Laura believed things were going well, and they would be disappointed, but we were running out of options.

When Abe arrived, I explained what had happened with Jimmy O'Brien, and we needed to rethink our strategy. He agreed that things had gone well for us, and we had the advantage with Simple Simon as the judge. We could continue the trial and hope that would be enough to get an acquittal. But by continuing the trial, we risked things turning on us, especially with the Feds monkeying around.

After a long discussion, we decided to continue with the trial without telling Marty about the thumb drive, at least not until McNulty had testified.

CHAPTER 94

The next morning, we all met at the Worth Street Coffee Shop, and I explained to Richie and Laura what had transpired the night before. Naturally, they were upset, and they didn't feel any better when I said they needed to prepare themselves to talk about a plea deal. As much as they thought they were prepared to have the discussion, they weren't. Talking theoretically about going to prison is a hell of a lot easier than talking about actually going to prison.

Richie probably understood the gravity of the situation and what going to prison would mean. That was why he initially refused to consider any deal that involved prison time. But I was sure Laura didn't know what it would mean for her if Richie went to prison. It's difficult explaining to a wife what her life is going to be like with her husband in prison. There's a lot more involved than the husband simply being out of the house.

The psychological impact is usually the worst part of it. When we talked about a plea deal, I'd have to be blunt with Laura, and I wasn't looking forward that.

By the time we left the coffee shop at nine-fifteen and headed across the street to the courthouse, we were all in a funky mood. Since there wasn't much to be optimistic about, our moods weren't likely to improve anytime soon.

When we got to the courtroom, the judge's law clerk announced there'd be a slight delay in the proceedings. Before either Marty or I could ask why, the clerk retreated into the judge's robing room.

As the minutes passed, everybody started getting antsy. It wasn't so much the delay itself that was getting to me; it was not knowing why we were delayed. Usually when there's a delay starting the trial, the judge or the judge's clerk lets the attorneys know why. But we were being left in the dark, and that worried me.

The delay wasn't helping anyone's mood. With nothing to do and nothing to occupy everyone's attention, it was easy to start thinking negatively, and that seemed to be happening. Abe and I were at counsel table with Richie, and Laura was seated behind us. No one was talking, which is never a good sign.

Hoping to break the tension, I asked Laura how the girls were doing. That turned out to be a colossal mistake. It seemed Richie had forbidden the girls from coming to New York for the trial, and that resulted in a big fight between him, his daughters and Laura. Okay, wrong topic. Maybe silence wasn't the worse thing in the world.

I glanced over at Marty sitting at the prosecutor's table. I noticed earlier he kept looking at his watch and glancing back at the courtroom door. I suspected he was waiting for McNulty to arrive because as the minutes passed, he was definitely looking nervous. The nervous look one gets when one's witness hasn't shown up on time.

I knew Marty was dying to check with his office, but using cell phones anywhere inside the courthouse is prohibited. If Marty wanted to make a call, he'd have to go all the way outside to the street. Not only would that take time, he'd have to go through security coming back into the building, and that would add at least ten minutes to the trip. He couldn't risk leaving and not being back before Judge Morganstern took the bench.

It was getting close to ten o'clock, and there was still no word from the judge why we were delayed. The only good thing you could say about Judge Morganstern was that he was timely, so I suspected the delay was the fault of one of the jurors.

We were still sitting there, waiting and wondering what was going on, when at ten-thirty the law clerk appeared and said the judge wanted to see counsel in his chambers. As we walked back, Marty and I exchanged puzzled glances. What had happened now?

CHAPTER 95

Judge Morganstern greeted us and asked us to take seats. I noticed he wasn't wearing his robe or his suit jacket, so I suspected that we weren't going into formal session anytime soon. I was right.

The judge had been informed earlier that Deputy Chief William McNulty had been shot numerous times leaving his apartment that morning. Wow, that was certainly shocking news, especially for Marty Bowman, who turned pale at the words.

Knowing McNulty was on his way to testify, the judge had decided to delay the start of the trial until McNulty's condition was known. I don't know why he didn't tell us this before. Did he expect McNulty to show up wounded?

We were in chambers because the judge had just received word that McNulty had died from his injuries. The news just kept getting better and better. Maybe not for McNulty and poor Marty, but certainly for Richie. If McNulty was dead, so was the case against Richie, and everybody in the judge's robing room knew it, and that included Simple Simon.

Judge Morganstern asked Marty what he intended to do. Naturally, Marty claimed he couldn't make any decisions without talking with his boss, so he asked for an adjournment. I had no objection, and the judge adjourned the trial until the following morning.

I danced my way back into the courtroom where Abe and I explained it all to a jubilant Richie and Laura. I was 99% certain the case would be dismissed, and even if it wasn't, I was now 99% certain we could win it. We'd withhold the formal celebration until the case was officially dismissed, but I knew it was over.

The judge called the jury into the courtroom and explained that, due to a legal complication, the case was being adjourned. He thanked them for their understanding, and instructed them to return the next morning.

As we left the courtroom, I told Laura and Richie to wait for me outside the courthouse, and then I went and spoke with Marty. Marty was fairly certain his boss would agree to dismiss the case because, without McNulty's testimony, his chance of getting a conviction was slim. Slim? I told him he was daydreaming if he thought he had any chance of winning. Marty smiled, knowing I was right; he just hated to admit it.

I'll tell you one thing. As much as I believe in God and miracles, this was above and beyond miraculous. Never in my wildest dreams would I have imagined the case ending that way. Which makes sense since my wildest dreams usually involve sex and not legal cases.

As I walked out of the courthouse and down the long staircase to the street, I saw Abe, Richie and Laura engaged in what was clearly a happily animated conversation. When I joined them, it was all hugs and laughter. And there were some tears. I won't say who was shedding them, to protect the identity of the macho.

CHAPTER 96

An hour later, as Laura, Richie, and I sat in my office, Marty called to inform me the DA was dropping the charges against Richie. The case was officially over. Laura kept thanking me until I told her, "Don't thank me, thank the guy that shot McNulty."

That afternoon, we had a big celebration luncheon at Shoo's Restaurant. Linda Chow and Abe joined us. Only Tommy was missing, but he wasn't forgotten, and we raised a glass in a toast to him.

When lunch ended, Laura and Richie headed back to Long Island, their long nightmare finally over. The next day I'd appear with Marty Bowman before Judge Morganstern, and the case would be formally and officially dismissed. I'd move to have the record expunged and the arrest record sealed. Marty wasn't likely to object, but if he did, I was counting on Simple Simon keeping it simple.

Linda went back to work, and Abe and I ended up in my office. I liked working with Abe and toyed with the idea of asking him to join with me. Before I could say anything, Abe said it was time for him to retire, again. Working on Richie's case, he realized that the per diem work he had been doing wasn't really practicing law; it was just going through the motions. He had been doing it to fill the void in his life left by his wife's death. But the law meant more to him than just going through the motions, and that was why he would retire.

I told him I'd be honored to have him as a partner, but he smiled and said, "It's too late. I'm too old to work that hard, and I really don't want to." He had accomplished everything he had set out to do when he graduated from law school. But more importantly, he didn't want to practice if he couldn't perform at his best. He had a daughter in California, and he'd start his second retirement by visiting her and her family. If things worked out, maybe he'd move there. Or maybe not.

I asked him about Mrs. Goldberg in the DA's Office. He smiled and said, "Who knows?" That was Abe.

EPILOGUE

It would be six months before I learned anything more about McNulty's murder, other than what was reported in the newspapers at the time. The local newspapers called the incident random street violence. The reports referred to McNulty as a recently retired high-ranking police official, who was the unfortunate victim of a random shooting. There was no mention he was on his way to testify at Richie's trial when he was shot. After two days of media coverage, the story died.

Six months later, I was walking on Doyer Street when I ran into Detective Chen. It was just in front of the Nom

Wah Tea Parlor, and Chen asked if I'd join him for a cup of tea. Suspecting he had something to tell me, I accepted his invitation.

Over a cup of bo-lay tea and a plate of fried sesame balls with lotus seed paste, Chen told me what he had learned about McNulty's murder. At the time of the shooting, only the very top brass at NYPD knew anything about McNulty's deal. Everyone else had been told McNulty had simply retired, and any rumors about an IAB investigation were untrue.

The McNulty homicide case was assigned to the Detectives at the 20th Precinct on the Upper West Side of Manhattan, which was where the shooting had occurred. Chen had a buddy on the Detective Squad who kept him informed on the investigation.

From the start, the Detectives had a hard time with the investigation because someone at One Police Plaza kept putting roadblocks in their way. For one thing, the top bras told them that the rumors of an IAB investigation of McNulty were untrue, and they should drop any leads in that direction.

Finding that road blocked, the Detectives changed direction. Knowing McNulty had been involved with the infamous Madison Street brothel raid, they sought to investigate Sam Yeoung and the Hop Sing Tong. That's when they hit the next roadblock. At that point, it became apparent that the brass wasn't interested in solving the case, so the investigation was soon closed and filed as a random act of violence.

From the start, it was Chen's belief that Yeoung was responsible for the murder. Recently, one of his confidential informers confirmed that Yeoung had put out the contract on McNulty. It seemed Yeoung wasn't sure what McNulty was going to say when he testified in open court, and he wasn't going to take any chances.

That made sense, and so did the fact that the NYPD was under pressure not to bring Yeoung to justice. If Yeoung was arrested, he was in a position to reveal the contents of the thumb drive, and the CIA wasn't going to let that happen. The easiest way to resolve the whole matter, once McNulty was dead, was to just drop the case, which is exactly what happened.

It also meant that Sam Yeoung wasn't going to be looked at too closely by the NYPD for the brothel operation, or anything else. But not everything the Task Force had done was in vain. The brothel stayed closed, at least on Madison Street, but the Hip Sing Tong did remain in business.

As for Richie, he was reinstated and went back to work at the 7th Precinct. But after a couple of months back on the job, he put in his papers and retired. I think the whole affair left a bad taste in his mouth, and after spending almost thirty years on the job, he was ready to get out.

After retiring, he did some security work, part-time, and even took up golf. The last time we got together, he said that he and Laura were considering moving to South Carolina. He assured me if they did, I had a standing invitation to visit. I reminded him that I didn't like traveling to Long Island to visit him, so why in the world would he

452

think I'd go all the way to South Carolina to visit? I should also mention, Richie and Laura promptly paid my bill when I finally got around to sending them one.

Tommy recovered fully from his gunshot wound and went back to work with Linda Chow. We still work together on cases, although I've vowed never to let him do anything that could get him shot. Tommy laughed when I told him that, not realizing I have his grandfather on my side.

Me? I'm still doing my thing. I'm handling 18B Panel cases and working for some private clients to pay the bills. Nothing has changed between Gracie and me. It's all good and God willing, it will stay that way. The good news is, since Richie's case, I haven't been mugged.

Oh yeah, I'm still sober.

Made in the USA
Middletown, DE
11 March 2018